What could be more refreshing on a lazy, sultry afternoon than this sexy quartet of summer novellas? Chris Kenry, William J. Mann, Andy Schell, and Ben Tyler transport readers from the balmy Hawaiian Islands to the breezy Atlantic coast, from the sizzling California desert to the brisk Rocky Mountains, where the boys of summer share far more than fabulous vacation houses. . . .

SUGAR DADDY SUMMER
by Chris Kenry

It's August, and Aspen is crawling with wealthy Walter's castoffs, from fey fashionistas Keith and Derek to macho Jake, back from the brink of death. Now, just in time for Summerfest, they're all under Walter's sprawling roof—along with Walter's latest flame, nubile newcomer Brian. Whirling on the merry carousel of tea dances and cocktail parties, the eclectic housemates are about to discover that romance has a way of popping up where—and with whom—you least expect it!

THE PERFECT HUSBAND
by William J. Mann

Look out, P-Town, here they come! Boyfriendless and bound for the Cape, Troy Palmer and Adam Krywinski are on a serious manhunt this year. The old college pals have never shared anything more than an annual beach house, a single stolen kiss, and a mutual crush on their roommate, the delectable Peter Youngblood. Now both Troy and Adam are on the verge of finding Mr. Right—and he's much closer than either of them ever suspected. . . .

THE OUTLINE OF A TORSO
by Andy Schell

Six years ago, three teen-aged friends spent a memorable vacation in Maui, sunning and surfing by day and sharing whispered confidences by night . . . until the decidedly straight—and therefore unwelcome—Ethan Prater crashed their provocative party. History seems destined to repeat when the original threesome, boyfriends in tow, are reunited in Maui—only to be joined by a familiar fourth wheel. But this time, Mr. Macho will stun them with a startling confession. . . .

SATISFACTION
by Ben Tyler

Summertime, and the livin' ain't so easy for Dusty, who has just discovered his lover in a compromising situation involving a hot tub and a hot stranger. Plunged headlong back into the dating pool, Dusty juggles corporate LA weekdays with laid-back Palm Springs weekends. When he falls for handsome, brilliant, fabulously wealthy Jon, Dusty can't help feeling that his newfound soul mate is too good to be true. But the budding couple has more in common than either of them ever imagined. . . .

Books by Chris Kenry

CAN'T BUY ME LOVE

UNCLE MAX

Books by William J. Mann

THE BIOGRAPH GIRL

Forthcoming

WHERE THE BOYS ARE

Books by Andy Schell

MY BEST MAN

Books by Ben Tyler

TRICKS OF THE TRADE

HUNK HOUSE

Published by Kensington Publishing Corporation

SUMMER SHARE

Chris Kenry

William J. Mann

Andy Schell

Ben Tyler

KENSINGTON BOOKS
http://www.kensingtonbooks.com

KENSINGTON BOOKS are published by

Kensington Publishing Corp.
850 Third Avenue
New York, NY 10022

All Kensington titles, imprints and distributed lines are available at special
quantity discounts for bulk purchases for sales promotion, premiums, fund
raising, educational or institutional use.

Special book excerpts or customized printings can also be created to fit spe-
cific needs. For details, write or phone the office of the Kensington Special
Sales Manager: Kensington Publishing Corp., 850 Third Avenue, New York,
NY, 10022. Attn. Special Sales Department. Phone: 1-800-221-2647.

ISBN 0-7582-0088-9

First Kensington Trade Printing: May 2002
10 9 8 7 6 5 4 3 2 1

Printed in the United States of America

Contents

Sugar Daddy Summer

Chris Kenry

Chapter One

"We deserve a vacation," Derek proclaimed, dropping his bag on the floor and taking a stool next to Keith at the bar.

"Too true," Keith agreed. "Too true." He lifted his Cosmopolitan and slid the one he had already ordered for Keith over to him.

"And after last weekend," he went on, "I deserve one. Do you know they made me work the white sale, even though it has nothing to do with my department, and they made me come in at eight o'clock!"

"In the *morning?*" Derek cried.

"Yes! Doesn't that just suck? My eyes were puffy *all day long*, and at the end of my shift I was even too tired to work out!"

"No!"

"It's the truth," Keith said. "Just lay on the couch watching *E!* Barely had enough energy to go to bed."

"Well, it's just as bad at the restaurant," Derek said, taking a fortifying sip of his own drink. "François treats me like a white slave. He made me work *two* lunches last week, and then I had to work both Friday *and* Saturday night! Yes, we definitely need a vacation."

The two friends had been meeting once a week for drinks and conversation since their friendship began, some three years ago. The drinks and the topics of their conversation were on a continual rotation, but the time of their meeting (five o clock on Thursday) and the location (The Grand on 17th), were always the same.

On this particular day, the topic was vacation and the fact that Derek had, while perusing one of the gay papers that afternoon, found the perfect place for them.

"Aspen Summerfest," he said, setting the paper down on the bar in front of Keith and pointing to the article.

"Summerfest," Keith repeated warily. "What's that?"

"It's supposed to be like a summer version of Gay Ski Week," Derek explained, "but it probably won't be as big a deal."

And about that, Derek was right. Whereas Gay Ski Week was a very big deal, flooding the town of Aspen with gays and lesbians from all over the world, Summerfest was lucky to bring a few of them up from Denver for the weekend. It was, at best, an attempt by the local gay community to try and liven up the otherwise stagnant summer social life of a traditionally winter resort. The "festivities" consisted of loosely organized brunches, hikes, and mountain bike rides during the day, followed by the usual round of cocktail parties and dances at night. It was nothing spectacular, and yet, for many reasons it appealed to Derek and Keith. The first of these was that Aspen was relatively close and so it would not require great expense to get there. Second, because they had a mutual friend, Walter, who owned a house in Aspen, at which they hoped they could stay for free. But most important, a weekend in Aspen appealed to them because they were gold diggers, and each knew that there were few places more ideally suited to dig for it than a former mining camp turned resort. It was sure to be filled with lots of well-off, older men in need of youthful, hard-bodied companionship, and Derek and Keith, although no longer exactly young, were certainly good-looking. They had beautiful bodies, with muscles that were ridiculously well defined, topped off with the square-jawed faces of fashion models. In addition, they had a knack for inane, cocktail party conversation and a highly refined sense of style. In short, they had everything necessary to ensure success at an event like Summerfest, so they resolved to go. And yet once they'd decided, several small hurdles presented themselves. The first and lowest of these being how they could get the time off from work at such short notice.

"Of course I wish I didn't have to lie about it," Keith said, taking another sip of his drink. "But it can't be helped. I shouldn't really feel bad; I mean, it's not like I don't *deserve* a vacation! I'm going to have the flu."

"And I'll have food poisoning," Derek said. "I'll tell them I got it from eating the slop they try and pass off as an employee meal. No way they can argue with that!"

Once that was settled, the next and slightly higher hurdle was money. Or, to be more precise, their absolute lack of it. Neither had a savings account, nothing squirreled away for a rainy day, not even anything they could really pawn. Which is not to say Keith and Derek were poor, for they were not. At least not in the conventional sense. Rather, they were "financially frustrated," meaning they made money, just never enough. They did not make enough to live in the manner to which they felt themselves entitled, and yet they charged on through life (in the real and plastic sense), affecting to be rich—always a step ahead in fashion and a month behind on rent. They were not unaware of their monetary situation (indeed reminders of it were sent to them on a monthly basis from their friends at Visa and Mastercard), but each saw himself as largely powerless to change it. They worked (Derek waiting tables and Keith in the men's sportswear section of a department store), but only to the extent that was absolutely necessary, for each knew that his current job was not to be his salvation. No, salvation would have to come from something else, and that something would be beauty. Beauty and, well, an innate fabulousness that each felt certain he possessed in abundance. They both knew that one day their value would inevitably be "discovered," much like the proverbial movie star who was discovered while sitting on a bar stool at a soda fountain. Their savior, usually envisioned by them in the form of David Geffen or Barry Diller or Tom Ford, was sure to find them sooner or later, and would lift them out of the mundane, banal, pedestrian mire that was their current state of existence. Until then, it was important to maintain the façade and keep up appearances. If doing that meant accepting help along the way from a number of generous men, usually older, less attractive, and wealthier than themselves, they were certainly not above it.

"I suppose we should call Walter," Keith said, picking up his bag and retrieving his cell phone. Walter was an independently wealthy man of fifty who, by happy chance, owned a small house in the hills of

Aspen. He knew and liked them both, and if he was approached in the right way, they felt sure he would help them out.

"Yes, call him," Derek said. "If we are going to go, then we better get the ball rolling. But he's got that new boyfriend, so he might not want to go. You know how he is—always afraid we're going to poison the well."

Keith laughed.

"But do call him," Derek said again. "If he doesn't want to go maybe he'll at least let us use his house."

Keith began dialing, but then a thought occurred to him and he quickly pressed the disconnect button. He frowned and looked over at Derek.

"But . . ." Keith said, "it would be better if he went, don't you think? I mean, we do kind of *need* him to go."

Derek wrinkled his brow.

"I guess you're right," he said, removing the cherry from the bottom of his empty glass and popping it into his mouth. "We can't go the whole weekend without eating."

"Or drinking," Keith said, downing the remainder of his own drink and motioning for the bartender to bring two more.

"Call him," Derek said, "and be nice."

Keith nodded and began to dial again.

"If that doesn't work I guess we'll just have to tighten the thumb-screws."

There was no answer, so Keith left a vague message asking Walter to call him back. The next round of drinks arrived and Keith proposed a toast.

"To our successful and profitable vacation."

"I'll drink to that," Derek said, and then added grimly, "I just hope the little boyfriend doesn't muck it all up."

"What do you know about him?" Keith asked. "Walter hasn't told me a thing."

"Me neither," Derek said, "but what's to wonder about? You know he's probably like all the rest of them: some dumb little twink night-mare. I do know that his name is Brian, but only because every time I call to see if Walter wants to take me to lunch he says 'I'd love to but I'm meeting Brian for coffee,' or 'Brian and I are going to San Diego for the weekend.' It's always 'Brian, Brian, Brian.' Makes me want to vomit."

"Well, they can't be going out much," Keith said. "Because I haven't seen Walter out at all, and you know what a bar fixture he is."

"Yes, it must be serious," Keith said gravely, and then they both burst out laughing. To think of Walter being serious about any boy was as believable as thinking Bill was serious about Hillary. It would be easier to give a cat a bath than tie Walter down, a fact that each knew from personal experience, having each, at different times, been Walter's boyfriend. Derek had replaced Walter's first boyfriend, and then Keith had replaced Derek. Since then, there had been far too many of Walter's young men for either Keith or Derek to count, but the two had, for various reasons remained in his life as friends. They labeled themselves, and all the others who had been a boyfriend of Walter's, as "B.O.Ws." to signify that they had endured the tribulation of being in a relationship with Walter and had emerged, scarred, but intact. It was a badge of sorts, that each wore with something like a veteran's pride. It wasn't that being with Walter was so difficult, on the contrary, both Derek and Keith would admit that he was even-tempered, generous with his money, and always well dressed and groomed. No, the only problem they had with Walter was his libido, and the fact that when he dated them he was either unable, or unwilling, to control it. He loved to woo and seduce young men and he was good at it, but he seemed to lose all interest in them once they had been thoroughly wooed and seduced. For Walter the joy was evidently in the battle. Victory always seemed to leave him feeling bored.

When Keith's call from the bar came through on his cell phone Walter did not answer. He heard it ring, looked at the caller ID, and then silenced the ringer. He remembered that it was the evening that Derek and Keith always met for drinks, and knew that if they were calling him, it was probably because they didn't have enough money to pay their tab or that they wanted him to take them out to dinner. More often than not, and especially if he was between boyfriends, he would go with them when they called. Money was not a big issue with him, and he found their odd brand of humor so consistently entertaining that he never minded bankrolling their outings. But when he did have a boyfriend and if he made the mistake of bringing him along, well, that was another story. On those evenings, Derek and Keith would suddenly change from being his friends, to being his ex-boyfriends, and the transformation was not a pretty one. The horns sprouted and the verbal knives came out, and by the end of the evening the poor boy he'd brought along was usually cut to ribbons.

No, Walter thought, as he looked down at the incoming call. They're on their own tonight. And he returned to the bedroom where Brian was waiting, wrapped in the sheets.

Unlike the empty-headed Abercrombies Walter usually dated, Brian was bookish. He had just graduated from college and was set to begin a masters program at DU in the fall. In addition to being smart, he was handsome, but, ironically enough, in an unstudied way: his hair, longer than the fashion, was rarely combed with anything other than his fingers, and his tall lanky body was completely unacquainted with the workings of any Nautilus machines or free weights. All of that, topped off with a wardrobe from the off-the-rack collection at Goodwill, made him resemble nothing so much as a porn star from the 1970s.

Since Brian and Walter had met at the beginning of the summer, they had spent nearly all their free time together to the exclusion of all others. Usually, with the boys Walter dated there was a pattern: he spent about a quarter of the time wooing a boy, a quarter of the time enjoying his company, and the remaining half of the time trying to figure a way to weasel out of the relationship. With Brian, he realized, it had been different. There was none of the trapped, suffocating feeling that usually came upon him, no urge to flee. It was now August and he was still interested in and attracted to him. If anything, he was worried about keeping Brian interested in and attracted to him.

For that reason when Keith and Derek called again with the Summerfest proposition, he had replied without hesitation, "No. Absolutely not."

"Oh come on," Keith had pleaded. "It'll be fun. We haven't seen you all summer and we both want to meet Billy."

"Brian."

"Yes."

"No," Walter said. "You'll have to meet him another time." And with that he hung up.

Brian, having heard his name mentioned from where he lay, yet again wrapped in the bed sheets, asked Walter what it was all about. Walter shook his head and returned to the bed.

"Nothing," he said, taking Brian in his arms. "Just some silly friends of mine who want us to go away for the weekend."

Walter hoped that was the end of it, but in the back of his mind he knew that Keith and Derek would not be so easily put off. The phone continued to ring and later that day Brian asked him about it again.

"Oh, it's some gay thing in Aspen," Walter said, with a dismissive wave. "I have a house there and they want to stay in it."

"So, why don't you let them?" Brian asked. Walter hesitated.

"Well, er," he stammered, "someone else, a friend, lives there sometimes, like a sort of caretaker, and he doesn't really like them. Besides, they're moochers. I love them, but I know they only want me to go because they probably don't have any money."

Brian smiled.

"Then you really don't want to go?"

"No, definitely not. Why . . . ?" Walter asked, somewhat afraid of the answer.

"Well," Brian said, shrugging his shoulders, "it could be fun. I haven't met any of your friends . . ."

Nor will you, Walter thought to himself. If I can help it.

". . . and it *would* be nice to get away before I have to start school."

"Fine. Great!" Walter replied, eagerly. "Let's go to Paris then, or Bermuda, or if you're set on mountains, how about Switzerland? Just not Aspen, not with my friends."

"Walter?" Brian asked, his voice full of mock terror. "You're not . . . ashamed of me, are you?"

"You? Please! It's not you I'm worried about, it's them."

But instead of putting him off the idea, Walter's reluctance seemed to intrigue Brian.

"Oh, it's hard to explain," Walter said. "They like to embarrass me. You know how old friends can be. It's all good fun usually, but sometimes they don't know when to stop. It can get pretty brutal."

"I think I could handle it." Brian laughed.

"Don't bet on it," Walter said, shaking his head. "You haven't met these two."

"No, but I'd like to," Brian said. "They sound interesting."

"Oh yeah, they are that!" Walter said with a laugh. "Interesting. Like spiders in a web. You just don't want to get too close. I love them to death, but . . ."

"But what?" Brian asked. "If they are your friends I'd *like* to meet them. Come on," he pleaded, "I can hold my own. We've been seeing each other for three months and I've hardly met any of your friends. Are you planning to get rid of them, or me?"

Walter studied the boy, and said nothing. As much as he'd have liked to, he knew he couldn't stay cloistered with him forever. If their relationship was going to last they would eventually have to bring it out of the bedroom and expose it to the harsh light of day. It was a risk, but one he supposed he had to take.

"All right," he said, throwing his arm over Brian's shoulder. "You want to go to Aspen with my friends, we'll go to Aspen with my friends. But don't say I didn't warn you."

The next time the phone rang Walter answered it.

"Okay, you win. We'll go. But you're not riding up with us," he said sternly. Then his tone changed and he added, "And you have to be nice. Please. Please be nice."

"Don't be silly," Keith said. "We're always nice."

"Of course you are," Walter groaned, rubbing his temples.

Chapter Two

One simply cannot arrive in Aspen by public transportation. It is just not done. Probably is not even possible. And yet, since Walter's refusal to allow them to ride with him, public transportation was an idea that had actually crossed the minds of Keith and Derek. It crossed them and kept on going. They could not bring themselves to do it. Just could not picture themselves on a bus with all the other members of the proletariat. In the end they decided to take their chances with Derek's wheezing Nissan.

Derek had bought the car a few months earlier from a handsome used car salesman on South Broadway. His office, a small trailer actually, stood behind a large sign proclaiming, "No credit? No problem!" And that was good enough for Derek. He wandered the lot with the man, kicking tires and staring blankly down at the engines, and in the end selected the Nissan on the basis of its paint color. He gave it one spin around the parking lot, and then returned with the man to the trailer and signed his name, again and again and again, at the bottom of several sheets of paper. Paper filled with lots of small-print mumbo-jumbo about the car being sold "as is, no warranty," and vaguely detailing the forty-five percent interest rate.

The Nissan was in bad shape when Derek acquired it, but under his ownership it had only gotten worse. In his mind, the words "routine maintenance" meant re-filling the gas tank. Oil changes, tune-ups, and tire rotation were viewed as frivolous extravagances—expensive medicine wasted on a dying patient.

Best not to indulge the thing, Derek thought to himself.

In spite of that philosophy, he had, earlier in the week, made a decision to fix the violently wobbling rear wheel which, mysteriously enough, wobbled only when the car was driven between the speeds of ten and fifty-five miles per hour. If he drove slower than ten, or faster than fifty-five, the wobbling ceased and the car sputtered along smoothly. Nevertheless, Derek thought it prudent to have the wheel repaired before embarking on what was to be a mountainous journey. With that intention, he drove down to the local repair shop, only to be told when he arrived, well after noon on a Thursday, that they could not even look at his car until the following Monday.

"Monday!" he cried, staring wide-eyed at the greasy man behind the counter. "But I need the car tomorrow."

Without looking up from his computer screen the man blandly repeated, "Monday."

"Look," Derek said, removing his sunglasses and leaning on the counter, his voice softer, almost pleading. "Can't you maybe just squeeze it in? It's a small car, really, and the problem can't be that big. It's a wobbling wheel. Probably just needs tightening or something. I'd do it myself if I had the tools, and, well, if I knew how. But look at you, I'm sure you could have it fixed in a couple of minutes."

"Monday," the man repeated, and then turned and disappeared through the door leading to the garage.

Annoyed by this snag, Derek left and walked across the parking lot to the mall. In less than an hour the problem with the car was all but forgotten, which was just as well, really, since in that hour he managed to spend all of the cash he had previously set aside to fix it. As he loaded the trunk with his purchases he sighed and said to himself, "I guess I'll just have to remember to watch the speed."

The two set out the next morning at ten o'clock. They would have started earlier but it was Friday after all, and that came after Thursday, which was the night they met for drinks, and after that, they never got up early.

The most common way to get to Aspen from Denver is to take Interstate 70 West, over the Continental Divide. It is a taxing drive for any car, but was especially so for the Nissan which had been ridden hard and put away wet so many times in its lifetime that it no longer had the ability to make such an extended, uphill journey.

The ride out of Denver, which was flat and level, went smoothly enough and Derek began to feel encouraged. But once they reached the foothills the problems began. As soon as they went uphill, the car would lose speed and the wheel started wobbling. It got so bad at one point that it seemed more like they were riding in an unbalanced washing machine than a car, and Derek found it almost impossible to hold the steering wheel. In an attempt to remedy the situation, he shifted down into third gear. This increased the car's speed and stopped the wobbling, but it made the engine squeal.

Keith tried to ask what was wrong, but Derek couldn't hear him.

"What?" Derek yelled. He glanced over at Keith, but then quickly returned his eyes to the orange needle of the speedometer.

"I *said*, why is it shaking so much!"

"What?" Derek yelled again, shaking his head this time. "I can't hear you at all!"

The needle fell to fifty so Derek pushed the accelerator to the floor. The engine squealed even more and made any communication between the two impossible. Realizing this, Keith sighed, rolled his eyes, and gave up. He lowered his sunglasses, eased back into the seat and tried to resume reading his copy of *Men's Fitness*.

Derek glanced out his window and saw that they were near the top of the divide. At that point, the road leveled off and went through the mile-long Eisenhower Tunnel. Derek knew that if they could reach that point they would probably be okay. He shifted the car into second gear and again pushed the accelerator to the floor. The engine screamed and the tachometer went to the end of the red zone. Derek could see the mouth of the tunnel ahead, and he began lunging forward with his body, like a child on a swing, in a vain effort to help the forward momentum. When they finally reached it, and he was able to ease up on the accelerator and shift into a higher gear, the car gave a sigh and ceased shaking. They drove through at an even sixty-five and Derek felt his shoulders relax.

And yet, when the tunnel ended things got worse. At that point, as they emerged into the sunlight, the road began a steep descent, a descent so steep that it is notorious for burning out the brakes of heed-less semi-trucks, busses, and RVs, sending them on a wild and usually deadly ride. For that reason, the powers that be have constructed a se-ries of gravel-filled ramps off to the side of the highway, into which the brakeless vehicles can, with any luck, steer themselves. The gravel is very fine and very deep, so that when the vehicle hits it, in theory, it will sink up to the axles and stop.

The Nissan exited the tunnel and began its descent. Its speed in-creased, and so, to Derek's dismay, did the wobbling. He eased up on the gas and glanced down at the speedometer. It was hovering around ninety.

I'm going faster than fifty-five, he thought, feeling annoyed. It should not be wobbling like that.

But wobbling it was, and soon the unbalanced agitation began again, shaking the whole car and making it almost impossible to hold the steering wheel. Keith removed his headphones, a look of concern on his face. Derek shrugged. He decided to apply the brakes, hoping that if he slowed down the shaking might stop. It didn't. As soon as his foot touched the brake pedal there was a loud snap, followed by an awful scraping sound, and the car lurched to the left. Derek screamed and gripped the wheel. Keith screamed and gripped the dashboard. The wobbling wheel popped away from the car and the bare axle, drag-ging along the pavement, leaving a trail of sparks behind them. The car fishtailed down the center of the road. In a panic, Derek again tried the brakes, but when he did so the other wheel popped off and they went into a spin. Somehow, his frantic steering led them off the road and into one of the truck ramps, in which they did, in fact, sink, and come to an abrupt stop.

The two stared straight ahead for some moments, too stunned to speak. The wobbling wheels, now free and on their own, bounced past them, almost joyfully, and then rolled off into the trees.

"You all right?" Derek asked, looking over at his friend.

"I think so," Keith replied, looking down at his arms and legs almost surprised to see that they were still there. Then he noticed something terrible and gave a shriek.

"What?" Derek cried, expecting to see bone jutting out of flesh. "What's the matter?"

"God damn it!" Keith whined. "My sunglasses are broken!"

"No!" Derek said, snatching the broken frames from his friend and examining them in disbelief. "You just bought them!"

"You don't have to tell *me*," Keith said angrily. "They're not even paid for."

"Oh, sweetie," Derek soothed. "We'll just take them back and say they're defective. It's a clean break. Look. It'll be all right. There's got to be an Armani store in Aspen. We'll take them in and get a new pair."

"If we ever get to Aspen," Keith said grimly, smacking the dashboard.

Derek tried his door but it wouldn't budge. He sighed, rolled down his window, and squirmed out. Keith grabbed the window crank on his side and began turning, but to no avail. It went round and round quite easily but with absolutely no effect on the window, so he crawled over to the driver's side and went out the same way Derek had gone. They took a few steps away and then turned and looked back at the nearly submerged car.

"At least we can still get to the trunk," Derek said, and he moved forward with difficulty, his feet sinking in the loose gravel, and released the elaborate set of bungee cords that were used to keep the trunk closed. It sprung open and the two began unloading their many bags and arranging them neatly next to the highway. That done, they were suddenly at a loss as to what to do next, and stared at each other dumbly, each holding his cell phone.

"Hmmm," Derek mused. "I'd usually call you if I was in a pinch like this."

"Oh my God, how funny!" Keith chuckled. "Same here!"

Then they nodded their heads in unison and Keith dialed Walter's number.

Several miles down the interstate a phone rang, shattering the cool tranquility in Walter's Mercedes. Walter looked at the incoming number and then quickly pushed a button to silence the ringer. He gazed over at Brian, still asleep in the passenger seat, the sun shining on the clear, smooth skin of his face, and the breeze from the air conditioner gently blowing his hair.

Good, he thought. Still sleeping.

He was just reaching over to brush a stray lock away from the boy's creaseless forehead, when again, the phone rang. Again, huffily this time, he silenced the ringer, and stuffed the phone into the console between the seats. A moment later he heard it ringing again, albeit muffled. He sighed, shook his head, and answered it.

An hour later, the giant Mercedes arrived at the runaway-truck ramp, in which Derek and Keith were laid out, like Speedo-clad corpses, tanning themselves on beach towels. Introductions were made, bags were stowed, clothes were put back on, and soon, all four were again on their way.

"Well," Keith said, lifting his cracked glasses and examining Brian. "So you're the latest Bambi."

Brian looked back, confused, then over at Walter, who just shook his head and stared off down the road, gripping the steering wheel with both hands.

It's already beginning, Walter thought to himself. They haven't been in the car for two minutes and already the cobra sisters are beginning to hiss and spit.

"Bambi?" Brian asked.

"Yes," Derek said, "Bambi. You know: the young, wide-eyed fawn."

"Ahh," Brian said, and his face relaxed into a smile.

"Yes," Derek repeated. "You're the Bambi and Walter is the Bambi hunter."

"He's had lots of experience tracking game and using his big gun," Keith said, in a high-pitched, cartoonish voice.

"I wonder . . ." Keith said, laying a hand on Brian's shoulder. "Was there much of a chase, or were you fairly easy to bag?"

"Please," Walter said, his hands gripping the steering wheel even more tightly. "You promised you'd be nice. Please."

"Oh, but we are, Blanche, we are being nice," Derek soothed. "We're just complimenting you on having trapped such a lovely young Bambi."

"I'll say," Keith added, stroking Brian's cheek. "This one still has its spots."

"I'm not that young," Brian said, turning to face the two in the back-seat, "if that's what you mean."

"Oh, please!" Keith protested. "You re still shitting yellow!"

"I'll bet you can't even ride a two-wheeler!" Derek laughed. "You're still a tender young chicken. Not like us tough old birds."

"You can't be much older than me," Brian said, hoping that compliments might soothe them. "I mean, you both look so young."

They laughed grimly, but were somewhat flattered.

"Eye cream, sweetie, and lots of water," Keith said, giving Brian's shoulder a pat. "Remember that. Clinique eye cream and eight glasses a day. Start now, and when you're my age you'll be better preserved than King Tut."

"Too true," Derek said, nodding. "The things I wish I'd known. I could write a book. I'd probably still be with Walter today if I'd started my preservation regimen back then. You did know that we dated? No? Walter! Well, we might as well get all the cards out on the table."

Walter groaned.

"You see," Derek continued, leaning closer to Brian, "we've both held your position."

"Yes," said Keith, "we've both had our turn in the front seat."

"We've both been B.O.Ws."

"We've both occupied the royal bed."

"Ha ha," Derek laughed. "That's funny! It is like a royal succession, isn't it? Walter is like that one king, the one who's always eating turkey legs."

"Henry the Eighth," Brian offered.

"Yeah, that one, and we're all Anne Boleyns, and Margaret Thatchers, or whatever the other queens were called."

Brian bit his lip to keep from laughing and even Walter smiled, although he turned his face to the window to hide it.

"I was one of Walter's first," Derek said haughtily, placing his hand on his chest and fluttering his eyelids. "Until this one," he said, elbowing Keith in the ribs, "wrestled the crown away from me."

"But mine was a brief reign," Keith interposed. "I was on the throne less than a year before I was forced to abdicate by that foreign queen."

"Ah, yes," Derek said. "Who can forget Rogelio, the Guatemalan lawn boy."

"After Rogelio," Keith went on, "the speed of succession increased.

There was Tom, who seemed to skateboard for a living and then James, the waiter from The Grand."

"And don't forget about that backsliding seminary student, what was his name? James? Jimmy?"

"Joseph."

"Yes, that's it, and after Joseph, well, I forget, actually."

"Not surprising," Keith said. "I mean, who could possibly keep track of them all?"

"True."

"But you needn't worry," Keith said reassuringly to Brian. "Walter has settled down in his old age. He's kept you hidden from view, which, in an odd way, says a lot."

"Yes," Derek agreed, "we haven't seen him all summer."

"You'll probably wear the crown and hold the scepter for many years to come."

"But just to be safe," Derek said, "I'd start with the eye cream and the water."

When they arrived at Aspen, two hours later, the sun was just beginning to set. Walter drove through the town with the easy familiarity of one who had once lived there, and pulled into a convenience store to fill up the car and to get some provisions. Derek and Keith immediately ran to the bathroom to unburden their bladders of some of the eight glasses of water, and Brian got out and stretched and looked around, amazed. The evening light had made the shadows long and the light golden. The green peaks surrounding the town looked as smooth and rich as velvet.

"It's beautiful," Brian said, and then turned to Walter and smiled. "Thank you again."

Walter smiled back and said, "You sure you still want to be with me after the picture those two just painted?"

Brian nodded and grinned. He studied Walter and remembered all the catty banter about him on the way up. It had hardly changed his feelings. On the contrary, he felt it validated all of his reasons for wanting to date only older men; there was never much to talk about with boys his age, never much he felt he had in common with them. Brian liked to think of himself as an old soul, and for that reason, among many other Freudian ones, he felt that he naturally gravitated to older, more experienced men. Men from whom he could learn something.

"Look up there," Walter said, pointing to the hillside. "That's the house."

Brian turned and followed his gaze. He saw a large drum-shaped structure perched on the hillside, its huge, monolithic glass front shining like a beacon in the setting sun.

"Good Christ!" Brian exclaimed. "That's your house?"

Walter nodded proudly.

"When I was a kid," Brian said, "our vacation house was a rented tin-roofed shack in the Catskills. This is quite a step up."

Walter laughed.

The two co-travelers returned from the bathroom, refreshed, and they all piled back into the car and continued on their way, following a winding dirt road up the hillside to the house.

Once inside, even before all the bags had been unloaded, Derek and Keith immediately began criticizing the interior decor.

"Walter, really!" Derek exclaimed, fingering the outdated plaid upholstery on the sofa. "What were you thinking? Yuck!"

"Too true," Keith chimed in. "Bad in any decade! Bad!"

"Hey." Walter shrugged from the kitchen, where he was unpacking some liquor bottles. "My wife picked it out."

"Which one?" Derek sneered.

"My *real* wife," Walter answered. "Brenda, the one I was married to for ten years and to whom I still pay a hell of a lot of alimony."

Keith and Derek made the rounds, passing judgment on the rest of the furnishings before finally claiming as their own the bedrooms they found the least offensive, which also happened to be the largest. Once installed, they set about the arduous and lengthy task of unpacking and selecting a suitable outfit for the evening.

While Walter was busy in the kitchen, and the other two were in the shower, Brian also took an inventory of the place. His eyes focused on different things than Keith and Derek noticed, but with a gaze that was no less discerning. On entering the house, in the foyer, he had no-

ticed the sports equipment, scanning and absorbing it with a greedy
excitement: the muddy hiking boots by the door, the snow shoes and
cross country skis hanging from a rack on one of the walls, the fly rods
and creels, and the mountain bike. All things he recognized and knew
about but, being a city boy, things he had never actually touched or
used. It was like an exotic museum to him and he was thrilled to know
that all of these things belonged to Walter. It was a side of him he'd
never suspected.

In the living room Brian immediately spied the large bookcase, and
he went directly to it. He gazed up and down the spines of the mostly
paperback library, reading the titles, and then he too passed judgment.
Unlike Keith and Derek's, however, Brian's judgment was much more
favorable to Walter. Older, masculine men always excited him, but
older, masculine men who read literary fiction gave him a serious
woody, and the shelves of this bookcase were packed with some of the
heaviest hitters.

When he'd finished looking them over, Brian said nothing but went
into the kitchen where Walter was putting away some groceries. He
came up behind him, encircled Walter in his arms and pressed his
body against his back so that Walter could feel he had a hard-on. A
devilish grin spread across Walter's face and he turned to kiss Brian.

"Which bedroom is ours?" Brian asked feverishly, between kisses.
Walter said nothing, but quickly led him out of the kitchen and down
the hall, undoing buttons as they went.

Forty minutes later their door was forced open by Derek and Keith.

"Gross!" Keith cried, as Brian and Walter peeped out from under
the sheets. "Get the hose!"

"I am so sure!" Derek said, his voice full of matronly disapproval.
"Like, you couldn't even wait!"

He then strode boldly into the room and grabbed a corner of the sheet,
whipping it away from the two before they had a chance to stop him.

"Now get up!" Derek said in the voice of an angry mother, afraid her
children may miss the bus. "The Double Diamond opens at eleven
and we've got to do some serious cocktailing beforehand. Up, up, up!"
he cried and gave Walter's bare ass a slap.

"Ow!" Walter cried, collecting his clothes from the floor and scrambling to cover his nakedness. "Look, why don't you two go along; I think we're going to just stay here tonight."

The response to this was decisive and swift for, in addition to having no car, Keith and Derek had very little money and were depending on Walter's largesse to pay the cover charge and to furnish their hands with Cosmopolitans.

"Oh, no," Keith said. "No, no, no. The time for love is *way* over. It's time for cocktails and for man trapping. You two little love hermits better come out of the cave. We want you showered and dressed in no more than fifteen minutes."

That said, they closed the door and disappeared, not waiting to hear any arguments.

An hour later they all went out. And they stayed out. Until nearly three o'clock. They had gone to a cocktail party at the Caribou Club, skipped dinner, and then mixed and mingled at the Double Diamond where Walter was pleased to notice several envious glances cast his way whenever he linked his arm in Brian's. And yet, whenever Brian went to the bathroom, or off to the bar to get more drinks, Walter's eyes could not help wandering. The bar was full-to-bursting with youthful beauty. More than he'd seen since, by lucky chance a few years before, he'd found himself in Cancun during spring break. He scanned the room in Brian's absence and was generous with his winks and smiles.

The next morning, around eleven, Brian and Walter were shaken awake by the sound of blaring disco music. They both sat up in bed, bleary-eyed.

"I guess they found the stereo," Walter said, getting up and pulling on a pair of sweatpants. Brian groaned, and fell back on the bed, covering his head with the pillow.

"I'll make us some breakfast," Walter said. "You stay here and I'll bring it in. They'll probably go out soon and then we can be alone."

In the kitchen, Derek and Keith were dancing around and mixing up their protein shakes. They were dressed for a workout so Walter gathered they had, in their socializing the night before, discovered the location of a gym.

"Did you bring any grape juice?" Derek asked, when he noticed Walter.

"No, I think I bought orange, why?"

Keith frowned. "Because you're supposed to drink grape juice with this in order to get optimum results."

Walter looked at the bottle of powder they were each spooning into their mouths.

"What is this stuff?" he asked.

"Creatine," Keith said. "The magic powder that will turn us both into gods."

"You look fine, for Christ's sake," Walter said, shaking his head and looking at their bulging arm muscles rippling beneath the sleeves of their shirts. They were beautiful, he thought, there was no doubt about that, but in an almost too idealized way, with the result that they looked somewhat plastic. And yet, as good as they looked, and as hard as they worked to look that good, Walter knew they would never be satisfied. They would never be big enough for themselves, but would instead focus on bulking up their too-slender ankles, or evening out their obviously lopsided (obviously lopsided to their eyes only) pectorals. Walter often wondered what they could do if only they channeled even a tenth of the energy they put into working out, into their professional lives.

"Speaking of stuff," Keith said, pulling a brown glass jar out of the refrigerator and holding it up for all to view, "what is this?"

Walter looked at the jar, read the label, and then stuck it back in the refrigerator.

"It's, uh, Jake's," he said softly. This was followed by an awkward silence in which the pulsing beat of the disco music seemed especially gaudy and inappropriate.

"Oh," Keith said gravely. "I didn't know."

"No, no, it's okay," Walter said. "He's okay. I talked to him last week to see if we should stay somewhere else but he, uh, said it was . . . okay."

Silence again.

"We'll probably see him around later on," Walter said, brightening. "He's staying just down the road at Lily's. I'm sure he'll go to some of the events."

"Good," Derek said. "Good. I always liked him. In fact, he's the only B.O.W. that I was really jealous of."

"Too true!" said Keith. "I hope we do see him."

"Well," Walter said, pouring himself a cup of coffee and changing the subject, "what's on the agenda for today?"

"I thought you might ask," Derek replied, "and I am prepared." He disappeared down the hall for a moment and returned carrying several sheets of pink paper. He handed one to Walter, one to Keith, and kept one for himself.

"I grabbed these schedules last night from the bar, since I was evidently the only one sober enough to see them."

"Now," Derek continued, adopting a business-like tone and addressing Walter, "our attendance at these events is, of course, subject to change at a moment's notice, so you might want to keep that in mind. If, say, the Portuguese tycoon I met last night should decide to whisk me away to his Canary Island villa, or if Keith's Teutonic love interest, about whose wealth I have my doubts, invites us to a private party, then you and The Bambi are, I'm afraid, on your own. However, if neither of those things pan out, you will certainly find each of us prospecting at any of the events I have taken the liberty of highlighting. And let me stress that we do hope you'll join us at these events, since, as you well know, neither one of us has a single red cent to call his own."

Walter smiled, set down his coffee cup, and returned to the bedroom. He emerged a moment later and gave each of them a fifty-dollar bill.

"Bless you," Keith said, making the sign of the cross on Walter's forehead. Derek bowed down and kissed his hand. Walter waved them away, trying to hide his smile.

"We're off then!" Derek said, and they grabbed their gym bags and bounded for the door. "There's a cocktail party at the Jerome tonight at five so we'll be back here no later than four to get ready. If I were you I'd take The Bambi out and get him some new clothes. Emphasis on the word 'new.' Ciao for now!" And they went out, slamming the door behind them.

Walter shook his head and allowed himself to smile. They were something else, those two. A financial liability mostly, but they were entertaining and could always make him laugh. He realized then how much he valued that, and how much he had missed seeing them over the summer.

He started making breakfast for Brian, humming to himself as he gathered eggs and bread and jam from the refrigerator. Again, he noticed the bottles of medicine in the back and stopped humming. He picked one up and looked at it, wondering if maybe it hadn't been wrong to bring Brian here. Jake had said it was fine, said he didn't mind at all, but then what else could he say, really, since it was, after all, Walter's house?

Jake had gotten sick a year after they'd broken up, so, technically, Walter really had no obligation to him. Anyone looking at it from the outside would agree, would say that Walter had done more than was expected, at least in the material sense. And yet, he still felt terrible about his part in it all. Yes, he had given Jake a place to live, but he had also actively avoided any contact with him beyond what was absolutely necessary. They spoke about the house and repairs that were needed, bills that needed to be paid, but nothing beyond the mundane, always tiptoeing around the issue of AIDS. Oh, Walter always inquired after his health, but Jake, probably knowing how uncomfortable the topic made him, replied with the meaningless words, "fine" and "okay."

Walter put the bottles back in the refrigerator and closed the door. He considered calling Jake and inviting him over, even went so far as to pick up the phone, but then he thought better of it and returned the phone to its cradle. It would seem odd to invite him back to the house he had been living in for years. No, better to go out to dinner, he thought. That way they'd be on neutral territory. He would call over to Lily's that afternoon and invite him.

As if on cue, he heard his cell phone ringing in the bedroom. He set the food down on the counter and ran to retrieve it from his pile of clothes on the floor. He answered it just in time, before it went to voice mail.

"Hello."

"Hello, is this Walter?"

"Yes. Who is this?"

"This is Gene, down at Dillon Towing. I've got a car here belongs to a Mr. Reynolds. State Patrol had me tow it out of the truck ramp on I-70."

"Yes," Walter said, somewhat impatiently. "That's Derek's car. Why are you calling me? How did you get my number?"

"Yeah, uh, Mr. Reynolds gave it to me," he said, his voice uneasy. "He, uh, told me you'd take care 'a the cost 'a the towing and take care of the other, uh, little issue."

"Wait a minute," Walter said, his blood pressure rising. "He said *I'd* pay for it? He told you that *I'd* pay for it?"

"Well, yeah, but not until his two other cards got declined."

Walter groaned.

"He said I could just have the car," the man continued, "said he didn't want it anymore, and that would be fine. The amount I'd get from the salvage company'll cover most of it, but then there's the little, uh, issue, like I said before."

"Yes, well, I don't know what you're talking about," Walter said impatiently, digging in his pants pocket for his wallet. "How much is the towing? I'll just give you a credit card number and we'll be done with it."

"Well, let's see, it's two-twenty-five, but like I said, I'll take out some in trade for the salvage, so that makes, say one-twenty-five."

"Fine," Walter said, "I'll put it on Amex; are you ready to take down the number?"

"Uh, excuse me, sir, but you can give me that when you come down to the garage, if you'd like. That way I can give you a receipt and you can come get the little item that was left under the front seat, and we'll be all free and clear."

"What? No," Walter said, shaking his head. "I'm not coming all the way down to Dillon. Whatever it is under the seat you can just leave it there for all I'm concerned."

"Sir. I'm afraid I can't do that."

"Why not?"

"I'm afraid I can't do that."

"Good God, why not? What is it?" Walter asked. The man was silent for a moment.

"Sir, uh, you are speaking on a cell phone, right?"

"Yes, why?" Walter snapped.

"Well, I guess you just gotta be sorta delicate about some things, ya know, when you're talking on a cell phone."

"Oh God! What is it?" Walter demanded, wondering what the hell Derek could have shoved under the seat.

"Hmmm. How to say this? Okay, okay, I got it, I got it, hee, hee. It comes after corned beef . . . but before browns."

Walter was silent. He rubbed his eyes and shook his head.

"Look," he said, as calmly as he could, "I don't follow you, and I'm a little bit hungover so please, no riddles."

The man chuckled.

"Okay, okay," he said. "How to say this . . . It's a brick, if you know what I mean."

"*Hash?*" Walter cried, suddenly comprehending the situation. Derek had been dating a Dutch drug dealer a month or so back and, Walter surmised, the hash probably belonged to him.

"Look, I don't want no trouble," the man said. "I wouldn't 'a touched it if I'd known. I got a record and I don't want trouble, see?"

"Oh, Christ," Walter sighed, hunting around for paper and a pencil. "Give me the address."

Once he'd written it down, he hung up and immediately dialed Derek's cell phone number.

In a locker room, far off in the corner of the Aspen Athletic Club, deep in the darkest recesses of Derek's gym bag, the purple phone rang its French can-can ring, unheard by anyone. Walter left a curt message instructing Derek to call immediately, and then he hung up and dialed Keith's phone. In the locker just next to Derek's, a teal phone rang, this time playing the familiar bars of Beethoven's Fifth Symphony. It repeated them four times and fell silent. Walter hung up without leaving a message and began singing his own tune of curses.

"What's the matter?" Brian asked, running into the kitchen, alarmed by all the noise. Walter was nearly purple with rage, but when he saw Brian, dressed only in boxers, his hair still styled by sleep, his expression softened.

"It's those fucking brats again," he moaned, beating the back of the sofa with his fist. "Listen," he said, giving Brian a quick kiss on the forehead and then returning to the bedroom to get dressed. "I have to go find them, but I'll be back. Shouldn't take more than an hour at most."

"Do you want me to go with you?" Brian asked.

"No." Walter smiled, pulling on his pants. "No, no, no. You just stay here. I'll explain when I get back. Get yourself some breakfast. Relax. I'll be back before you know it. Hopefully we can settle this without going all the way back to Dillon."

Walter finished dressing, kissed Brian again, and went out the door, slamming it behind him. Brian watched, bewildered, as the car drove down the winding road, disappearing in the town below.

The house, filled with noise all morning while Brian had been trying to sleep, was empty and silent now that he was awake. For a while, he paced around wondering what could have happened, but soon those thoughts were usurped by his appetite and he went about fixing his breakfast. After he'd eaten, he paced around some more, again wondering what to do, but decided he'd better take a shower so he'd be ready to go when Walter came back. While he was in the shower, the phone rang, and, like the can-can ring and the Beethoven's Fifth ring, this mundane, average, unexciting ring was heard by no one.

Brian got out of the shower, put on a fresh pair of boxers, and again paced and waited. He thought he might read to pass the time so he wandered over to the large bookcase and gazed sideways at the spines. He ran his fingers along the titles, wanting to choose something masculine, a Hemingway or a Jack London maybe, something to fit the mountainous setting, but then he spied a faded copy of *Jane Eyre* and gave a little gasp of pleasure. It was a book he'd read so many times he could almost recite it from memory, but to which he never tired of returning. Almost timidly, he took it down from the shelf, looking around to see that no one was watching. He flipped through a few pages, smiling as he read, and then wandered into the kitchen and made himself a cup of tea, returning with it to the living room and settling into a sunny spot on the sofa by the window. He read less than a chapter before his eyelids got heavy and he fell asleep.

When he awoke, it was to see a strange man staring down at him. He sat up with a start, his heart racing.

"Hold on there," the man said, extending a large hand, his voice rough and gravelly. "Don't be scared. I didn't think anyone was here. I, uh, called," he said, looking back over his shoulder at the phone, "and there was no car in the drive, so I just . . ."

Brian moved back into the corner of the sofa, still not quite awake.

The man gazed down at him, smiling, and Brian observed that he was blind in one eye. His weathered face, thin to the point of gauntness, was very tan, and had the pronounced racoon-eye tan lines from his sunglasses, which now hung from a short purple cord around his neck. He was dressed in a pair of khaki pants and an unironed plaid shirt, whose rolled up sleeves revealed arms that were surprisingly muscular. He seemed to Brian to emit both vitality and fatality at the same time, in a mix that was not unattractive.

"I can tell, just by looking at you, little puppy," the man said with a rough laugh, "that you belong to Walter."

He then turned his head to look at the book Brian was holding.

"*Jane Eyre*," he said slowly, and then paused and looked out the window, as if trying to remember it. "You like that one?" he asked.

Brian glanced down at the book, embarrassed, and then back up at the man. He nodded.

"Yeah, me too," he said in a husky voice, and then turned and walked purposefully toward the kitchen. "Although I have to say it's been a while since I've read it."

Brian watched him disappear and when he did not soon return, he got up from the sofa and went into the kitchen himself. He found the man squatting down in front of the open refrigerator.

"Excuse me," Brian said, as politely as he could, "but who are you?"

"Huh?" the man replied, turning and looking over his shoulder.

"I mean, I guess you're a friend of Walter's since you know his name, but I don't know you. My name is Brian," he said, extending his hand.

"Brian," the man repeated, setting his bottles on the counter and shaking his hand. "Brian the puppy. Shake, Brian. Shake. Good boy!"

He then turned his attention back to his bottles and began placing them in a paper grocery bag. Brian waited for the man to introduce himself but when it didn't happen he asked again, "And, uh, who . . . are you?"

The man looked up, a devious grin on his face.

"Walter didn't tell you about me?" he asked.

"Well, no," Brian answered, shaking his head.

"Nothing?"

"No, I'm afraid not."

"Hmm. Well, then I guess I'll have to tell you," he said, and spying the copy of *Jane Eyre* that Brian had set on the counter, tapped it and said grandly, "My name's Jake, but you can call me the first Mrs. Rochester."

Brian looked confused. The man's smile disappeared and his shoulders fell, disappointed that Brian had not understood his literary reference. His voice lost all its grandeur and in a bland tone he said, "I'm Walter's ex."

"Yes, of course!" Brian said, and then laughed.

"Yes, I'm the afflicted one, the one the family doesn't know what to do with. The first Mrs. Rochester. The crazy one they stuck up in the attic."

Brian nodded and laughed.

"Have you ever noticed," Jake went on, his voice becoming animated once more, "that all those retards and psychopaths in books and movies are always stuffed away in the attic? Either that or the cellar, or the rickety old house at the end of the block. Think about it," he said, starting to count on his fingers. "There's crazy Mrs. Rochester, Norman Bates and his mother, old Boo Radley . . ."

"Don't forget the portrait of Dorian Grey!" Brian chimed in.

"Yes, good!" Jake said. "But now, come on, does that one really count? It's a picture, not a real person. But it's a nice idea, isn't it: put all your aging ugliness in the attic while you wander the streets looking beautiful. As you can see I'm the reverse of that: I keep the beautiful portrait of myself in the attic and roam the streets displaying my gargoyle visage."

Jake laughed heartily at his own joke, but it made Brian a bit uneasy, like when black people used the word "nigger."

"Not that I complain," Jake went on. "Ha! Far from it. My little attic here," he said, gesturing at his surroundings, "is nothing to whine about. In fact I'm pretty lucky to have fallen into this gravy boat."

"You've obviously taken advantage of Walter's library," Brian said, smiling now. For a moment Jake looked confused.

"*Walter's* library," he said with a chuckle. "That's a good one!"

Now it was Brian's turn to look confused.

"You mean they're . . . not . . . Walter's books?"

Again, Jake laughed.

"Please! Walter hasn't cracked the spine of a book in all the years I've known him," Jake said, "unless he knew there'd be dirty pictures inside."

The phone rang and Jake immediately answered it.

". . . Jake?" Walter asked, surprised. "Is that you?"

"Walter. Yeah, it's me. I guess you want to talk to the puppy," he said, handing the phone to Brian without waiting for an answer.

"Hello," Brian said.

"Hey, it's me. When did Jake get there?"

"Just now, I think," Brian said, rubbing his eyes. "I was asleep."

"Awww," Walter sighed, remembering the drowsy image of Brian as he'd come out of the bedroom that morning.

"What's up?" Brian asked.

"Well, I went to the gym and I found them. They're showering and then it looks like we have to go back to Dillon. Oh, here they come now. Look, I'm so sorry about this. I'll make up for it tonight, I promise."

"Don't worry about it," Brian said, nervously twirling the phone cord, aware that Jake was staring at him. "I'll find something to do."

"Okay," Walter said. "I'll get back as soon as I can. Do you still . . . love me?" he whispered.

In the background Brian heard Keith and Derek making exaggerated kissing sounds and repeating in high pitched voices, "Ooooh, Brian, kissy kissy, do you still *love* me?"

"Uh, yes, of course," Brian whispered, turning away from Jake. "Do what you have to do. I'll be fine."

"Okay," Walter said. "Let me talk to Jake again."

Brian handed the phone back to Jake and returned to the living room where he pretended to read. A few minutes later, Jake emerged, carrying his bag.

"Get dressed," he said. "Walter's asked me to show you around and I've decided to oblige."

Five minutes later Brian and Jake were driving back down the hill in Jake's ancient Jeep. In town, Jake parked on the street and the two got out and walked up and down several streets, popping in and out of shops on errands that Jake needed to run. Several people along the way waved at Jake or stopped and said hello, and Brian realized that Jake was evidently quite popular among the locals. Eventually their walk led them to Lily's shop just off of Main.

"Hello, Lily," Jake said, in a booming voice, as he opened the door. "I've come for lunch and I've brought a friend."

The small shop they entered sold jewelry, and had glittering glass display cases along each of the walls. From behind one of these cases a woman rose and came toward them, smiling. She was very short, with short, spiky black hair, and long, pendulous silver earrings. She smiled at Jake and then turned her alarmingly blue eyes on Brian.

"My goodness," she said, walking completely around Brian and eyeing him up and down. "Where on earth did you find this little gem?"

Brian blushed and smiled.

"He's Walter's," Jake replied. "He's on loan for the day. It's a shame, isn't it?"

"Walter ought to keep him locked away," she replied. "This is the kind of jewel you only bring out on special occasions. I'm Lily," she said, pausing in front of Brian and extending her ring-laden hand. Brian shook it and blushed even more.

"We were hoping we could get some lunch, and then I told Walter I'd take Brian out and show him some of the sights in our little village."

"You ought to take him fishing," Lily said, in an almost scolding tone to Jake. "What does he want to see in town? Make him take you fishing, Brian."

"Lily, stop!" Jake said. "We're not going fishing. Brian doesn't want to go fishing."

"Well, actually," Brian said suddenly, his interest piqued by the idea, "I've never been and I've always wanted to."

"See!" Lily cried. "He wants to go! Oh, I like this Brian already; come with me, sweetie." And she took Brian by the arm and led him to a staircase at the back of the store. "We'll get you some lunch and then you two can go fishing."

"But . . ." Jake started. He was cut short by Lily.

"Jake, don't be a dick. Lock the door and flip the sign."

The stairway led up to a sunny loft above the store, in which Lily lived. For Brian, it was like stepping into a Stevie Nicks album cover, full of colorful scarves, and hanging houseplants, and long-haired cats, several of which were lounging on the pillow-covered window seats.

"Welcome," she said, shooing one of the cats away and offering a chair to Brian. "I'm an old friend of Jake and Walter's, although I really don't see much of Walter anymore."

They heard Jake coming up the stairs. Lily leaned in close to Brian and cupped her hands around her mouth.

"Please make him take you fishing," she whispered. "More for his sake than for yours."

Brian nodded hastily and Lily pulled back, but not before Jake had seen the interaction.

"Conspiring already," he said, raising an eyebrow.

Lily patted Brian's head and then turned and took Jake by the arm, hustling him over to the kitchen where the two busied themselves fixing lunch.

"Can I help?" Brian asked, rising with difficulty from the pillowy chair.

"No, no," Lily called. "Sit. We'll have it all ready in a minute."

"Sit, Puppy, sit!" Jake commanded.

Brian rolled his eyes at Jake and then eased back into the chair, surveying the busy surroundings. Three walls of the loft were covered with blobby paintings and odd-shaped ceramics Lily had obviously made herself. The fourth wall was one large bookcase, the shelves of which were crammed with candles, seashells, rocks, and bunches of dried flowers. On the sari-covered table next to him there was a lamp with an elaborate, fringed shade, and under this stood several framed photographs. Brian fixed his attention on these: a group shot from the days when Jake and Lily were on the ski patrol; several photos from weddings; pictures of nieces, and nephews, and kitties . . . but then Brian's eyes settled on a larger picture behind all the others that appeared to be of Jake. He made sure that Jake and Lily were still occupied in the kitchen and then he picked up the picture and studied it closely. It was a picture of Jake, standing in the middle of a stream, fly fishing. An idyllic shot, taken in the late afternoon sun, the reflection off the water illuminating his face and the glistening line arced high above his head. It was an amazing photo, but what was really amazing about it was how it only vaguely resembled the Jake that Brian could see standing next to Lily in the kitchen. He glanced up at Jake, and then back down at the photo, and shuddered, nearly overcome by a feeling of pity. He'd always known what AIDS is, but only in an abstract sense. As he looked at Jake and at the photo he saw, for the first time in his life, just exactly what AIDS does.

During lunch, the conversation was mostly about Brian, about whom, the boy was flattered to observe, Lily seemed genuinely interested.

"I just graduated this past spring with a BA in literature and I'm set to start a graduate program in the fall," Brian said. "I really want to be a professor so I'll probably go right on from there and get my Ph.D."

"Wait a minute," Lily said, a concerned look suddenly clouding her face. "You're saying you just got your undergraduate degree and you're jumping right into grad school with nothing but a summer in between?"

"Well, yes," Brian answered, somewhat startled by her reaction. "Why?"

"It just surprises me, that's all," she said, shrugging and poking at her salad. Brian waited for her to say why it surprised her, and when, after several moments, she did not, he asked, "What . . . if you don't mind my asking, is surprising about it?"

She pushed her food around on the plate, thinking it over.

"I don't know," she said. "I mean, I may be wrong but I just think you're awfully young to be on the fast track to tenure."

"No, not really," Brian said, becoming defensive. "It's a very competitive field. The younger I start, the better my chances. It's important to stay focused."

Lily and Jake exchanged an amused look but were silent. Brian was confused.

"I'm getting the sense that you disapprove," Brian said.

"Oh, no, it's not that really. You're a smart kid, ambitious, I can tell that. And it's good to have goals . . ."

"But . . ." Brian said, supplying the transition.

"Just make sure you get some living in there somewhere," Lily offered. "Some of the most boring professors I ever knew were the ones who went straight through from kindergarten until they got their

Ph.D. They didn't—how do I say this?—they didn't really have a lot to bring to the table, you know? No life experience."

Brian nodded. He had never really thought of it that way before.

"There's a whole world outside of books, Puppy," Jake said with a smile. "Just make sure you grab some of it."

After lunch, Jake returned to Walter's to retrieve the fishing gear (which, Brian was surprised to learn, did not belong, as the books had not belonged, to Walter, but to Jake). Brian stayed behind and helped Lily with the dishes.

"Is Jake okay to go fishing?" Brian asked, washing and rinsing the plates, and then handing them to Lily. "I mean, he seems so reluctant to go."

"He's fine. Really. It'll be good for him."

They were silent for a moment.

"Was he . . . very sick?" Brian asked timidly. He had no knowledge of death or illness, his father having died when he was only an infant, and both sets of grandparents were still going strong.

"Very," Lily said. "It looked grim for a while. The cocktail came around just in time. He was really ready to die, you know what I mean? So it's been hard for him to come back from that."

Brian nodded but said nothing. He looked down at his arms in the hot soapy water and noticed they were covered in goose bumps.

"Physically he's been strong enough for a long time," Lily went on, "and he's getting stronger every day. Really! I'm amazed. But he's lost a lot of confidence, and that's why he's not doing such a great job at getting back."

Jake returned just as Brian and Lily were finishing. He and Brian thanked Lily for lunch, said goodbye, and then took off in the Jeep. They drove out of town for about half an hour, during which time Jake was silent. Partly this was due to the fact there was no roof on the Jeep, so the wind and the noise from the wheels on the road made conversation difficult, but Brian also sensed that maybe Jake was a little nervous, whether from excitement or apprehension, he couldn't tell.

From time to time Brian looked over at him. His eyes wandered down Jake's sleeve to the large forearm. It was tan and hairy, and the muscles and tendons flexed as he shifted the Jeep through the various gears. Brian then looked down at his own arms, folded in his lap and thought, sadly, how much they looked like nothing so much as pale, thin twigs in comparison. He glanced over again but this time Jake caught him looking and smiled. Without any warning, Jake lifted his large hand from where it had been resting on the gearshift knob and placed it squarely on Brian's thigh. Brian looked at the hand and then over at Jake. Jake's eyes were on the road but his lips were curved up into a smile.

Eventually, they went off the pavement and drove along a winding dirt road. After a few miles on that road they went off onto a stretch of dirt that could hardly be called a road, littered as it was with boulders and fallen trees. They traveled on for about fifteen minutes, and then Jake pulled off and parked the Jeep under a tree. He gave Brian's thigh another pat and hopped out.

"Come on," he said, collecting the poles and waders from the back of the Jeep. "You can use my old waders. They should fit you and I'm pretty sure they don't leak."

Brian got out and watched as Jake eagerly removed his boots and stepped into his pair of hip waders. He took the pair Jake gave to him and gingerly put them on. To Brian, there was something almost erotic about the whole process, like borrowing someone else's underwear, and he felt an unmistakable stirring in his own underwear as Jake knelt down in front of him, fed the rubber straps through Brian's belt loops, and then snapped them into place.

"Okay," Jake said, when the last snap was fastened, "you're good to go." And he gave Brian a slap on the ass. He then handed him an enormously long pole, a smelly creel, and a small dip net with a bottle of bug spray in it.

"Now, this is a great spot I'm taking you to and no one else knows about it," Jake said, "so if you tell anyone, I'm going to have to kill you."

He picked up his own creel and pole, and his net and ran off excitedly through the woods. Brian followed, as closely as he could, but found it difficult to maneuver through the bushes in the heavy rubber boots, and he never quite figured out how to carry his pole so that it didn't keep snagging in the tree limbs overhead. He was busy trying to remedy this problem, walking forward but looking up, when he tripped over something and fell, facedown on the ground. He sat up, looked back, and saw that what he had tripped over was Jake, who was also lying facedown. Jake lifted up his head and Brian saw that he was afraid.

"Guess, uh, I got a little too excited," Jake said, pulling himself up and brushing the dirt and pine needles off of his chest. His breathing was erratic and his eyes were wide. "I forget I can't see very well."

Brian remembered Jake's reluctance to go fishing in the first place and suddenly knew that this was the reason for it. He knew that Jake was afraid he wouldn't be able to make it, was afraid that something just like this would happen. Brian also knew that his being there and witnessing it made it even worse and could easily break the man's already brittle confidence. Almost without thinking, Brian pulled himself up, brushed the dirt and pine needles off his own chest and then grabbed Jake by the arm and pulled him up.

"Watch it next time," he said, in a tone of mock anger. "If you're going to take off running like a kid after the ice-cream man and leave me trying to keep up, the least you could do would be to call out when you decide to face plant so I don't go down with you. Or was that part of the plan?" he asked, reaching over and giving Jake's ass a slap. Jake's grin returned. He swatted Brian's hand away, straightened his cap, and then collected his creel and pole and net. When Brian had retrieved all of his own accessories, the two set off again, more slowly this time, toward the river. Jake seemed a little unsteady so Brian stuck close behind him, ready to assist if the need arose.

Ironically enough, it was Brian who needed all the assistance once they arrived at the river. They sat down on the bank and Jake took out his fly box and a spool of leader. He showed Brian how to tie the clear leader onto the thick, yellow line, first demonstrating the knot, and then undoing it and handing it to him so that he could do it himself. Knot tying was completely foreign to Brian, so his hands were naturally clumsy. But Jake was a patient teacher, and after several unsuccessful attempts to join the two lines, Brian was finally able to do it himself. The feeling of elation and accomplishment he got from this small, intricate task was immense, and he gazed down proudly for several seconds at the two strands joined by his knot. The next task, attaching the fly to the leader, seemed easy by comparison and he leaned forward eagerly as Jake selected flies and showed him how to do it.

"Okay," Jake said, when they were up and at the edge of the river. "Now fly fishing is all about the rhythm, just don't overdo it. Make an arc and aim for the sweet spot."

He took his rod in his right hand, accordioned several feet of line in his left, and set the rod in motion, waving it above his head three times before pointing it forward and releasing the line. It shot out over the water, the fly hitting first, followed by the clear leader, and then the yellow line. He let the fly float for a moment on the ripple, watched as the water carried it downstream, and when it had run its course, slowly reeled it back in.

"Now you try," he said to Brian, setting down his pole and coming over next to him.

Brian took a deep breath and grasped the cork handle of his pole. He accordioned the yellow line, just as he had seen Jake do although not nearly so neatly, and then leaned back and whipped the rod back and forth. There was a slashing sound in the air overhead and then a splash as the tip smacked the water. The line was all bunched up at the tip of the rod. Brian reddened and looked down. He shook his head and quickly untangled the line. He was sure Jake would be laughing, but a moment later he was aware of Jake's arms encircling him, and felt his breath on the back of his neck.

"Let's try it again," Jake said, placing his right hand over Brian's on the cork handle and using his left to again demonstrate how to accordion the line. When they were ready, Jake moved the rod, and Brian's arm with it, back and forth several times in a slow and graceful motion until Brian was able to absorb the rhythm. Jake then gave his shoulder a squeeze and stepped off to the side. Brian was so nervous, his hand was shaking. He wanted to succeed, wanted desperately not to look foolish in front of Jake, wanted to learn. He bit his lip, furrowed his brow, and tried to focus on all the things Jake had said, while at the same time aiming for a spot on the water. He rocked the rod back and forth, four or five times, trying to relax. When he felt the rhythm was right he leaned forward and released the line. It wasn't the prettiest cast, and it hardly came close to the "sweet spot" but it did get the line out into the water without making a splash.

"Good, Puppy," Jake said, his eyes on the river. "Good! Now let it float a little, natural-like, and then reel it in real slow. That's it, that's it."

Brian made three more casts, each better than the last, but got into trouble with the fourth. He rocked back and forth several times but when he shot forward the line didn't follow. He looked back and saw it snagged in the willow bushes behind him. He yanked and pulled on the rod, trying to free it, but that only seemed to make it worse. Jake, who had wandered out into the middle of the stream with his own rod, looked back at Brian's distress and smiled.

"Welcome to Fly Fishing 101," he called, and then turned back to the stream leaving Brian to fend for himself. Five minutes later, Brian was still tugging and yanking, now cursing at the line. Jake noticed him, laughed, and waded slowly back toward shore.

"Need some help?"

Brian nodded, wiping the sweat from his face with his sleeve. Jake stepped forward, took a pocket knife from his creel and cut the line.

"Sometimes you just gotta start over," he said. He gave Brian some more leader and another fly and left him to tie them together, wading back out into the river and heading downstream. Brian watched enviously from the shore as Jake caught several fish, and he tried to hurry tying his knots, as if he thought Jake would get all the fish from the stream and leave nothing for him. When he was done, Jake was nowhere to be seen. Brian waded out into the stream, far away from the menacing willows, and began casting once again. He recited all the things that Jake had told him, over and over again like a mantra, and when he felt the rhythm, he shot the line forward. It was easier now that he knew he was not being watched, and with each successful cast he made, his confidence inched up. When he caught his first fish, he didn't believe it, thinking that the fly must have snagged a floating stick, or gotten wedged between some rocks. It was only when he felt the insistent tug, and then saw the fish jump completely out of the water, that he realized what it was. He panicked. His legs trembled and he became flustered, clinging to the cork handle with both hands while the line sped out of the reel with a buzzing sound. It was by no means a huge fish, probably no more than eight inches, but he could feel it tugging on his line and saw it bending the tip of his rod and to

him, at that point, it might as well have been Melville's white whale.
Just then, Jake reappeared, coming round the bend in the river downstream.

"Reel him in!" he called out. Brian nodded several times.

"Yes, yes, reel him in, reel him in, reel him in," he repeated to himself, and began frantically turning the crank on the side of the reel.
The fish fought back and Brian watched, awestruck as the line moved,
with an almost ghostly power, from one side of the river to the other.

"Slow down!" Jake called. "Reel him in slow!"

Again Brian nodded and slowed his turning. He took several deep
breaths and tried to relax his shoulders, reeling slowly and steadily.
Soon, the fish was less than ten yards away. At times Brian could even
see it. When it jumped, making a showy splash in the water, Brian was
so startled he nearly dropped the pole.

Net, he thought feverishly to himself. The net. Get the net.

The net was attached to his belt loop and he fumbled with his left
hand to get it undone. The fish jumped again. Brian immediately returned both hands to the rod and in the process dropped the net. He
watched, horrified, as the current caught it and carried it rapidly
downstream. Jake saw all this and waded slowly out into the middle of
the water, grabbing the net as it floated by. Jake was smiling and was
calling something out to him, but the roar of the water was too loud,
and Brian couldn't hear. He went back to reeling, and soon the fish was
there, right in front of him, weaving frantically from side to side. Brian
didn't know what to do. But he knew he wanted to bag this fish, almost
more than he'd ever wanted anything in his life. He reeled in some
more line and then tilted the pole high in the air. The fish popped out
of the water, flapping wildly in the air before him. He held the pole
with his right hand and reached out in front of him with his left, trying
to grab it. He managed to grab the line above it and then pulled it
closer. It swung toward him suddenly and he felt a wet smack on his
cheek. The reel and handle were now completely submerged, and
Brian grasped the pole tightly between his legs, holding the line with
one hand and grasping at the fish with the other. He caught it, but it
was so slimy and slippery it shot up out of his hand like a wet bar of
soap. He tried again. He moved the line in closer, grasped again, and
this time got it. He brought it in close to his body and held the flap-

ping thing against his chest. With his other hand he tried to unhook the fly from the fish's mouth. It was lodged deep and he had to put his hand inside and pull. The feel of the tiny teeth was almost too gross, but he persevered, and by grasping the fly and twisting it back and forth, he managed to remove it. He held the fish fast to his chest, painfully aware that the line no longer held it, and reached with his free hand for the creel resting on his opposite hip. He moved it around in front of him, opened it, stuffed the fish inside, and quickly snapped it shut. He realized he had been holding his breath for some time so he released the air and relaxed his shoulders. He looked downstream. Jake was still standing in the middle of the river, holding his pole and Brian's net, smiling proudly. Brian was elated. He pulled his pole out of the water, shook it off, and strode downstream toward Jake, a broad grin on his face.

And then it happened. In truth it could have happened, and often does happen, to even the most seasoned fisherman. Brian stepped on a rock covered with that particularly slimy type of algae and his feet went out from under him. The waders filled with water, were caught by the current and pulled him under. It was not especially deep water, maybe three feet at the most, but it was swift and cold. Bitter cold. Water from just-melted snow. He surfaced a moment later, gasping for breath, blowing the water out of his nose. His head ached from the cold, like when he had eaten ice cream too fast, but worse, much worse. He stood up, still clutching the pole, and was surprised to realize that his first concern was about his fish. He peeked in the creel and was relieved to see its speckled body still there. He crept with difficulty back to the shore and sat down on a rock, water pouring out of his waders as he did so. Jake was hurrying toward him now, still smiling, but looking concerned. Brian's teeth began to chatter.

"You all right?" Jake asked, as he waded up to Brian.

"I still got him!" Brian shouted, and then proudly opened his creel to show Jake. "I can't believe I got him! Did you see that?"

"I did, Puppy. You did great! But we gotta get you out of those clothes. Come on."

Jake took his pole and stepped onto the shore. He led the shivering Brian to a grassy clearing where the sun was shining brightly and

helped him off with his waders. The light breeze that had been blowing now felt to Brian like an Arctic blast and his whole body began
trembling.

"Stay here," Jake commanded, his voice low and serious, "and take
off your wet clothes. I think I've got some others in the Jeep. I'll be
right back."

Brian was far too cold to be shy at this point so he peeled off his wet
shirt and then quickly undid the buttons of his jeans. He was struggling to pull them off his legs when Jake returned, carrying an old,
wool army blanket.

"Here, let me help," Jake said, grabbing the legs of Brian's jeans and
pulling them off. He then stood up and said, "Come on, skivvies too."

"No way!" Brian said, shaking his head. "You give me that blanket
first."

Jake shook his head. He picked up the blanket and took several
steps backward, grinning.

"I just fell in ice-cold water!" Brian whined, but was smiling in spite
of himself. "I'm not showing you anything until it's back to normal
size. And probably not even then! Come on, give me the blanket."

"I won't look," Jake said, putting his hand over his eyes. "I promise.
I can hardly see anyway."

"No!"

"Well, suit yourself," Jake said, and then turned and walked away
with the blanket.

Outraged, Brian pulled off his wet underwear. He rolled them into a
soggy ball and then threw them as hard as he could at Jake. They hit
him in the back of the head with a smack. Jake spun around and
looked back at Brian, who was peering at him from behind a rock.

"I suppose I deserved that," Jake said, bending down and picking up
the underwear, "but you'll still have to come and get the blanket." And
he turned once again and walked back down to the river. Brian, shivering,
cupped one hand around his shrunken genitals and marched out after
him, snatching the blanket away and quickly wrapping it around his
shoulders. He felt like he should be mad, but he could not stop smiling.

"Sit down in the sun," Jake said, laughing and pointing to a large
rock. "I'll spread these out so they'll dry, and then I'm going back out

and try and catch some more. If there are any more, since you probably scared them all away with your little swim."

Brian, warming now wrapped in the wool blanket, watched Jake as he returned to the water and began fishing. It was late afternoon, and the sun was reflected off the water much the way it had been in the photograph at Lily's. He is a beautiful man, Brian thought to himself, but there was something more. Something he couldn't quite put his finger on. A masculinity, a strength, a capability; something almost archetypically male that he couldn't find the right word for, but which he found irresistibly sexy. And then there was his patience and guidance, his desire to impart knowledge for no self-serving reason.

Brian was falling in love, and he knew it. It was the knot tying that had done it, that and the feeling of Jake's arms around his, guiding the rod and teaching him the rhythm. It was a slightly sexual feeling, yes, but that was almost secondary. It was mentoring, of the type he'd only read about in his studies of the Greeks, and scarcely dared ever hope for. Yes, that was it! Jake had been a mentor, and that was something Walter, or any of the other men he'd known, had never done. Oh, they gave him things, they took him places, but this was different, this was more. Maybe it was because fishing was on his mind, but he remembered one of those trite little sayings just then, and was surprised at how well it put into words what he was thinking.

Give a man a fish and you feed him for a day.
Teach a man to fish and you feed him for a lifetime.

Brian saw that so far in all of his relationships he had been given fish. That was all very well and good, and definitely had its advantages, but he saw then that not much growth had come of it. In Jake, he saw someone that could teach him to fish (indeed, in the literal sense, already had). Someone who was strong, and who could give him confidence. Someone who was smart, funny, and attractive. Someone he could admire and respect. But the way he really knew he was falling for Jake was the feeling he got when he imagined not seeing him again. It was a hollow, vacant, almost sad feeling. He looked out at him fishing, so focused and intent, and Brian knew that he wanted him. He wanted him and, he decided, he would go after him.

About an hour later Jake came back around the bend and returned to shore. He squatted down along the edge of the river and began gutting the fish. Brian retrieved his now-dry underwear from the rock, put them on and went over and sat next to him. Jake looked up and smiled.

"There's some beer in the river over by that tree," he said, nodding to a large pine tree about twenty yards off. Brian tiptoed along the rocks and then peered down into the water where Jake had pointed. There, like hidden treasure, were two bottles of beer, their gold caps shining in the sunlight. He pulled them out, held them aloft while the water dripped off, and then quickly brought them back to Jake.

"Can I do that?" Brian asked, pointing to the bloody mess in Jake's hands. Jake looked up at him in disbelief.

"You *want* to gut the fish?" he asked. "You're not supposed to want to do this. This is like picking up dog poop, or shoveling snow. Nobody wants to do it."

"Well, I do," Brian said, crouching down next to him and pulling one of the dead fish from the creel. Jake finished the fish he'd been working on, rinsed off his hands in the stream, and then handed the knife to Brian. He showed him where to start the cut and where to stop, how to reach in, grasp the slimy guts and pull them out. It was disgusting work, and more than once Brian felt himself starting to gag, but there was something primal about it, something so many people, himself included, just took for granted.

When he finished, Jake opened the beers and they lay back on the blanket in the evening sun. The beer was ice-cold and at that moment it was the best beer Brian had ever tasted. He looked over at Jake, admiring his jagged, sunburned face, and his large hands. He made his move.

Jake seemed surprised by the kiss, and for a moment, after Brian pulled away and saw his expression, he thought he might have made a mistake. But then he felt Jake's hand on his shoulder guiding him back, and he knew it was all right.

It was dark by the time they had the Jeep loaded up and were headed back. They held hands most of the way, when Jake wasn't busy shifting, and Brian cursed the Jeep for having bucket seats. When they got back into town Jake stopped before they reached the drive leading to Walter's. The lights were on in the house and the Mercedes was parked next to the garage. Brian crawled over and kissed him. They kissed for a long time, with the urgency that only kisses with new lovers have. Jake eventually pulled away.

"We better get you back home, Puppy," he said, repositioning his baseball cap.

Brian nodded and fell back in his own seat. This was trouble, he knew that, but he also knew what he wanted.

"I want to see you again," he said, looking over at Jake. Jake smiled and turned the key. He turned and drove up the drive and then stopped next to the Mercedes.

"Look," he said. "I want to see you again, too. But . . ." He hesitated a moment, trying to find the right words. "But this could get messy. Maybe we better just keep it as a real nice memory."

"No," Brian said emphatically. "I don't want that. I want to see you again. Whenever I can."

Jake lifted his hat and scratched his head. He started and stopped several times. Eventually he said, "Look, I know you know I've been sick. Lily likes to paint a bright picture of my future and I am better now, but it's not gone. It's not going away. It'll get me in the end."

"I don't care. That doesn't matter," Brian said, but as he said so he realized, by the lump in his throat, that he did care. Very much. The thought that Jake's time was limited made him want time with him all the more.

"You're twenty-three," Jake said, "of course you don't think it matters, but it does, it will. Most of my life is taken up with trying to prop myself up. You're young, you don't want that. You hardly even know me."

Just then Walter, who had heard the Jeep in the driveway, came out the front door. He peered into the darkness.

"Jake? That you?"

"Yes," Jake said. "It's me. And I've got a little puppy here that I'm about to spank with the paper if he doesn't get out of my car."

Brian scowled. Walter came down the front steps and stood next to the passenger side. He put his arm around Brian and kissed his forehead.

"I'm sorry about today," he said. "Did Jake here show you around?"

"Yes," Brian said coldly, his eyes staring angrily at Jake. "He took me fishing."

Walter turned his attention to Jake.

"How have you been?" Walter asked. "You look good."

"Thanks. Yeah, I'm doing okay," he replied.

"Thanks again for showing him around. It was a real disaster this morning. You know how those two are," Walter said, motioning back to the house from which the repetitive thump of disco music could be heard. Jake nodded and smiled.

"Listen," Walter said, "why don't you come to dinner with us tomorrow night. I got a reservation at Antonio's at eight. I'll call and make it for one more."

"Yes," Brian said eagerly. "Come."

Jake hesitated, looking awkwardly at Walter and then almost angrily at Brian.

"Uh, I'll see," he said. "I think Lily might have something planned. If I'm not there don't wait."

"Come," Brian said, placing his hand over Jake's on the gearshift. All three gazed down at this.

"I'll see," Jake said, and then moved his hand and started the ignition. Brian got out of the Jeep, and then turned and walked up the steps, Walter's arm around his waist. Jake turned the Jeep around and went down the drive, waving as he turned onto the road.

Walter stopped on the step and turned Brian to face him. "Again," he said, "I am so sorry about today."

"No, don't be silly," Brian said. "How did it go?"

"Well, it's over anyway. That's the good part. I found them at the gym and we all drove down to Dillon and got the hash. Did you know about that?"

Brian shook his head. They sat down on the steps and Walter explained the situation to him.

"I insisted they throw it away immediately, but of course they don't listen to me, so while I drove they sat in the backseat and smoked some. They made this clever little pipe out of an old soda can; ingenious, really, I'll have to show it to you. Anyway, they were giggly for a while, singing along with the CD player, but by the time we hit Vail they'd passed out, which made the rest of the ride pleasant enough. I left them asleep in the car and they only just woke up an hour ago. Of course they're starving and want us all to go out to eat but I said I'd leave it up to you, since you pretty much got shafted today."

Brian blushed.

"Uh, yeah. I'd like to go. To eat, I mean. With them. I'm starving, myself. We ate lunch at Lily's house but that was ages ago."

Going out with Derek and Keith would be a relief, Brian thought. He was already suffering a guilty conscience and felt like every word he said to Walter was a lie. He was no expert when it came to concealing his feelings and he knew that if they all went to dinner he really wouldn't have to talk much at all. Derek and Keith would monopolize the conversation just like they always did, and he would hardly be noticed.

"You sure you want to go with those two?" Walter asked once more before entering the house. "Because we could certainly go out alone, or I could even cook here."

"No, really. Let's all go," Brian said. "It'll be fun."

So Brian hurried inside, showered and changed, and all four went out to dinner.

The topic at the dinner table was the evening's manhunt, and as Brian predicted, Derek and Keith hardly gave anyone else a chance to speak. They had wasted a day with the silly Nissan/hashish business, so they were determined to make up for lost time that evening.

Earlier, while waiting for Brian to return, they had chosen their battle dress, and were now fully outfitted in what were essentially identical outfits: oversized jeans, tight wife-beaters (which would, at some point in the evening, be removed and tucked into the waistband of the oversized jeans), and pre-distressed, pre-formed baseball caps, emblazoned with the A&F logo. Accessories consisted of a few silver rings and coral chokers. It was the standard issue club boy uniform, but a uniform in which they looked better than most—and knew it.

While they waited for Walter to pay the bill, Derek and Keith reviewed their strategy:

"Listen up," Derek said to Keith. "I'll go after my Portuguese guy. I'm pretty sure I saw him get out of that Porsche last night at the bar so I don't think he was lying about the villa. I could tell he was about to talk to me at the gym today, before we were so rudely snatched away.

He'll probably send me a drink tonight, but if not I'll get some money from Walter and send him one. It's probably a safe investment, don't you think?"

"I do." Keith nodded. "I do. You're not going to put out, are you?"

"No way! It's far to early in the game to show my cards. I've got to make sure the Porsche is his and see pictures of the villa before he even gets a glimpse of God."

"I don't think I will either," Keith said. "I'm going to keep working on my German. He said he wants to take me shopping. I'll wait till after that."

"The German . . . ?" Derek asked, wrinkling his forehead. "The thin German with the bad haircut and the Rolex?"

"Exactly."

"Un-uh," Derek said, lowering his eyelids and shaking his head. "Don't waste your time. The only place he'll take you shopping is Wal-Mart."

"What? No!" Keith cried. "He's loaded!"

"Honey, no, he's not. It's not a real Rolex. I looked. And believe me, I know about these things, you know I do. It's some dumb knock-off. He probably bought it on one of those sex tours of Bangkok, and who knows what else he picked up there. No, you need to go after the Jap. Now he's the one with money, and he was pissing it away like water last night on all the dumb twinks. He needs someone to manage his accounts, that's what I think, and why, my friend, shouldn't that someone be you?"

"You really care, don't you," Keith said, his eyes misting up. "You're always watching out for me. That is so cool."

"I'm your friend," Derek replied warmly, reaching across the table and taking both of Keith's hands in his. "I don't want you going after a bone with no meat on it. I want you to be happy."

If he had been following this conversation Brian might well have lost his dinner, but he wasn't listening. Although seated right next to Keith, his mind was elsewhere. He was remembering the day with Jake and wondering what Jake was doing just then; wondering what was Jake's favorite color, and what kind of food Jake liked; wondering if Jake had read *Walden*, and what he thought of it; and wondering what songs he would put on the mix-tape he would make for Jake. But most of all he was wondering how long it would be until he could see him again.

Walter, who had been flirting shamelessly with the young host while waiting for his credit card to clear, returned to the table and finished his glass of port, oblivious to all the plotting that had transpired.

"Are we ready to go?" he asked, taking a final sip.

"Locked and loaded!" Keith replied, giving Derek a high five.

"You all right?" Walter asked, looking at Brian, whose mind was still back in the woods. Brian snapped back and smiled.

"What? All right? Yes, fine, why?" he said nervously.

They all looked at him queerly, so to speak.

"I was just, um, thinking," he stammered. "About my ID. I thought maybe I forgot my ID, but here it is. Never mind."

Walter rose from the table with the others and shrugged, feeling a bit guilty himself but suspecting nothing of Brian. Together they all left the restaurant and strolled down Main Street to the dance bar called The Edge.

Keith and Derek immediately put their plans into action, drinking and dancing, showing just enough skin, and promising just enough access to that skin, if the price was right. Walter and Brian stood off by themselves. Brian was tired and felt bad lying to Walter, and Walter felt bad because it seemed as if Brian was not having a good time.

"Why don't we go home?" Walter yelled. "It's been a dumb day. I promise tomorrow will be better."

Brian nodded and the two snuck out of the bar unnoticed. When they got home Brian went straight to bed, saying he had taken too much sun and had a headache. Again, Walter suspected nothing. He kissed Brian's forehead, tucked him into bed, and then went and had a wank in the shower, imagining himself and the young restaurant host, who, Walter was flattered to note, had hastily added his phone number to the bottom of the receipt.

The next day was busy for everyone. Derek had a date to go on a picnic with his Porsche-driving Portuguese, and Keith had arranged to go shopping and have dinner with his new Japanese friend, Mr. Kawanishi. As for Walter and Brian, they would take an early trip out to see the Maroon Bells. After that, they would do some shopping, have a leisurely lunch, and then, if Walter had his way, they'd go back to the house and stain some furniture. As for Brian, he wanted to ditch them all and find Jake.

For Derek and Keith the day started out promisingly enough. They got up early (at ten), and mixed their protein shakes, and ate their spoonfuls of Creatine. After that, they returned to the athletic club and were both able to get in a lengthy, and this time uninterrupted, workout. After steaming and showering and dressing with the utmost care, they exchanged airy kisses, wished each other good luck, and went their separate ways.

Derek's date had been at the gym as well, so Derek waited for him in the lobby. When the man had showered and dressed, the two went down to the garage and hopped in the Porsche. It was a beautiful car, a new 911 Cabriolet, and didn't appear, Derek noticed, to have rental license plates. Nor did Derek find, when they stopped to fill up the tank and he checked the glove compartment, anything resembling rental paperwork. This he took as a good omen, and was not sorry he had brought lube and condoms.

Derek studied the man as he washed the windshield. He wasn't exactly pretty, that was certain. He was a little thick around the torso, wore his thinning hair a little too obviously combed over his bald spot, and had the skin of an avid smoker. But, on the plus side he did appear to *own* a Porsche 911 Cabriolet, promised to show pictures of his villa in the Canaries, and was very free with his cash. As they drove away from the gas station Derek weighed the positives and the negatives and decided they were just about equal.

On the way out of town they stopped at one of the little stores only a town like Aspen can support: a gingham-curtained Victorian house out of which the proprietors sold, among other esoteric items, elaborate pre-made picnic baskets. Exorbitantly priced picnic baskets containing fresh bread and fruit, various tinned delicacies from the south of France, Belgian chocolates, and a chilled bottle or two of The Widow. The Portuguese bought one of these baskets, an extra bottle of champagne, and then sped off into the hills, promising to show Derek "a most special place. A place almost as special and beautiful as you."

Well! What more could a beautiful-bodied, vain, easily-impressed-by-flattery-and-money, not-so-young-man want to hear? He was putty in Portuguese hands. Granted, he was a little alarmed by the lines of coke the man had done before they left the parking garage, and was dismayed by his insistence on opening and consuming one of the bottles of champagne while driving at a high rate of speed up Independence Pass, but maybe, Derek thought, that was just a European thing. They're always more relaxed about substances. Probably nothing to worry about.

After parting from Derek, Keith left the gym and walked over to the Ritz-Carlton to meet Mr. Kawanishi. He inquired for him at the front desk, they called, and Keith was told he would be right down. A half hour later, Keith was still waiting. He inquired again, they called again, and again he was told Mr. Kawanishi would be right down. Ten minutes after this second inquiry, the man arrived. The elevator doors opened and he and his pimply trick from the night before emerged into the lobby. They lingered over a sloppy kiss (during which Keith, hidden behind a potted palm, noticed the boy's enormous tongue-piercing), and then parted. When the coast was clear, Keith approached.

"Good morning," Keith said as brightly as he could.

"Ah, goomolning, goomolning," Mr. Kawanishi said, nodding rapidly.

Derek had noticed his teeth in the bar last night, but in the light of day it was much more obvious that they were false. And the smell! It seemed to be coming from his mouth, but it smelled just like old socks.

"You leady go shopping?" he asked.

"Ready and willing!" Keith replied, taking him by the arm and leading him outside.

"Good, good, let's go! But maybe better have a dlink first," he said, turning and leading Keith back toward the bar.

A half a bottle of Suntory whisky later, Keith again attempted to lead him outside of the hotel. This time he was successful and they headed down to the street where all the high-end shops were located.

As for Walter, he had gotten up with Derek and Keith that morning and given them a ride down to the gym. On his way back he stopped at a small market and bought some things to make a surprise breakfast in bed for Brian. He returned to the house, humming cheerily to himself, and immediately began frying bacon and scrambling eggs. He made toast, filled a little compote with lingonberry jam, and even squeezed some fresh orange juice. He arranged his creation on a tray with a little vase of Columbines, and tiptoed excitedly to the bedroom door. He opened it, tiptoed over to the window blinds, turned the tiny rod, and saw . . . that Brian was not there.

Despite his plea of fatigue the night before, Brian had lain awake most of the night, his heart aching. He heard Walter get up in the morning, heard them all talking in the kitchen, and then heard them all leave. As soon as they were gone, he vaulted out of bed, threw on a pair of shorts and a shirt he thought might pass for running clothes, and sprinted out of the house and down the hill, arriving ten minutes later, panting and sweating, at the door of Lily's shop. A "closed" sign was in the window, but he ignored it and knocked hard on the door. The shop opened at noon, said the sign, but Brian had no idea what time it was since, in his haste to get out of the house, he had forgotten to put on his watch.

When there was no answer to his first knock, he knocked again, longer and louder this time. Still nothing. He turned around and began scanning the gutter for pebbles. When he had a handful of a suitable size, he stepped back into the middle of the road and tossed them at the upper windows. The kitties gazed down at him, flitting their tails, unconcerned, but no Lily. He gathered more ammunition and tried again. He was just about to lob a big pine cone at the window when he heard Lily's voice behind him.

"Hey! Stop that! What are you doing?" Brian spun around, hoping to see Lily *and* Jake, but he was disappointed. It was just Lily. His heart sank.

"Oh, it's you," she said, relieved, when she recognized Brian, and her face relaxed into a smile. She was carrying two bags of groceries. She approached, handed him one, and nudged him toward the sidewalk.

"You're going to get hit standing in the middle of the road like that. Come on."

She led him over to the door of the shop and handed him the second bag of groceries. She began searching in her purse for her keys.

Brian, who had wanted so desperately to speak to her, now had no idea what to say, or how to begin.

"I just saw Walter," she said, a wry smile on her face. "He told me you were sleeping late and he was going to make you breakfast. He doesn't know you're here, does he?"

Brian shook his head.

"Come inside," she said, ushering him in and locking the door behind them. Like she had the day before, she ushered him through the shop and up the stairs. She took the groceries from him, motioned for him to sit in the same chair he'd occupied yesterday, and then went and poured out two cups of coffee. She returned and handed one to him. He set it down on the table next to Jake's picture. Lily stood before him, holding her blobby ceramic mug in both hands, blowing on the contents and gazing down at him over the rim. She seemed to be waiting for him to speak.

"Is Jake . . . here?" Brian asked, peering beyond her into the kitchen. She shook her head.

"Jake went down to Breckenridge," she said. "He's got some friends there."

Brian nodded.

"Will he be back?" he asked hopefully. "I mean, soon?"

"Hmmmm, probably not. He said he might stay for a couple days—since Walter's at the house, and since he's not wild about my cats. Why?" she asked, again concealing everything but her eyes behind the rim of the mug.

Why indeed, Brian wondered. What could he tell her? What would he have told Jake? He had wanted to see him, wanted to touch him, wanted to talk to him, but evidently Jake didn't want the same thing. Jake had gone to Breckenridge, and from the sound of it he wasn't planning to come back until after Brian had gone. They would probably pass each other going the opposite direction on I-70. He leaned forward, put his face in his hands and groaned.

"Ohhh, kiddo," Lily said with a sympathetic laugh, "you got it bad!"

Brian nodded. She set her cup down and gazed at him, a broad grin on her face.

"This wasn't really in your fast-track-to-tenure plan, now was it?" And she gave his shoulder a pat. He shook his head.

Crestfallen, he returned to Walter's and tried to pretend he'd been out for a run. He ate the breakfast Walter made, and then rode with him out to see the Maroon Bells, but he hardly tasted the food, and did not appreciate the slanted majesty of the peaks. Life for him had become as bland and colorless as a bowl of oatmeal.

Walter, somewhat concerned with Brian's listlessness, but preferring to think it just the lingering effects of a hangover, drove him back into town and, on the advice of Derek and Keith, said he would take him clothes shopping. Normally, Brian would have balked at this. He didn't mind a little gift now and then, but he definitely didn't like the idea of being completely outfitted at someone else's expense. He was always bothered by the money that Walter spent on him, and tried, whenever he could, to pay his share. But, on this particular day, he really didn't care. He allowed himself to be led into Banana Republic and did not protest as Walter and the eager sales girl outfitted him in clothing that was nicer and newer than anything he'd worn since his confirmation. He stood there like a mannequin while she held up shirt after shirt against his chest so that Walter could determine which one best complimented his eyes, eyes that were staring out the plate-glass window at the sporting goods store across the street and wishing they would see Jake emerge.

Had he not been daydreaming, Brian might have noticed a short, blond man saunter by on the sidewalk below, on the arm of a drunken Japanese man. Or, he might have noticed an electric blue Porsche 911 Cabriolet as it whizzed past several miles above the posted speed limit with a vacant passenger seat. But Brian did not see these things. His gaze was vacant and his mind was in the past. He was remembering the feel of Jake standing close behind him in the river, his firm, yet tender grip on Brian's rod.

Once they left Banana Republic, the rest of the afternoon went quickly for Walter and Brian. They bought some shoes, walked around looking in the shops, and then Walter stopped and looked up at the sun.

"Well, it's probably five o'clock somewhere." He chuckled. "What would you say to stopping in at the Jerome for a drink?"

Brian nodded. A drink. Yes. Why not, he thought. Might as well. They walked to the Jerome, had two cocktails each, and then went home to dress for dinner. Walter was feeling amorous, and Brian, now loosened with liquor, decided he might as well go through the motions. But his heart wasn't in it and he had to fantasize about the day before in order to get a hard-on. If he could only speak to Jake, he thought, see if there was any point in pining away. But Lily did not know the name of the friends he had gone to visit, and Jake had not left their phone number.

When the sex was over, Walter and Brian showered, dressed, and had another drink, watching the sunset from the back terrace. It had only been two days since they were at the gas station below looking up at just this spot, Brian thought, swirling his highball, but he didn't even feel like the same person. All the plans he'd made, all the goals he'd set seemed much less important, almost silly, to him now.

"Are the boys meeting us?" Brian asked, as they drove down into town. He was hoping they would be. He needed to get his mind off his troubles and hearing of their antics would probably do the trick. It would also take the burden of conversation off him, and he wanted that desperately.

"I don't know," Walter replied. "I guess that depends on how their day went. If they don't come, we'll probably meet up with them later at the Double Diamond. I wonder if Jake will come. I haven't heard from him, so probably not."

When they got to the restaurant Jake was not there. Keith, however, was already at the table, well into a bottle of Chianti.

"Well," Walter said, taking a seat next to him and examining the wine label, "and just how did you intend to pay for this if we didn't show up?"

"Be nice," Keith moaned. "Please. I've had a devil of a day."

"Hmmm, 'be nice. Please, be nice,'" Walter said, looking up at the ceiling thoughtfully. "Seems like I've heard *that* somewhere before. What happened?"

"Oh, it was so gross," Keith said, emptying his glass.

"Do tell!" Brian urged, eager to hear about someone else's misery.

The waiter arrived bearing two more glasses and some bread sticks. Walter ordered another bottle, and poured out the remainder of the first. Keith took a sip and cleared his throat. He told them all about waiting in the lobby, and the pierced trick, and the half a bottle of Suntory.

"Then," he went on, "when we actually did go shopping all we did was shop for his wife and daughter and some business colleagues! Now don't get me wrong," he said, holding up a palm. "I'm a great personal shopper, and I picked out a fabulous Fendi bag for the wife, and a funky little charm bracelet for the daughter, but whenever I'd select something for myself, even just a shirt, or a belt, he'd give a little grunt and say, 'No, we find something more better for you.' Well, of course we never did. He bought me some dumb key chain, and one of those pens you turn upside down and the man's swimming suit disappears, but that was it!"

"So then you came here," Walter said, thinking Keith had reached the end of his story.

"I wish!" Keith said. "He kept promising we'd go out later that evening and said we would find something for me then. I should have just bagged it but I figured I was in so deep I might as well stick it out. So anyway, we went back to the Ritz so he could change and take me to dinner but before we went up to the room he had to stop at the bar and get 'another little dlink.' Well it was more like four little drinks and the more he drank the more he got all touchy-feely, which would have been annoying anywhere but was especially annoying in the Ritz bar surrounded by straight people. I figured I better at least get him back to the room. I was pretty much resigned at that point to just dumping him and going. I know it sounds pathetic but it took me that long to realize how stupid and gross it all was. Anyway, the only way I could get him back to the room was to whisper promises of sex in his ear, which, unfortunately, he repeated loudly while we were in the elevator with several old women. So I got him to the room, and he started undressing, and trying to get his tongue in my mouth. It really was pathetic. He was so drunk I'm sure he couldn't have done anything. Anyway, I excused myself and went in the bathroom. I stayed there for about twenty minutes, until I couldn't hear him anymore. Then I crept out and sure enough, there he was, passed out. And thank God because it was not a pretty weenie."

"You saw it?" Walter asked.

"I did, I'm afraid. Before I left I pulled back the sheet and looked at the equipment. Just to see what I would have had to work with. Ugh! It was one of those tiny, button mushroom weenies. It's sad, really. That wife deserves her Fendi bag. All I got for my trouble was some dumb key chain and a porno pen. Whoopee! I did steal a ten from his wallet though, and ran right down to the drugstore in the lobby and bought some Listerine."

Just then, both Jake and Derek arrived. Brian, who was only half listening to Keith's narrative, saw them first and his stomach flipped. Derek was sweaty, and dusty, and the sleeve of his shirt was torn. They were standing at the host stand and Jake was laughing with one of the waiters. When the manager saw them, he approached Jake and gave him a hearty clap on the back. Jake said a few words to him and was then pointed in the direction of the table. He and Derek approached.

"Look who I found," Jake said, his arm around Derek, "hitchhiking on the road into town."

"Jake!" Keith cried, rising and giving him a hug. "I thought that was you!" Then he turned to Derek and his expression fell. "Oh, honey, what happened?"

Derek shook his head and rolled his eyes. "Don't ask me to explain. At least not until I've had a glass of wine. Please. It was too stupid."

Keith smiled gently, led his friend over to a chair and went to ask the waiter for another glass. Walter rose and gave Jake a hug, during which Jake looked down at Brian and winked.

Once they were all seated again, and Derek had relaxed, Walter asked him again what had happened.

"What *did* happen?" Derek replied. "I still wonder, myself. We drove up in the mountains and had our little picnic, but as soon as that was over he just went berserk, pushing me down and ripping my clothes. Now I like a little slap and tickle every now and then, just as much as the next guy, but this was too much. It wasn't even fun! I tried to calm him down, but that really made him mad and he started shouting all this Spanish at me."

"I think it was probably Portuguese," Walter corrected.

"Whatever. He started yelling and kicking at the dirt. I was getting a little bit scared but it was also pretty funny, like watching a kid throw a tantrum, and I'm afraid he saw me laughing."

"Oh, no," Keith said, hiding his face in his hands.

"And then what happened?" Brian asked.

"Well, nothing. He got in his car and sped away, with my cell phone still on the seat! I sat down, ate the picnic lunch and then started walking. It took me a couple hours to get to the main road and I was on that for about an hour before Jake picked me up."

"And where were you headed?" Walter asked. Jake hesitated. Brian looked over at him intently.

"I was, uh, coming back from Breckenridge."

Walter nodded, thinking nothing of it.

"What were you doing there?" Brian asked.

Jake grinned. "Just visiting some friends," he said.

"Short visit," Brian said, raising an eyebrow. Again Jake grinned, but did not reply.

All through dinner the mood around the table, aided by good wine and good food, was high. Walter was particularly glad to see an upward shift in Brian's spirits but thought it was probably on account of the spirits he'd consumed that evening. Again he attributed the boy's earlier moroseness to nothing more than a hangover and had no suspicions of Jake.

Unbowed by their earlier failures Keith and Derek began to plot out their last night over dessert.

"Look, let's be honest," Derek said. "Summerfest has been pretty much a failure in the sugar daddy department. We need to just cut our losses and move on."

"Agreed," Keith said. "We need to set a new goal and just focus on that."

"Yes. Forget Summerfest. Tonight, we need to find some rich local with a place we can stay at during Ski Week," Derek said. "That's when all the really rich guys will be here. None of these Germans with their faux Rolexes."

Brian excused himself from the table at this point and went to the bathroom. He was washing his hands when he looked up and saw Jake reflected in the mirror. Brian spun around and smiled. He took a paper towel from the dispenser and dried his hands. He wanted to speak, had rehearsed all the night before and all that day what he would say, but now that the time had come he couldn't remember anything. He locked the bathroom door, turned, and kissed Jake, long and hard, for some minutes. He put his lips next to Jake's ear and whispered, "Thanks for coming back. I don't know if it was because of me or not, and right now I don't care. I just wanted to see you again."

"Me, too," Jake whispered, and kissed him again.

"Look," Brian said, pulling away and leaning back on the sink. "I'll be honest. I'm drunk, and I'm worn out from worrying I wouldn't see you again so I'm going to be blunt. I don't love Walter. I—I love you. I know you think I'm young, and melodramatic, and all that. Fine. But I know I love you. It's like a bell rang in my brain yesterday and suddenly it was all clear. I love you, Jake, and I'd like to know more about you, and spend as much time as I can with you."

Jake approached, lifted him up, and kissed him, but when he pulled away Brian saw there was a look of concern on his face. Brian worried that maybe he'd been too forward and scolded himself for drinking so much. It was like the dam had burst and he could do nothing to stop everything from just pouring out. He thought he'd probably said too much, or said it in the wrong way, but he went on, figuring at that point he might as well say it all.

"I don't know what you feel," Brian said. "Maybe you think I'm just some dumb kid, some 'nice memory,' like you said yesterday. I don't know. And I don't want you to tell me. Not right now. It's all been so perfect. Yesterday, and even this, right here, in this tiny bathroom. If it has to be a memory I don't want to hear anything that'll ruin it."

He walked over to the door and grabbed the handle, but paused before turning it. He said nothing for a moment, debating in his mind if he should say more. He turned and looked back at Jake.

"The others are all going out tonight," he said, his voice low and serious. "I won't go. I'll stay at Walter's. If you are interested in pursuing this, something with me, then come by. If not, well, you know how I feel and I wish you the best in your life."

He gave Jake one last kiss, barely touching his lips, and left the bathroom.

When everyone was reassembled at the table, they all tried to convince Jake to go out with them. All except Brian, that is. But Jake declined, saying he was tired from all the driving that day and wanted to get a good night's rest. Walter paid the bill and then they all said goodbye to Jake on the sidewalk and watched him drive away. Then all four piled into the Mercedes and returned up the hill to Walter's.

As soon as they were in the car, Brian began laying the foundation of his plan, saying that he'd had far too much to drink, and was getting a headache. By the time they were back at Walter's, waiting for Keith and Derek to dress, it had grown into a full-blown migraine.

"I'll stay here with you," Walter said, as Brian lay writhing on the couch. "You need some taking care of."

"No. Don't," Brian replied, "I'll be fine. Really. I just need to lie in the dark for a while. You go. It's the last night with your friends. Ohh, owwww," he moaned. "Please go. Really. Have a good time."

Walter said nothing. He rubbed Brian's shoulder and looked down at the boy gripping his head. I know I shouldn't, he thought, but I *do* want to go out. It's just one night, only a couple of hours, really. I'll make it up to him when we get back in town.

"Weeellll," Walter said cautiously. "If you're sure you want me to, I'll go."

"I do."

"But I'll keep my phone with me so if you need anything, if you want me to come back, all you have to do is call."

Brian nodded. "Go. Have a good time. Those two deserve one after the day they had. I'm just going to go lie down," he said, limping to the bedroom.

As soon as he heard the tires of the Mercedes leave the gravel drive, Brian got up. He turned out most of the lights in the house and went out on the front porch. He stared down at the road.

Relax, he told himself, he's probably waiting to make sure they're gone. He'll come. At least I hope he'll come. Oh God, what if he doesn't?

Brian thought about his life, and his future plans all so neatly mapped out. Again, the plan for grad school seemed dull, which he couldn't understand. He'd thought he was looking forward to it but now it just seemed like a lot of work for something he was no longer sure he wanted to do. School was safe, he realized, and maybe that was why he'd been reluctant to leave it for anything more than a summer.

He heard the engine struggling up the hill and then he saw the headlights. The Jeep stopped at the bottom of the drive and Brian knew Jake was trying to see if the Mercedes had gone. A moment later he pulled up and parked in the garage. Brian's first instinct was to run down the steps, but he forced himself to wait. He'd been demonstrative enough and didn't want to scare Jake away. Best to play it cool, he thought. Just play it cool.

Jake got out of the Jeep and slowly crossed the gravel drive.

"Brian?" he whispered, when he saw that there was someone on the steps. "Is that you?"

Brian made a barking sound in reply, and then laughing, said, "Yes, it's me."

He grabbed Jake by the hand, pulled him close. They stood kissing on the porch, but then both grew more anxious and went into the house, shedding clothes on the way to the bedroom.

"Why did you come back?" Brian asked, after the first frenzied round was over and they were both lying on their backs in the dark. It was a question he'd wanted to ask since dinner that night.

"I think you know why I came back," Jake said, giving Brian's leg a squeeze.

"I guess wh—I mean—what I want to know is, do you feel anything for me, other than lust, I mean?"

Jake laughed, and then pulled Brian close to him.

"More than you know," he said. "That's why I went away. I had such a great time yesterday. Better than I've had in a long time and I got scared, I guess."

"Why scared?"

Jake hesitated. "It's hard for me to say this," and then he hesitated again. "But it's been so long. I've been on my own for so long. I was afraid of what I felt, so I went away. I wasn't going to come back until you'd gone, but . . . but I couldn't."

Brian hugged him tightly. He remembered what Lily had said the day before about Jake being strong enough but not having much confidence, and again, the little bell went off in his head and he knew clearly just what he wanted: he wanted to stay, and he wanted to try and make Jake feel like the man Brian saw in him.

"I want to stay," Brian said, sitting up and looking down at Jake.

"Here with you. If not in Walter's house then somewhere else, but I want to stay."

Jake's expression grew serious. He ran his hand along Brian's cheek.

"But what about school?" he asked. "What about the rest of your life? I don't think you know what life with me would be like."

"You're right," Brian said resolutely. "But I'm going to find out."

Jake sat up and leaned his back against the headboard.

"Hey, let's be serious a minute," he said. "I'm not all that bad to live with personally, but some days it's no picnic. My life is totally scheduled by my medicine, and the times I have to take it, and some of the side effects are not so pretty. Some days I'm so tired by eleven in the morning I have to go home and take a three-hour nap. As you can imagine, for those reasons, and a lot of others, I'm not much of a partier anymore. But you're young! You should get out there. Have lots of different experiences while you can."

"If you're trying to dissuade me," Brian said, "you're not doing a very good job. I'm not much of a partier myself, as you've probably noticed. I can't even keep up with Walter, let alone two like Derek and Keith! And as for school, well . . . it's not going anywhere. You and Lily told me so yourselves just yesterday. I can always decide to go back if this doesn't work out."

"And the other thing . . . ?" Jake asked.

"Look," Brian said, almost impatiently. "I know you're not totally healthy . . ."

"That's an understatement."

"Fine, I know you've got AIDS. I know you've been sick and I know you'll more than likely get sick again, probably even die from it, but don't you see!" Brian cried, pounding the bed with his fists. "That's just what I mean! School can wait. Other things in my life can wait. Spending time with you, getting to know you; who knows how much time there is to do that. I want all I can get. It's selfish, really. I know it sounds crazy, and to anyone looking at it from the outside it probably appears crazy, but to me it makes perfect sense. I had a better time with you in the few hours we were together yesterday than I've had with any other guy I've ever been with. Is it so hard to believe I'd want more?"

When Brian was finished he stared down at Jake, waiting for him to reply, but he did not. At least not with words. He pulled Brian down and kissed him.

Twenty minutes later Jake, exhausted from his trip, and Brian, exhausted from anxiety and the numerous glasses of wine to which he was not accustomed, fell into a warm, satisfied sleep.

Chapter Three

About one o'clock in the morning, Walter returned to the house alone. He had been doing tequila body shots with some of the strippers brought in for the closing night festivities and thought he had better leave before the situation got out of hand. He stumbled up the steps, as quietly as he could and was careful to remove his shoes as soon as he entered so as not to wake Brian. He went to the kitchen to get a drink of water, then to the bathroom to pee, before finally tiptoeing off to the bedroom. He removed his clothes in the dark and then gently pulled back the blanket and the sheet and slipped into bed.

Jake woke up. He was aware of a hand around his waist, gently caressing his belly. He opened his eyes. Brian was in front of him, facing away from him.

Walter, feeling a hairy body instead of a smooth one, immediately stopped his caresses. He opened his eyes and looked at the head of hair in front of him.

"Jake?"

"Uh . . . no?" Jake replied.

Walter whipped back the covers, got up, and switched on the light. For a moment he was too shocked to say a word. Jake stared up at him, a guilty expression on his face, and Brian had pulled the sheets completely over his head.

"Somebody better tell me what the hell is going on here!" Walter shouted.

Just then Derek came walking up the road. His plans to find a sugar daddy for Ski Week had failed and he was returning, feeling tired and somewhat humiliated. As he turned onto the drive he was surprised to see the house completely lit up, and he hoped that Walter had not invited all of the strippers from the club back to the house for an impromptu after-hours party. He climbed the steps to the porch and it was then that he heard the shouting.

"How could you?"

Derek leaned closer and listened. It was Walter's voice, and from the sound of it he was angry.

"After all I've done! I let you live here, rent free, and you thank me by screwing my boyfriend?"

This was good, Derek thought, a devilish smile spreading across his face, and he moved over into the bushes so that he could see into one of the windows. There were Walter and Jake, standing in the living room, both red-faced and waving their arms. And there, in the middle of it all, was The Bambi, seated on the sofa just shaking his head.

"Fishing!" Walter sneered. "Fishing in *my* pond! You're the last person I would have expected to do this."

"Oh Christ!" Jake fired back. "I don't know why you're surprised. I had a good teacher when it comes to infidelity, remember? I wasn't the one who brought a case of crabs home from every business trip!"

Derek's attention was then diverted away by the sound of a car door slamming at the bottom of the drive. He looked back in time to see a taxi turn around and head back down the hill. A moment later he saw the figure of Keith approaching. He waited until he had almost reached the porch and then whispered, "I wouldn't go in there."

Keith was startled and jumped back. He peered into the bushes. "Derek?"

"Shhh," Derek whispered, "somebody's been defiling The Bambi and it's a somebody that we both know."

"No!" Keith said, rushing into the bushes next to Derek and looking in the window. They watched the scene in silence for some time.

*   *   *

"Stop it!" Brian cried, rising and putting himself between the two men. "There's no point in pulling your past out of the coffin and killing it again. Stop it! This is about now. Today, Walter," Brian said, turning his attention to the older man and softening his tone. "I know this looks bad."

Walter gave a contemptuous snort and folded his arms across his chest.

"Okay, it is bad," Brian conceded. "There's no getting around that. I shouldn't have done all this under your nose. I'm sorry. But it was me, not Jake. None of this would have happened if I hadn't made it. It's my fault. I've done some things in the past forty-eight hours that even I can't believe. I don't know what's happened to me." He looked confused and he closed his eyes and massaged the sides of his aching head. Then he opened them again and smiled at Jake. "I don't know what's happened to me," he said again, "but I'm sure glad."

"Great!" Walter sneered. "I'm happy for you. Really fucking happy!" Then he spun around and marched into the bathroom, slamming and locking the door behind him.

"That crafty little fawn!" Keith whispered. "I didn't suspect a thing."

"Me neither. I knew he didn't really have a headache tonight—that was a pretty poor performance, if you ask me—but I thought he just wanted to stay home and read, or some geeky thing like that."

Keith laughed.

"Why are you back?" Derek asked. "You looked pretty hot and heavy out on the dance floor with that tall guy."

"It didn't work out," Keith said. "Oh, it probably could have, but when the lights went up I decided I didn't want to even try. Why is it all the ones with money are such jerks, or so gross?"

"Tell me about it," Derek groaned.

"What happened to you?" Keith asked.

"I couldn't do it either," Derek said. "I looked at the guy I was working on and just thought 'Blick! I'd rather have another evening alone with Rosy,' so I left."

Keith laughed again.

"I guess we better not go in," Derek said, looking back at the scene inside that was still in the process of unfurling.

"Probably not."

"But I'm getting cold!"

"Me too," Keith said, heading out of the bushes. "Come on. Maybe there are some coats or something in the garage."

He walked down the steps and over to the garage, entering it through a side door. A moment later he emerged carrying the army blanket from the back of Jake's Jeep.

"This was all I could find," Keith said, returning to the porch and shaking it out. They draped it over their shoulders and huddled under it on the porch.

"You know," Keith said thoughtfully, "money would be nice, but sometimes I just want someone that doesn't annoy the shit out of me."

"I know."

"I mean, why is it that eight out of ten guys with money are just un-bearable?"

"And the other two aren't interested."

"Yeah."

"I don't know," Derek said, putting an arm around his friend's shoulder. "I don't know."

"After this weekend," Keith went on, "all I want is someone who's not a jerk! That, and someone with their own teeth."

"Preferably white ones!"

"Yeah." Keith chuckled. "And someone that likes the same music I do."

"That'd be nice."

"And someone with good taste in clothes."

"Mmmm."

"And someone who takes care of their body . . ."

"A body you don't have to turn the lights out to have sex with," Derek added.

"Yeah."

They fell silent for a moment. Even the yelling inside seemed to have quieted. The sky was clear and all the stars were twinkling above.

"Um, Derek?" Keith asked.

"Hmmm?"

"Is . . . that . . . your hand?"

"Mm-hmm. Is it all right?"

"It is."

Walter remained in the bathroom ignoring the knocks and conversation on the other side of the door. He was angry, yes, but more for being made a fool of than anything else. He could just imagine the chiding and teasing that was sure to come from Derek and Keith as soon as they found out about it. But underneath the anger he had to admit that what he felt was relief. Relief that he had been given an exit from his relationship with Brian. Granted, it was an exit that had come earlier than he would have liked, and in a way he didn't at all like, but in his heart he knew that the desire for it would, like the sunset, have inevitably come. He was too flirtatious, his wanderlust was too strong, he did enjoy the chase. The thing with Brian would have ended badly. That much he knew. Maybe this was better. He turned on the light, looked at himself in the mirror and chuckled. He got up, splashed some water on his face to simulate tears and headed back out.

The next morning, Walter was the first one to wake up. He lifted up his head from where it had been resting on the arm of the sofa and cursed whoever it was that had invented tequila. The room was flooded with morning sun and it hurt his eyes. Squinting, he got up and hobbled over to the kitchen to find some aspirin. He shook three out of the bottle, and popped them in his mouth, washing them down with a shot of vodka. He gasped, shook out his jowls, and then started fixing breakfast.

A few minutes later he was joined by Brian, dressed in his boxers and an old T-shirt. Without a word, he jumped in and began helping, taking a fork from one of the drawers and using it to poke at the big slab of bacon frying on the stove. Walter glanced up at him from where he was standing at the counter busy cracking eggs, but then returned his attention to what he was doing.

"I want to thank you for last night," Brian said, looking over at him. "It was good of you to be so understanding."

Walter did not look up. He grunted, shrugged his shoulders, and began scrambling the eggs in the bowl.

"I don't want to harp on it," Brian went on, "but I really do love Jake, and I want to make him happy."

Walter looked up, a kind expression on his face. He stopped his scrambling.

"And I really hope you can do that," he said. "Because I sure did the opposite when we were together."

Just then Jake burst into the kitchen.

"You gotta see this," he said, motioning them both to come with him. They set down their utensils, and followed him back through the living room. He led them over to the front door but before opening it he turned and held his finger to his lips, warning them to be quiet. Then he opened the door slowly and they all crept out onto the porch. Jake pointed down to Walter's car parked just below.

On the hood there were two neatly folded piles of clothes, and below, on the gravel, were two pairs of shoes. In the backseat, only partially covered by the army blanket, were the naked bodies of Derek and Keith, the latter resting his head on the shoulder of the former.

"Oh, good Lord," Walter said, looking down at the scene the way most people would look at a three-headed frog. "And I thought *I* had too much to drink. Isn't that incest, or something?"

"I don't know about that," Jake said, putting his arm around Brian. "But I do know that blanket is going to need a cleaning."

Later that morning, after Derek and Keith had been roused from the matrimonial Mercedes, they all gathered in the dining room for breakfast. The two new couples billed and cooed at each other over their eggs, while Walter skulked around the table, refilling juice glasses and coffee cups, pretending to be disgusted by it all.

It would seem a sad, lonely ending for poor Walter, but really he was not sad. In fact, as he returned to the kitchen for more juice, there was, despite his hangover, a noticeable spring in his step. His mind was already on the future. He refilled the juice pitcher, buttered some more toast, and was about to return to the dining room, but then paused at the door. He looked down at the breast pocket of his shirt and smiled. It was the same shirt he'd slept in, the same one he'd worn to the bar the night before. He pushed the door open a crack and peeked into the dining room. All still billing and cooing. He set down the juice and the plate of toast on the counter and picked up the phone. With his free hand, he reached in his shirt pocket and removed three crumpled bar napkins, each with the name and phone number of a new Bambi written on it. He selected one and dialed the number, his heart racing.

"Hello, uh, Jason? Yeah, hi, this is Walter. We met last night. You gave me your number . . ."

The Perfect Husband

William J. Mann

A Cold Morning in February That Suddenly Got Even Colder

Oh, he was gorgeous all right. Dark hair, olive skin, big pouty lips, an upturned nose, abs for days. We even fell asleep in each other's arms, him first, me lying there with my nose in his hair, smelling his shampoo, listening to him breathe. Do you know how long it had been since I'd done that? Fallen asleep with my nose in some guy's hair?

I'd even sucked his toes. Damn, that pisses me off now. I so totally wish I hadn't sucked his toes. Oh, he *loved* it. It drove him *crazy*. He said nobody had ever done that to him before. I was the first.

Oh, man, I wish I hadn't sucked his toes.

Because he slipped out before morning. The sound of the latch on my door woke me up. The jerkface bolted without saying goodbye, without leaving a note, without even so much as a kiss on my forehead and a tousle of my hair, saying, "I'll call you sometime," or at least, "Thanks for a good time."

I sat up, still smelling him in my bed, the sheets beside me still warm. I tried to convince myself he'd just gotten up to take a pee. But his jeans were no longer crumpled up on the floor. His shoes were gone.

And immediately I was thinking about Adam again.

"*Men*," I spit, throwing the blanket off me and placing my feet against the hardwood floor. "They're all fucking alike."

My feet froze against the floor. It was cold. *Way* cold. You have *no idea* how cold it was that morning in my apartment on West Newton Street in Boston's South End. And you also have no idea just how much I had been looking forward to waking up on that cold Sunday morning with a dreamy boy next to me keeping me warm and toasty in my bed.

Well, fuck him. I walked across the room and cranked up the heat.

It was 7:35. I couldn't go back to sleep now. Even though all I'd had was maybe three and a half hours, tops, all I wanted to do was rip those goddamn sheets off my bed and wash them in scalding hot water. Creep probably had crabs. The little buggers were probably crawling through my pubes even as I stood there.

I stepped into the shower and let the water revive me. Thank God I didn't have a hangover. I could be grateful for that much at least. Maybe my anger had evaporated all the alcohol out of my body. Naw, it was simply that I knew my limit. I had three cosmos and then cut myself off. It wasn't a big party night, just a night out at Buzz with a couple friends. I'd gone with no intention of meeting anyone, of bringing anybody back home.

At least that's what I'd said. It's what I *always* say, actually. "I'm not even going to *look* at anyone," I announce on the way to the bar. "I'm just going to dance."

See, that way, if I end up going home alone, it's like I planned it that way. Like that's the way I really wanted it. The friends I was with last night totally believed me. Adam, however, had he been along, would never have bought it. Adam would have said, "Girl, you are so hungry for a husband you have been known to squeeze over two dozen cantaloupes in Star Market's produce department just to cruise some hottie who's lingering by the lettuce. The store manager hates to see you coming. He throws a tarp over all his fresh fruit."

Okay, so maybe there's some truth to that. But it wasn't two dozen, maybe just six or seven cantaloupes—and like Adam *doesn't* want a husband? Like Adam hasn't forced me to go to church with him— *church!*—because he had the hots for some guy he thought would be there. It was last summer in Provincetown, and the guy had said always went to the Unitarian-Universalist Meeting House on Sundays. So Adam drags me along, all groggy-eyed and messy-haired from the night before, and we can't even spot the guy. Everybody's singing away and praising God and there we are, peering through the pews for some guy with a buzzcut. Adam wasn't even sure at that point that he could recognize him again. "It was dark on the dance floor," he pleaded.

"I can't believe we are here cruising guys in *church*," I'd whispered, a little too loud, for a couple of lesbians in the pew in front of us turned around to glare.

So don't tell me that Adam isn't as bad as I am. He's actually *worse*. He's been this way ever since college. For our entire junior and senior year, he had a different boyfriend every three weeks. Each one he was convinced he'd grow old with. And inevitably, at the end of each failed relationship, he'd act like his entire life was over, that the one great love of his had just slipped through his fingers.

"You're *nineteen*," I'd finally said to him, exasperated. "You haven't even been alive two whole decades!"

See, Adam and I did things like that for each other. We could talk to each other that way. We kept each other in check with reality. Adam knew me better than anyone in the whole world, and me him. That's why we were sisters. Why the fuck did he have to go and move to Hartford?

It had been a job offer he couldn't resist. We saw each other maybe twice a month, instead of the twice a *day* routine it had been when he lived in Boston. Plus, of course, there was our week together in Provincetown every August. We'd been renting a house there for Carnival Week for the last few years, and I fully expected we'd do it again this year.

But still, when things happened like that idiot bolting out on me that morning, it was always Adam who came to mind. He was always the one I thought of when I wanted to talk. If it hadn't been so early I'd have called him. I figured I'd at least wait until ten o'clock.

But then, at eight, the phone rang, and it was Adam.

Didn't I tell you? We're on the same wavelength, Adam and me. Things like this are always happening. I'll be thinking of him, and he'll call. That's the way it's been ever since that first night, toward the end of sophomore year, when we made love together out on the lawn behind the student union. I can still see him above me, the moonlight in his hair, his eyes reflecting the stars. Oh my God, I have never tasted anyone whose mouth was as sweet as Adam's. And his skin, so smooth, like silk. Really, I am not exaggerating . . .

I stopped myself. Why did I always do that? Why did I allow myself to think that way about Adam? We were sisters. *Sisters!*

"Troy," he was telling me over the phone, "I had the absolute worst night."

"You too? Make room in the club."

So he proceeded to tell me about the asshole who flirted with him all night long at some club in Hartford, totally leading him on, and then went home with somebody else. And I told him about Mr. Out-the-Door, cradling the phone with my shoulder as I pulled the sheets off the bed.

"At least you got laid," Adam griped.

"I sucked his toes," I admitted in a little voice.

"*You sucked his toes?* Troy! You never do that on the first night! That's a reward that shouldn't come before the third night, at best!"

"I know, I know," I said, pressing the guy's pillowcase to my face briefly. I could still smell him. "It was just that he was *so* cute."

Adam sighed. "I'm so over cute guys. I'm going after the ugly ones from now on. Bet they wouldn't leave before morning."

"Bet I wouldn't want to suck their toes either."

I stuffed the sheets into my laundry bag. Spending the morning at the Laund-O-Rett was hardly the day I'd imagined. I'd pictured me and What's-His-Name (I refused to even *think* his name, hoping I'd quickly forget it) sipping caffe lattes at Francesca's, gazing into each other's eyes lovingly while pretending to read the Sunday *Globe*. All my friends would be seated around us, glaring at me enviously.

"Troy," Adam said suddenly. "Let's do the whole summer this year."

"What?"

"The whole summer in P-town," he said. "Not just Carnival Week."

"Adam. We can't afford the whole summer."

"So we'll get another roommate. Come on. Let's do it. We can go up every weekend. We owe it to ourselves. Let's just have a wild summer, you and me. Come on, Troy."

"I don't know . . ."

"We're not getting any younger, Troy. In three more years we'll be thirty. Let's do it now."

Okay, a little background. Our week in P-town has always proved to be a blast. And round about Thursday or Friday we always turn to each other and say, "Next year, let's do the whole summer." Lots of guys we know do. You really become part of the rhythm of the town that way, and you get to meet so many more people. Every summer I've fallen in love with some guy who lives too far away to ever pursue anything with. The first summer it was San Francisco. The second summer it was Berlin. As in Germany. Last year it was Philadelphia, which, after Berlin, seemed to be right around the block from Boston. But after a couple of phone calls, our summer ardor kind of fizzled out. Guess that happens.

"Who knows?" Adam was saying. "If we go for the whole summer, maybe we'll actually find husbands, somebody who's not too far away, who will actually stick around."

I thought I spied a crab in the sheets, a little brown speck moving sideways. I gasped, grabbing it between my fingers. It was a speck of lint.

"Okay," I said to Adam. "Let's do it. So long as we can find a third roommate to share the costs."

There was a pause before he said, "I already got somebody."

"Who?"

"You sitting down, Troy?"

I scowled into the phone. "Who *is* it, Adam?"

"Peter Youngblood."

I hung up on him.

Why I Could Never Share a House With Peter Youngblood

Okay, some more background. I am twenty-seven years old, Irish and English mixed. Not bad-looking—in fact, actually, kind of cute. Five-eight, not too tall, not too short, dark hair, blue eyes. I go to the gym four times a week, so I'm pretty toned, not too big, not too small. If you saw me, you wouldn't drop your jaw or anything, but you also wouldn't be embarassed to show up with me at a party in front of your friends.

Adam is the same age as me, but blond, a little taller, a little more built but not by much. His hairline's starting to recede just the slightest bit. Adam is Irish and Polish. I think he is very handsome, handsome in the way I wish I could be, but he's not soap-opera beautiful. Your jaw wouldn't drop for him either, but Adam has no trouble scoring tricks. His failure of the night before was definitely an aberration, which was probably why he was so upset about it.

So we're both slightly better-than-average-looking guys with decent bodies. Decent for gay life, that is: both of us look far, far better than our straight brothers, both of whom have gotten little beer guts and wear their hair too long. And they're a year younger than we are.

But the point is this: Peter Youngblood is definitely A List, and we maybe make B-plus.

So there is absolutely, positively *no fucking way* I could ever share a house with Peter Youngblood.

Look, the guy has been driving me crazy for years! Ever since I moved to the South End four years ago, in fact. Peter's in his thirties, probably thirty-five, maybe even thirty-six. But guys like him don't age. Sure, when he smiles, there are a few creases around his eyes, but even his wrinkles drive me nuts to see them. *Everything* about the guy sends me into orbit.

Everybody's got a Peter in their lives: the dreamboy, the trophy that can never be won. I would watch him at Buzz or at the A-House in Provincetown, peeling off his shirt, every single muscle on his torso standing out, his shoulders rippling, his eight-pack perfectly defined, those scrumptious lines of his abdomen leading down into his low-cut pants. His butt is high and round and hard, the kind Madonna said you could serve drinks from. Peter's a model (big surprise) and occasional actor: I've seen him in commercials and in some local Boston theater productions. (I don't remember the names because, let's face it, I wasn't going for the plot. I was going for the moment when Peter obligingly removed his shirt for some reason or other.) He's got dark hair, green eyes, and a dimpled smile that reveals the whitest, most even teeth you can imagine. I have no idea what Peter's ethnicity is. People say there's a mix of African-American, Native-American, Brazilian, Iranian, Italian, Greek, and Spanish. He is, without question the most beautiful man I have ever seen in my entire life.

And I'm supposed to share a house with him?

It's Hard to Imagine a
Summer House in the
Winter When It's Cold and
Dark and Wet

"It's really very cute," the realtor was saying, "once you hang a few drapes and sweep out the sand."

Neither Adam nor I had been prepared for the cost of Provincetown rentals. Every year they seemed to jump another grand. The only ones in our price range were little cottages behind bigger houses, converted garages with small windows and bad plumbing. This one was off Commercial Street in the West End, tucked in between a basketball court and a motel. At least maybe we could watch hunky boys play shirts and skins.

True, all the way down here I'd been dreaming of luxury, renting a place for the season with a large deck overlooking the bay, maybe with skylights and a sumptuous sunken living room. But neither Adam nor I had that kind of money. Though we had good jobs—I work in the loan department of a major bank and Adam works for an insurance company—we were also still paying off student loans, making car payments, and all that. So the best we could do was seven grand. Especially because Peter wasn't able to put in anything.

"What do you say?" the realtor was asking.

Adam looked at me. I grimaced. The place was truly a dump, at least by my standards. I'd gotten used to our one-week rental, a fabulous condo with an entertainment station, Jacuzzi, and washer and dryer. This was hardly more than a wooden shack with cardboard walls separating two jail-cell-sized bedrooms, a tiny living room, and a kitchen with a miniature refrigerator and convection oven. The shower stall was rusty and cramped, and the toilet shifted when you sat on it. Given Provincetown's water problems, the owners of the house had posted a sign over the toilet that read, "If it's yellow, let it mellow. If it's brown, flush it down." Classy guys, our landlords.

But the house *was* within walking distance of the Boatslip, and a six-minute bike ride would get you to Herring Cove beach. I just wished I could picture the place during summertime, with the windows open, the sun overhead, and boys walking by with their shirts off. Instead, it was cold and damp. The day had darkened and there was the threat of snow.

"All right," I said. "Let's take it."

"Excellent," the realtor said. "Come on back to the office and we'll do up the paperwork. Will you be able to leave a check?"

Adam said he'd write it. He'd better, since it was he who'd promised to cover for Peter.

I was still waiting for the details. Finally, over coffee after the lease was signed, Adam explained how it had all come to be.

"He's friends with a girl I work with, and I met him at her house. Oh, Troy, he was *so* thankful when I said I'd cover for him until he started working! He'd been going *crazy* trying to find summer housing. It's not easy, you know." Adam smiled slyly at me. "He even kissed me."

"Peter Youngblood kissed you?"

"Yes, he did." Adam looked very smug. "And maybe more before the summer is over."

"You're playing out of your league," I told him, feeling suddenly resentful.

He laughed. "Worst case scenario is we get to look at him lounging around the house in his 2(x)ists."

I shuddered. "I won't make it past Fourth of July."

"He promised he'd pay me back, and I'm certain he's good for the money," Adam said. "It's just that he's between shows right now."

I shook my head. "You just fell into those dreamy green eyes, didn't you?"

Adam sniffed. "He is going to be performing in 'The Rocky Horror

Show' this summer in P-town. It's a three-month gig. He'll have the cash then."

"'The Rocky Horror Show'?" I asked, leaning in over the table. "Will he play Rocky?"

Adam smiled. "Yes. He'll stand there shirtless for the whole time. And he's promised us a season pass."

I took a long sip of my coffee. I pictured Peter Youngblood's torso. It was tattooed in my mind, even if we'd never even exchanged a hello. "What was he like?" I asked. "Did you get to talk with him much?"

"Just for a few minutes," Adam said. "But he seemed very nice. Not stuck-up at all."

I thought of something. "But, Adam, there are only two bedrooms and there are three of us."

"Well, he'll have to take the couch when we're there," Adam said. "That way, when we get up in the morning, we can ogle to our heart's content." He smirked. "Of course, I told him during the week, when we're not there, he can use one of our rooms. Think about it, Troy. Peter Youngblood sleeping in your bed."

I shivered. "Correction," I said, draining my coffee. "I'm not going to make it through Memorial Day."

In Springtime a Man's Fancy
Turns To . . .

Sex. It turns to sex.

It was the longest, horniest three months of my life. I wasn't getting much. The city seemed to pull inward. Nobody seemed to be going out. The winter seemed to drag on and on, giving us one last slap across the face with a sudden snowfall in early April. Thankfully the snow lasted only about twenty-four hours before it melted off the daffodils. Oh, man, I couldn't *wait* for summer to begin.

"It's going to be our best summer ever," Adam kept promising. "We are going to meet the men of our dreams. And if not, at least we can take turns rubbing sunscreen into Peter Youngblood's back."

I had marked off the days until May 15 on my calendar at work. I can't even begin to tell you how excited I was about spending this summer in P-town. See, I'd always wished I'd spent a summer there during college, or maybe taken some time off between graduation and going to work. Being a houseboy at a guesthouse for a summer would have been awesome. During our annual one-week stay, I would watch the boys who were in town working for the summer. They'd be knotted together outside of Spiritus Pizza at 1 A.M., sharing their secret jokes, their mysterious knowing smiles. There was such a camaraderie, such a kinship, that I always felt envious. We were the outsiders, the drop-ins, the clueless tourists. They were the boys everybody wanted to meet, nameless celebrities Adam and I christened with our own little epithets. One year there was Snake Boy, because of the tattoo of a cobra on his shoulder. Another year there was Roy Rogers, because he always wore a cowboy hat. Finally, last year, there was Stand by Me, because this guy was just the spitting image of a young River Phoenix.

Hey, maybe this summer, people would actually make up names for Adam and me—although I really couldn't think of anything unique about either one of us that it could be singled out and turned into a nickname.

Of course, my mother couldn't understand the appeal of renting a house for the entire summer in one place. Here's me calling to tell her of my plans.

"You're paying how much?" she asked.

"Seven thousand," I repeated.

"Well, I hope it's a *mansion*," she said. "But won't you get bored doing the same thing every weekend?"

Although it was true that life in P-town *did* settle into a kind of routine, I assured her the town was a never-ending kaleidoscope of people and activities.

She wasn't even listening. "How many times can you go on a whale-watch? After a while, don't all the whales look alike?"

I supposed a better question would be, "After a while, don't all the boys look alike?"

Maybe so, but I didn't care. I was going to snare one this summer. I might be heading into P-town alone, but I was determined I wouldn't be coming out that way.

Blue Skies and Speedos

We spied the the Monument as we rounded a curve on Route 6 in Truro, and the outline of Provincetown came into view, glittering under a sharp blue sky. The town is the final sandy finger of Cape Cod, delicately curling around on itself into the bay. It was here that the Pilgrims first landed, before heading on to Plymouth, and the monument built in their memory rises up into the sky, a tall phallus of gray mortar. We cheered when we saw it. We had arrived!

It was a dazzling start to our summer adventure. The sun was high and warm, and the town swelled with new arrivals: gay boys from Boston and New York and Hartford and Providence, lesbians from everywhere, heteros from down Cape coming up to shop and to gawk. We collected the keys from the realtor and drove up to our little bungalow. As I'd hoped, it looked far more inviting in the sun and the warmth, and the owners had left a bouquet of orchids and a bottle of champagne to welcome us. Maybe they *were* pretty classy after all.

"Maybe we can have a little kickoff dinner tonight," I suggested, admiring the champagne. "Just you and me, Adam."

"Sure, sure," he said, not really listening to me, hauling in his suitcases. "Which room do you want?"

"They're both the same," I said. "Take whichever one you want."

Peter wouldn't be joining us until next weekend, which I was glad about. It gave me a little time to settle in before preparing myself for his arrival. I was also happy that I'd get some time alone with Adam. We'd both been so busy these past couple of months that we'd hardly seen each other. Both of us had been working longer shifts and would continue to do so Mondays through Wednesdays, so that we could leave early on Thursday and enjoy three-day weekends for most of the summer. I was grateful we had such accommodating bosses. I knew we were luckier than most.

I looked around our little shack. It was actually kind of sweet. A warm spring breeze tickled the yellow curtains at the windows. Yes, I thought I would enjoy it here. The summer seemed filled with promise. And I could think of no better way to kick it off than a quiet night with Adam, sipping champagne, catching up, finally having the time to just talk, just be with each other. Sisters needed to do that every now and then. Just be with each other. Maybe we could take a walk on the beach later.

I thought back to those days in college, when Adam and I would sit around my dorm room, smoking pot, talking about life. He was the first person I'd ever really opened to, ever really confided my secrets. How my parents had always favored my younger brother because he was the athlete in the family, the good old boy they could be proud of.

"I don't like my brother all that much either," Adam said. "He's Mr. Golden Boy too. Gets all the trophies in baseball and all that shit. Dad totally favors him."

It was that night that Adam and I made love out behind the student union. We were so high, I mean higher than Jesus, and we'd gone for a walk. We just sat down on the grass in the shadows and started kissing and messing around. There are nights I still wake up with a big old hard-on, dreaming of that night. The sex was awesome. I remember how Adam kissed my neck, little flickers of his lips down my throat and all the way down my chest. When he took my dick in his mouth I thought nothing could ever be better than this.

I actually thought Adam and I were going to become boyfriends after that, but see, at the time, he was in the midst of a way powerful crush on this guy named Brad, who he ended up dating for about a week. By then I'd moved on to somebody else myself, and so we never got back around to considering each other as boyfriend material.

Except we did become best friends. Brothers, to replace the fucked-up models we already got. Actually, in gay lingo, we became *sisters*.

So it was only natural that I was looking forward to having time this summer to recapture some of our college intimacy. I mean just sitting around, the two of us, smoking pot, talking about ourselves and what we were feeling, what we hoped for, what we dreamed about. All that kind of stuff. It would be kind of like having a boyfriend, except without the sex.

"How about if we barbecue some chicken on the grill tonight?" I called into Adam's room, where he was fast dumping his socks and underwear into a drawer of the dresser.

"Troy!" he exclaimed. "You've got to come in here and look at this!"

I hurried into his room. His window looked out onto the deck of a house pushed up close to ours. There, sunning themselves in all their glory, were three incredible hotties, each in a different colored Speedo. It was like one of those ads you see for gay cruises or guesthouses.

"Okay, we *have* to go out there," Adam said.

"We don't even know them," I protested.

"Not yet we don't," he corrected me. "Come on. Isn't this what we rented this place for?"

"Well, that and maybe a few other things," I said. He didn't respond, just darted out of the room.

I shrugged, and followed him out around the house. We stopped at the side of our neighbors' deck, leaning our elbows against the railing.

"You boys care to join us for margaritas?" Adam called. "We're just setting up our blender."

All three of them shot up at once as if they were controlled by hinges. "Sure!" squealed the one closest to us. Nice body, but as queeny as they come. The other two just smiled. I noticed one had a gold navel ring set among a set of hard abs, the sun reflecting off it as he moved.

They all toddled over to our place. We didn't have a deck, but there was a small front porch where we all settled into wicker chairs. Adam, suddenly energized, brought out the tequila and the blender and plugged it into an outdoor switch. The boys introduced themselves.

"I'm Robbie," said the queeny one. The others were Todd and Track.

Track was the one with the abs and the navel ring. Adam was already cooing up to him, staking his claim. "That's a cool name," he
said, pouring in the margarita mix.

"My full name's Lautrec. I'm French-Canadian." He did indeed
have the accent, a delicious little twist to his lips.

I took my place beside Todd, the third and least talkative of the
group. Handsome, great body. So let Adam have Track. This one would
do well enough.

They were all working here in P-town for the summer, Robbie explained. Houseboys during the day and bartenders at night. Robbie
also juggled a couple shifts as a waiter.

I couldn't take my eyes off Todd's body as he leaned in to accept the
margarita offered him by Adam, then settled back in his chair. He was
wearing a Speedo, remember.

"Awesome day, huh?" Robbie was asking. "Feels like August already."

"Here's to the whole summer being awesome," Adam said, his eyes
on Track.

"When it's this nice to start," Todd finally said, "it means the rest of
it's gonna suck."

Okay, so he tended to be a bit gloomy. But with a waist and shoulders like that, who needed light and cheerful?

Robbie suggested we all head over to their deck, so we could look
out over the bay. Adam whipped up another round of drinks and carried the blender with us. It wasn't even two o'clock in the afternoon
and already I had a buzz.

"Talk about fate, huh?" Adam whispered to me as we trotted over to
the deck. "Not here an hour and already we've found boyfriends."

"Um, Adam, you may be rushing things just a tad," I cautioned.

"You mean to say you didn't catch the electricity between me and
Track? Honey, I already know how *my* night is going to end." He
grinned, his eyes flashing.

I made a face. "I thought we were going to stay in our first night,
just you and me and the barbecue."

He looked at me as if I were crazy. "Troy, what would you rather
have? Me—or Todd in his bright blue Speedo?"

I didn't have time to answer. We had arrived on the deck. "*Voilà!*"

Robbie was announcing, gesturing with a dramatic wave of his hand. "Provincetown Harbor, with a view of Long Point."

It was the very end of Cape Cod, where the land curled around in one last spiral, crumbling into sand and marshes. At the very tip stood a lighthouse. I'd been out to Long Point before, a couple summers ago when Adam and I had packed a lunch and rented a boat. We'd had a great time, just the two of us, talking about stuff, laughing. The day had been as spectacular as this one was, with a full blue sky and a soft sea breeze.

"People died out there," Todd said suddenly.

We all looked at him.

"On Long Point," he said. "I wonder if you could hear their screams from here."

"What?" I asked.

Robbie made a face. "Todd's been obsessed with the story of the Long Point settlement ever since we read about it at the museum. There used to be houses out there, a whole little village, back in, like, the 1800s or something. But during the winter it was harder to get fresh water out there, so they floated all the houses back over the bay to Commercial Street. Todd has imagined a whole community perishing of thirst. It's just his way. He imagines himself a playwright."

"Interesting," I said, moving closer to this hunky poetic character. "What kind of plays?"

"Plays about death," he said, turning his face bleakly toward mine.

I backed off. "Sounds fun," I ventured.

"There is no escaping death," Todd intoned, lifting his margarita in the direction of Long Point, "no matter what we try. No matter what we humans do in the pursuit of living, as the Pilgrims were doing in their exploration and settlement of new lands. Death is always a tragic corollary to any story."

"Oh, bravo, Sir John Gielgud," quipped Robbie. He looked over at me. "He always gets this way after a couple of drinks."

I turned to look at Adam, but he and Track were gone. Todd settled down on a lounge and closed his eyes against the sun. He looked like a beautiful corpse.

Robbie motioned for me to sit down next to him at the table. "Hon, you should really put on some lotion," he said. "We've been here for a few days so we've got a pretty good base. But you're still pale as a ghost."

I glanced down at my skin. Suddenly I was feeling terribly depressed. "I guess you're right," I said.

"Here." Robbie has produced a tube of sunblock No. 23 from his satchel. "Start off slow. That's the only way. Otherwise you'll look like a leather jacket by the time you're thirty."

I sighed, accepting the lotion from him and slathering it on my shoulders and arms. "I had wanted to get a tan quickly this year," I mused.

"Sweetheart, you know that we shouldn't be tanning anymore. Especially here. There's no more ozone left over New England."

We sat there for a while not talking. Eventually Todd got up and went inside without saying anything. It was just Robbie and me left now.

"Adam your boyfriend?" Robbie finally asked.

"No," I said, registering shock. "We're *sisters*. Why would you think we're boyfriends? I mean, he took off with Track, didn't he?"

Robbie shrugged. "Who knows what games boyfriends play here in P-town? I only asked because I can tell you're steamed he took off on you."

"I'm not steamed. Adam can do what he wants."

"Okay. Whatever you say. I've just met you."

I scowled. "Do *you* have a boyfriend?"

"Just got dumped." He looked at me deliberately. "By Track."

"Oh," I said.

"It's no big deal, really. The relationship only lasted a little over a month. I knew coming here for the summer would kill it. I mean, how can you expect to stick to just M&Ms when you walk into a candy store and everything is marked 'free'?"

I sighed. "I thought Adam wanted a different summer, that's all," I said. "We said we wanted to meet new people. Date. Find boyfriends." I paused. "And spend time together."

"Honey, P-town in the summer is a *great* place to find a boyfriend." He waited a beat before adding, "Somebody *else's*, of course." He slapped his thigh in laughter.

When he saw I wasn't joining in, he leaned across the table at me. "Sweetie, the summer is the time to be carefree. To forget all your worries, all your goals. Put 'em on hold and just go *mad*. That's what I decided to do. I'm just going to have *fun* this summer. If Track and me are meant to be, he'll be back after Labor Day."

I smiled, but he could tell I wasn't convinced.

"You want to go grab a burrito at Big Daddy's?" Robbie suddenly asked.

Why not? Who knew how long Adam and Track would take? Such a beautiful day and they were inside, fucking.

So maybe I *was* steamed. Here I was, eating a chicken burrito with black beans with some queeny guy I didn't even know, my first day of my long-awaited P-town summer. And Adam was off with some guy with a navel ring. Whatever.

Yes, I had sex with Robbie, but that's another story for another time.

The Arrival of Peter Youngblood

And of course Peter has to look even better than I remembered. It was the second weekend of our summer, and Memorial Day weekend to boot. The town was jammed with tourists. People were everywhere, crowded along the sides of streets three and four deep, making it difficult for cars to pass and nearly impossible for anyone on a bike. The main drag swarmed with families, nervous-looking dads, their arms filled with packages, trailing behind crisply efficient moms pushing strollers, pausing to stop at every boutique and gift shop and chatting up the queens who ran them. There were plenty of gay boys strolling by in tank tops, but Memorial Day has traditionally been more for the girls. Thousands of lesbians, every other one with the exact same haircut, parading down Commercial Street, loud and proud.

I was determined this weekend would go better than the first. I'd hardly seen Adam at all last week. True to his prediction, he and Track had fallen madly in love and spent the entire two days taking long walks along the beach or making out on the dance floor. Driving up to P-town on Thursday afternoon, ahead of all the traffic, I vowed I'd have a good time whether Adam was around or not.

But then Peter shows up.

"Hello? Anyone home?"

I had just arrived. I panicked. Adam wasn't here yet. I would have to face Peter on my own.

"Hi," I ventured, staring up into his bronzed face, his green eyes reflecting the sun. "I'm . . . Troy."

"Hey, Troy," Peter said, shaking my hand heartily. I nearly melted. "What's happening?"

He was shirtless, already tanned, his smooth, hard, rounded pectorals situated over a sharply delineated set of abdominals. Peter wasn't bulky or huge. He was simply chiseled out of the finest marble. He smiled, flashing the whitest teeth I'd ever seen.

"So this is our place, huh?" Peter was looking around. "Not so bad. A little hideaway I can call home for the next three months." He winked at me. "Which one is my room?"

"Um," I said, faltering. "Well, I thought Adam had talked to you about —"

"I'd prefer this one," he said, indicating mine. "It's a little removed from the street. I might need quiet to study the script. Did Adam tell you I was in 'The Rocky Horror Show'?"

"Um, yeah." He had tossed his backpack down on the dresser and had flopped himself down on my bed.

"Man, I am beat," Peter said. "Partied a little too long and too late last night. Think I'll catch some zee's. Hey, it was awesome meeting you, Troy. Hope we have an amazing summer together."

"Yeah," I said. "Me, too."

He shut the door.

The Curse

So what the fuck was I supposed to do? Kick the man of my dreams out of my bed? I'd figure out later where was I going to sleep.

I headed out to the beach. It wasn't as warm as last weekend. There was a crisp sea breeze that made me shiver. I spotted Robbie and Todd heading toward me. I waved.

"Hey, sweetie," Robbie called. Todd was silent in his greeting, just nodded.

"What's going on?" I asked.

"Just out for a morning stroll," Robbie said. "Finished our chores at the guesthouse and now we're just killing time until Tea Dance."

"Killing time," Todd said. "A phrase that reveals the truth of death never being very far away."

"Oh, *please*, Mary," Robbie said.

I looked over at Todd. "Why are you always so gloomy?" I asked.

"Give me a reason not to be," he said.

"Well, here we are, on the beach, and the sun is out, and we have the whole summer ahead of us," I offered.

Yet my words carried little conviction, I have to admit, because I was feeling a little gloomy myself, what with having just lost my bedroom. Pointing out the brighter side of life to Todd, however, made me see my situation more clearly myself. Things weren't so bad. The hunkiest man in the world had just slipped between my sheets. That I wasn't in them at the time was merely a minor quibble.

"The whole summer ahead of us," Todd intoned. He leveled his eyes at me. "Apparently this is your first summer here."

"Well, my first *whole* summer," I admitted.

He stopped in his tracks. "So you have no idea of the horrors to come?" Todd proclaimed dramatically.

"Oh, here he goes again," Robbie said, rolling his eyes.

"The horrors?" I asked.

"Welcome to the world of the Lost Boys," Todd said. "A world of aimless washashores, flitting from one job to the next, always running to escape the cold breath of winter on our necks. We go to South Beach, to Key West, to Los Angeles, to St. Croix, to Puerto Rico for the winter. But we return here faithfully to Provincetown every May, like the swallows to Capistrano." He paused, smiling grimly. "Welcome to our world."

"Well, I'm not exactly part of it," I said. "I don't flit."

"But you aspire to be one of us, do you not?'"

I said nothing, just looked over at Robbie, who shrugged.

"As one of the Lost Boys, you will descend deeper and deeper into our world," Todd informed me. "You will not discover a substance that cannot be abused. Your blackest hours will be spent crying on the shoulders of strangers. Your heart will be used and ultimately abandoned. You will confide secrets only to have them exposed mercilessly, when you least expect it. You will discover you have nothing to offer and nobody wants what you have anyway."

"Doesn't he sound as if he's casting some gypsy curse?" Robbie laughed.

I shuddered. He did indeed. "If you've had such miserable experiences here before," I asked, "why did you return this summer?"

"This is my *fourth* summer," Todd intoned, eyes looking out to sea. "That is the cruelest part of all. You are doomed to repeat your mistakes again and again, hoping against hope, year after year, that this time you will meet Mr. Right and settle down into happy and blissful domesticity."

I shivered.

Robbie slipped his arm around me. "Not Troy. I opened Troy's eyes to all that. He's heading into his first summer in P-town with his eyes wide open."

I was glad when Todd sauntered off alone down the beach. Pretty as he might be to look at it, he made me uneasy. He was one odd duck. But his words had an undeniable impact on me. I'd already set myself up for a fall this summer, and I appeared to have taken it. I'd hoped to spend time with Adam, and already he'd deserted me. I'd hoped to have someplace I could call my own, and now Peter had taken my room. All because I'd been too intimidated to speak up.

And yes, I'd gone into this summer hoping maybe I'd meet a boyfriend, the Holy Grail for so many gay men these days. Everybody I knew seemed to want to find a husband. The few couples I knew were hardly stable, with one partner usually cheating on the other, or else both of them caught in a highly dysfunctional arrangement. And to think gay men had the gall to demand the right to be married! Why was it that so many gay men found themselves in this predicament, seemingly unable to find a relationship and, when they did, so ready to fuck it up?

Robbie and I began walking down the beach. He took my hand in his. *Yikes.* Had our little roll in the sack last weekend given him the wrong impression? That I was *interested* in him? Oh, the sex had been okay. I'd enjoyed it. Robbie has a nice body and is fairly handsome, but I could never date a guy as queeny as he is.

That's when it hit me. I was just like so many of the guys I knew. Here I was, shaking my head over Adam's cavalier involvement with Track, when I'd fallen very quickly and easily into bed with Robbie. Had I led Robbie on in the same way I was certain Track was leading Adam on?

"Listen, Troy," Robbie was saying, "don't let Todd get you down. He's been burned pretty bad and is bitter. Pay him no mind."

"How'd he get burned?"

"He let himself fall in love with someone who just wasn't interested, who just could never see him as husband material." Robbie smiled ruefully. "Who was hung up on someone else."

I looked at him. It was like I had ESP or something. "You," I said.

He sighed. "You got it, sister. Todd's in love with me and I'm in love with Track, who's in love with Adam. At least for right now. Track usually has two or three loves per summer."

"Jeez," I said. "The world sure is out of sync, isn't it?"

"Yeah. Sometimes I wish somebody could just give it a shove and push it all one degree to one side, then everything might fall into place."

I laughed. "Or maybe just push it too far in the opposite direction."

It was Robbie's turn to laugh. "How about you, Troy? Who are you in love with?"

I shrugged. "Nobody. That's the problem."

"Oh, come on. Everybody's in love with somebody."

I thought of Peter, back home snoozing in my bed. I told Robbie about him.

"No," Robbie insisted. "You're not in love with Peter. He's your celebrity. Everybody's got one of those, too. You idolize celebrities from afar. You're not in love with them."

"I guess you're right. I could never play in Peter's league."

"You sell yourself short," Robbie scolded. He kissed me. I kissed him back. It felt good kissing him. Honest. He'd just admitted his feelings rested with someone else, and I'd admitted I had none at all. So we could fool around all we liked. I felt better about it.

We had lunch again at Big Daddy's Burritos, sitting out on the wharf watching kids fly colorful kites down the beach. Then we hopped on our bikes and rode out to Beech Forest, spying a red fox among the gnarled trees. We found a spot in the dunes where we made out a little while watching sea gulls glide lazily overhead. Back to Robbie's place, where we mixed up a batch of margaritas and got showered for Tea Dance. I realized I still hadn't seen Adam all day.

That changed at the Boatslip, where I spotted him with his arms linked with Track's, leaning up against the rail out on the deck and talking with Peter.

"Well," Adam said, "finally a sighting of our third roomie."

"When did you get in?" I asked Adam.

"Hours ago. Guess you've been out flitting around." He looked over at Robbie with the weirdest look on his face. As if he were . . . *jealous?* But how weird would *that* be?

"We went for a bike ride," I said simply.

"And made up the best margaritas ever," Robbie added.

"Whatever," Adam said. He turned and swallowed Track's face.

Peter smiled over at us. "They seem to do that a lot," he said.

Then Track suddenly spotted some guy across the room. He pulled out of Adam's embrace and exclaimed, "Oh! There's Ricardo! I heard he was going to be bartending here! I've just got to go and say hello. We go way back."

I watched as Adam's face registered discomfort, even a little embarrassment, as Track rushed off. But he tried to feign disinterest, just leaning back against the railing and closing his eyes against the sun. I observed Track's beeline across the deck, and saw the way he threw his arms around a shirtless guy with muscles for days. *Years*, actually. Then they disappeared into the crowd.

I brought my eyes back to our little group. Of course, Robbie's jaw was still on the floor as he stared at Peter. Everyone was coming up to Peter, grabbing at him, throwing their arms around him. Guys would spot him from across the deck and scream, "Oh my God! Peter! Welcome back!" Everyone knew Peter. One guy came up and started gushing so much over Peter that he actually stepped between us, his back pressed up to me as if I were a wall or something. I tapped him on the shoulder. He gave me one eye.

"Allow me to introduce myself," I said. "I'm another person on the deck."

He just took Peter by the arm and moved him away from us.

I sighed, leaning in beside Adam. "You want to get out of here?" I whispered to him. "Just you and me? Go get some dinner and maybe rent a video?"

He looked at me as if I were crazy. "What? Do you think Track isn't coming back?"

I shrugged. "Adam, I'm worried that maybe you're going to get hurt."

He laughed. "Having a relationship means learning to *trust*. Track will return in a couple minutes, Troy. You'll see."

"I hope so. I just think maybe you ought to take it a little slower . . ."

Adam looked at me all annoyed. "Just back off, okay, Troy?" He actually moved a few feet away from me to lean once more against the rail, turning his face to the sky and closing his eyes again.

"What's the matter?" Robbie asked, leaning into me.

"Nothing," I lied.

"Come on. What is it?"

"Really, nothing. It's just—" I hesitated. "I just keep thinking about what Todd said. I think maybe I had expectations that this was going to be a different kind of summer than it's turning out to be."

"Hon, it's only Memorial Day. You've got *three whole months* to make it what you want."

That was just it. What exactly *did* I want? I looked over at Peter, swarmed by a sea of admirers. I looked back over at Adam. Track had indeed returned and they were now back to a state of liplockedness, oblivious to everyone and everything around them.

"Let's dance," Robbie said. He took my hand, leading me out onto the small dance floor. We passed into the crowd, blending in, fading out, two more gay men bouncing up and down to Madonna among hordes of others who looked and acted not much differently from all the rest of us. From a distance, none of us would have been distinguishable from anyone else.

The Provincetown Shuffle

Not to be confused with the Provincetown shuttle, which picks you up along Bradford Street and drops you off at Herring Cove beach, the Provincetown shuffle is the routine one finds oneself in when one rents a house for the summer. Here's how it goes, and indeed how it went for me in the first several weeks leading into June, the days getting progressively longer and hotter and sunnier:

I arrived on Thursday night, usually a little worn and weary from work. My weekdays had taken on a kind of a blur. I *lived* for my weekends: everything led inexorably to them, and nothing else mattered quite so much. My apartment in Boston became a pigsty, undusted, unvacuumed. I laundered only those clothes I'd need for the following weekend. I ate Cheerios every night for dinner rather than buy any groceries.

In the office, I did my work as if by rote. I was cramming more hours into every day so that I could have Fridays off. Not many guys could arrange a deal like that. I was lucky, I kept telling myself. Meanwhile, I was falling asleep over the copy machine at seven o'clock on Wednesday nights.

But when I got to P-town, I left all that behind me. My spirit soared. Just what was it about this place that so energized me? Maybe it was the way the light reflects off the water from three directions all around you. Maybe it was the fact that P-town is at the very end of the earth, at the point farthest out to sea. Maybe it was the long history of art and creativity that exists in this place, nurturing artists and writers, musicians and people on the fringe for hundreds of years. Maybe it was the sheer beauty of the dunes, their golden windswept majesty standing in contrast to the white-capped blue of the sea.

And maybe I'm just getting a little too highfalutin'. Maybe it was simply the heady sense of abandon. Maybe it was escape from drudgery, the headlong plunge into hedonism that inspired me. I did indeed become one of the Lost Boys, despite my gainful year-round employment and the fact that I did not flit to warmer climates every fall. I became one of the Lost Boys and reveled in that status. People knew my name on Commercial Street. I was certain that tourists recognized me as one of the town clique, probably already spinning their own nickname for me. I felt "in," I felt cool, I felt embraced. That such feelings came because of the margaritas and cosmopolitans and marijuana and Ecstasy seemed not to matter. Not at first.

Every Thursday I'd meet up with Adam and Track and Robbie and we'd mix a batch of whatever had been deemed the drink of the evening. We'd wind up, a little twisted, at Spiritus Pizza at one in the morning, eyeing the crowd, picking out the new faces and waving at the old ones. Sex rarely happened on Thursday nights; I'd just fall asleep, dead to the world.

On Fridays I'd sleep in until almost noon, finally dragging myself out to the beach where I'd sleep some more. Herring Cove is like nowhere else in the world. You've got hundreds of lesbians clustered together at the start of the beach, followed by as many (or more) gay men. Some clueless hetero wandering by would certainly furrow his brow and wonder why the men and women were so segregated.

Out on the beach, I'd meet Adam and Track and Robbie and Todd, one or more of whom had usually brought along some lunch and a pitcher of vodka martinis. We'd blare dance mixes from our portable CD players while we watched boys walking past in tight colorful squarecuts.

Around three we'd trudge back down the sand and ride our bikes back home, where we'd shower and primp for Tea Dance. First stop was Mussel Beach Gym, however, where we never seemed to get the machines we wanted, having to work in with six other guys at a time. I kept vowing to get to the gym earlier, like maybe first thing in the morning before the crowds descended, but it never seemed to happen. I always slept straight through the mornings and besides, everybody had to get to the gym just before Tea for their party pump.

From Tea we often made a beeline to Power Tea, then grabbed some dinner and smoked some pot. On the days we skipped Tea, we shopped along Commercial Street—not so much for clothes or trinkets, but for *boys*. It's amazing how easy it is to meet guys along Commercial Street. Just a look, a smile, then a hello. People I'd seen for *years* in Boston who never gave me the time of day would stop and chat and shoot the shit with you in P-town.

Before going out for the night, of course, we needed to shower and primp again, so between nine and ten-thirty we were all invariably back home, making one last change before the night was over. That's when Track or Todd or somebody would always turn up with the drugs, usually X or once in a while some K. Depending on the night, we either headed to the Crown and Anchor, the A-House, or Purgatory. Since the clubs didn't start hopping until eleven at the very earliest, sometimes we popped into the Monkey Bar or the Porchside for a couple drinks first. Given that closing time in P-town is 1 A.M., you have to learn how to stretch out your party time in creative ways.

If you scored at the club, you went home directly with your trick of the evening, usually some cute tourist guy from Phillie or Baltimore or Albany. If you had no such luck, you trooped with everybody else down Commercial Street to Spiritus—or Stare-At-Us, as wags liked to call it. A slice of pizza at one in the morning is not a good idea if one wants to ward off love handles, but it's surprising how often I ordered my cheese-and-pepperoni, standing there and trying to eat it gracefully in front of a thousand watching eyes. By two, when the pizza joint closes, most of the crowd had wandered off, some back to their homes or their guesthouses, others to private parties, still others to back alleys or the docks for a little anonymous *amour*.

That's when I usually headed home, the typical ending to my P-town day. I'd be pretty wasted, and preferred falling asleep alone. Occasionally I'd meet someone and trick. This is where the P-town shuffle can be disrupted and the schedule changed. Once, for example, I met a guy from Toronto at After Tea and we'd spent the entire

evening in bed, foregoing any dinner or clubbing. I actually started liking the guy, but then learned he had a boyfriend. "It's okay," he said.
"We have an open relationship." Well, it wasn't okay with me. When
he called the next day I had Adam tell him I was out.

Another time, I met a guy at the beach. His name was Zachary, and
he was from Chicago. Another sweetheart at first meeting. We went
back to my place, starting fooling around on the couch, and then Peter
walks in the door. Of course, Zack forgets all about me and before I
know it, the two of them are in my room, in my bed, with the door
closed. I looked at the clock. It was almost six. Time to rejoin the
P-town shuffle in mid-progression; I met Adam and Track and Robbie
at the Pied for After Tea.

One night we all broke routine to attend the premiere of "The
Rocky Horror Show." You did that every so often, to catch a show
everybody was talking about or a comic who'd enticed you into attending with one of his or her flyers. Like Varla Jean Merman.
Everybody had to see Varla. Of course, everybody had to see Peter, too:
Peter as the shirtless, hunky, man-made Rocky. Peter sure had his
groupies in this town, guys who always seemed to be walking a few
steps behind him, who showed up with him everywhere. They cheered
and whistled when he appeared on stage, and afterward they closed
ranks around him, keeping him protected from the unwashed
masses—that is, the rest of us.

So far, it hadn't really been a problem with Peter taking over my
room, except for that afternoon with Zack. Truth was, Peter was often
not around, so I just slipped into the bed, inhaling deeply his aroma
from the sheets. One time I even found a pair of his DKNY underwear
in the bed. No, I'm not so pathetic as to have *done* anything with
them, but I'm also not going to deny that I left them there, under the
sheets with me. I figured it was as close as I'd come to being in bed
with Peter.

As for Adam, I saw a good deal of him, but nearly always with Track.
They were inseparable. There was a lot of drinking, and often the
nights would just blur together for me from six or seven on. But we
seemed to be always laughing. Adam and Track and Robbie and me.
The Lost Boys. How much fun was this?

Then, one night, all at once, without warning, I suddenly had this clear moment, when I realized I didn't know *why* we were laughing. We were just this bunch of goofballs laughing at dumb jokes. Was this really the kind of summer I'd wanted, all mindless games?

I turned to some guy sitting next to me, some friend of Robbie's I barely knew. I think his name was Will. I started telling him how I felt, how suddenly I was so unsure of everything. How, after all, we were all really just looking for love. I actually began to get somewhat emotional, the drugs and alcohol slurring my words. Will (or whatever his name was) listened for a while, then got up and walked away.

I wiped my mouth. I had been slobbering. I heard Will across the room telling somebody that I was so twisted I was carrying on like a crybaby.

Your blackest hours will be spent crying on the shoulders of strangers. Your heart will be used and ultimately abandoned. You will confide secrets only to have them exposed mercilessly, when you least expect it. You will discover you have nothing to offer and nobody wants what you have anyway.

I looked across the room and there was Todd staring back at me. It was as if he could read my mind. Everything he'd predicted was coming true.

The First Disaster

It was a late Friday afternoon toward the end of June that a startling chain of events was first put into motion. I was just back from the beach with Robbie, and was showering off the sand in our outdoor stall. I was already thinking of what I'd wear to Tea Dance. I could hear Robbie in the kitchen whipping up margaritas.

But when I stepped out of the shower stall, my towel wrapped around my waist, I was greeted by Adam.

"Troy," he managed to say, and then his face twisted, as if he might cry.

"What's the matter?"

"It's Track." Adam closed his eyes tightly. "I just saw him. With another guy."

Your heart will be used, abused and ultimately discarded. Another of Todd's curses coming true.

"Oh, man," I said, putting my hand on his shoulder. "Maybe they were just hanging out."

"They were *kissing*," Adam said plainly. "Track's hands were down his pants. They *weren't* just hanging out."

"Oh," I said in a small voice.

"I went into the house to surprise Track and spotted them on the couch together."

"Did they see you?"

He shook his head. "No. I don't think so."

"Who was it?"

Adam scowled. "That musclehead bartender Ricardo. Track was always saying how hot he thought he was."

"So what are you going to do?"

Adam ran his hands through his hair. "I don't know. What *can* I do?" He sat down on a deck chair. "Maybe it's for the best anyway. I was starting to think Track wasn't the guy for me."

I was conscious of the fact that my towel wasn't all that secure around my waist. "Let's go inside," I said.

He shook his head. "You know what, Troy? I just can't face Robbie right now, do the whole margarita thing. You guys are going to Tea Dance, right?"

"Well, we had planned—"

"That's okay. You go on ahead. I think I'm just going to take a walk by myself."

"No, Adam, wait." I looked at him intently. "Robbie can go on without me. You and I haven't spent any real time together yet. And I think you need a friend right now."

He smiled. "Thanks, Troy."

Robbie seemed a little miffed, having mixed a whole batch of margaritas and everything, but when I told him that Adam and Track were *finis*, a little sparkle flickered in his eyes. *Maybe I can get him back,* I could tell Robbie was thinking. So let *him* take on Ricardo, I thought. I hurriedly dressed and headed back out to Adam, who was already halfway down the beach.

The surf washed in quietly at our feet. There was a little nip to the air as the sun sank lower over the rooftops. Adam suggested we head out to the breakwater, a jetty of granite that provides a shortcut to Long Point, the very tip of the Cape. It also serves as a barrier to prevent the tides from wrecking the fragile marshlands. We've always loved the spot. In years past we used to make up picnic baskets and head out over the breakwater to the quieter beaches on Long Point, away from the crowds at Herring Cove.

"We can watch the sunset," Adam suggested.

I smiled over at him. God, it was nice to be doing something just the two of us, for a change.

On the breakwater the wind was a little frisky. I was glad I'd brought along a sweatshirt. Adam was just in a T-shirt, so he nestled in between my legs and I wrapped my arms around him. It's okay; sisters can do things like that without there being any sexual tension. So what if passersby assumed we were lovers? Adam and I had been friends since we were *teenagers*. We'd long passed any nonsense getting in the way of intimacy.

"I'm actually glad it's over," Adam said. "I mean, it was distracting me from the real reason I came here this summer."

I smiled. "And what might that reason be?"

He shrugged. "I'm not sure, but it sure as hell wasn't getting drunk every night and acting stupid."

I nodded. "I've been starting to feel the same way myself."

"Track isn't like us," Adam said. "I mean, he doesn't think about things the same way. Doesn't process, doesn't feel."

"I'm sure he *feels*," I offered.

"Maybe, but you'd never know it."

The sun had dropped lower, sending long blue shadows across the rocks and reflecting a pinkish glow off the surface of the water.

"We're not Lost Boys, you and I, Troy," Adam told me. "We have *lives*. We have *jobs*. We're not like them."

I just sighed. Adam was right. We'd been playacting. And for what reason? To fit in? To feel part of things?

"I guess I was just so eager to find a boyfriend, I jumped at the first opportunity that presented itself." Adam turned around to look up at me. "You tried to tell me to slow down."

I smiled. "I was worried I was just being envious because I hadn't found someone like you had."

"Let's make a pact," Adam said. "No more jumping into things. No more partying until our brains are fried."

"It's a deal."

We sat there for another hour or more, just talking—talking and laughing like the old days. A couple of times people smiled at us as they passed, and I was certain they thought we were lovers. In the gay world people often mistake sisters for lovers. But it didn't matter what anybody thought. I was convinced we'd gotten our summer back. I'd prove Todd wrong in the end.

A Great Guy

"**I** have met *a great guy*," Adam insisted, all out of breath.

I was rubbing sunblock on Robbie's back out on the deck. I looked up at Adam warily.

"I thought we weren't jumping into things," I said.

He suddenly looked defensive. "I'm not. He's just a great guy. That's all."

Robbie lifted an eyebrow. "Name? Age? Rank? Serial number? Dick size?"

Adam folded his arms across his chest. "I'm not going to tell you. Just so I can prove that I'm not jumping into anything."

"At least tell us where you met him," I said.

"On the bike trail. We were both just out riding our bikes. I mean, how great is that? No bars, no sleazy cruising scene. Just a couple guys out riding their bikes in the sun."

I rolled my eyes. "You're jumping, Adam."

"I am *not* jumping," he huffed.

"*Please*," Robbie concurred. "You've practically married him already."

Adam sniffed. "I'm never telling you guys anything ever again."

"Sure, sure," Robbie joked. "Promises, promises."

"I won't tell you that he's handsome, that he's successful, that he has a *real* job and a *real* life, that he's smart as well as good-looking, that he uses words like 'egregious'—words you two couldn't even *spell* if you tried looking them up in the dictionary."

"*Egregious?*" Robbie asked, making a face at me.

"I won't tell you that both of you would fall *instantly* in love with him if you met him." Adam smiled. "Or that he's taking me out to dinner tonight. At Front Street, the fanciest restaurant in all of P-town."

"Well, I'm glad you're keeping all that to yourself," I said.

"Just to prove that I'm not jumping into anything," Adam said, disappearing into the house.

Disappeared, all right. I would hardly see him for the next two weeks, so completely did he jump right into his latest Great Guy.

Oh, What Explosions I Saw on the Fourth of July

So it was the Fourth of July, and Adam headed over to his Great Guy's waterfront condo to watch the fireworks from his deck. Of course, the Great Guy had a waterfront condo. I was sure he also had a sportscar, a six-pack of abs, and a nine-inch dick.

And at long last, I'd have the chance to find out—about the car and maybe the abs, if not the dick—since Adam had consented finally to share him with the rest of the world, inviting me to come along to watch the fireworks. "His name is Paul," Adam had admitted. "I think I can now safely admit that yes, we *are* in love."

But you know what? I just didn't have the heart to tag along. Maybe indeed Adam had found his Mr. Right, his true love. Maybe he *had* fulfilled his summer goal of landing a boyfriend. Well, whoopee for him. I tried to be glad for him. I really did. Adam was my best friend, and this Paul guy certainly seemed to make him happy. But I just couldn't go. I had horrible visions of sitting there on Paul's deck feeling like a rusty third wheel trying to keep my eyes on the fireworks while other combustible activities were going on between Adam and Paul. It would be a miserable time, I was certain.

So instead I accepted Robbie's offer to watch the fireworks from the beach with him and Track and Todd. It wasn't much better. Todd pronounced the red and blue gunpowder show as an arrogant display of American arrogance, and Robbie sat all night mooning over Track, who was completely preoccupied with cruising some hunky redhead one blanket over. Just when and where he'd dumped Ricardo the hunky bartender I wasn't sure. Neither did I care.

So I staggered back to our house after all the popping and booming had ended, declining Todd's offer to get twisted and head out to the bar. I determined that I'd go home, go to bed, and get up early for a long bike ride out through the Province Lands. There's more to do here in P-town than party and sleep with cute boys. I'd explore the dunes, pick wild cranberries, catch a sighting of a rare blue heron . . .

But when I got home my plans took a decided turn.

I figured I'd have the whole place to myself for the night. Peter hadn't been around for days, and I was certain Adam wouldn't be coming home. Indeed, when I got there, the little house was quiet, except for the occasional hooting from Commercial Street and the leftover home-made pyrotechnics still going off all over town. I crawled into bed, wiggling in my earplugs. I fell asleep trying not to think about Adam and Mr. Great Guy drinking champagne and planning their life together.

I was awakened by hands. With my earplugs in place, I hadn't heard a thing. All I knew was that someone was in bed with me, and whoever it was, his hands were in my Calvin Kleins.

I jumped, pulling out my earplugs. "Baby," a voice in the dark purred, and suddenly warm wet lips were covering mine.

A slice of moonlight revealed a profile. Oh my God.

It was *Peter.*

And he was making love to me.

There are moments that rock one's world. This was one of them. Peter Youngblood—in bed with me! Naked! Kissing me! His hands in my pants! To say I was stunned would hardly describe what I was feeling. My hands anxiously settled onto his hard rippled back. This was beyond belief. My nose brushed his hair. His scent drove me out of my skin.

"Baby," he murmured again.

He tasted so divine, better than I could possibly have imagined. How many guys get the chance to actually *taste* their celebrity?

I tried to stay in the moment, to savor what was happening—but that was impossible. I mean, all sorts of thoughts started running through my head. *He just couldn't resist me. He's been wanting me all along. He waited for the right moment to make his move. He came home, found me alone, and dove in to get what he's been lusting after for almost two whole months. . . .*

"Baby," he moaned, kissing me again.

I went with it. I kissed him back, suddenly delirious. "Peter," I kept repeating, over and over, as if to convince myself it was really him. My hands explored his face, his shoulders, his chest. I turned him onto his back and kissed him all the way from the hollow of his throat down to his navel. I followed the happy trail of hair that led to his crotch. The torso I had so long admired from afar was now actually mine to touch, to lick, to kiss. His dick stood at a hard seven inches. I swallowed as much of it as I could.

"Oh, baby," he moaned.

I drove him wild. Then I got a wicked idea.

I scooted down the bed and lifted his right foot to my face.

"Baby?" he asked.

I popped his toes into my mouth. Man, would I give him the best toe suck he'd ever had in his life. He writhed in pleasure, grabbing at the sheets. I sucked each toe of each foot in turn, even going so far as swallowing the little pieces of lint I tasted in between. Go ahead, gag all you want—*but this was Peter Youngblood!!*

Now for the finale. I pulled open the drawer of the bedside table and withdrew a condom, slipping it over his cock. His head thrashed back and forth on the pillow, his eyes rolled back into their sockets. I sat myself down on him, filling myself up with the man I adored. As he thrust hard and furious I leaned down to suck his mighty pectorals into my mouth. We came at the same time.

I collapsed, exhausted, next to him.

"You are awesome," he told me.

"No, *you* are," I told him, putting my head down on his chest and listening to his heartbeat.

In that hour, my whole world changed. How had it happened? I had fallen asleep feeling alone and unwanted. I awoke to find Prince Charming in bed with me.

"You really are awesome," he said again.

I kissed him. "I've had a crush on you for *years*," I admitted. "You're everything I could ever want in a man. Oh, Peter, has this really been as wonderful for you as it has for me?"

He nodded. "You are awesome. I love you."

Forget for a moment that such words at such a moment are beyond absurd. Forget for a moment all my lectures to Adam about jumping into things. The dam of my heart just gave way to the rushing flood of feeling behind it. If I sound goopy and crazy, I was. Who wouldn't be, after finally having sex with Peter Youngblood?

"*I love you, too!*" I cried, pulling him to me, kissing him furiously.

I fell asleep in his arms, certain my life would forever be different from then on. Adam may have found a great guy, but I had found The Greatest Guy of All Time.

Peter Youngblood was mine!!!!!

THE BREAK OF DAY

Until about ten-thirty the next morning, that is.

"Good morning, sleepyhead," I called, carrying in a tray of croissants and a big mug of coffee I'd just freshly brewed.

He opened one eye. "Uhhhh," he groaned.

"I know how much you like chocolate croissants, so I went out and bought you some."

My voice sounded ridiculously chirpy.

"What time is it?" he managed to rasp.

I set the tray down and sat beside him on the bed. I ran my hand through his hair. "Did I really leave you so whipped, baby?" I asked.

He opened one eye to look at me. "Troy?"

"Of course it's me, sweetheart." I smiled. "I thought maybe we could take a bike ride."

"Oh, man, my head is killing me," he groaned. "Shut off the light." He pulled the sheet over his head.

That's when it all became crystal clear to me. When I realized what a fool I'd been.

Peter had been drunk. And now he had one killer of a hangover.

I stood up. "Let me ask you one thing," I said.

He grunted from under the sheet.

"Do you remember what happened last night?"

He peeked out from under his sheet. "What?" he asked. "Did I puke or something?"

I stiffened. So he *didn't* remember making love with me.

Or rather, he didn't remember *screwing* me. *Making love* was hardly the way to describe it.

And I'd sucked his toes!

"Yes," I told him, suddenly feeling particularly nasty. "You puked all over yourself on Commercial Street in front of hundreds of people."

"Oh, man, no!"

I nodded. "Yes, you did. All over the place. It was quite the scene."

He sat up in bed, and winced at the pain behind his eyes. "Was Brian there? Did he see?"

I had no idea who the fuck Brian was, but figured since Peter had asked, he was no doubt somebody who *mattered*. Unlike me.

"Yes," I said. "Brian saw the whole thing."

"Oh, shit," Peter grumbled, falling back down and covering himself with the sheet.

Later, I told Peter the truth. I'm not that mean a person. I told him I had no idea whether he'd puked, or whether Brian, whoever he was, was there to witness it or not. I did *not* tell him, however, that we had had sex. It wasn't something I really wanted him to know.

I wanted to forget it myself.

Why Adam's My Best Friend

You're probably wondering at this point why exactly Adam is my best friend. I mean, I've portrayed him as kind of fickle, kind of flighty, a kind of fair-weather friend. But that's not really true. And here's a good example of what I mean.

I was sitting out on the deck feeling pretty glum about what happened with Peter when Adam shows up.

"You okay, Troy?" he asked.

"What the fuck does okay mean?" I snarled. "Yes, I'm okay. I have my health, I have a job, I have an apartment, I have a house in P-town for the summer. I have a small savings account, I have a 401k, I have a car that runs. Sure, Adam. I'm okay."

He sat down next to me. "You're not okay."

"Go figure."

"You want to talk?"

I wasn't through being snarly. "I'm not sure that what I have to talk about would fit conveniently into whatever pocket of time you have available. I assume you're here just to change clothes and then you're off to see your Great Guy again."

Adam sighed. "Paul thought we'd go sailing on his boat."

"He has a *boat*, too? Why am I not surprised?"

"Troy, what's the matter?"

I put my nose in the air. "Don't you trouble yourself. Wouldn't want you fretting about me while you're sunning yourself on the Great Guy's yacht."

"It's a catamaran," Adam said, heading into the house. I heard him on the phone. In a few minutes he was back on the deck, settling himself on a lounger beside me.

"Aren't you leaving?" I asked timidly.

"I figure I can catch rays right here just as well as on any old boat," he said.

See? *That's* why Adam's my best friend. "So I slept with Peter last night," I said after a long silence.

"*What????*" Adam practically fell out of his chair.

"He was drunk," I said bitterly. "He doesn't even remember."

"Oh, Troy," Adam said.

I looked at him. "I sucked his toes," I said sheepishly, unable to hold back a grin.

Adam tried to stifle his laugh, but then it just bubbled out. "You've just *got* to stop going around sucking toes at random," he said.

I laughed along with him. Suddenly it *did* all seem so absurd.

"Listen," Adam said, "I had my heart set on being on the water today. How about you and me renting a boat and heading over to Long Point?"

It was the most awesome idea I'd heard in weeks. So we packed up a couple bottles of wine, some strawberries and cheese and hurried over to Flyer's. We picked out a simple little motorboat and piled in with our stuff. Starting the boat's engine was like starting a lawn mower, yanking on the cord until it kicked in. After several attempts, Adam handed it over to me. I got it to roar on my first try.

We cut a fast path through the water, and the day overhead opened into the sharpest blue sky we'd seen all summer. "Just look at that light," Adam said, gesturing toward the water, where the sun reflected off the bay. "Nowhere else in the world does it look like that."

Adam explained that the light in Provincetown, being surrounded by water on three sides, was unique. That's one of the reasons the place had attracted painters and other artists for over a hundred years. Here one could see better, more clearly, than practically anywhere else in the world. Here things were illuminated in a way like no place else.

I was feeling more clear-headed myself. I watched as Adam un-corked the first bottle of wine. We had our first toast while still at sea.

"I want to meet somebody who I can do things like this with," I said.

Adam nodded. "That's why I feel so lucky that I met Paul. We do things like this all the time. Oh, Troy, I can't wait for you to meet him."

For a moment I felt downhearted again. Just why, I wasn't sure. Was it the reminder that yet again Adam had found somebody and I hadn't? Or was it the fear that outings like this one with Adam were likely to become extremely rare now that he had Paul?

"You'll meet somebody soon," Adam said, as if reading my mind. That's often the way with us. We can totally tell what the other is thinking. "I'm sure of it, Troy. Very soon. Before the summer is over."

"How can you be so sure?"

"It's just your turn," Adam said. "Won't it be fun, you and your boyfriend, me and Paul, hanging out together?"

I couldn't imagine it. We docked the boat at Long Point, the very end of Cape Cod, and stretched out on the sand. Adam was soon asleep in the sun, but I remained awake, trying to visualize "me and my boyfriend." I couldn't see a thing.

The Boyfriend Dilemma

Why has the search for a boyfriend become such a Holy Grail for gay men? Why is that whenever you pick up a gay magazine there's some article on how to find the perfect boyfriend? Why is it that entire books are written about the subject, with crazy titles like "Finding the Husband Within" and "My Search for Mr. Right"? Why does conversation always revolve around husband-hunting at every gay dinner party I go to, and why does every gay man alive seem to have an opinion about why gay relationships do or do not last?

I have had three boyfriends. I've dated a whole bunch of other guys, but boyfriends, for me, have to at least pass the one-month mark. My first boyfriend was a guy named Clarence. Can you imagine? Clarence Abernathy. What a name, huh? The relationship started during my senior year in college. Adam thought he was a big priss. He was indeed, as it turned out. He never liked me to see him come and wasn't especially into seeing me. He was the kind who consider semen "yucky." He'd clean off immediately after orgasm and always made me shoot aiming away from him. Our relationship, such as it was, lasted exactly five weeks.

My second boyfriend was a guy named José Acosta. He was the best-looking guy I ever dated. I thought we'd grow old together. José lasted almost three months. I was totally in love with him for the first two. Then he got a job in San Diego. He announced it one night while we were having dinner at Bertucci's Pizza. He was all casual about it, as if he were simply telling me he had to pick up his shirts at the dry cleaner or something. "And then I'll be moving to San Diego at the end of the month. Hey, can you pass the grated cheese?"

Why I didn't dump him then and there, I don't know. I hung around for the rest of the month, writing him little love notes and putting them in the pockets of his jackets, hoping he'd find them when he got to San Diego, realize how much he missed me, and fly back to my waiting arms in Boston. All I got was one postcard after he left. Adam said he'd never liked José from the start. But I played the part of the bereaved widow for weeks. Almost as long as we'd been together.

My third boyfriend lasted the longest: five months, three weeks, and two days. Damn, was I pissed that we couldn't at least make it to the six-month mark. His name was Pierce. Isn't that awesome? Pierce Richardson. And he was everything you'd expect a Pierce to be. Sharp, funny, handsome, a great dresser. What he saw in me I'm not sure. But, man, did I ever feel like hot shit walking into Club Cafe with him. So many of my friends wanted Pierce. What I didn't know was how many were actually *getting* him. Adam finally had to break the news to me after Pierce hit on him. Turns out Pierce had slept with at least three guys I knew. You can imagine the royal shit fit that I threw.

"But I really *loved* him," I bawled to Adam. "I really *loved* Pierce!"

"No, you didn't, Troy. You loved the idea of him. What he represented. You want to *be* Pierce as much as be married to him."

I suppose that was true. But if Adam could be so wise about my affairs, how come he was so bad at picking husbands for himself? His list of ill-fated relationships stretched on even longer than mine. And I'd be there to counsel and advise, just as he counseled and advised me.

At least Adam could reply, when asked about his longest relationship, "Oh, about a year." He and this guy Danny lasted ten and a half months, almost eleven, which I figured gave him permission to round it up when asked. Me, I hadn't even broken the half-year barrier.

My parents, on the other hand, have been married for forty-one years. They dated for three years steadily before that, so by gay reckoning, their relationship has lasted for forty-four years. When they were my age, they'd already been married five years, together eight. When it comes to gay and straight relationships, time continuums are significantly different.

I work with a couple of lesbians who have been together twelve years. This is cause for great comment among people we know. "Twelve years!" they'll exclaim. "Twelve years together! God bless you!"

Even when Adam says his longest lasting relationship was "about a year," he still gets grins and claps on his back, as if to say, "Wow, you sure are lucky." Doesn't it seem a trifle odd that we gush over relationships of such relatively short duration when in the straight world a couple just hitting their one-year mark is still treated like a pair of newlyweds?

So the boyfriend dilemma continues. Suffice to say that by midsummer I'd pretty much given up all hope, figuring I was destined to end up one of those old aunties, living alone, fretting over the younger set, bedecked and bedizened with rings, and smelling of cologne. It was not a pretty image.

My Own Great Guy

O f course, it's when you least expect it that it happens.

It was the second week in July. Turns out that Adam's grandmother died on the night of Fourth of July, so he had to go home for the funeral. He'd have to miss a weekend in Provincetown. I considered not going down myself, staying in Boston for a change. My apartment was in dire need of a cleaning, I had laundry piled up everywhere, and it might be nice to see friends other than the P-town crew for a change.

But habits are hard to break, and Thursday night I sat in traffic in a rainstorm on the Sagamore Bridge. "Why?" I kept muttering to myself. "Why am I so drawn here every week? So far all I've found is casual sex, booze, drugs, and heartache. Why do I keep thinking things will change?"

Well, they did.

We met cute, as they say in the movies. It was still raining buckets when I got to town. I'd had no dinner, so I hurried down to the pizza joint. I must have looked a wreck, my shirt and pants splashed wet, my hair dripping down around my face. And who do I run smack-dab into but Peter.

Peter and this very handsome blond guy with a goatee.

"Hey, Troy," Peter chirped, still oblivious to our intimacy of a week before. I gave him a small smile as I ordered a couple of slices.

"Troy's my roommate," he was telling the blond guy.

Peter leaned up close to me, pretending to ask for a refill of his Coke, but in fact he pulled in to whisper in my ear, "Pretend we've got plans, okay?" he asked. "This guy's been after me all day and I want to shake him."

I turned to look at the guy. Why anyone would want to shake him I couldn't fathom. But then again, Peter wasn't anyone. I guess one had to be of Brad Pitt quality to pass muster with Peter. Damn, was I ever still pissed at myself for sucking his toes.

"Hi," I said to the blond guy, feeling a little cocky. "Haven't seen you around. What's your name?"

I could see Peter out of the corner of my eye shaking his head.

But then the most amazing thing happened. The guy smiled, reaching out to shake my hand. Our eyes met. I realized in that instant he had transferred his interest from Peter to me.

Me!

I think Peter realized as well. Oh, sure, he must have been grateful, since he'd been wanting to get rid of the guy. But there had to be a little bit of an ego bruise as well, to be so quickly forgotten and replaced. Especially by me, so clearly out of Peter Youngblood's league.

"My name's Alistair," the guy said. Our handshake was held for as long as our eyes continued to lock. It's an awesome experience, and most gay guys can relate: it's that moment when you realize somebody you're attracted to is attracted by you. Your head spins with the possibilities. *It's happening,* you think. *It's happening!*

"You here for the week?" I asked, suddenly aware that my voice was a little uneven, my heart racing in my chest.

"No, for the season," Alistair said. "I have a place in the east end."

"Cool," I said. "Me, too, except my place is in the west end."

"And your name?" he asked.

"Troy."

His eyes seemed to dance and he grinned. "Well, hello, Troy," he said. "Care to join me at my table?"

I turned. Peter was nowhere to be seen. I imagined he had snuck out in humiliation. To be thrown over, even by a guy he wasn't interested in, was probably just too much for him to bear.

Of course, eating pizza in front of a guy you're hot for is not a smart idea. I was constantly wiping my mouth, paranoid that cheese was stuck in my teeth. But he watched my eyes, not my lips, and I fell into his dreamy gaze easily.

He was thirty-one, an investments counselor, and he *owned his own home* in Jamaica Plain. None of my friends owned their own homes. This guy was a *catch*.

And he was so handsome. I mean, *really*. Soft brown eyes, dimples when he smiled. Best of all, he seemed really interested in me. Alistair asked lots of questions about what I did for work (I tried my best to make processing bank loans sound interesting) and about my family (you know, the usual, how many brothers and sisters, if your parents know you're gay, all that stuff) and about what kind of summer I'd been having so far.

"Well," I admitted, "I'm not sure. It's so easy to just get sucked into a kind of mindlessness here. There are a lot of games."

"Don't I know it," he agreed. "People of substance are difficult to find."

"Most everybody who's here for the summer is just out for a good time." I laughed. "I suppose there's nothing wrong with that."

"Nothing at all." Alistair narrowed his eyes thoughtfully at me from across the booth. "But you're looking for more than just fun."

I nodded, wiping my mouth and crumpling my napkin on my now-empty plate. "Yeah," I said quietly. "I'm looking for more."

Our eyes held for several seconds.

Alistair smiled, seemingly more to himself than me. "I remember thinking to myself, 'Wouldn't it be nice to fall in love this summer?'" He sighed. "But that might be too much to hope for."

"Why too much?" I asked. "Why should that be so difficult?"

"I'm not sure," he said. "Maybe we just make it more difficult than it needs to be."

I looked at him. Could he be true? A sensitive, good-looking, successful guy? One with no obvious substance-abuse problem? One who was single and looking for a commitment? I had given up hope that any such men were left on the planet.

The rain had let up and now just a light mist hit our faces as we left the pizza joint. The fog was heavy and rolling in off the bay. The lighthouse was sounding from Long Point. The scent of a salty low tide was thick. I could even taste it on my tongue.

We decided to take a walk along the beach. I hadn't even been home to primp, but somehow this guy seemed to like me just as I was. At one point he took my hand in his.

"You have such pretty, bright eyes," he told me, stopping to look at me.

Pretty eyes. No one had ever told me I had pretty eyes before.

We kissed. My mind had stopped thinking. I was completely engulfed by the moment. I trusted it. I trusted him. I should have been more skeptical, I suppose, given what had happened with Peter. I had trusted *that* moment as well, only for it to turn out completely bogus. But Peter had been a fantasy. Alistair in my arms felt warm and real, flesh and blood.

We walked all the way down the beach to the east end. The fog continued to thicken, and we'd occasionally pass people who became visible only when we drew within a few feet of them. There seemed to be no landmarks behind us or ahead of us. It was as if we were walking through time, with only the sound of the surf to guide us.

At Alistair's house, we made love for hours. Never before had I experienced such passion. He entered me gently and I felt subsumed by him, completely overwhelmed. It was a heady rush and I wanted to cry. His skin tasted sweet and pungent at the same time. The taste of a man.

But still . . . something stopped me from *sucking his toes.*

When we were finished, we lay back in each other's arms, exhausted. "Will you spend the night?" he whispered.

"I'd love to," I replied.

Alistair smiled. "I'm glad."

I fell asleep against his chest, listening to his heartbeat.

Oh, Joy! Oh, Rapture!

I woke up to the bright rays of the sun filling the room.
Alistair's room overlooked the bay. With the fog of the night before, I hadn't seen what a spectacular view he had. I sat up in bed, stretching, marveling at the panorama of sun and sky and sand and sea. It was low tide, and it appeared from here that one could actually walk out to Long Point.

My great guy was still asleep beside me. How unbelievable it had been, sleeping beside him all night. Do you know how long it had been since I'd slept in a man's arms, all night long? He looked even more beautiful in the morning light. His lips were slightly parted and his breathing rose and fell gently under the sheet. I ran my hand softly across the downy blond fur on his chest.

Well, *he* might look gorgeous in the morning, but I was sure *I* looked a sight. Stealthily, I crept out of bed and tiptoed into his bathroom. The mirror confirmed my worst fears. I patted my hair down with some water from the faucet and scrubbed my face, trying to make the morning puffiness of my eyes disappear. In Alistair's medicine cabinet I found a tube of toothpaste and squeezed out a glob, spreading it over my teeth, using my finger as a brush.

He caught me. He stood in the doorway and smiled. I jumped, blushing a little, then I filled my hands with water from the tap and swished the toothpaste away.

"I thought maybe you had snuck out on me," he said.

Oh, that he even would think so! And *care!* It just showed what a great guy I had found.

We kissed. I didn't even care that his breath was a little rank from sleep. At least I knew mine was minty fresh.

"Would you like to spend the day together?" Alistair asked.

Would I like to spend the day together? Could this fairy tale get any better?

We rode our bikes out through Beech Forest. We climbed up onto the observatory deck at the Visitors' Center to get a view of the dunes. We watched a six-seater plane take off from the tiny airport. We trekked out to Hatches Harbor and watched the seals sun themselves on the beach.

At midday we headed over to the Boatslip for Tea Dance. Alistair pushed his way into the crowd around the bar to buy us drinks. I spotted Robbie and Todd. I waved them down.

"Hey, girl," Robbie said, embracing me. Todd just gave me one of his solemn nods.

"I want you to meet this guy," I told them. "He's awesome."

Robbie beamed. "You see? Didn't I tell you you'd meet someone?"

"He's a great guy," I said, realizing how much I sounded like Adam.

I smiled to myself. Had it just been just a week ago that Adam had ventured to imagine us, each with our own boyfriend, doing stuff together? I'd dismissed the idea then, but now it seemed so possible.

"He's like a dream come true," I told Robbie.

"Dreams can do that sometimes." Robbie grinned at me. "My own beau will be here soon as well."

"Who is he?" I asked.

Robbie gestured with his head. "Here he comes now."

I looked across the deck. Track was making his way toward us.

"*Track?*" I was stunned. "You mean, you and he—are back together?"

"Yup." Robbie looked at me with glee. "It happened just the other night. It's *perfect.*"

I was happy for him, even if I didn't care all that much for Track. I watched as the two embraced and kissed. Maybe things *were* falling into place. Maybe the world *had* gotten back in sync. Robbie and Track. Adam and Paul. Alistair and me.

But then my eyes caught Todd, still leaning against the rail, watching Track and Robbie move off to the dance floor. I remembered what Robbie had told me, that Todd had feelings for him. So, no, the world hadn't yet shifted for everyone. And maybe it never could. Maybe a few would always be left out. Maybe there just weren't enough boyfriends to go around.

"A penny for your thoughts," Alistair said, coming up behind me, two bottles of beer in his hands.

"Oh, hey," I said, accepting one of the bottles. "I was just spacing a little. I'm still a bit in a daze from last night."

He kissed the tip of my nose. "It *has* all happened so fast, hasn't it?"

"I wanted you to meet my friends," I said. "This is Todd, but Robbie's gone off with . . ."

"Off with his Prince Charming," Todd finished my sentence for me. "But the Brothers Grimm failed to tell the truth of what came after the end. 'Happily ever after' is merely modern wish-fulfillment. In truth, Cinderella became a battered wife. The Prince left Snow White for one of the dwarves." He snorted. "Robbie's shining knight will prove just as unreliable."

"Todd, why are you always so pessimistic?" I had had just about enough of him. "Some things *do* turn out well, you know."

He just rolled his eyes, taking a sip of his beer.

"You tell him, Bright Eyes," Alistair said, grinning, pulling me to him.

"Let's dance," I said, anxious to be away from Todd's gloomy energy.

I led Alistair out onto the tiny dance floor, squeezing ourselves in next to Robbie and Track. They seemed oblivious of us. I understood. As far as I was concerned, despite the crowd, there was no one else in the entire room but Alistair and me.

Joy and rapture. There is nothing quite like that first day of being in love.

Real Life Has a Way of Getting in the Way

We spent the whole rest of the weekend together, and then Alistair drove with me back to Boston. He'd flown down, and could have flown back, but he said the two-hour ride would allow us to spend even more time together before we had to go back to four days of real-world lives and jobs.

Come on, could it get much better than this? A guy willingly sitting in traffic on Route 6 *just so he could be with me?*

I could hardly concentrate on my work. All day long I kept checking my e-mail to see if Alistair had written to me. About four o'clock I got a note (in response to one I'd sent). "Thinking of you, too, Bright Eyes," it read.

Thinking of you, too.

"Go ahead," I said to Adam when I reached him on the phone. "Tell me I'm jumping. I don't care. This guy is awesome."

"He sounds it. Just go slow, Troy. Remember how I waited a couple weeks before I allowed myself to get in very far with Paul."

"This weekend, how about the four of us going out to dinner?" I asked, nearly cutting him off, hardly listening to his words. "Some really fabulous restaurant. Like Front Street or Chester."

"Sounds good. I do really want you to meet Paul finally."

"And I really want you to meet Alistair." I remembered something. "Hey, how did the funeral go?"

"How is a funeral supposed to go? They said some prayers and put her in the ground. I just hope I live so long. She was ninety-one."

"Wow. And your grandfather is still alive?"

Adam laughed. "Sure is. They were married seventy-two years."

"Seventy-two years!" My mind couldn't embrace the idea. "Can you imagine?"

"I'm starting to be able to," Adam said. "I just got an e-mail from Paul, just telling me he was thinking of me and missed me."

I smiled. "And I just got an e-mail from Alistair, too. Isn't that cool? Do you think we've finally found our Mr. Rights?"

Adam had to go then. His boss was at his desk. I hung up and re-read Alistair's e-mail. Just six simple words, and how they'd made my day. *Thinking of you, too, Bright Eyes*.

I loved that he called me that.

I finally had my nickname.

Comedy of Errors

It felt like one of those old movies, or an *I Love Lucy* episode where everything keeps going wrong. I stopped by Alistair's house as soon as I got to P-town on Thursday. He wasn't there. I left a note pinned to his door. "Bright Eyes was here. Call me."

When I got to the cottage, he had left a message. "Troy, guess I just missed you. Call me." So I did, but got his machine. "Guess you just stepped out," I said. "I'm home. Call me."

That's when Adam arrived. We barely had time to greet each other when his cell phone rang. It was Paul. They exchanged some kissy-kissy lovers' talk (which, since meeting Alistair, no longer seemed quite as nauseating). "Sweetheart, I was hoping maybe you and me and Troy and Troy's boyfriend could have dinner tomorrow night. Is that cool?" Paul must have agreed, for Adam gave me the thumbs-up sign.

I wondered if Alistair had a cell phone. He must. Everybody did, except me. I resolved to get one this week, just so it would be easier to stay in touch with Alistair.

Finally Adam hung up with Paul. "Let's plan tomorrow night at seven," he informed me. I said I'd check with Alistair.

"So what are you doing tonight?" Adam asked. "Paul's making me dinner at his house."

How sweet. I hoped Alistair would make me dinner sometime.

"Well, I'm not sure what we're doing, but I'm certain it will be something *wonderful*." I smiled. Just then the phone rang. *"Voilà!"* I said, and indeed, it was Alistair. "Hi, baby doll," I gushed into the phone, determined to sound just as mushy as Adam had. "I have missed you so much!"

Adam just grinned and headed into the shower.

"I've missed you, too, Bright Eyes," Alistair said. "Sorry I wasn't here when you stopped by."

"That's okay. Hey, you want to do dinner tomorrow night at seven with my friend Adam and his boyfriend?"

"Sure. But hey, about tonight . . . I'm really beat from a hard day at work and need a nap. Can we meet late, like at eleven?"

I was disappointed. I had hoped he'd be as eager to see me as I was to see him. But if he needed a nap . . . "Okay," I said. What else could I say?

It was a long evening. Adam spruced himself up and headed out on his own date. I stayed in, watching the Game Show Network on television. I considered going out for a couple hours for a drink before meeting Alistair, but figured Robbie was with Track and I really didn't want to hang out with Todd. So I just hung around the house, smiling at Brett Somers and Charles Nelson Reilly camping it up on "Match Game," keeping my eyes on the clock as the hands moved ever so slowly toward eleven.

A little after ten, Adam came home. He looked utterly dejected. "What's the matter?" I asked.

"Nothing, really," he announced, flopping down onto the chair beside me. "We had a lovely dinner, and a nice walk, and we even made love . . ."

"So why are you home so early?"

"Paul suddenly got a headache. He needed to go to bed. I offered to stay with him, to play nurse—but he insisted that he gets these migraines every once in a while and just preferred to be alone. So I had no choice but to come home."

"That's odd," I agreed.

He shrugged. "So what are you doing? Want to go over to the Crown, just you and me?"

I stood, looking at the clock. "Sorry, Adam. But I've got to shower. I'm meeting Alistair at eleven."

"Oh. Okay. Well, have a good time."

We did, too. Alistair, refreshed from his nap, was his usual charming and happy self. He had bought chocolate-marshmallow ice cream, and we ate it from one huge bowl between us in the middle of his bed. He scooped some onto my dick and licked it off. I had the idea of putting some on his toes, but nixed it. Funny how I could suck all these strangers' toes but was leery about doing it with Alistair.

In the morning, however, Alistair had some work to do on his computer ("Can't get away from it," he apologized) and suggested we meet later that afternoon. Reluctantly I trudged home, thinking maybe Adam and I could climb to the top of the Pilgrim's Monument. It was a crystal-clear day. We'd have a view all the way down the Cape, maybe even out to Boston.

But Adam and Paul had plans to go bike-riding. "His headache is better, I take it," I observed. Adam nodded, promising to be back in time for the four of us to have dinner.

It didn't quite work out that way.

I sat around all day waiting for Alistair to call me, regretting my lack of cell phone more with each passing hour, feeling tied to the house by the phone lines. I called him once, but got his machine. "I know you're probably on-line working," I said, "but call me when you can. Do you want to take a walk before dinner? Maybe a bike ride? Call me, okay? Soon as you can?"

I knew I probably sounded pathetic. Hey, the guy has a life. That's what made him so attractive. He was *real*. He was *grounded*.

Unlike me, who sat there on my deck with the cordless phone in my lap, checking every once in a while just to make sure the ringer hadn't gotten accidentally switched off.

"I have bad news," Adam announced, scaring the shit out of me, coming up behind me.

The sun had dropped lower in the sky. Adam's face had nice color, the result of an afternoon of horseriding.

"What?" I asked. "I don't like bad news."

"We're going to have to cancel dinner." Adam looked as if he might cry. "Paul has gotten his migraine back."

"Oh, I'm sorry," I said. "Does he want to be alone again?"

Adam nodded. "You guys mind having a third wheel for dinner?"

"Not at all," I said, pulling him in close for a hug. "Adam, you're my best friend."

The phone finally rang. It was Alistair. "Hey, Bright Eyes, I'm finally done with this stupid work," he told me. "Why don't you come over?"

Adam had gone into the house. "Alistair," I said, "looks as if it will be just three for dinner. Paul's got a headache."

"So it's just going to be you and me and your roommate?" Alistair groaned. "Any way out of it, Bright Eyes? I've been missing you so bad all day. I'd like it to be just you and me. I'd love to cook you some dinner, here at my place."

I thought of how envious I had been last night when Paul had cooked for Adam. I'd never had a guy make me dinner before. "Well," I said, "it's just that I don't want Adam to be alone . . ."

I wasn't aware that Adam had come back outside. "Don't worry about me," he said. "You guys do what you want. We can have dinner another time."

I'm not proud of the fact that I didn't insist we keep our plans. I should've told Alistair that as much as I'd like to spend time alone with him, I wasn't going to leave my best friend alone on a Saturday night. But I didn't. I accepted the out Adam was offering me, and headed over to Alistair's, who cooked me the most delicious pepper-crusted salmon with sundried tomatoes.

It was only later that I realized the irony of the weekend: I'd still not met Paul, Adam had still not met Alistair, and I'd spent exactly one half my weekend alone.

Weirdness

Okay, so maybe I'm a big old dumb-ass. Maybe you can read the handwriting on the wall better than I can. But I was head over heels in love. *Love!*

The following weekend was hot. Hot like the surface of Mercury. The dog days of August, they call them. On Commercial Street somebody took up the old bet of cracking an egg on the sidewalk and seeing if it fried. It just made a big gooey mess. But that didn't mean the day wasn't hotter than hell. And humid. My underwear was sticking to my thighs. The humidity was the real problem, but if I heard one more person say, "It's not the heat, it's the humidity," I was going to punch them in the snout.

I hadn't seen Alistair on Thursday night; he'd called to say he'd be getting into town too late. Now, it wasn't that I didn't trust him or anything, but I rode my bike by his place around ten. I noticed that there were lights on in his condo. So maybe he had them set on an automatic timer. For a fleeting second, I considered stopping my bike to peer through the slats on his garage to see if his car was inside, but something persuaded me against it. I just kept riding past.

When I got back home, Adam had left a note saying he was out with Paul; he wouldn't be back until morning. I flopped down on my bed and fell asleep without even taking off my clothes. I dreamed about Alistair, and something about the dream seemed really important, as if I needed to remember it when I woke up. But I didn't. I lay there trying for several seconds, then gave up.

I hopped into the shower, called Alistair, who seemed in a hurry to get me off the phone. "Yes," he said, "come by around ten." Then he hung up abruptly. Maybe he was in the middle of something on his computer; maybe I'd interrupted him. Adam came home a few minutes later, a bit in a mood because he said Paul had to work this afternoon. That's why he agreed to Peter's request to help him break down the set for "The Rocky Horror Show." It had completed its run; now Peter was out of work. Like I had any time for sympathy for him. All I could think about was seeing Alistair again.

He greeted me warmly and effusively, making up for his brusqueness on the phone.

"Bright Eyes, I've missed you," he said, kissing me deep.

In moments we were naked and going at it on his bed. A ceiling fan circled overhead, but our bodies quickly grew sticky and damp. I didn't care. Making love to Alistair was the best sex I'd ever had. We thrashed about for nearly an hour, then collapsed into each other's arms. Neither of us had orgasmed; we just needed to take a little breather.

"You want something to drink?" Alistair asked, getting up out of bed.

"Some water," I panted.

He headed out into the kitchen. I sat up, looking out the large picture window down at the water. The bay was dotted with white sailboats.

"Maybe we can rent a boat today," I called into the kitchen. "It's probably cooler out on the water."

"No need," Alistair replied, coming back into the room, handing me a glass of ice water. I accepted it gratefully and drank quickly. "I have a boat."

"Really?" I was thrilled. "A sailboat?"

"Well, a catamaran. It's small but it does the trick."

He smiled at me. I smiled back at him.

We started to kiss. I pulled back at one point and looked him deep in the eyes. "I know it's far too early to think beyond the moment," I said, "but I want you to know I *really* like you. Before I met you, I was in this place of really, really wanting a relationship. I was so tired of being single. I wanted someone to love. You fill a very big part inside me, Alistair. I just want you to know that."

He gave me a small smile. "Are you saying you're falling in love with me?"

"Maybe. Maybe I am."

"Wow," is all he said.

"I don't want to freak you out," I said quickly. "It's not like I want to get married or anything. You're just a really great guy. You have everything I want in a boyfriend. You're grounded. You're successful. You're smart. You're funny. You're sexy." I grinned. "And you have a boat!"

I began kissing down his chest, flicking my tongue against his nipple. I kissed down the line of hair to his navel, then kissed all the way down his leg. I got to his feet. I kissed his toes.

Then I stopped.

"What kind of boat did you say you had?" I asked.

"A catamaran."

"Right." I thought of something. "Paul has one, too. Adam's boyfriend."

"Oh."

I pulled up close to him again. "I really want you to meet Adam. He's my best friend. It's so weird that we haven't been able to hook up."

"Summer schedules are crazy."

"Yeah."

He started to kiss my neck.

"Maybe tonight?" I asked. "You haven't even seen my place yet."

"Sure," he muttered, as his mouth found its way down my chest and into my armpit. I surrendered to the sensations, forgetting any weirdness. I wasn't sure what I'd been thinking anyway.

A Discovery

So we didn't hook up with Adam that night. We also didn't go sailing on Alistair's catamaran. Instead, we took a long drive in his Range Rover down Cape, exploring the Wellfleet ponds, and stopping for a lobster roll at P.J.'s take-out.

"Sometimes I just need to get out of Provincetown," Alistair said. "It just feels too confining for me sometimes. There's the whole rest of the Cape to discover. Too many folks just stay in P-town and never see what else there is to offer."

Yet as much as I enjoyed the ponds and our ride down Cape, I was intrigued by Alistair's apparent discomfort. Provincetown "too confining?" That was the first time I'd ever heard anybody call it that.

While he was in getting our lobster rolls, I opened his glove compartment. I took out his registration. ALISTAIR P. MCKENNA. That "P" intrigued me. I'm not sure why, but it did. When he got back in the car I asked him what his middle name was.

"Why?" he asked.

Did he seem suddenly anxious, or was it my imagination?

"I'm just curious," I replied. "I want to learn more about you."

"Philip," he said quickly, then handed me my lobster roll.

I watched him devour his ravenously. "How come I haven't met any of your friends?" I asked, not even starting to eat yet. "Not only haven't you met Adam, but I've never met any friends of *yours* either."

He shrugged. "I keep to myself mostly."

"Hmm."

We backed out onto Route 6. A car cut us off as we did so. Alistair leaned on his horn and called the guy a prick. "I hate it when people do that," he snarled. "I find it so egregrious."

"What did you say?"

"*Egregious.*" He laughed. "It means offensive."

"I know what it means," I said quietly.

He reached over and tousled my hair. "What's going through that little brain of yours, Bright Eyes?"

Suddenly my little nickname seemed absolutely appropriate. I was starting to see more clearly. More clearly than I had in weeks.

Peter Turns Out to Be Good for Something

It was Peter Youngblood who gave me the key. But that's getting ahead of the story. Let me start at the beginning.

The next weekend, I was out on my deck brooding. Alistair had just called. He had a cold. He didn't think we ought to go out on the boat today as we'd planned. We'd have dinner tonight instead, after he had a good long nap. "And maybe take in a movie," he suggested. "How about if we go down to Hyannis?"

Hyannis???

So I was brooding. Pissed, really. It was a perfect day for sailing. The bay was studded with boats. Lots of catamarans. And I knew Adam was out there with Paul.

Paul, who I'd never met.

Paul, that no-good bum.

You see, I'd run into Robbie last night. He was a wreck. He was snorting and sniveling coming down Commercial Street, looking as if he could tear through a brick wall if he came up against one. Lots of townies looked that way in August—those who worked in town called it "Augustitis"—but Robbie was particularly agitated, gnashing his teeth and growling like a bear.

"Whoa, Robbie!" I called. "What's up?"

"I should have known," he spit. "*I should have known!*"

"What? Tell me!"

I steadied him with my hands on his shoulders. He let out a long sigh and wiped his eyes with the back of his palm.

"It sure wasn't the first time he did this to me. We dated before, you remember, and he did it to me then, too!"

"Track?" I asked.

He nodded. "I just saw him with another guy, hand-in-hand, and they were nuzzling each other as they walked down the beach."

"Oh, man," I said. "I'm sorry. It's just what he did to Adam."

"Yeah, well, Adam is going to be pissed all over again."

I made a face. "Why?"

"Because the guy Track was holding hands with was *Paul*."

"Are you sure?"

"Oh, yes. Adam introduced us a couple days ago when I saw them on the beach. I remember Paul seemed mighty anxious being around me. Now I understand *why!*"

So Paul was two-timing Adam. As Adam's best friend, I needed to tell him, but how?

Still, there was one last bit of information that had yet to slide into place.

I was starting to doze off on the deck when Peter came up behind me.

"Um, Troy," he said.

"What?" I grunted. Being cordial to Peter took work. Ever since that night, I had given him the cold shoulder as often as possible. I even installed a lock on my door so I could sleep in peace. He made no protest. On the nights he showed up at the house, he just slept on the couch.

"Can I talk with you a minute?" he asked.

I opened one eye. "What about?"

"I've got a problem," he said.

"You're just figuring that out?"

He sighed. "It's Adam. I need to tell him something about that guy he's seeing."

"If it's about Paul and Track, I already know."

"*Track?*" Peter seemed genuinely surprised. "Is Paul fooling around with Track, too?"

I sat up and glared at him. "What do you mean, *too*? Are you sleeping with Paul?"

He held his hands up to me, seemingly desperate for me to believe in his innocence. "No way! I wouldn't do that! Adam's been really good to me, putting up the cash for me for stay here this summer and everything. I wouldn't do that to Adam." He paused. "But see, I didn't know it was Adam's boyfriend. I tricked with him once, and now he keeps calling me. I saw him one day with Adam and realized it was the same guy. What should I do?"

I sighed. "I suppose I need to talk to Adam."

"Well, tell him I never did anything with him after I found out who he was." Peter's eyes suddenly lit up as he appeared to think of something. "Hey, you can vouch for me!"

I narrowed my eyes at him. "Why would I do that?"

"Because you saw me turn him down! That day at the pizza joint. He was coming on to me and I asked you to help me get rid of him."

In that moment it still didn't register. I just glared at Peter.

"What are you talking about?" I asked in a small, low voice.

"Troy, you talked to Paul that day. When I left, the two of you were talking."

I felt the blood drain from my face. "That . . . that wasn't . . . Paul . . ." I managed to say.

"Yes, it was. I thought you knew. I thought you must have met him, being Adam's best friend and all."

Of course, I did know. Somewhere I had known, I think, ever since he'd told me he had a catamaran. The "egregious" should have clinched it, but although I had become suspicious, I wasn't sure what I was suspicious about. When you don't want to see something, you don't. It's like my mother about me being gay. Of course she knew, but she was still stunned when I told her. You make it real by speaking it. And Peter had just made it real.

It made sense. All those attempts at getting the four of us together—they didn't work because *there were only three of us!* All those times when Adam would come home just as I was heading out to see Alistair. It was like a revolving door.

Alistair was Paul. Paul was Alistair.

And he knew it. He was playing us off each other. And not only us, but Track, too. And Peter. And who knew how many else?

No wonder P-town was getting too confining for him.

So how do I describe the emotions that suddenly took hold of my mind and my body? Anger, surely. Grief, definitely. Shock, mostly. I wanted to swim out into the middle of the bay, climb up on his catamaran, and expose him in front of Adam.

But all I could do was cry. I didn't want Peter to see me—the last thing in the world I wanted was pity from Peter—so I hurried into the house, got dressed, and jumped into my car. I drove back to Boston, the tears running down my face and dripping off my chin. I'd practically told that faker that I loved him! I'd gotten all mushy with him—while he was sitting there laughing out of his ass at me, watching the clock to see when my shift ended and Adam's began.

Yet the worst feeling of all—the one that kept me awake all that night—was that this whole brouhaha just might destroy my friendship with Adam. That was the worst of it, the very worst. That I could lose Adam.

What a great summer it had turned out to be, huh?

The Truth Will Out

I never did have to break the news to Adam. He had his own re-sources.

I'd gotten through the entire week without talking to him. He never once called to ask why I'd left Provincetown early. That in itself was strange. Over and over in my head I tried working out a way of talking to him.

Then, Wednesday night, my buzzer sounded. It was Adam. He'd driven up to Boston from Hartford.

I knew when I let him into my apartment that he knew the truth. We just looked at each other. Then finally we embraced.

"How did you find out?" I asked.

"Things had been getting too weird," he said. "I think I knew before I even admitted it to myself." He made a wry face. "Then, his mother called."

"His mother?"

Adam nodded. "He was in the shower. So his machine picked up. She starts out, 'Hello, Alistair . . .'" He sighed. "Then it all made sense."

"So did you confront him?"

"No," Adam said. "I wanted to talk with you first. But you had left town. I've been so freaked ever since. The worst thing that could come of all this is that I could lose you. My best friend."

I fell into his arms. "That was the worst fear for me, too."

"We've both been used," he said.

I told him about Track and Peter. Adam just shook his head.

"So Alistair . . . or Paul . . . or whatever we should call him . . . still doesn't know we're on to him?" I asked.

Adam looked at me. "Are you planning something, Troy?"

I smirked. "Of course I am. This can only end well if the tables are turned."

"Maybe we just ought to move on," Adam said.

"Oh, no. We've both been through enough this summer that we're entitled to a little fun." I smiled. "Tomorrow is the Carnival Week parade. You call Paul and tell him you have to work, that you can't get down for it. He said to me last weekend that he didn't think he could make it in time for the parade. Let's see if—after your call—he sings a different tune."

I waited an hour after Adam's call to place my own to my beloved Alistair. "Oh, baby," I said, "I was *so* wanting to watch the parade with you tomorrow."

"Well," he said, reveling in his generosity, "maybe I *can* arrange to get off in time to meet you there."

"Oh, thank you!" I cheered. "Let's meet in front of the post office at five o'clock!"

"See you there, Bright Eyes!"

I hung up the phone and looked over at Adam.

"Oh, yes," I said. "We'll see him there all right."

Carnival

Every year, the parade is a riot. Almost literally. People line up five and six deep along Commercial Street to watch the floats and the stilt-walkers, the dykes on bikes, and the drag queens tossing pixie dust and condoms. Shirtless circuit boys with tribal tattoos are carried around on each other's shoulders. People honk horns, pass around balloons, eat cotton candy. There are cheers, hoots, whistles. It is a scaled-down Mardi Gras. Lots of flesh, fantasy, and fun.

I found a spot in front of the post office. I was worried Alistair-Paul wouldn't be able to spot me in the crowd. I stood up on the steps keeping my head high.

I needn't have worried. He found me easily.

"Bright Eyes," he called.

A little twinge of sadness shot through me. How much I had loved that nickname.

But I stayed on course.

We kissed. "I'm so glad you were able to get down for the parade," I told him.

He smiled. "When I realized how much it meant to you, I was glad to do it."

"You are *so* thoughtful," I said.

A float filled with queens in leopard prints passed by us then. "Hey, boys," one of them called to us, gyrating to Mariah Carey blaring from the loudspeakers. Alistair blew her a kiss.

That's when Adam made his appearance, appearing out of the crowd as if from thin air.

"Hey, baby," he said sweetly. "I thought you had to work."

"Uh," Alistair stammered, finally caught between us, unable to think fast enough.

"Hey, Troy," Adam said. "I see you finally met Paul."

"Paul?" I responded, in well-rehearsed outrage. "*Paul?* This is *Alistair.*"

"No, this is *Paul*," Adam insisted, arms akimbo, mirroring my outrage.

"Please, guys, um . . ."

People around us had begun to look quizzically at him. Alistair-Paul's face turned a deep shade of purple.

Though I enjoyed his discomfort, we certainly weren't going to give him the satisfaction of fighting over him. Instead we surprised him by suddenly laughing. "You *mean,*" Adam gushed, "we've both been dating *the same man?*"

I slapped my leg in mirth. "Wow! Who'd have guessed?"

"What a hoot!" Adam clapped his hands together. "That's a good one!"

"Look, guys, I was going to tell you . . . I just didn't know how . . ."

"Hey," I said, easing into him. "It's no big deal. Right, Adam?"

"Not at *all,*" Adam agreed, moving in on his other side. We each had an arm around his shoulder. "In fact, I think it's kind of *hot.* Don't you, Troy?"

"Totally," I said.

"You must have thought so, too, huh, Paul?" Adam asked. "Or do you prefer being called Alistair?"

I swatted his nose playfully. "I remember you saying once how people of substance were difficult to find. Hey, now you've got *two!*"

"*Two?* Why not try *three?*" It was Track, suddenly appearing from the crowd, right on cue, grinning like a madman.

I laughed. "Hey, the more the merrier."

"Great," came yet another voice, from behind us this time. "Then how about if we try for *four?*"

It was Peter, who proceeded to give Alistair a big smack of a kiss on the cheek. The four of us surrounded him now. I thought he was going to pass out.

"One big happy family," I said cheerily.

"Please," he said in a little voice. "Let me go."

Many in the crowd had turned away from the parade to watch our little drama. People were laughing. Robbie and Todd emerged now. "We could join in and make it *six*," Robbie offered.

"If we keep going," Adam suggested, "I'll bet we can draw the whole damn town in."

"You guys are crazy," Alistair grumbled, breaking free of us. He turned back once and shuddered. "You guys are really crazy," he repeated, before pushing off into the crowd.

We all cracked up. We watched the rest of the parade in high spirits. Afterward, we went back to Robbie's where he mixed up a great batch of cosmopolitans and we got totally wasted. The merriment was starting to wear off me, and I think for Adam, too. We were back where we started. Alone. And drunk.

I had hoped for so much with Alistair, allowed myself to dream . . .

I got very drunk. And I ended up in bed with Peter again.

A Rejection and a Revelation

"I have something to tell you," Peter said, lifting his face from sucking my cock and looking up at me with those dreamy eyes of his. "I remember doing this before."

"You never did *that* before," I said drunkenly. "I did that to you, but you never did that to me."

"No, I mean, the whole thing. Having sex with you. I never forgot. I just didn't want to acknowledge it."

I felt my hard-on start to wilt. "Why not?" I asked. "You acted like you were too drunk to remember."

"I know. I just didn't want it to turn into anything. I didn't think you were . . . you know, my type. Not to date, anyway."

My dick softened even more. "Not in your league."

He shrugged. "But after seeing the way you were today, planning this whole little ruse against Alistair, I saw you were really pretty cool."

I smiled tightly. "I proved that I was good enough for you."

"Yeah," he said, completely oblivious to his arrogance. "Yeah, I guess so." He grinned up at me. "Hey, suck my toes for me again, okay?"

Now, remember that I was drunk. I *had* to be, for I got up out of bed, got dressed, and walked out on Peter Youngblood. *Peter Youngblood!* I rejected Peter Youngblood after he'd pledged his affection for me. *His affection!* Who knew where that might have led?

Except that I *did* know.

It would have led exactly *nowhere*.

And, see, I was tired of going nowhere. Drunk as I was, I could still think clearly enough to know that once again, I was barking down the wrong path. Or heading up the wrong tree. Or whatever that goddam cliché is. Hey, I was pretty twisted. Give me a break.

I walked out into the night. Peter was still a big jerk. Sure, he was gorgeous, but maybe that was my problem. Maybe I was still single after all these years because I'd been too blinded by the superficial to see what I was really looking for. I thought about Robbie. We'd started off the summer sleeping together, but I'd never allowed myself to think of him as a potential boyfriend. Why? Because I'd deemed him too queeny. He didn't fit the image I was carrying around in my head of what a boyfriend was *supposed* to be. As if Peter Youngblood had fit the image. As if Alistair-Paul had.

How many other guys had I let get by me who might have made excellent husbands? Sure, Robbie carried the torch for Track, but who knows? If we had permitted ourselves to see beyond our limitations, maybe we could have eventually fallen in love. Robbie was a good guy. There were *lots* of good guys out there, I was suddenly convinced, and I'd been spinning my wheels chasing after jerks.

"Don't step on me," came a voice suddenly.

I looked down. There, on a blanket spread out on the sand, lying there staring up at the moon, was Adam.

"What are you doing out here?" I asked.

"I had to clear my head. Too much for one day."

I sat down on the blanket beside him. "I just walked out on Peter. We were doing it again. He admitted he remembered the first time. He'd just been pretending not to."

He sat up, shaking his head. "What an asshole."

"Totally." I sighed. "And I'm tired of assholes."

"The problem is," Adam said, choking up, "I miss him. Paul. Or whatever I should call him."

"I know. I do, too." I let out a long sigh, putting my arm around Adam and pulling him close. "But you know what? It's like what you told me when Pierce and I broke up. We weren't in love with him. We were in love with the *idea* of him."

"I guess you're right."

I laughed a little. "At least I can say one thing, though."

"What's that?"

"I never sucked his toes."

I felt Adam's body start to tremble. I thought he was crying. But when I looked over to see his face, I saw that he was laughing. A small chuckle that grew and grew, bubbling over so much that he had to cover his mouth with his hands. It made me laugh too. We both started laughing so hard that we fell down onto the blanket, me on top of him.

That's when I started to kiss him. He kissed me back.

We made love on that blanket under the stars, Adam and I.

Sisters. Best friends.

We made love.

There's Got to Be a
Morning After

Of course, I freaked out the next day.

"Adam!" I shrieked to Robbie, my head pounding with a horrible hangover. "I had sex with *Adam!*"

"So? It happened once before, didn't it?"

"When we were *teenagers!* When we were in *college!*" I paced the room. I had left the house before Adam woke up. "But we're *adults* now! *Best friends!* We should know better!"

"Know better why?"

I wasn't listening to him. "I feel like I should pull a Peter and claim not to remember. But I can't! Adam and I just talked about that. I can't do that!"

Robbie was shaking his head, looking at me. "Sweetie, was it good?"

I was aghast. "You can't ask me that. I can't even —"

"Was it good?"

"You're talking about me and Adam! My sister! It was *incest!*"

"Was it *good?*" Robbie insisted, folding his arms over his chest.

I sat down on his couch. "Yes," I admitted. "It was good." I closed my eyes. "It was awesome."

Just as it had been the first time. Just as it had been in my dreams, so often, in the intervening years.

"You love Adam, don't you?" Robbie asked, sitting down beside me and taking my hand in his.

"Yes," I said. "But as a friend . . ."

"Look. Sex has ruined many a beautiful friendship. And I know you wouldn't want anything to ruin your friendship with Adam."

I nodded, unsure where he was going with this.

"But maybe sometimes what we think of as friendship limits us. Maybe it blinds us to possibilities . . . Troy, I've seen the two of you together all summer. I've seen how the two of you can't wait for each other to get to town. I've seen how happy you are when he walks into the room, how alive he seems when he spots you on the dance floor. You can't deny that he's the first person you think about when you wake up every morning, can you?"

I considered it. Even during those few weeks with Alistair, yes, indeed, it had been Adam I'd always thought of first. Just as it had been with all my other short-term boyfriends.

"Maybe your perfect husband has been right here all the time," Robbie offered.

I couldn't pretend anymore. Not to him or myself. Maybe I *had* always loved Adam, and as more than a friend. "But Adam . . . I don't know how he feels . . ."

"Then go ask him," Robbie said. "Go. He's back there waiting." I hesitated.

"*Go*, girlfriend," Robbie insisted. He seemed to consider something. "I have something I need to do myself."

But when I mustered up the courage to march across the way and into Adam's room, I found his bed empty. There was a note on his pillow.

Troy—I've gone back to Hartford. See you next weekend.
Adam.

I've Never Believed in Phony Happy Endings

Not believing in them, however, didn't mean I wasn't desperately hoping for one. You don't know how hard it was not to call Adam all week. Actually, maybe it wasn't so hard. My feelings were so jumbled. Fear, joy, anxiety, embarrassment. All of them, coming over me in successive waves. My boss made a comment about how glad he'd be when the summer was over and I could finally get my mind back on my work. I wondered if I would ever think clearly again.

So that following weekend, the last one in August, the second to last of our summer season, I sat quietly in our little living area waiting for Adam. The door opened and I looked up anxiously. But it was Peter.

"I just came to say good-bye," he said. "I've packed up all my stuff. I'm heading to Fort Lauderdale. We're going to do the show there."

"Good luck," I said.

"Hey, thanks. Say good-bye to Adam for me, okay? Tell him I'll try to get him some money soon."

I just nodded.

Peter paused in the doorway. "For what it's worth," he said, looking over his shoulder, "I think I'm more out of *your* league than you are out of mine. You're a good guy, Troy. Some guy's gonna be lucky to get you."

I wasn't sure I trusted his sincerity, but I smiled anyway.

"You know what?" he said. "You and Adam would make a great couple. I can see the two of you married, with a house in the suburbs, having a dog. No more of this party life for you. Just the two of you, watching TV, going to bed early, mowing your grass, going grocery shopping. I can totally see that, Troy." He flashed me a big grin, a grin that would certainly continue breaking hearts for many more years. "Hey, take it easy, man. Thanks for a great summer."

I sat there not moving after he left.

Mowing the grass?

Grocery shopping?

Then I heard Adam's car crunch the gravel in the driveway outside. I swallowed, bracing myself for the worst. I remembered feeling that the worst thing about the whole mess with Alistair would be losing Adam. That didn't happen, but it still might. I could still lose Adam, but it wouldn't be because of Alistair.

It would be because of me.

Adam came into the house looking as fearful as I felt. We exchanged small smiles. He sat down opposite me.

"So," I said.

"So," he echoed.

We fell into silence. How many of you would know what to say to your best friend after sleeping with him? Part of me just wanted to say, "Hey, we were drunk," and move beyond all this, going back to the way things were. But another part of me didn't want to go back. Robbie's words had enlightened me. I wanted to go forward, not back.

So I waited for Adam to speak. And finally he did.

"I've never told you this, and I should've," he said, "but the time you and I had sex in college . . . was the best sex I've ever had in my whole life." He smiled. "Until the other night."

I felt like crying. "Adam, me too."

He came over to sit beside me on the couch. We embraced. "I've thought about you all week," Adam said. "How much you mean to me. How much fun we have together. How I can tell you things I can't tell anyone else."

"Me too," I said. "How you know me better than I know myself."

He looked at me. "But can we . . . *do* this?"

"I don't know," I admitted.

"You want to try?" he asked.

"Yeah," I said. "I think I want to try."

We kissed for a long time. When he pulled back he looked me in the eyes.

"What's so awesome is that we both want the same things," he said. "Commitment. A life together. A home . . ."

"It . . . doesn't have to be in the suburbs," I asked, "does it?"

Adam didn't answer. He just pulled me close to him. "I love you, Troy."

I touched his face. "I love you, too, Adam."

Giving It Our Best Shot

So who knows? It's Labor Day weekend, the biggest crush onto the Cape of the whole season, and here Adam and I are—holding hands!—walking through gads and gads of hetero tourists with their baby strollers and shopping bags. It's something both of us have always wanted to do. Have a boyfriend and hold hands in public on Commercial Street. And now we're doing it.

Sometimes we just look at each other and burst out laughing, as if we've just realized how ridiculous we're being. Maybe we are. Maybe once the summer is finally over we'll see it was just a big silly goof and we'll go back to being sisters. But other times we look at each other and we won't laugh at all. We'll just start kissing each other, deep and passionate, in a way I've never kissed anyone in my whole life.

I just don't like it when images of mowing the grass and going to bed early pop up. How long has it been that I've wanted a boyfriend and now—now when it seems like maybe it's really *happened*—I'm scared of what it might bring. Suddenly all those years of marriage for which I was envying my parents and Adam's grandparents seem so—so—*long*. I can't seem to get out of my mind the image of my dad falling asleep in his chair wearing his argyle socks and watching the nightly news. Suddenly I wish the summer wouldn't end.

"I don't want to be a Lost Boy when I'm thirty," Robbie says.

"I don't know," I say, looking over at him. "Didn't we have fun this summer? Going out? Dancing? Tricking? Playing around? Didn't we?"

Nobody says anything.

"Come *on*," I say. "There are worse ways of being, you know."

"Name one." Robbie laughs. He's walking with us down Commercial Street, dodging the kids and the bikes, as he holds hands with his own new love. *Todd.*

"I listened to the advice that I gave to you, Troy," he'd said, "and I saw what I'd been overlooking *myself* for so long."

Man, you should see how Todd has changed. He's smiling, actually singing, as we trot down Commercial Street. *"Fairy tales can come true, they can happen to you,"* he warbles at the top of his voice, prompting lots of stares as we pass down the crowded street. Most smile when they see how happy he looks.

"What do *you* think, Troy?" Adam asks. "Is this where we all fade off to live happily ever after?"

"Well, sure," I say. "But happily ever after doesn't have to mean we fade off the planet, does it? We can still rent a place next year, can't we? We can still have *fun*."

"Or maybe," Adam tells me with a grin, "we ought to save our money for a down payment on a *house*."

My hand goes a little clammy in his.

"Let's not get a dog," I say. "And remember, I like to stay up late. *Real* late."

We all laugh, and head over to Tea Dance one last time.

The Outline of a Torso

Andy Schell

"Ethan?"

Thank God I don't say anything more. It could be an exceptionally stupid and screenplay moment. Something like, "Ethan? Ethan Prater? Is that really you?"

We, meaning my college boyfriend and I, are walking along the path above Makena beach, Big Makena mind you—the straight Makena. It is the first time I've been back to Maui since that summer. You know: that summer. Haven't we all had one? Like in *The Opposite of Sex*, when Dedee Truitt mockingly says, "I was never the same again after that summer." It's just a voice-over, but you can practically see her rolling her eyes and sticking her finger down her throat.

"Hey . . . Rusty," Ethan says tentatively. His surfboard is propped against a tree and he stands beside it, his surf shorts slung low on his hips. My pulse surges, not just in my heart but in my whole body. I have to catch myself from staring too hard. With his hair buzzed short, he's even more sexy at twenty-two than he was at sixteen. My first thought is that I must look pretty stupid, gawking at him. My second thought is that I'd like to send my boyfriend on some meaningless errand and pull Ethan's surf shorts down right here, right now, and spank him like I should have six years ago. But something's wrong—he looks humble. Believe me, humility was a personal trait that Ethan was incapable of having the last time I saw him.

"I'm Brandon," my boyfriend says, tossing no judgment toward me regarding my failure to introduce him to Ethan. Brandon's black hair is thick and shiny, and it falls over his face as he shakes Ethan's hand. Brandon has an exotic face. His grandparents are from Eastern Europe. Great body. Really great body. His stomach is almost as flat and gorgeous as Ethan's. His Speedo is teal, just right for his coloring. Everyone tells me what a catch he is.

"Hey," Ethan says, shaking Brandon's hand. Ethan Prater is still the only guy I've ever known who can take a one-word sentence and lay it down like it's a horizontal billboard for him to crawl on top of and display himself. Humble or not, I guess the old Ethan is still intact.

"So how do you guys know each other?" Brandon asks.

Ethan squints from the sun in his eyes. "Rusty's and my parents were friends."

"My dad used to be Ethan's father's attorney," I tell Brandon.

"Are you alone?" Brandon asks him.

One of the reasons people tell me Brandon is a catch is because he's not only great-looking and smart, but he's also friendly to everyone he meets. At the moment, that's not such a good thing, particularly when Ethan nods that he's alone. But it's a wounded nod, a body action that appears to be an undecipherable metaphor of some kind. Or am I just reading into the situation? The truth is, the last time I saw Ethan Prater he couldn't even spell *metaphor*.

"Great," Brandon says, smiling at Ethan. "We're headed over to Little Makena. Want to join us?"

"Karl and Robby are here," I say quickly. It's also their first time back since that summer, and the last person they're going to want to see is Ethan. He *has* to know that.

"I saw them," Ethan tells me.

Maybe that's why he's wounded. Maybe they told him to hop on his surfboard and paddle the fuck out of here.

"But I don't think they saw me, so I'm just hanging out."

Interesting. Ethan may not be such a dumb jock anymore if he's smart enough not to flag down Karl Grant and Robby Edelman.

Brandon presses on. "You know Karl and Robby? Great. Come on, join us for the day."

I fully expect Ethan to decline, grab his surfboard, and perhaps even catch the first flight back to the mainland. He doesn't. He looks at me and shrugs, like I'm supposed to make the decision. How can I invite him along? He ruined my life—for a time. How can I not invite him? He's been splayed across my brain for six years. Karl and Robby aren't going to believe it—or tolerate it. I just can't imagine them, even now, as college graduates, with their boyfriends by their sides, being magnanimous to Ethan Prater.

Robby Edelman, Karl Grant, and I were in heaven that summer. It was the first summer vacation that our families took together where we guys got to have our own house, separate from the adults. Our dads were senior partners in the Los Angeles law firm, Edelman, Doonan, Grant, and Staad. The three of us were all the same age: sixteen. But more important, we were all gay and we knew it. Well, at least Karl and I knew it. Robby was the biggest fag of the three of us, but at that point he insisted on being undeclared. As if a guy who entered a raffle on the Internet for Trent Reznor's used jockstrap can call himself undeclared.

Robby's family is Jewish, though I really didn't know what that meant at the time. I'm not sure his family knew what it meant either. My mom said the Edelmans were Los Angeles Jews, and that Jewish people in LA were different from those of other places. They didn't have to go to Chinese restaurants and pretend they didn't know what they were getting in order to eat pork. They just went to the supermarket and bought big slabs of it—roasts, bacon, hot dogs, and chops. And they ate it all for Christmas dinner. The Edelmans always had a Christmas tree, and lights on their house. My guess is that they drew the line at caroling only because Mrs. Edelman had one of those voices that sounded like a wounded borzoi.

Robby wasn't soft, but he wasn't hard. He was middle material. The kid in the beige shirt in the center seat in the center row. He was incredibly unpretentious for a guy whose father was the apex of the firm. He wasn't into any of the flash his parents displayed. His mother's hands were so topped with diamonds she suffered load displacement. It always looked like her arms were falling out of her shoulder sockets. His dad was pretty decked out too. Gold everything, including the necklace he always wore (which was a Star of David, so I guess he really was Jewish). Robby didn't wear any metal at all, except his glasses. Small, neat, wire-frame glasses that perfectly fit his perfect nose. My mother said Robby had the most gorgeous nose she'd ever seen. I think she was right.

Karl's family was descended from Germany, like the Staads, who didn't have children and avoided these once-a-year senior partner family trips. Only in LA could you find a law firm headed by Jews, Germans, and the Irish. My dad always said it was a good thing that Mr. Edelman and Mr. Grant never got into fights, because he'd be too drunk to help them out. Then again, the Grants, Karl's family, were about as German as the Edelmans were Jewish—which was about the same degree that my family was Irish. The truth is, nobody is much of what they are in southern California, genealogically speaking. The weather just takes all that history right out of you. You get a nice car, and if you're lucky a nice house, and you live your life in shorts.

Karl was quite the boy, with his blond hair, blue eyes, kissy lips, and a body that was halfway to becoming a man. To be honest, Karl really was the biggest fag of the three of us, not because he acted like it, but because he was absolutely obsessed with sex (and had been since the age of three, according to his memory). The guy could make a sexual reference out of raindrops on a rock. He conjured genitals and body parts in everything he saw. It was amazing. Robby and I still hadn't had the big *coming out* talk with our parents, but Karl would never have to. You'd have to be as blind as a newborn kitten not to see it. Since the age of six his head had been spinning full circle on his neck anytime a halfway hot guy walked by. By first grade he was flirting with the dads on Parent Night at our private school. He just seamlessly transitioned into being *openly gay*, whatever the hell that means, around the age of nine or ten, and that was that. To be so comfortable around Karl, Mrs. Edelman and my mother thought Robby and I were the representatives of a new, open-minded generation. They didn't know we were comfortable around Karl because he had the best porno.

The guys and I had really worked on our parents all year to let us have our own house for this vacation. Actually, we'd hoped for a different locale. The three of us pored over the gay travel guide that Karl had shoplifted from the adult book store in The Valley, and decided that each of us should lobby for a different place. We figured there was strength in multiple numbers. Meaning, if we gave them three different suggestions, they'd pick at least one. So when the families were trying to decide on where the annual get-together would be, Karl begged for Fire Island. He said his mom (who's a blond babe herself) just laughed him off and told him to wait until he was in college to visit Fire Island. But Karl was smart. He knew he'd see more action as a sixteen-year-old than he would as a college boy. Still, he couldn't convince his parents to go east.

Robby and I just didn't have the same freedom of expression, or so we thought, that Karl did. We tried to pick places that could go either way. Robby went with Key West (for the great snorkeling), and I proposed Puerto Vallarta (for the food—as if you couldn't get great Mexican food in California). Robby's and my mother had to be in total denial not to catch on to our queerness, but they didn't seem to have a clue, and both agreed to take our suggestions up with all the dads.

In the end we landed in Hawaii, on Maui, land of straight honeymooners and vacationing families. There wasn't even a decent gay bar where we could use our fake IDs and drink rum and Cokes. Oh well, it wasn't like we had to have a bar. After all, we had our own house. While the parents roosted in a five-bedroom monstrosity that actually had two fireplaces (in Hawaii?), our all-boy homestead was a two-bedroom bungalow separated from the main house by nearly an acre of lawn and a swarm of mosquitoes.

In case you didn't know, the island of Maui is shaped like the upper half of a person. It's a head and a torso, basically. And Robby's dad insisted that we stay at this new swank area on the head (where his own bald spot was), near Kapalua, because there was an airport there and we could fly right in. But we had to take a commuter propeller plane from Honolulu, and Mrs. Edelman spent the whole flight talking about every recent air disaster she could think of. Our commuter plane didn't have a stewardess or drinks, so Mrs. Edelman had to swallow her anti-anxiety pill with her own spit.

A couple of weeks before, Robby and I had met at Karl's house, while his parents were out at some fundraiser for women who throw up, and we pored over the Hawaii section of the stolen gay travel guide. It recommended Little Makena beach over all the others for *cruise action*. It said that there was an area above the beach, in the trees, where gay men cruised and *hooked up*. It was our goal to get to Makena, even though our guesthouse was up in the bald spot of Maui, and Makena was down in the chest and nipples of the island. The trek would involve twenty or thirty miles of winding coastal road, and though we didn't have a car, or even scooters, we vowed to get there.

In our bungalow, we cranked Alanis Morissette's *Jagged Little Pill*, and danced around in our surf shorts, our balls hanging low from the heat of the island sun (Karl's hanging lower than Robby's and mine because he'd traded blow jobs with the sacker-boy in the bathroom at Safeway the day before). We opened all the windows and let the ocean breeze be the conductor. And if Alanis drifted too loud on the trade winds, and our parents wanted to say something about it, we figured they could come and say it.

Karl took out his huge stashed bottle of Captain Morgan's spiced rum, and we poured it into our Cokes. "Where the hell do you hide a bottle that big?" Robby wanted to know, chopping vegetables for our first dinner.

"Up my ass," Karl answered, swaying his butt to Alanis and pumping out the words.

Robby laughed, then he cried when slicing the onions.

Robby's cooking was incredible. I'd never had a sit-down dinner made by a friend before. Frozen pizza, takeout, whatever, but never a real meal made with real stuff that you cooked together. Robby even ran barefoot over to the big house, and somehow slipped in and stole a bottle of wine from our parents without them knowing it. So there we were, no shirts, no shoes, and no parents. Just the three of us in our surf shorts, eating glazed chicken in a papaya sauce (don't tell me he learned that from his mother) with sweetened caramelized onions, wild rice, and buttered green beans. The stolen white wine was one that he thought would go well with the chicken, and it did. And for dessert he'd made chocolate mousse, which we paired with Kona coffee spiked with rum. We waited until after the meal to toast. Raising our coffee mugs into the air, we clinked them all together and Karl said, "Here's to boys like us." And right then, in our first gay guesthouse, I knew that being gay was going to be good.

*   *   *

Karl and Robby, as nude as everyone else on the beach, bolt up and practically run away when Ethan approaches with us. "What the fuck is *he* doing here?" Karl hisses under his breath, though we plainly hear him. Somehow Robby and Karl maintain their naked civility, though they refuse to shake his hand or look him in the eye. Ethan is gracious toward Robby and Karl's snub, though obviously uncomfortable. Their boyfriends, Nathan and Jeremy, rely on their good breeding (and ignorance of who Ethan Prater is) and each offer Ethan a handshake that he gratefully accepts. When we strip naked, it's apparent that Nathan and Jeremy would gladly shake more than Ethan's hand; they have to struggle to keep the sand off their tongues when they get a load of Ethan. Robby and Karl grow angrier.

"Hey, Rusty, I think I just sighted a Hawaiian dodo bird," Karl chirps. "Come on, I want to show you."

Before I lie down on the blanket, Karl pulls me away. We start walking down the beach. It's hard to play defense against Karl, so I start with a strong offense. "This is as much a surprise to me as it is to you. Brandon and I were walking along, and Ethan was just sitting there. I swear."

Karl's too furious to check out the hot dudes spread out along the beach. He's even too enraged to strut and exhibit himself as he usually would. "And you asked him to *join* us?"

"Brandon did," I say. "You know how he is."

"Yeah, I know how Brandon is—he's nice," Karl tells me. "And he's the first guy you've dated that isn't a shit-stirrer. And here you are, showing up with the *original* shit-stirrer. Wasn't it bad enough he dropped into our lives *once*?"

"Carolyn! Carolyn, it's Abby! Hi!" My mother was waving and yelling across the restaurant.

A man and woman with their son, who looked to be exactly the same age as me and Robby and Karl, maybe a year older, came over to our table. And without asking anyone's permission, my mother said, "Have you eaten?" And before these people even answered, I saw that this kid was checking me and the guys out, not in a sexual way, not even in a friendly way, but in a competitive way. Like if we were dogs, he'd have sniffed our butts, then made a point to hike his leg higher than the rest of us and take a big pee. I looked across the table at Robby, who appeared immediately uncomfortable, and then I glanced at Karl, who I figured was already lusting after this kid, whoever he was, because it was obvious the guy was a total stud, but instead Karl actually looked kind of like Robby at that moment, which was a bad sign, and I wanted to stick my starched napkin into my mom's mouth and shut her up. But it was too late.

"Join us! We've got room."

The guys and I had had the smarts to band together down at one end of the table, and of course my mom suggested that the Praters' son, Ethan, squeeze in with us on our end, while his parents sat at the other end beside my parents. As the bus boy (a local island boy our age that Karl had been giving the eye to) brought him a chair, Ethan gave a tough-boy sneer and took the chair without saying thanks. It wasn't a studied tough-boy sneer, but the real thing. "Nice shirts," he said, slamming our matching Polos while sitting down next to me.

Robby didn't say anything. Karl gave this look, like *what an asshole.* "Our moms made us wear them," I explained, trying not to sound like a chump.

"You guys always do what your mommies say?" Ethan asked the question like we were titty-baby losers. Reaching back without even looking, he took the menu from the busboy and flipped it open, still refusing to make eye contact with anyone. He was short, about five feet seven, and his face was compact, like a handsome pit bull. Small rounded ears, short nose, square chin, tight mouth. His head was muscular, if you know what I mean. Brown hair and brown eyes. He was a stud. He wore a tank top in defiance of this upscale restaurant, and it felt like he was daring the manager (or his parents) to say anything about it. His forearms were cut with muscles. *His forearms.* His biceps were ripped and each had a big vein going down the center. His shoulders were brawny and solid, and the right one was tattooed with an elaborately patterned surfboard. He had a thick neck and his Adam's apple stuck out like a luscious piece of fruit.

It was the fastest boner I ever got in my whole life. My erection

sprang up so fast I thought it would knock the underside of the table
and spill everybody's water glasses. I pretended that I was looking at
my menu, but I was looking at him. And I think he knew it. Because he
finally glanced up from his menu and gave me this look that said if I
didn't stop fagging off on him that he'd bust my fucking chops, which
scared the shit out of me but made my dick even harder.

As soon as we all ordered (Mrs. Edelman requested some Hawaiian
fish that sounded like *ohfuckme*), my dad looked down the table to us
and said, "Hey, guys, let's head out to the deck and check out the wind
surfers." The restaurant overlooked one of the best sailboarding spots
on the planet. Riders from all over the world came to this spot for international competitions.

"Jack," my mother scolded. "We just ordered. They're going to
bring the salads."

He laughed her off. "We're Californians. We'll eat them after the
meal." He stood and motioned to us. "Come on, guys. It's male bonding time."

He was right about that. My maleness was bonded to my stomach.
While Robby and Karl gladly pushed back their chairs for the escape, I
quickly yanked my Polo shirt out from my belted shorts, and slowly
stood while holding my napkin in front of me. As I backed away from
the table my mom said, "Rusty, your napkin."

Why did my mother always have to be so on top of everything?
She'd admitted to me that she smoked pot in college, so why couldn't
she go back to smoking, and mellow out? If I wanted to hold a napkin
in front of my crotch, why would she care? "Oh, right," I said timidly. I
kind of threw the napkin into my chair and turned away. And as we all
made our way to the door, the four dads and the four sons, Ethan
turned to me and said, "You gotta take a leak?"

Why me? Did he see the bulge in my shorts? Why not ask Robby or
Karl, or the dads if *they* had to pee? Was he going to take me into the
men's room and punch my face? Of course I should have turned him
down. I was rock-hard still, and if I stood at a urinal with him, he'd see.
But I didn't refuse him. I couldn't. "Yeah," I answered, trying to sound
casual.

"Rusty and I gotta take a leak," Ethan announced, as the others
headed to the deck. All I could think was that Ethan had called me by

my name. He'd told the others that he and *Rusty* were going to go pee together. Robby gave me this unbelieving look, and Karl carefully gave me eye contact that I couldn't decipher. Mr. Prater said, "OK, see you out there."

Ethan just kept right on walking toward the john, like an alpha dog that always led and never looked behind because he *knew* the other dog was right on his butt. At this point, if I were telling you this to create maximum tension, I'd say that once we got inside the john there was one of those pee troughs, and I was forced to expose my boner and my queerness to Ethan Prater. But the truth is, I was saved by those divider screens secured between the urinals (Karl called them *Mormon screens* because when our families went skiing in Utah we noticed they were in every public bathroom, and we decided it must have been the law to have those things in every men's room in the state, so guys couldn't look at other guys' dicks in Utah—and now the Mormon missionaries who came to the islands didn't want anyone checking out the local meat either).

We were standing there, draining, and Ethan said, "Are those guys gay?"

I knew right away that he meant Robby and Karl, and I couldn't believe he was asking me because he'd just busted *me* for looking at him before we ordered our food. "Who?"

He turned his head, his brown eyes looking over the divider screen. "Those other two guys at the table."

"They're my friends," I answered, watching him look down and shake himself off. His motions were bigger and slower than mine were.

"I think they're queer," he said, looking back up at me and letting go of his underwear so that I could hear the snap of his waistband against his stomach.

"No way," I said, doing my best to give a short laugh of disbelief. I maneuvered my bone back into my pants, struggled to zip up, and pulled my shirt farther down in front of my crotch.

"You're so full of shit," he said, kicking open the bathroom door with his foot.

Out on the deck we watched the windsurfers torpedo over the waves, but Karl kept glancing down to the beach below because there was a group of guys changing out of their wetsuits. I felt a knock against my shoulder, and looked at Ethan. He had that sneer on his face again, and he nodded at Karl watching the dudes peel out of their wetsuits and flash their perfect white asses. Ethan looked at me again with this *I told you so* look, then turned his head and spit onto the deck. I don't know why I did it, but I gave a little nod to Ethan to say *yeah, you're right*. I even thought about spitting too, but instead I turned my view back to the sailboarders on the sea, and for a moment, watched them skim over the surface without really touching it. Then, very carefully, without anyone noticing, I looked down at Ethan Prater's spit. It sat on a two-by-four in a clear wad, shining in the late sun of that endless summer day.

The water is the perfect temperature. From the first wave we're swimming in bliss. It is so fine to feel the saltwater just sweep over our whole bodies, no shorts or wetsuits to detour the ocean from sliding across every inch of us. And bodysurfing isn't the big macho thing that surfing can be, so the energy of the participants is different. Nobody owns a wave, and if twenty people happen to hop on and ride, then all the better. That's just twenty people being carried along by life, screaming their guts out, and for that eight-second ride they're each connected to the ocean and to each other in a way that they'll never duplicate again in their whole lives, because once a wave is gone, it's gone forever.

It's these waves at Makena that bring us together again. I'm not sure when it happens, but at some point I realize we are all looking over our shoulders, waiting for the next beauty to come rolling along, and when it arrives it literally lifts up our bodies with its power, and our souls too, and we're friends again, screaming to each other, laughing, and sharing naked high-fives in the shallows before we go racing back toward the next perfect possibility. Well, the truth is, our *boyfriends* rush to give Ethan high-fives, but neither Karl, Robby, nor I extend ourselves. I want to make contact with Ethan, but I don't know what his response will be. When everyone is tired and ready to head for shore, Ethan stays and floats beyond the break. It may be my only chance.

"Aren't you coming?" Brandon asks.

"In a minute," I tell him. "I'm going to play catch-up with Ethan."

"I don't blame you," he says with a devilish smile. "I'm out." Then he jumps onto a wave and rides toward shore.

Everything is blue: the sea, the sky, an umbrella on the beach, and Ethan's mood. Maybe that's what I saw when Brandon and I first spotted him today, maybe that was what I translated as humble. "So, Ethan. *Really*, what are you doing here?"

"I live here now," he says, floating on his back. He studies the sky, but the sky is empty, not a cloud in the blue.

"You *live* here? Since when?" I stay upright and tread water so that I don't lose the view of Ethan floating naked on his back in front of me, even though I should be swimming for the hills.

"A couple months, I guess."

"But school's only been out a month," I tell him.

He closes his eyes while fanning his perfect arms back and forth to stay afloat, as if he's making a snow angel in the water. "I didn't finish."

"You didn't finish school? But you were about to graduate." A drip of saltwater runs down from my hair and lands on my lips. I clear it off with my tongue.

He opens his eyes. "My parents found out I'm gay."

I laugh. "Ethan, you're *not* gay."

Now Ethan laughs, but not like he thinks it's funny. "Great. That's exactly what my dad said when I told him."

I should be ashamed for reacting like some stupid parent in denial, but I find it hard to believe that Ethan Prater is gay. I wasn't sure what he was when we were sixteen, and I'm not sure what he is now. And I've always thought that when you can't figure out a person's orientation, it's because they can't figure it out themselves. But if it's true, and he is? My heart starts thumping so hard in my chest I sink down a little in the water so he won't see.

"Then he hit me in the face, made me give up my car keys, and kicked me out of the house. And you know how they say moms are usually cooler than dads? Not mine. My entire life, all she worships is the almighty dollar. But I tell her I'm gay and she goes all Christian on me. She starts calling the priest of *our* church—the church we've gone to about once every three years. And in the end it's total rejection."

Even wet, my head feels the warmth of the sun. It's a strange warmth when coupled with the breeze that flows between Ethan and me. "I'm sorry," I tell him. Am I? If ever there were an example of someone's karma hitting him in the face, this was it. "So you came back to Maui?"

He lets his body collapse into the water until he's vertical. Like a beautiful seahorse, he treads water while inching closer and closer to me, until we're face to face. "I had to come back," he says, his breath still having the essence of the mango juice he drank on shore. "This is where it all started, Rusty. This is where I fell in love with another guy for the first time." He looks at me with such longing that I wonder if it's he or the ocean that will melt me, as if I'm a chunk of ice being dissolved.

"Yes, yes, yes!" Brandon screams, his head thrown back while the water from an offshoot of Waimoku Falls washes through his hair as if he's starring in a shampoo commercial.

We're outside of Hana, at the top of Oheo Gulch (the navel of the island), in a natural pool beneath a waterfall that comes crashing down from a cliff that's at least four hundred feet straight above us. It's a hot and gloriously sunny day, and the continual mist of water that escapes the falls mixes with the air and forms silver filigree that suddenly becomes a rainbow when you stand at right angles to the sun.

"This is dick-shrinker water," Karl yelps, standing in the pool up to his thighs. Jeremy creeps up behind him and throws himself onto Karl's back, taking them both down, below the surface. Karl blasts up through the water and nearly jumps the four hundred feet to the top of the cliff. He screams, "Woo!" Jeremy reemerges, laughs and gives him a dripping kiss on the lips. Karl laughs too and pushes Jeremy back under.

A guy and a girl (Germans, I think) slightly older than us, probably on their honeymoon, sit beyond the pool on a rock. They watch Karl and Jeremy's brief kiss, then look at each other and smile, amused.

Robby and Nathan stand on the side of the pool, their toes barely wet. "Come on, you sissies," Jeremy yells to them, bolting up and swimming toward them. "Get in."

"We're not sissies," Nathan declares. "We're Jewish princesses, and we're not going to mess up our hair."

"You didn't mind it yesterday when we were bodysurfing."

"That was then, this is now," Robby tells him. He sticks out his tongue, not as a response, but to catch the mist.

"Girly boys," Jeremy sings.

"Like you can talk?" Nathan laughs. "We heard your head slamming against the bedroom wall last night."

Karl looks proudly responsible for the slamming, and Jeremy draws back his arm and takes a nice slash into the water that splashes the two Jewish princesses, who both go scrambling for higher ground.

The straight couple (who obviously understand English) look at each other and try not to laugh.

I push off a large rock and sink into the ice-cold water. As I swim to-ward Brandon the breath is squeezed out of my body. The closer I get to him, the worse it gets. I decide the only way to acclimate is to dive under. As I break the surface, Brandon disappears from view, and I fol-low my hands to the bottom of the chilly pool. The shock to my sys-tem lasts but a moment, and when that moment is over I feel totally powerful, like a battery recharged.

We're hiking back down the two-mile trail; our hair is still damp on our necks. The trail is perfumed with the smell of overripe guava that falls from the trees and crushes beneath the soles of our shoes. In areas where the brush and trees are dense, and the air is thick, the smell of the rotted fruit is overly pungent, almost sickening. When we reach a clearing, and the breeze funnels through to disperse the scent, it's light and heavenly.

"I'm surprised we didn't see Ethan today," Brandon tells me, as we leave the open trail and enter into the bamboo forest.

I look to see if Karl and Robby have heard him. They haven't. They're ahead of us, but I slow my steps, just to be sure. "Why would we see Ethan?" I ask. Daylight quickly disappears as we enter into the swath cut through the seemingly impenetrable giant bamboo that grows so thick and tall around us that we lose sight of anything but the man-made path ahead.

"I told him we were coming here today," Brandon answers. "I sug-gested he join us."

The wind must be blowing outside the forest, because the leafed tops of the bamboo, at least seventy feet overhead, start to stir. Then the thick stalks of bamboo knock against each other throughout the forest, and it is as if we are walking inside the world's largest wind chime.

"Listen to that! Awesome," Karl yells ahead.

"Karl and Robby would have killed you if Ethan had shown," I quietly tell Brandon.

"What about you?" he asks.

Ethan is all I've been able to think about since I saw him yesterday. "I never heard you invite Ethan," I say. But then I remember when we'd said goodbye to Ethan, and we were back in the parking lot, loading up the car, Brandon suddenly had to take a leak—or so he said. He had run back toward the trail again. It must have been to find Ethan, and invite him here. "Why did you?"

"I thought it would be nice."

"Not for Karl and Robby."

"I thought it would be nice for *you*. And Ethan. Why do you care so much about what Karl and Robby think?" he asks me.

It's a good question.

That night it's back to the water—in the form of a hot bath with bubbles. Brandon sits behind me in the tub and we soak together. He's brought a Japanese washcloth that shreds my skin like a dull cheese grater as he scrubs my back. "So what's the story with Ethan? Karl and Robby really hate him, huh?"

"He did something pretty awful." He's pressing a little too hard. "Less pressure, Brandon."

Brandon backs off, but my skin still burns a little. "What did he do?"

"What's that soap you're using? It smells incredible."

He picks up the bar and waves it under my nose. "Satsuma."

I think I've eaten Satsuma tangerines before. They were really good. "What did Ethan do?"

"He outed me to my parents when we were sixteen."

Brandon stops scrubbing. "What happened?"

"His family was here on Maui and we ran into them in a restaurant. The next thing I knew, my mom had invited them to stay with us. His parents took a room in the main house, and Ethan moved into the guesthouse with me and the guys."

Brandon switches the Japanese cloth for a cotton washrag. He dunks it in the water, then squeezes it out over my back, and the scent of Satsuma washes down my skin. "That must have sucked—being forced out to your parents."

Brandon is headed for law school at Duke in the fall, but his vocabulary is still loaded with words like *suck* and *bogus*. I worry that those eastern intellectuals will obliterate his easy-going demeanor and California vocabulary. Of course, my worries are his parents' hopes.

"It was awful at the time. My parents weren't ready to hear it, but Ethan outed me. Actually, he outed Robby too. And believe me, Robby had it even worse than I."

"Wow," Brandon says, squeezing more water over my back. "What made him out you?"

"Ethan and I messed around. He started it, but it freaked him out, so I think he reacted by throwing stones at Robby and me—Karl too, but that was no surprise to anyone."

"But Ethan's not gay, is he?"

I laugh a little. I didn't tell Brandon much about my conversation with Ethan in the water, but not because I think it would worry him. I don't think it would worry him at all to know that Ethan is gay—and available. Nothing seems to threaten Brandon. Actually, nothing seems to *penetrate* Brandon. It's strange. "Switch," I tell him. We turn, and now I take the Japanese washcloth and shred his back. "Why do you say he's not gay?"

"I don't know. He just had that *outsider* feel, standing there by his surfboard when we walked up. He watched us like we were foreign in some way. Like he was curious, but not really one of us."

"I think he does want to be one of us."

"Harder," Brandon tells me, as I scrub. "What makes you think so?"

"Just a feeling."

Brandon sighs. "Well, maybe you're right. We all remember that outsider feeling, huh?" He's silent for a moment while I rub the grating cloth in circles on his back. "So, what are your feelings toward Ethan?"

Maybe it will be good for Brandon to go east after all. Those East Coast professors will teach him not to ask so many questions about *feelings.* "Ethan is Ethan," I answer. Does anyone ever get over his first love? It's common not to, so why make a big deal out of it?

"You know, Rusty, I'm moving away at the end of the summer." I squeeze water over his back as he did mine, only I stick with the Japanese washcloth. "Maybe you need to rekindle your friendship with Ethan."

I take the washcloth full of water and squeeze it over Brandon's head.

"Hey!" He laughs, turning and grabbing the washcloth from my hands. He dips it into the water then pushes it onto my face.

I peel it off, careful not to shred my face, then wipe my eyes. "Why did you use the word *rekindle?*"

"Karl and Robby say you've never gotten over Ethan. Even after what he did to you."

"That's bullshit." I hate it when Karl and Robby gang up and think they have me figured out. The truth is, *they're* the ones who've never gotten over Ethan. Look at the lousy way they're treating him. They haven't let the whole thing go at all. Besides staying neutral, I've been downright decent to Ethan. Maybe that means I *am* over him. "Wait a minute," I say. "If Robby and Karl told you I'm not over Ethan, *even after what he did*, then you already knew the whole story."

Brandon answers, "Just doing a little cross-examination."

"And I thought you were too sweet and honest to make a good attorney," I say, pinching one of his nipples.

"Ouch!" He swats my hand away.

"Don't play dumb with me, Brandon. You already knew the whole story. And don't tell me to make an overture toward Ethan, just because you're moving away. Nobody is that perfect and understanding. Even you." I reach around him, to the drain, and pull the plug.

The six of us are riding in the *rental ship*, as Karl calls it. We've rented a Lincoln Navigator, and it's about as big as the cruise ship we see chugging out of Kahului Bay in the distance. We're driving with the windows down through the pineapple fields outside of Kahului, making our way toward Haleakala Crater Road, a winding two-lane road that ascends the great volcano of Maui. Jeremy sticks a Britney Spears CD into the player, and starts singing along.

"Oops, he did it again," I say. We had to listen to Britney yesterday during the ride home from Makena. "We're college graduates, guys. We all have boyfriends now. When do we get to stop acting like teenage girls?"

"What do you prefer instead, Rusty?" Karl asks from behind the wheel. "Metallica or Pearl Jam?" He's taunting me. Metallica and Pearl Jam were Ethan's favorites that summer. Ethan came into our bunga-low and tossed practically all our CDs out the window. It was goodbye to Paula Cole, Tori Amos, and Sheryl Crow, and hello to heavy metal and grunge. While *Rage Against the Machine* blared from the speak-ers, he lined up his three surfboards against the living room wall. He had a thruster that was seven feet long, and two big guns that were at least eight and a half feet. He wasted no time making fun of our dinky boogie boards and swim fins.

I ignore Karl's taunt (and Britney's belting) by sticking my head out the window and letting the trade winds wash my face with oceanic oxygen. As the Navigator plows ahead, the smell of the fecund pineap-ple fields throws me into reverse.

It was just 3 A.M. and the road was dead. The blacktop blended into the night, and all I could see were those painted white lines that looked like the lines I followed along the floor at the hospital when I went to visit my grandmother after she fell and broke her hip and was dying. Ethan and I followed the line along the side of the road, neither of us talking because we were both so tired we couldn't think of any-thing to say. We'd have ridden our skateboards but what was the point? Right when Ethan kicked a pebble and said, "Let's forget it," I saw a beam of light start to glow under my feet.

I turned around and saw headlights a mile away, coming toward us. "No, look!" I said, using every bit of power in my brain to stare at those lights and will them to stop. I crossed Ethan and stepped roadside and held up my skateboard with one arm while waving with the other. It was an old beater of a pickup truck, with peeling red paint and a dented passenger door that seemed to buckle further as it whooshed past us.

But the truck's brake lights flashed, like a good warning, and it pulled over.

"Come on," Ethan said, and we ran to the truck as it idled by the side of the road ahead. The truck's bed was piled high with plant stalks, and as we approached the driver's window, I made out the silhouettes of three heads in the cab. Where would we sit?

The driver was Hawaiian and had to weigh at least three hundred pounds. His face was huge, but even as the full moon was nearly falling out of sight, I could see he was friendly. "Howzit, brah? You headed to crater, yah?"

"Da'kine," I said, speaking the only pidgin I knew.

The guys in the cab started laughing. They were all blood brothers, I was sure. They looked like big bread rolls that had been placed too close on a baking sheet and had all connected to each other while baking. The driver said, "Hele on, we got a baby pidgin, yah? Hop onna cane. We take you to Thirty-Seven."

So Ethan and I ran to the back, stepped onto the bumper, and piled atop a huge load of cut sugar cane. We smashed ourselves down into the stalks while the truck slowly rolled out onto the highway again. As the old Chevy picked up speed, we lay there, side by side, on our backs, and looked up at the stars while the wind whistled through the sugar cane at a constant pitch, and the leaves of the stalks rustled as if birds were flying out of them. There was a scent I'd never smelled before. It was both earthy and sweet, and with the humidity of the piled plants creeping up around us, we were wrapped together, like two vines that escaped their boundaries and crept their way into a sugar field and twisted their way around the cane. I don't know which one of us fell asleep first, or who woke first. All I remember is Ethan's leg draped over mine, and my arm across his chest, and then the driver yelling out the window to us, "OK, brah, lesgo. You at Thirty-Seven. Bimbye someone you kine take you up right now."

We unwrapped our sweaty bodies from each other, grabbed our skateboards, and thanked the pickup driver while jumping off the truck. There was a steady stream of cars turning up the junction of Highway 37 that headed out to the Haleakala Crater Road. We hadn't stood in the darkness for a minute when one of those common Pontiac rental cars stopped. Inside was a guy and a girl from Oregon, and as soon as we got into the backseat Ethan kicked my foot and made a motion with his hands to indicate that the girl had huge tits. The rental car reeked of skunkweed. "It stinks," the girl told us, "but it's great shit." She turned her breasts toward Ethan and handed him the joint first, and he sucked a good long hit before handing it to me. I imitated him completely. I even blew my smoke out exactly like he did. The weed made us both sleepy again, and Ethan unlaced the top of his surf shorts to get comfortable. With the top edge of his pubic hair showing, he slid his legs out toward me while shoving his pelvis forward to slink down in the seat and sleep.

The moon still shared enough of a glimmer that I could see him, even in the darkened rental car. The hairs on the inside of his thighs were slightly darker than the sun-bleached hairs on his shins, and they moved inward over his leg muscles in this gorgeous pattern, like a Zen garden, as if they'd been raked toward his crotch. His arms were crossed over his chest, pushing his hulking pecs toward his chin. He had a big scab on his left elbow, and the skin around the scab was pink. The rest of him was golden and tan and more filled out than other guys our age. His feet were wide, and his toes fanned out in perfect proportion.

And there was his package. It was more obvious than ever, with the fabric smashed against it as he slumped in the seat. But Ethan didn't know I was staring at it. He just slept, his arms crossed over his chest, while the car wound back and forth, up the two-lane highway, like a snake climbing the volcano.

I listened to the girl from Oregon talk about how Haleakala was a natural conductor of cosmic energy, and how even the U.S. Air Force did research that proved Haleakala is the strongest power point in America. I wanted to tell her she was wrong, that the strongest power point in America was *Ethan Prater's crotch.*

When we got to the summit parking lot, we left the weak masses of people and hiked up to the top of the volcano. There were about twenty other people around. It was freezing. We'd gone from sea level to over ten thousand feet. Ethan and I were the only ones in T-shirts, and I was sure that I was going to ice over. I'd drawn my arms into my shirt, and my body was shivering and shaking. Ethan just stood there, his hands on his hips like he wasn't even cold. We stood in the dark and everyone was hushed. Then it got really quiet as a general wash of light began to lighten the night sky and everybody could feel that it was about to happen. And the next thing I knew, Ethan began to take off. "Where are you going?" I asked, starting to follow.

"Stay here. Watch my board." He dropped his skateboard and took off down the path, behind the silhouette of the girl from the rental car.

I scanned the small group of people on the summit, and tried to find her boyfriend's outline or shadow. Finally I think I did. But it looked like he was just staring out onto the horizon. Then I turned back and saw Ethan and the girl disappear below, behind some rocks off the trail. Should I follow them? Were they going to smoke some more weed? "Oh my God," I heard someone say in the dark. And by the time I turned around I'd missed it. I'd fucking missed it. The first pierce of new day had risen over the curve of the earth and broken through while I was looking for Ethan's shadow.

I stood for a while, shaking from the cold, and watched the rest of the sun rise up and burn the edges of the earth, and I told myself I'd remember what I saw so I could tell Ethan what it was like. It was probably another ten minutes (and full morning light) before he jumped up behind me, smashing his sandals into the lava and scaring the shit out of me. "Fuck, where were you? It was incredible." He stuck his fingers up my nose and I winced at the smell. "Whoa."

"Hey, man, at least you know what it is." He laughed. "I was beginning to wonder if you were like your little friends back there at the house."

"I've had pussy on my fingers," I said, like any guy who hadn't was a loser.

"Well, stop wrinkling your nose, fag boy, or I'll make you smell my dick too." He said it like he meant it, and he swallowed me with his brown eyes like he had the day before when he peered over the Mormon screen in the men's room.

"The rising sun was incredible," I told him. "You should have seen it."

＊   ＊   ＊

We huddle together like a box of popsicles, the six of us standing at ten thousand feet above sea level while the wind rips across the top of the Haleakala Crater. Our windbreakers flap violently, as if we are standing inside the jetstream and we have to push ourselves into it to stand upright. But it is an awesome sight, no less majestic than the first two times I was here. We see all of Maui poured out in front of us: cattle land, sugar cane, pineapple fields, beaches, and mountains. We see it as God does, from above the world. We can actually make out the curvature of the earth on the far horizon. And out there in the emerald and cobalt ocean sit Oahu and Molokai off one side, and the Big Island off the other. And whatever those other little islands are close by, I never can remember their names.

"This is awesome," Brandon says, standing with his legs slightly apart to brace himself against the wind.

Jeremy shakes his head. "We really are just little specks of nothing, aren't we?"

"For Christ's sake," Robby moans, pointing at the guy sitting over on the rock, his legs pulled up to his chest. It's Ethan.

Karl rolls his eyes. "*He's* a speck of nothing."

Robby turns to me. "What is he doing up here? Has he turned into a stalker?"

"Did you tell him we were coming up here?" Karl asks me.

Why is everyone looking at me? "No."

"Why don't you give the guy a break?" Nathan says to Karl and Robby. "Weren't we *all* pretty fucked up at sixteen?"

"Not like him," Robby says.

"I don't believe anything he told Rusty yesterday," Karl snipes.

Brandon dragged it out of me this morning at breakfast. With everyone sitting at the table, he used his magic powers to gently lure the truth to the table—or at least the information Ethan shared as the truth. I knew it was a mistake to tell everyone. I hadn't been able to conceal my sympathy for Ethan, I know it.

"Well, I believe Ethan. And we're all grown up now so I'm going over to say hi," Brandon says jauntily. He breaks from the pack and heads over the rocks toward Ethan.

I watch Brandon go—and wonder if he somehow got in contact with Ethan since yesterday, and told him we were coming up here. I want to follow, but I don't. I know Karl and Robby would kill me if I did. I can't stop thinking about what Ethan said at Makena. *This is where I fell in love with another guy for the first time.* It was the same for me—if that's what Ethan meant. I'd had crushes before, but I fell so hard for Ethan that I couldn't get up. I lost my self-respect. Robby and Karl lost their respect for me too. And my parents did as well.

Like a dumbshit girl I would write Ethan's name on a piece of paper, over and over. My mother would find pieces of paper, napkins, matchbook covers—whatever I could write on (including my hand)—strewn around the house or in the car. She'd silently throw them away (or make me wash my hand). I'd skip out of school and drive over to Ethan's school, park around the block, then sneak in and try to catch a glimpse of him without anyone seeing me. I'd call his house from payphones and hang up when he answered. I'd go to his wrestling matches and slink anonymously into the far bleachers, careful that his parents didn't see me, and my heart would pound as he wrestled in his skintight singlet. I drove Karl and Robby crazy, because there was a girl that I was kind of friends with at Ethan's school, and she'd give me the heads-up if she knew where Ethan was going on a Friday night or whenever, and I'd rope Karl and Robby into going someplace with me and I'd pretend to be surprised when Ethan just happened to be there. After a while they caught on and stopped going anywhere with me. I guess I was pretty obsessed. In all, it took me several years to smooth the wrinkled linen, as my grandmother used to say.

We watch from behind as Brandon approaches Ethan on top of the crater. Ethan looks up to see Brandon, then looks over his shoulder at the rest of us. He sheepishly gives an abbreviated wave, then turns back to Brandon and starts talking to him.

"Maybe your boyfriend is *too* nice," Karl growls.

"And maybe mine isn't nice enough," Jeremy chides, poking Karl in the ribs. "Come on, let's hop down to the visitor's center."

"Shouldn't we tell Brandon where we're going?" Robby asks.

"He's a big boy," I say, herding everybody down the trail. "He'll figure it out."

"And you're just going to leave him here with Mr. Trouble?"

Nathan laughs. "He looks about as threatening as Mr. Bubble."

"I'd love to see him *covered* in Mr. Bubble," Jeremy whispers in a low voice.

Karl thumps him on the head as I push them all forward.

Outside the visitor's center, I sit on the ledge of the rock wall and look into the crater as the guys browse inside. Before the sunrise trip all those years ago, Ethan and I had come up in the daylight with our parents earlier that week. At about the same place that he and Brandon sat right now, Ethan had put his arm over my shoulder, like buddies do. "I told my dad you're supposed to come up here in the dark, before sunrise. And then you're supposed to watch the sun come up over the curve of the earth, right over there." He had pointed with his free arm to the east. "*That's* supposed to be awesome. My friend, Griffin, did it. And I'm going to do it too."

The weight of his arm on my shoulder was as much paradise as the island we stood upon. I didn't dare move. I wanted to stay there, on top of the heart of Maui, with Ethan Prater's arm draped over me for the rest of my life. "It's too late," I had said. "We missed it."

He had leaned over, kept his arm around me, and even though there was no one around and the wind whistled so loud that it almost drowned us out, he'd whispered in my ear, "I'm going to get up at 3 A.M. and hitchhike back up here. Wanna come?"

He'd whispered so close to me that my ear got warm and moist just for a second. I couldn't turn and look at him, because I knew if I did I wouldn't have been able to control myself and I'd have kissed him. So I just stood there with his arm around my shoulder and gazed beyond the fringes, to the deep blue mystery beyond the island, while the wind chilled his wet breath in my ear.

I feel an arm wrap around my shoulder. "Hi, sweetheart," Brandon says, pulling my thoughts out of the moon-like crater that opens in front of me. "Where are the guys?"

"Inside," I say, reaching behind him and giving his ass a swat. "Have a seat."

He swings a leg over and simply straddles the wall while gazing upon the cinder fields of Haleakala. "This is so unbelievable. Here we are on a hot tropical island, and we're practically numb with the cold."

I look at him and try to decipher his impish grin. "So how is Ethan?"

"Ethan's fine," Brandon says, still grinning. "We had a good talk."

"About what?"

"Life."

I'm hoping not to think about life, at least for a couple months. We all just finished up at UCLA, and we're faced with the big *what's next*. It's weird. Our boyfriends seem to know exactly where they're headed. Nathan and Jeremy have rounded up venture capital to start an online business that rates the quality of everything from lightbulbs to business jets. And the VC is from an *old economy* company, so they may have a genuine shot at building the business. Brandon's going straight on to law school, and it's solely his idea and not his parents'. But Robby, Karl, and I are lost. Robby intends to get a graduate degree in world history but he's not sure where to get it, which means he's too late for fall enrollment anywhere. Karl wants to take a year off to travel, and then get his MBA. I graduated film school, with my studies directed toward screenwriting. So I guess I'm supposed to start writing great films that change the world. But the truth is I'm too paralyzed by my possibilities to write anything at all.

"I'm telling you, he's a pretty good guy, Rusty," Brandon says. "He's definitely not the jerk that Karl and Robby portray."

Yes, but he *was*, I try to remind myself. And I don't blame Robby and Karl for being leery of him. Still, I trust Brandon—he's a good judge of character. And the fact is, I *want* Ethan to have improved. I want Ethan's wounds to take away some of his steam, because the Ethan Prater that I knew had way too much steam anyway. "I don't have anything against him, not anymore," I tell Brandon.

Brandon ignores the other tourists and kisses me on the cheek. "You're a good guy, Rusty Doonan. You're going to make somebody a fine wife one day."

I shove him, and he laughs as he rolls off the wall and lands onto the hardened lava, as if a benevolent horse has tossed him gently onto the ground.

"It's Opakapaka," Robby yells to us from the kitchen. He smiles while holding up the fish.

"Oh whatta whatta?" Karl asks.

"It's a local fish," Robby yells. He has to project his voice over the whir of the blender. It is our last night on the island and Brandon is making a rum concoction with pineapple juice, banana, coconut milk, mango, and ice. "You're going to love it. I'm grilling it. We're having it with a wasabi soy sauce, steamed kale, and jasmine rice. I made a coconut cake for dessert," Robby finishes, a little satisfied smile on his face. It was his idea to have a final special dinner before we say goodbye to Maui.

From the sofa in the living room, Nathan coos over Robby, "No one's voting *you* off the island, Martha."

"Except maybe Hitler," Robby offers. "I think he and Eva retired somewhere on Maui, didn't he?"

"It doesn't matter," Karl says. "Even Adolph Hitler is voting Ethan Prater off the island before the Jews."

Brandon turns off the blender and lines up seven glasses. He starts pouring the golden frothy mixture into them, one by one. "I like Ethan. He's got character."

"I'll say," Jeremy growls. "And monster pecs."

Karl squints at Jeremy and hisses like an angry tomcat.

It's strange to me that Karl is the least forgiving of the three of us when it comes to Ethan, yet Karl was the only one of us who wasn't newly outed that summer and whose home life upon return to the mainland was least affected by Ethan's lob of dynamite. Robby and I went through hell. Mrs. Edelman went into full-on drama alert, wrapping herself in the living room draperies and weeping like a four-year-old after a booster shot. First she didn't eat at all, and then she ate like a pig in the Borneo jungle. Robby said she'd go to Gelsons, grab two carts, and go up and down the aisles until they were brimming with hundreds of dollars worth of groceries and were so heavy she'd have to push one and pull the other. Then she'd tip the sacker-boy fifty dollars to ride home with her and help her unload them in front of Robby, and the whole time she'd say things to the guy like, "You wouldn't tell *your* mother you're gay, would you? *You're* planning on having children someday, *aren't* you?"

Robby's father just stayed at the office even longer each night. Basically that was his response.

My mom went into her typical airy-fairy mindset and pretended to be very accepting and spiritual about it while each day nudging me further and further toward seeing a therapist to *sort out my feelings.* After five weeks in a row of refusing the appointments she'd scheduled for me at her therapist's office, her gentle nudging exploded into "Kurt Cobain killed himself over this! He mentioned Freddy Mercury in his suicide note! Get the fucking therapy!"

Eventually I did, and I learned a lot. In just a few short weeks my mom's therapist helped me to understand that my mom is crazy— something she'd not yet been able to get across to my mom. The therapist also taught me that it's best to live life on my own terms and not worry too much about what other people think. I've been able to do that pretty successfully with my parents, who eventually support-grouped themselves into getting the whole gay thing. But at the moment, I'm feeling pressure from Karl and Robby, and it's hard not to worry about what they think of Ethan. I almost lost my friendship with them over it. And in retrospect that was a mistake.

"You are so naïve," Robby tells Brandon. "You believe what people tell you."

"Haven't you had some big event that changed your life forever?"

Robby is chopping garlic and he almost chops his finger off. "Like, duh!" he says, slamming the knife down. "The only son in a Jewish family being outed when he's sixteen? I think I can call that my big life-changing event. Thanks to Ethan."

"So what effect did it have on your life?" Brandon asks in his friendly but probing way. He carries two glasses of fruity rum cocktail out of the kitchen and hands one to Jeremy, the other to Nathan. I can't believe it, but this is the first time I realize that I'm basically dating my mother. Both she and Brandon spend half their lives probing everybody else's feelings.

"It *ruined* my life, Oprah," Robby answers, picking up the knife and moving his fingers out of the way while chopping the garlic as if it were Ethan's head.

Brandon returns to the kitchen. "To this day?" he asks, grabbing two more cocktails. He drops one off on the kitchen counter in front of Robby, then delivers the other glass to Karl. "I've seen you with your parents. You guys get along great."

Robby drops the knife again and takes a drink of his cocktail. "OK, it's not like my life is ruined today, not anymore. But it's not like things are perfectly normal either. And I can't tell you how bad it was the first few years."

"So how do you think Ethan feels? He just told his parents two months ago. How screwed up were things two months after your parents found out about you? Don't you think Ethan's probably going through a hard time?" Brandon carries two more drinks. He hands one to me, and takes a drink out of the other.

"Told them what?" Karl interjects. "That he preys upon innocent gay guys just before he goes over to his girlfriend's house and treats her like shit too?"

"None of us are the same as when we were teenagers," I say, realizing that the longer I stay out of this conversation, the guiltier I appear. "How much have *you* changed in the last six years?" I ask Karl.

"A hell of a lot more than Ethan has," Karl answers, slipping a Hapa CD into the player. Hapa is a Hawaiian duo that Jeremy has introduced into our lives after he heard them play an outdoor concert on Oahu a couple years ago. The music is light, breezy, and sung in beautiful harmonies. Coupled with our conversation it strikes a perfectly dissonant chord.

Robby puts the fish into the oven to bake. "Hey," he says to Brandon. He counts the people in the room and makes it to six. Then he looks at the seventh glass, full of rum cocktail, sitting there on the counter by the blender. "Why did you pour an extra glass? Who is that for?"

There's a knock on the door.

OK, if this were a screenplay I'd written in school, my professor would say, "You can't have the knock on the door come right after the moment when the character of Robby asks, 'Who's this extra drink for?' It's too staged, too much of a sitcom moment." But what am I supposed to do, change the story to make it believable? This *is* what happens, and somehow every single one of us knows exactly who's on the other side of the door.

"No fucking way," Karl says, putting his hands on his slender little sexy hips. His blue eyes turn the color of fire.

"No fucking way," Robby echoes, his rounded shoulders not carrying off the dramatic tension nearly as well as Karl.

"How original," Jeremy says, laughing them off. "Maybe you guys ought to go to law school with Brandon this fall and learn how to persuade the jury with a full vocabulary."

"Maybe Brandon ought to be sued for malpractice before he even has his license," Karl blurts.

Brandon picks up the cocktail glass by the blender and carries it over to the door. He opens the door and hands the rum cocktail to Ethan. "Aloha."

"Aloha," Ethan says, forced. He accepts the drink and quickly takes a sip. "That's awesome."

The blended cocktail leaves behind a foam mustache over Ethan's upper lip. Staring at it, Karl mumbles, "Got arsenic?"

"Thanks," Brandon tells Ethan, smiling. "It's my own secret potion. Come on in."

Ethan, wearing his dress-up surf shorts and a tank top, uncomfortably nods to everyone while Brandon shuts the door behind him. When he looks at me, he gives me a look that asks if it's OK to be here. I smile and try to let my eyes tell him it is. God, he's a babe. The two months he's been here have had their effect—he's darker than the rest of us. It's his feet that give him away. In his light blue, dime-store flip-flops, his feet appear even more browned than his gorgeous body.

There's a moment of awkward silence. "Nice house," Ethan says.

"It's great. Want a tour?" Jeremy asks.

"Sure."

The silence continues as Jeremy walks Ethan around the house. Finally the tour continues to the backyard. As Jeremy and Ethan exit through the sliding glass door, and walk out to the yard, Karl opens up. "What the hell did you invite him for? You had no right to do that without asking us first."

"You would have said no," Brandon says simply.

"That's right," Robby says. "And we'd have had good reason."

"Well what do you expect Brandon to do?" Nathan asks. "Uninvite him?"

"That's exactly what he should do," Robby says haughtily.

Nathan looks at his boyfriend with surprise. "What's gotten into you?"

"We don't have enough fish," Robby says.

"So we divide it seven ways instead of six. What's the big deal?"

"It's more than that," Karl says. "We don't want him in this house."

Brandon comes to Nathan's aid. "OK, so you had a difficult summer when you were sixteen years old. Who cares? Get over it. Move on. Who knows, maybe Ethan could become one of your friends now."

"And maybe the First Lady will conduct *How to Perform Better Fellatio* seminars during White House tea parties," Karl says, while Jeremy slides the glass door open and escorts Ethan back into the house.

Cocktail hour is more like *cocktail millennium*. If any of us had known that it would be this uncomfortable we'd have eaten the Opakapaka as sashimi and called it a night. Ethan still has chutzpah—which is for certain. If I were Ethan, I'd have left this party long ago. But he stays and manages to dodge the not-so-subtle arrows and snubs as Karl and Robby toss them. And while Brandon, Jeremy, and Nathan do their best to keep the conversation sparkling and as comfortable as possible, I can see that Karl's and Robby's patience is narrowing, and the tension in the room is ratcheting up.

When we finally sit down for dinner, Brandon is on one side of me and Ethan is on the other. It's as if everyone at the table is suspended on the same very thin wire that slices the crack of his ass, and if even one of us leans slightly to the left or the right, we'll all go crashing to the ground.

"To the chef," Brandon toasts, carefully raising his glass of wine.

"To the chef," several of us repeat, while raising our glasses and clanking them together. I notice that Karl and Robby purposefully re-tract their glasses as Ethan attempts to make contact with them. I still can't believe they're being so childish. We're twenty-two years old, for God's sake. High school is over; we all survived. And now college is over—at least for some of us—and it's time to grow up. The funny thing is, it appears that Ethan *has*. Even though Karl and Robby are regressing to high school behavior and treating him like he's outside of *the clique*, he's keeping himself together. The macho jock we all knew has yielded to being a patient gentleman. The old Ethan would have called them *dumb fags* and kicked their asses. Of course, the old Ethan wouldn't have attended one of these gay dinner parties because the old Ethan hadn't figured out he was gay himself.

"The Opakapaka is really great," Ethan says to Robby.

Robby ignores him.

"He's right," Brandon says. He slowly pulls a bite off his fork and savors the flavor. "What's the sauce?" he asks, with a mouthful of Opakapaka.

Robby thrusts his head slightly, and with a superior jut of his chin he answers, "Ginger, black bean, garlic, and soy sauce."

"I like how you seared the whole thing in oil," Ethan says, giving it another try.

"You *would*," Karl says.

"What's *that* supposed to mean?" Jeremy asks his boyfriend.

Karl spears his fork into his fish as if it is still alive and attempting to swim off his plate. "It means Ethan's more comfortable with things seared in oil—including other people's lives."

I drop my fork and can't help but laugh. "God, Karl, that's really the suckiest metaphor I've ever heard."

Karl pulls his fork out of the dead fish and slams it onto his plate. He aims his glare toward me. "Oh, I'm sorry Mr. Hollywood Screenplay Writer," he says, seething. "I'm sure you're banking every word for your future Academy Award winning screenplays. I wouldn't want to contaminate you with *sucky* metaphor."

"Well, you have," I snap. "And worse, you're acting rude and unkind to Ethan. Knock it off."

"Bravo," Brandon sincerely says to me.

"I've had just about enough out of *you* too," Karl says, glaring at Brandon. "You never know when to draw the line, do you?"

Ethan pushes back from the table. "I knew this was a mistake." He looks at me with intense eyes, then directs his words to Karl. "I can figure out when I'm not wanted. I've gotten good at it."

"Six years too late," Robby says, grinding salt.

"Man, what is it with you two?" Nathan asks, shaking his head at Robby. "Can't you just back off?"

"No," Ethan says. "They can't. And I think you guys should just say what you need to say, and I'll go. I don't think we'll be seeing each other again after tonight."

I look to Ethan with disbelief. Is this really it? I waited years to see him again. I dreamed and wondered what it would be like to be in his arms again, to have him be cool about it, to have him kiss me. I wondered if we would ever talk like friends, if we would study each other's faces and see the difference between sixteen and twenty-two. I wondered if he was really gay or not. And if he was, would he ever figure it out, and if he did, would he tell *me?* And now he has. And he is. And he did. And he's about to walk out! I've been stupidly holding back this whole time because I didn't want Karl and Robby to judge me all over again, and now it's too late.

"I'll tell you what I have to say," Karl says. "You fucking *ruined* the lives of my two best friends. Robby's dad didn't talk to him for two years. *Two years.* And his mom went totally stupid and used more Jewish guilt than the entire country of Israel has dished out in five thousand years. She forced him to go to a shrink in Beverly Hills every week until he turned eighteen."

"Dr. Lamequack," Robby blurts. "Who billed my parents about seventy-five thousand dollars in two years time in order to come to the conclusion that I was afraid of my sisters' pussies!"

Nathan starts laughing, and Robby, turning red with anger, picks up the fish head from the platter and throws it at Nathan who ducks just in time for it to whack Brandon in the face.

Now I laugh. I can't help it. It's funny. "Sorry, babe," I say to Brandon, who picks up the fish head while rubbing his cheek. I give Ethan a quick glance. He's not amused.

"Go ahead," Karl prods. "Tell them, Rusty. Tell *both* your boyfriends what it was like."

"It's *over*," I say to Karl. "Let it go."

I'm shocked when Ethan speaks up. "No. He's right, Rusty. I should know what happened, what I caused."

"I'll tell you later," I say, embarrassed.

"Tell him now!" Karl demands, sounding like Barbara Stanwyck in one of those classic films we'd dissect in school.

I let out a huge breath. "Jesus, Karl. Something's weird here. You were the least affected and you took this whole thing the hardest."

"Tell him what it was like," Karl persists.

I look at Ethan, but my eyes are empty of the fire raging in Karl's. If anything, my eyes are pools of sorrow for both Ethan and me—and every other gay kid who was ever sixteen and trying to figure himself out. Is there ever any forgiveness for us? "It was rough," I tell Ethan. "My mom made me do therapy too. But my therapist was pretty cool. She sided with me."

"And the kids in school," Karl prompts. "Did they side with you?"

"Well, that was awful. Yes. I guess you told the guys at your school, and they knew some of the guys at our school and told them. I was harassed by all of them."

"Every single day until we graduated," Robby adds.

Ethan nods his head, and I can tell he's really listening. He sighs. "I'm sorry, Rusty. You too, Robby."

"You weren't there the day six guys backed Rusty against the lockers in gym class and threatened to shove a banana up his ass," Karl spouts. "And you weren't there the day someone spray-painted the word FAG across Robby's locker."

"And you weren't there the night my dad hit me in the face and kicked me out of the house," Ethan says coldly. I'm glad to see some of his old fire, and that he's finally standing up to Karl's abuse.

"That's called karma, dude," Karl blasts. "Whether it takes six minutes or six years, what goes around comes around. Do you know how he outed us?" Karl asks all the boyfriends at the table. "He took our porno tapes to the main house. We were so stupid we'd all labeled our tapes with our names, so that when we traded tapes we could keep track of whose was whose. So we all gave ourselves away."

"And whose idea was the name labels?" I remind Karl.

"Whose idea was it to put a tape into the VCR so the parents could see what we were watching?" Karl blasts. "There they were, all the parents, watching two guys doing a sixty-nine rimming scene."

"Oh God," Jeremy laughs.

"It wasn't funny," Robby screams. "My mother still can't eat!"

Jeremy laughs harder, and Karl gets more enraged. "Maybe if you hadn't fucked up our lives, yours wouldn't be so fucked up now," he tells Ethan.

"Maybe," Ethan tells him.

"You shouldn't have come here tonight," Robby finishes.

"You're right." Ethan stands and walks toward the door. "I'm sorry to you both," he says to Robby and me. "I don't need Karl to tell me that I was fucked up and I tried to ruin your lives so that nobody would look too closely at mine. I admit it. Sorry, guys." He opens the front door and before he steps out he looks at Karl. "And I'm sorry that you've never forgiven me for what happened between us," he says, making some kind of a point.

Karl's anger turns to uncomfortable exposition. "Just get out of here."

Ethan looks at me, shrugs, and says, "Goodbye, Rusty."

As soon as he shuts the door, Brandon says to me, "Go after him."

Now I'm as angry as Karl is, but it's an anger that confuses me. Why is Brandon pushing me toward Ethan? Is he trying to dump me? It's as if the moment we ran into Ethan on the beach, Brandon's been making his graceful exit by slipping out of his own shoes and coaxing Ethan into them. OK, so I'm still attracted to Ethan, but what right does Brandon have to force me toward someone else when he's supposed to be the one who cares about me? "Excuse me. Are you my boyfriend or not?" I ask Brandon.

"Well, yeah. But what about Ethan?"

"What *about* Ethan?" Karl asks.

"I'm not talking to you," Brandon snaps, zeroing in on Karl. It's the first time I've ever seen Brandon somewhat lose his cool.

"And I'm not talking to you either," Jeremy says to Karl. "You acted like a total asshole."

"You too," Nathan says to Robby. "My mom says you never really know someone until you travel with them. I'm not liking what I see."

"Are you going after him or not?" Brandon asks me.

This is where human nature is truly sick. You see, I started dating Brandon because not only is he a babe to look at, but because everybody (Karl and Robby especially) told me I *needed* to date somebody like Brandon. And though he's really smart and funny and nice—he's not the kind of guy that stirs up the coals in my fire (if you'll allow me a sucky metaphor). The truth is, I've known all along that Brandon and I would probably not last through the end of this fall, when he would leave for school. And it's also true that I've never gotten over Ethan, regardless of the amount of pain he's caused me in the past. I've waited all these years for another chance at him, and here he is, but now I'm pissed off at Brandon for not wanting me—even though I really don't want him! And by the time I've thought all this out, it's too late. Brandon grabs a bottle of wine off the table and flies out the door after Ethan.

"You see!" Karl screams, pushing his chair back from the table so hard that it slams against the floor while the soothing Hawaiian music of Hapa plays in the background. "This is what Ethan Prater does to people. He doesn't even make it past dinner and Jeremy's mad at me, Nathan's mad at Robby, and Brandon's out the door. Ethan is poison, man. He's poison."

Jeremy gets up and grabs the car keys off the coffee table. "Come on, Nathan, let's go for pizza."

The two of them are out the door before we know it, and Karl, Robby, and I are left alone in our Hawaiian guesthouse, trying to sort out our feelings again, just like when we were sixteen.

I start clearing the table of uneaten food. "What the hell did Ethan mean when he told you he was sorry that you hadn't forgiven him for what happened between you two?" I ask Karl. "What happened between you and Ethan?"

"You know," Karl says, not looking at me.

"No, I don't. I think he was saying something."

Karl stands in the kitchen and takes the plates as I bring them in. He scrapes the food into the trash. "What happened between me and Ethan was no different than what happened between Ethan and the two of you," he answers, looking at Robby and me.

I shake my head. "No, there's something more."

*   *   *

It's 11 P.M., Jeremy and Nathan are back, and both angry couples are behind closed doors for the night. Brandon has never returned. I'm sitting on the back lanai and drinking a beer. The moist, warm air of the islands washes over me and lulls my aching ego. There are a million stars in the sky, and I don't have to wait but a few minutes in between watching one fall and burn out before another falls behind it. I can hear the ocean oscillating in the dark, beyond the boundary of the backyard and the beach thereafter. The cotton cloth of the chair holds me steadily and breathes beneath me. I still can't believe I didn't go after Ethan tonight. Mixed up with all that sicko ego crap floating around in my head was the simple pull of loyalty. Even with Karl and Robby's jerky behavior and lousy treatment toward Ethan, I still feel a sense of loyalty to my two best buddies. I never would have made it through high school without them. It was the three of us against everyone. We would have died without each other. Even though they got sick of my entire Ethan obsession, they never gave up on me. They stuck by me and stuck up for me when the other guys in school tried to mess with me. And even though they're both acting like a couple of jerks now, I can't abandon them or our friendship. I guess I really have matured since I was sixteen. There was a time when I thought I'd spend my whole life going after Ethan—like I did that summer.

We'd had to practically drag Robby by his heels. He *really* didn't like Ethan from the beginning. But Karl had helped me convince him to come along (maybe because Karl didn't want to be alone with Ethan and me). Mrs. Grant gave us a ride, and even a couple of beers to share on the way. Robby and Karl wanted to go back to Honokohau Beach, because the waves were compact and perfect, and we'd had all those good memories from the last week and a half, but Ethan said Honokohau had nothing but bullshit ankle snappers, and it wasn't worth wasting his time. He said Honolua Bay had total power lines that peeled the skin off your balls, and he wasn't going to miss it. So I talked the boys into giving Honolua a shot.

Ethan directed Mrs. Grant to turn down a little dirt road and troll through the pineapple fields. It was apparent he'd been there before and that he knew what he was doing. Finally he told her to stop and we all bailed out of the car, far above the waves. There were several paths down to the surf, but Ethan chose the most radical and dangerous one. It wasn't so much a trail as it was a steep eroded gully that twisted and turned and fell straight down the cliff. I sensed that during rain this gully operated as a waterfall. So down we dropped, precariously descending a dry waterfall. Ethan just took off without us, his thruster tucked under his arm and his ass crack peeking out of his low-hanging surf shorts. I don't know how he maneuvered it, because the three of us were sliding out of control on the hazardous terrain. At one point, Robby slipped and skinned his leg pretty bad. I yelled for Ethan to wait up, but he was out of sight and didn't hear me. So Karl and I waited while Robby collected himself, and Karl took Robby's board and carried it down for him, while I offered Robby my hand.

When we finally made it to the beach, it was totally worth it. The weather was burning hot, and the sand was sweet and white, and the waves were spectacular. They peeled off, one after another, just like Ethan said. The swells were about six or seven feet, big for me and the guys, but probably nothing for Ethan, who was over talking to a couple of locals by the time we made it down. The three of them watched the three of us, then Ethan trotted over, his board still slung under his killer biceps.

"Come on," he said to me. "We're going to Hookipa."

"We just got here."

"And now we're leaving. Are you coming or not?"

I looked at Robby who gave me a look that said he'd be glad to see Ethan go—and perhaps me as well. But when I looked at Karl he had that face again, with that cautious look he gave me at the restaurant, the one where he bit his lower lip. It was a look that said, "Watch your back." I didn't know what to do. Ethan explained that those local guys told him it was picture postcard perfect at Hookipa at the moment. That the trade winds were dead and the sailboarders were sitting it out. And those local dudes heard on their radio that there were perfect glassy peaks just peeling off, waiting for board surfers.

If Ethan and I wanted to catch a ride with the locals in their truck, we didn't have time to take any of the lunch food with us, and I wasn't sure Robby would have shared with us anyway. So we scaled the cliff trail, and this time Ethan told me to go first. I didn't want to be a spaz, so I tried really hard to go steady. But sometimes I'd slip or wasn't fast enough for him, and he'd take the palm of his hand and push against my ass. He didn't say, "Keep going," or "I'll help you," or anything. He just pushed against my ass from behind, without a word.

Keani and Chewy, the locals, were already waiting in their truck by the time Ethan and I made it up to the parking lot. Keani was a fine and babyish *hapa* boy with a lean, ripped body and black hair that he'd dyed halfway orange and spiked up. Chewy looked Filipino in ancestry, and was much larger than Keani. He nodded to acknowledge me, but there was something about his eyes that I didn't trust. There wasn't room for all four of us in the truck's cab, so I let Ethan sit with them while I rode in the back of the truck, with the boards. Traffic sucked and it took over an hour to get to Hookipa, and the whole way those guys cranked metal banger shit on the stereo, and they smoked what had to have been some gnarly weed because it smelled like burning theater curtains.

At that point I was feeling pretty stupid. It would have been a sweet day over there at Honolua, and I'd left my buddies to go riding in the back of a pickup by myself to land at a surf spot that was totally out of my league, with a guy that was, too. Or at least that's what I would have thought just from meeting Ethan. But since he kept *wanting* me to hang with him, and he'd *asked* me to go to Hookipa, I thought that maybe he wasn't out of my league at all.

When we got there we saw right away that the whole setup was bogus. The winds were blowing as hard as they were two days ago when we stood on the deck at the restaurant and watched from above. And again, it looked like there were about a hundred windsurfers out there. Same story as before. There were colored tails of sails flying in from everywhere, like back in Los Angeles when we were driving on the 405 freeway to get to the airport, and I looked up at those jets that were screaming into LAX from every direction and I wondered how they didn't all slam into each other and fall out of the sky. And the few board surfers out there in Hookipa were like those little propeller planes mixed in with the big traffic at LAX, the little planes I was sure were going to be smashed by the 747s going ten times as fast.

Ethan checked out the scene, and for the first time he didn't look so confident. He hadn't brought either of his big guns because he hadn't planned on coming to this beach, and the board he had wasn't right for the waves. But Keani and Chewy had already unloaded their boards and were laughing at Ethan's face. Chewy said to him, "Waddascoops, brah? Your balls shrinking?"

Ethan sucked it up and went for his board. "Fuck you," he snarled, and he wasn't smiling or kidding around like Chewy appeared to be. I thought it was a pretty ungrateful thing to say to a couple of guys who had just brought us all the way over here. Chewy's face registered unhappiness.

"Hey, brah," Keani cautioned. "You don't want Chewy's stinkface."

Ethan put his hands on his hips. "Yeah? Well, ask Chewy where the glassy fucking peaks are? Huh?"

"I not talk story, brah," Chewy said patiently. "I hear it on the radio, I come."

Ethan offered a fake smile. "Not a problem. I'll make the best of it, *dudes.*" He picked up his board and made for the beach.

Chewy and Keani watched him leave. "Mo' bettah we pau with dis one," Chewy said to Keani.

"Pau," Keani said, looking at Ethan as if he'd put a hex on him.

I wondered if Ethan should be heading down there, considering the situation—and considering that I'd let him drink the whole beer Mrs. Grant gave us to share, and he'd smoked all that burning curtains weed. I got the feeling he'd just made two new enemies out of his two new friends. It just didn't seem like a good idea for him to dive into this saturated sea space, all things considered.

I sat on my boogie board on the beach and watched him paddle out. I was feeling dumb again. It was beginning to dawn on me that I *was* acting like some stupid-shit teenage girl, as Karl had said. But there was no way I was going out there on a boogie board. I didn't even want to be out there on a yacht. It was radical, and it wasn't for me. I don't know, but maybe that's why I was so hot for Ethan. He was radical. And pretty much fearless. And all the stud. I'd never up to this point thought about another guy fucking me up the ass. But if I ever did let anyone do it, it would be Ethan. I wondered if he was trying to tell me he would when he was pushing against my ass back there at Honolua.

I started to get a woody just thinking about it, but it went down pretty quickly when I saw what Ethan was getting into. It was major predatory action going down. Local *wave ownership* happened in California, but it was nothing like in the islands. My friend, Koji, who's Japanese and looks totally Hawaiian anyway, got sliced and diced at a notorious spot near Kahului, right here on Maui. He was first up on a wave, but these locals dropped in and squeezed him like a vice, then chopped him. It was bad.

Just watching Ethan paddle out, I got nervous. Those windsurfers were exploding over the sea like surface missiles. And when Ethan was down on his board, paddling out, and those swells were rising over him, there was no way they could see him. He almost got it good before he even made it past the break. Finally he did make it out though, and positioned himself in between Keani and Chewy—or did they position themselves on either side of him? There weren't that many guys on surfboards where Ethan was lined up, maybe a total of eight. But I could tell, even from the beach, that the vibes were ramped up to a wicked level, like a wire that had been pulled taut, and twisted until the tension had made it nearly invisible. But it was there. And if the wire didn't snap, you could get sliced like a piece of cheese. And if it did snap, it could cut you all the worse because you'd never see it coming.

It seemed crazy to me that Ethan and those guys weren't off to the side, like another group of surfers in the distance. Ethan, Keani, and Chewy chose to plug themselves into the center of all those sailboard missiles, which required them to execute projectile takeoffs and launch themselves right into the hairy festivity with no warning. I could hardly watch. I was sure with the way Keani and Chewy were looking at Ethan that they were planning to take him down.

As the new set came in, Ethan passed on the first couple of waves, and let the locals hop on. That made me relax, and I figured that Ethan would play the scene and respect his place as a *haole*. But then, as the third wave in the set rolled in, and several guys were paddling onto it, I saw Ethan just barrel in, late. Keani fell away to yield rights to the first guy up, and another surfer hung for a couple more seconds, then begrudgingly bailed. But Ethan just popped up on his board, the last of the four, and started battling it out, even though he had no right to be there. I couldn't believe it. California, Hawaii, or your own fucking bathtub, it was the wrong etiquette. And the guy was gesturing to Ethan, telling him to get off his wave. They came within an inch of each other at one point, then it looked like Ethan lost his footing and he popped out, but only because of his lost balance, not because he did the right thing. He snaked the guy.

I could practically see the steam coming off the locals' heads. It was obvious from watching body language and arm movements that they were talking about Ethan, and then I could see they were talking *to* him. But it looked like he was ignoring them. He just got back outside as quickly as he could and inserted himself into the lineup. I noticed that Keani and Chewy had paddled away from him this time, and I realized I was wrong about those guys. They weren't trying to fuck with him. It was obvious they didn't want to have anything to do with him.

I swear he didn't even wait for a couple waves this time, he just jammed himself into the pack, and just like last time, he dropped in on someone else's wave. Only this time he was marked. Everyone had seen what he'd just done, and they weren't going to take it. A guy in red shorts, the one with the darkest tan, long black hair, and shoulders as wide as a house, just barreled down on Ethan from behind, stalking his prey. Then in one brilliant instant he cut back around, overtook him, and totally clipped Ethan from the front before bailing out at the perfect moment to miss the crash. Ethan went flying off the front of his board, smashed through the twisting vertical board left in his path by the other surfer, then took a hit from his own board from behind.

Everybody on the beach let out gasps. People said, "Whoa!" and "Shit!" And one guy said, "That fucking idiot deserves it." I stood up, put my hand to my eyes to shield the sun and get a better look, and waited for Ethan to surface. I waited a long time. And then some more. Finally, when I truly was about to panic, he came up. But his leash had snapped (or been cut) and his board was in the white water, thrashing around without him. I didn't know if he was in any shape to swim, so I grabbed my boogie board and ran to the water. I don't know what I was thinking, because I didn't have my flippers, and the whitewater inside was churning like a pissed-off washing machine in overdrive. But I paddled for Ethan like his life depended on it. It took me forever to get out there, and if it weren't for my little board I'd have drowned.

"Get my board!" he yelled as I headed for him.

Now we were *two* fucking idiots. I sure as hell wasn't going to save him on my tiny little boogie board. I changed direction and headed for his board. I swear it was taunting me. Every time I got close it launched into some rip and flew away. I wondered if I'd die out there myself. The sailboarders were *cruising* by my head. I could hear the turbine-like sound of their sails in the wind. And the surfers knew I was Ethan's buddy, so they didn't give a shit whether they ran over me, or whether I retrieved his board. We could both drown as far as they were concerned.

I finally got it, and straddled it with my little board, and rode the current of the inside foam back to Ethan. When I caught up with him, he looked a little panicked. He'd been riding the current in, but he was disoriented and out of air. And then I saw that his head was bleeding up near his temple.

There was a concrete toilet and changing facility down the beach, so I dragged the boards up past the tide line and grabbed our towels, and we headed for refuge. "That fucking bastard," Ethan said, putting his hand to his head, then taking it away to look at the blood. "He cut me off." He was still breathing hard, and his manly chest was heaving up and down. His stomach muscles rippled with each gulp of air, and the seawater dripped off his body as he walked.

"You cut him off first," I said, as we headed into the men's room.

"No fucking way," Ethan said stubbornly. "It's every man for himself. And that was *my* wave."

"You're bleeding, Ethan."

"I can see that, dipshit," he told me, going to the sink. There wasn't a mirror in the place, and when he tried to splash water on the cut, he missed.

"Let me," I told him, and he did. I had him bend his head down, and I took a look into the cut. It wasn't too bad, but it wasn't too good. I'm not sure if a fin actually sliced him or if he just took a good thump from his board. I filled my hands with water and opened them up on it. He winced, but I told him we needed to get the saltwater out of it, and

then it wouldn't sting anymore. I just made that up, but it was probably true. I rinsed it about six or seven more times, and he seemed to
calm down, and he even joked with me.

"Just let that fuck come to California," he grinned. "I'll eat his ass
for lunch." As I tried to figure out if that statement was totally macho
or totally faggot, he asked, "Is it still bleeding?" It was, and I told him
so. So he ordered me to grab my towel and follow him over to the john.
We got to a stall and he said, "Get in." Even with the bullshit I just
saw him pull, and with his blood fresh on my fingers, I wasn't about to
argue. I stepped in and he followed, locking the door. "Stand here," he
told me, indicating to stand to the side of the toilet. I did, and then he
undid his wet surf shorts right in front of me and dropped them to his
ankles. His dick wasn't as big as I thought it would be. Maybe it was
because he was cold and wet and injured.

When he took his dick in his hand, my heart started racing as fast as
his was. He sat down on the toilet, took his hand off his dick to spit in
it, then told me quietly, "Press your towel against my cut. You give me
pressure, while I send the blood somewhere else. That way we'll get it
to stop bleeding." And I swear to God he started sliding his hand over
himself, working it up. At first I was so stunned I didn't respond.
"Come on," he told me, guiding my hand. I put my towel to his cut,
and pressed. "That's it," he whispered, while stroking himself. Now I
realized that my first impression, back at the house, was right. It was
bigger than mine was, that was for sure. And it was bigger (and
thicker) than anything I'd ever seen in a magazine or a porno movie. It
was like taking *two* dicks and putting them together, the kind you can
hardly get your hand around. And it just continued to grow. I kept
thinking it would just rise up and bust through the bathroom roof, or
at least hit him in his chin. "Keep pressing," he whispered, as he in-
creased his stroke.

I was as hard as the concrete wall I was leaning against. I couldn't
hide it in my surf shorts, and I figured there wasn't any reason to. If
Ethan wasn't ashamed of his, then I wasn't ashamed of mine. I wanted
to do what Ethan was doing—but I didn't have a gash on my head.
And I didn't know if being a jane was enough of an excuse. So I pressed
and I watched. When he dried up, he spit in his hand again, but it
wasn't much. So he held his hand up to me and whispered, "Give me

some spit." I ran my tongue around the insides of my cheeks to get the saliva flowing, then bent my head over and spit into his hand, my spit mixing with his. He took it and went right back to it.

And when two guys came into the restroom to use the urinals, Ethan put his finger up to his lips to tell me to keep my mouth shut, and he just kept right on stroking. The two guys talked about some girl that one of them had gone out with, and how she had a perfect ass. As they spoke of the girl, Ethan looked up at me and his eyes kind of flashed and he pulled his dick back toward his stomach and shot four big straight lines. And then he leaned back and closed his eyes, and I just stared at it, dripping down his stomach. And before he opened his eyes, I reached over, and while keeping one end of my towel pressed against his temple, I used the other end to clean him up while he just laid back with his eyes closed and let me.

And when I took my towel off his temple, the bleeding had stopped.

When I wake, my wristwatch shows me it's after midnight. I look back into the house, and everything is how I left it. Brandon isn't back yet. The memory of that day at Hookipa is fresh in my mind, and even though I don't want to, my memories force me to doubt Ethan's sincerity. I remember what a scammer he was, and how he led me to believe that everything was cool between us right before he blew up my life by showing that video to my parents. What if Ethan is scamming me again with all this talk about being gay? I begin to worry about Brandon. What if his kindness and compassion have actually gotten him in over his head? I decide to go looking for Brandon and Ethan. They can't be far.

There's a half-moon hanging in the sky, but I decide a flashlight would be a good idea. I return to the kitchen and pull the flashlight out from under the sink, then head out, sliding the back screen door behind me, but leaving the house open to the breeze.

I walk quietly off the back lanai and step onto the grass yard that leads down toward the beach. The grass is prickly against the sides of my feet that hang over my rubber flip-flops. My body is the kind of tired that happens when you've slept only one-third of a night. My muscles ache, my eyes (even in the moist air) are dry, and I'm thirsty.

I'm tempted to simply walk straight out to the beach and lie down on the sand, but I have to keep going. I have to find him. But who am I trying to find? Am I looking for Brandon or searching for Ethan? It's a question I haven't been able to answer since I was sixteen years old.

I cross the boundary of the yard, and crouch beneath the twisted branches of a tree that looks like a giant piece of coral that has washed ashore. It's hard to see the branches in the half-moon's muted glow, especially as the huge billowing clouds that loom over the dark island pass between the moon and me. A branch takes a swipe at my face, and I fall back onto my ass, into the sand. I reach up and feel my face and I'm not sure if it's bleeding or if the skin's just raised. It might be brilliant of me to turn on the flashlight. Oh well, too late. I decide to crawl on my knees until I'm clear. As I crawl I start to imagine crabs waiting in my path of darkness, and I place my knuckles into the sand very slowly and carefully as I go, clutching the darkened flashlight.

In a moment I'm clear, and I stand up to greet the sea beyond the beach. The white froth of the waves as they dissolve onto the shore is my visual marker for where the sea meets the shore. My instincts lead me down to the water, and I wonder how many years ago it was that some form of mankind rose out of that sea and made it to land and grew legs and arms, and eventually started shopping at The Gap. Then I realize my instincts should be ignored, because I'm not about to crawl back into that sea and turn into some squishy anemone or whatever I was a million years ago, because it's doubtful that Ethan and Brandon have done the same, and most likely I'm going to find them nestled in the sand beneath one of those twisty trees that just scratched my face, and their boners will be anything but invertebrate.

I walk back up toward the top of the beach, and as my eyes adjust to the darkness, I spot something up ahead. It's either a huge piece of driftwood or a coffin. It's hard to tell. My heels sink into the sand first, then I roll my feet carefully after, so that I'm as silent as possible. As I get nearer I hear moaning—which rules out the possibility that I'm approaching driftwood. I slow down and crouch a little. The moaning continues, and now I can tell that the moans are pleasure—which rules out the possibility that I'm approaching a coffin. The moans are distinctly male, and I realize that my fears are validated.

I crouch all the way down, on my hands and knees again, and start slinking toward them like a tiger ready to pounce. It's Ethan, I think, that's on top. And he's riding Brandon like an unbroken mustang. Those jerks. Those stupid jerks. They didn't even go very far from the house.

"Ah-ha!" I scream, pouncing on Ethan's ankles.

The scream that arises beneath Ethan is so shrill and female that I'd laugh if I weren't so angry. It's obvious that Brandon has gotten in touch with his feminine side since dinner. Not only is he on the bottom, but he screams like a girl. And it's a powerful scream. Real women can't scream that loud, even in the movies.

"Hey, brah," the unfamiliar voice threatens in the dark. He rolls off the real woman beneath him. "You lookin' to get killed?"

It's obvious I've gotten in touch with my stupid side since I left the house. "My mistake!" I say, abandoning my tiger crouch to stand fully erect and bolt. "Sorry!" I yell over my shoulder as I take off down the beach in a brisk run, my flip-flops ripping off my feet as I go. Easy come easy go. I'll buy a new pair at the ABC store tomorrow—if I'm alive. My heart is thumping and I'm quickly out of breath. As soon as I'm far enough away I start laughing. God, what a stupid ass-wipe I am. Some of those Hawaiian guys *are* as big as coffins. And they could snap my neck two seconds faster than a giant wave. And any girl with a scream that strong could probably do the same. I quit running and stop, putting my hands on my knees while I bend over to gulp for the thick warm air that washes invisibly in from the dark throbbing ocean. I swear I can feel the glow of the stars on my back.

Maybe I should turn around and head for home. Then again, maybe I shouldn't. I'd have to pass the fornicating couple again. When I can breathe again I rise up and start walking. Truly, I feel like an idiot. I realize that I didn't even check the bedroom to see if Brandon had returned while I was sleeping out on the lanai. Maybe he's asleep in our bed and I don't even know it. If I were smart, that's where I would be. But I really don't want to pass those two people on the beach again, and the only way out of here is to continue the full mile and a half down the beach and take the path up to the road, then walk back alongside the ditch. I head back down toward the water and continue on while the ocean washes over my feet in a perfect rhythm. The outlines of the clouds against the inky sky are barely visible, but stunning in their subtlety. I wish that I could write something as subtle. Most of the time I feel so obvious and clunky and literal. Though, at the moment I feel disconnected to the reality of Brandon as I grasp for my familiar obsession with the unreality of Ethan.

But it's not unreal anymore. He's here—somewhere. The water feels soft, like warm milk soaking my feet. The lazy half-moon is reclining, leaning against the mirrored edge of an enormous silent cloud. From the darkness a wisp of fragrant, hot trade wind blows past, as if someone has opened the oven door after baking cookies. My skin is rehydrated, my eyes are clear again. How can the physical world be so perfect while my emotions are roiling?

I've walked the length of the beach, and as I head up toward the path I almost miss the two of them, Brandon and Ethan, their voices floating out from somewhere under the trees. "Come on," I hear Brandon say. "Why not?" I stop where I am, halfway between the shore and the trees. I stare into the dark, and strain to see what I think is the outline of a torso.

"Brandon," Ethan tells him. "Behave yourself."

"Why? We're on vacation."

"*You're* on vacation. I live here."

"So take a vacation tonight—with me." I hear what sounds like sloppy kisses, or groping, or the scuffling of cheap behavior.

"Cut it out," Ethan tells him. "I'm not into it."

From where I stand I flick the switch on the flashlight and aim it toward the trees. It takes me a couple sweeps, but I locate them, sitting together under one of the twisted trees, just like I pictured. But something's wrong with the picture—Brandon is pushing Ethan's arms away as they both squint into the flashlight beam. I walk up to them.

"There you are," Brandon says, smiling. When I get there I see that his shorts are off. He's naked. He doesn't even seem embarrassed. It's like he's almost proud. "I was just telling your boyfriend how cute he is," he says a little sloppily, squinting into the spotlight. Then he grabs Ethan's face and plants a kiss on it.

I turn the flashlight off and wait for my eyes to readjust. "He's not my boyfriend," I tell Brandon. "You are."

"He's drunk a whole bottle of wine," says Ethan, coming into focus as my pupils open to the darkness.

"So what?" Brandon says. "I know who Rusty is out here searching for."

"You," I tell him.

"Rusty Doonan, don't bullshit a bullshitter," Brandon laughs.

I've never thought of Brandon as a bullshitter. I don't think anyone who's ever met him has—even if he *is* choosing to be a lawyer. Then again, I've never thought of Brandon as someone who would try to seduce my first love.

"Tell us," Brandon says gamely. "Tell us who you were really trying to find out here."

"I should have brought him back," Ethan says. "After he drank all that wine."

"Oh, will you two get a fucking grip?" Brandon laughs. His shorts in hand, he crawls out from the tree and stands up. He pushes a leg through the opening of his shorts. "Oops." He catches himself from tilting and falling over.

"Let's get him home," Ethan offers.

"Enough!" Brandon says, putting his hand out in the international sign for *stop*. He stands there naked, with his shorts down around one ankle. "I'm fine and you know it." He steps out of his shorts, takes a stance, reaches back with his arms, and jumps into the air for a perfect pirouette. He lands in the same spot, takes a bow, reaches down, and grabs his shorts. "Satisfied?" he asks, slipping them on. "I'm going back now," he says, with a slur.

"We're coming with you," I tell him.

"I'm perfectly capable of walking a mile," he says. "Sure, I'm a little drunk. Who cares? I'm on a beach in Hawaii, guys. If I trip I'll land in the sand." Brandon gives me a loud smack on my ass. "You're staying here with Ethan."

I don't say anything.

"We should watch after him," Ethan cautions.

"It's non-negotiable," Brandon assures us, walking away. "I'm on my own."

"Don't walk by the water's edge," I call after him.

"Wear your rubbers!" he calls back, laughing.

Ethan and I stand there, in the atmosphere of Maui. We don't move. It's the first time we're alone since that summer. I look out toward the darkened sea. He does the same, perhaps to see what I'm looking for, or perhaps because he doesn't know what else to do. Then I look over at him, and we laugh out of nervousness.

"So what did he mean by *wear your rubbers?*" Ethan asks, joking around.

"You're supposedly gay now," I tell him. "You should know."

He knocks me on the shoulder.

I knock him back.

He puts me in a headlock. "That's right, sissy boy. And I'm a high school all-state wrestling champ, too."

"Former," I tell him, trying to twist out of it. I reach back to put my arms around him, and he loosens his headlock and swivels around me until we're face to face, our arms around each other. "I can't believe you're here," I whisper.

"I can't believe I'm here, either," he answers.

We stare at each other. One-Mississippi, two-Mississippi, three-Mississippi. We press our lips together. And in that brief moment, my roiling emotions equalize with the island's nocturnal tranquility. As my lips press into his, and our tongues slide in and out, I know that Brandon was right. It was Ethan I'd been searching for when I left the house.

Ethan and I are in up to our heads. The swells are small and steady, and they merely roll gently over the surface of the water as they pass. The moon is playing tricks on the clouds again, outsmarting them all so that Ethan and I have enough light to see each other's faces. "Why did this take six years?" Ethan asks.

"Because I was a love-struck teenage girl who drove you away," I answer, my toes barely touching the ocean's floor.

"And I was an asshole who drove you crazy," he says.

"That's pretty much it," I tell him, kissing him on the lips. Wrapped around each other like tangled seaweed, we're sort of treading water, sort of not. "Ethan, tell me something. Why does Karl hate you more than anyone? I mean, his life was the least altered by what you did. Get this—he told Robby and me that his mother told him what they were cued to see in the video that day. That's how we knew. And his mom was so hip, she just wanted to know from Karl what it felt like."

Ethan moans and laughs at the same time. "I did *not* cue that tape. It just happened to be on that scene. Man, Karl's mother has got to go down as the all-time coolest mom."

"She is. And nothing really changed for Karl when he got home that summer. So why does he hate you so much?"

"Because he loves you," Ethan says.

"Not like that," I answer.

A wave washes by and Ethan untangles from me in order to float on his back. I lean back and float beside him, and reach out and hold his hand. He tells me, "Karl came on to me that summer—before you did. The night all four of us drank that bottle of dark rum and watched the video of the surfing competition. When you and Robby were in the bathroom, brushing your teeth, he stuck his hand in my shorts."

"What did you do?"

"I just about busted his hand. And I told him if he ever tried anything again, I'd kick his ass all the way back to California."

Karl's venom for Ethan finally makes sense. "Hell hath no fury like a faggot scorned?"

"Something like that."

We enter a small current. I hold his hand tighter, so that he won't float away. The stars are so thick they almost touch. "I don't get it, Ethan. You threaten to kick Karl's ass, but the next morning you mess around with me in bed."

"Right before I go expose you to the world for being gay. Pretty fucked, huh?"

"Pretty," I say, still holding tight to him.

"I was so confused, Rusty. That day we met at the fish house, I knew you wanted me. And I *loved* that you wanted me. And I wanted to *kill* you for wanting me. I was totally fucked up. Being sixteen really sucked."

"Is twenty-two any better?" I ask honestly.

"It is for me. At least I know it's OK for me to love another guy now."

I abandon the moon and stars to collapse into the water and move toward him, and pull him down until we're face to face.

"Are you saying you love me?" I ask.

"Fuck no. I mean, I don't know. I haven't seen you in six years. I mean . . ."

"I love you, Ethan. I have since we were sixteen."

"Aw hell," he sighs. "Me too."

We ride the waves to shore and walk to the trees and lie down together.

When we woke, at the age of sixteen, we were side by side, both of us lying on our stomachs, Ethan's heavy muscular leg draped over mine, his knee hiked up under my ass. The truth is, I woke first, but for about a half an hour I just stayed put, under the pressure of Ethan. Finally he stirred, moving his leg up slightly to knee my ass before sliding it down again. I could tell he was hard by the way he was moving. I was hard too—like a rail. After he'd moved his leg up and down about three times, I gathered the courage to slide my hand under his stomach, then move it down.

Robby and Karl were already up, I could hear them. And there was coffee made, I could smell it. But the door to our room was closed, and Ethan didn't try to stop me when I started doing it. We didn't kiss, or say anything, or look each other in the eye. But we lit up like two matches stuck together, and we could have burned the sheets. The moment he pushed my head off I knew it all changed. His anger exploded at the same time his body did. He was ashamed to see me watch him in that moment. "Fuck!" he snapped, scrambling off the bed. He grabbed my T-shirt and covered himself. "What the hell are you doing?"

I couldn't answer him—I was too stunned. He knew what I was doing, what *we* were doing. He'd been doing it with me. But all of a sudden he was acting as if he'd had nothing to do with it.

He started calling me terrible things, and I hated what he called me because I wanted to believe that he was no different from me, but if that were true it now meant that he hated himself. I didn't say any-

thing. And when he got all his clothes on, and bolted out, I didn't try
to stop him—but I wanted to.

When we wake under the trees, we're stuck together like two spoons
that dried together in a drawer. The tree forms a canopy above our
heads, and the sky is straining toward periwinkle as the sun pushes
closer to the eastern horizon. Ethan is behind me, and he presses his
nose into my neck and kisses me over and over, very softly and very
quietly. I'm smiling but he can't see me. The waves are still rolling, and
the water is still lapping against the sand as it breaks onto the shore. I
fall back asleep with Ethan's lips on my neck.

"Shit! Ethan, get up!" I tell him. It's hot, full sun, and I don't have
my watch on. The guys and I are booked on a 9 A.M. flight back to the
mainland today. I scramble up from our bed in the sand while one of
those honeymooning couples jogs by in their matching running shorts
and matching tank tops (that are more queer than Ethan and I will
ever be) and I yell to them and ask them what time it is.

They both look at their matching watches at the same time and yell
in unison, "Eight-twelve!"

"Fuck," I say to Ethan. "I'm never going to make it!"

He bolts up, and we start running in the opposite direction of the
matching couple, and for a moment I have the funny thought that it
probably looks like we're running away from them because of their
outfits. But then I snap to reality again. "Come on," Ethan yells, picking up the pace. We run the whole mile and a half back to the house,
and I swear that my heart is going to explode. Turning up and heading
onto the lawn, I look through the windows for life inside the house,
but I know the guys are gone. The flight leaves in less than forty minutes and they've probably already turned the rental car in, checked in
at the gate, and are waiting to board the flight.

Without a word, Ethan helps me throw all my stuff into my bag. I
run to grab my boogie board from the back lanai (I can't believe they
wouldn't at least carry my board to the airport for me), while Ethan
jumps into the bathroom and sweeps up my toiletries. I throw on my

long pants and a T-shirt. It only takes a minute before we're done. "Come on!" he says, carrying my bag for me while I carry the boogie board.

We race outside and I follow him to a beat-up old pickup truck that reminds me of the truck that was loaded with sugar cane, the truck that carried us halfway to Haleakala. I throw my board in the bed of the truck, and Ethan throws my bag on top of it, and we hop into the cab.

Traffic sucks—even on Maui. We're caught in the morning rush hour. We don't say anything as we drive—I think because we're caught in the same predicament we faced six years ago. Our separation is premature and hasty and full of unspoken feelings. Only, this time, we're much clearer on what those feelings are and what we could possibly do with them.

When we finally make it to the Kahului airport, Ethan pulls the truck to the front curb and we both jump out. I grab the bag and the boogie board and he yells, "Go!"

"No," I tell him. "Can't you come with me?"

"To California? No."

"Well, at least come with me to the plane," I beg.

"What about my truck?" he asks. He turns and sees an airport cop. "Can I leave my truck here for a minute?" he asks.

"No way, brah," the cop tells him. "Security alert."

"What?" I say. "The honeymooners are going to overthrow the island?"

"I'll pull it into the lot," Ethan tells me quickly. "Get your ass up to the gate. I'll meet you."

At the gate, the plane is still there. And no one has gone aboard yet. "Shit," I say, my heart beating against my chest so hard I swear it's going to break my bones. Robby, Nathan, Karl, Jeremy, and Brandon are hanging out together, standing to the side of the crowded gate area.

Upon seeing me, Jeremy says to Nathan, "You owe me twenty bucks." It's clear that the two of them placed some kind of a bet on me. I don't want to ask who bet what.

I throw my stuff down. "Oh my God," I wheeze, clutching the wall beside them. "The plane was supposed to leave two minutes ago. Why aren't you on board?"

"Mechanical problem," Karl answers.

"DC-10," Robby says. "My mother says the DC stands for Death Cylinder."

"It's just a little problem with getting the cockpit windshield to heat. They've almost fixed it," Brandon says, smiling. "Where's Ethan?"

"I have to check in," I answer, heading over to the gate check-in counter. There are two people giving the agent a hassle. They're telling her that they're sure they'll miss their connection in Los Angeles, and because of that they want a first-class seat. The gate agent sees that it's more of a hustle than a hassle. She maintains her aloha and smiles sweetly while telling them that first class is sold out.

Finally they begrudgingly give up, and I step forward. "Rusty Doonan, checking in," I say, reaching for my wallet. Gone. No wallet. Shit, I know I left it in these pants. I didn't even check for it when I put them on back at the house, because I knew it was in them. I dig through all my pockets. Nothing. "I can't find my wallet," I tell her, still looking. She smiles but says nothing. I'm not sure if she's full of aloha or Valium. The phone rings at her counter as I continue to dig. She answers it, says, "OK," and hangs up. Then she grabs the P.A. microphone and announces, "Ladies and gentleman, I have been informed that our mechanical problem has been fixed and we are ready to board the aircraft."

I run over to the guys and say, "I can't find my wallet. Did you guys bring my wallet?"

"Maybe Ethan stole it," Karl says.

"Maybe he didn't," I tell him. "And I know why you've been such a shit about Ethan, and we're going to talk about it."

"Later," Karl tells me. "I have a plane to catch."

"Ooh, the plot thickens," Jeremy says. "Talk about it now."

Ethan comes running. "Whew!" he says, out of breath. "I just heard them announce your flight. I thought I'd missed you."

The Valium-laden aloha-smiling woman announces, "Passengers

seated in rows thirty-five through thirty-eight, please board at this time."

"That's us," Brandon says gleefully.

"I don't have my wallet," I tell Ethan. "I guess I lost it."

"I'll bet it's back at the house," he says. "We can run back and find it."

"Even so, I guess I won't make it on this flight."

"There's another flight in a few hours," Karl says, dry as dust. He picks up his carry-on and says to Jeremy, "Coming?" He walks toward the boarding door.

Jeremy reaches out to shake hands with Ethan. "It was nice meeting you. Anybody who brings out the worst in my boyfriend can't be all bad." He pats me on the shoulder. "I intend to pull the bug out of Karl's ass as soon as we're on the mainland." He turns and heads for the plane.

"Well," Nathan says to Ethan. "It's been fun. Next time we'll leave our boyfriends at home."

Ethan smiles and shakes Nathan's hand.

Then Robby steps forward, right up to Ethan's face. Oh God. What next? Robby answers my question by leaning over and awkwardly kissing Ethan on the cheek. I just about fall over. I think Ethan does too. "Sorry about dinner last night," Robby tells him. "That whole thing was stupid. The entire last six years have been stupid. A lot of it is my fault. Not *entirely* my fault, but you know what I mean. What I hate most about my life is my mother's cheap drama, and last night it was like I was turning into my mother. And I'm *way* too young to be turning into my mother."

Ethan laughs, and so do the rest of us.

"So I've decided to end the six-year war," Robby finishes.

Ethan reaches out to shake Robby's hand, and when Robby shakes it, Ethan leans in and kisses him on his cheek in return.

"Come on, Nathan," Robby says, "it's back to civilization."

Brandon is left. I turn to Ethan. "Can I have just a minute?" Ethan isn't the least hesitant. He reaches out to Brandon, earnestly shakes his hand, and politely steps away, out of the gate area and into the open air terminal. I turn back to Brandon. "I'm sorry about last night. I should have walked you home."

Brandon smiles that famous smile. "You couldn't have kept up with me," he says. "Besides, you shouldn't be apologizing. I was trying to seduce Ethan, remember?"

"I'm not upset. Ethan told me that you had drunk a full bottle of wine."

He looks at me dead-on. Still smiling. "It wasn't the wine. I knew exactly what I was doing."

The thing about Brandon that drives me a little nuts is that he's always so happy and sure of himself, even when he says potentially powerful statements that may actually be difficult for someone to hear. "What am I supposed to say to that?" I ask.

"I'd seen you approaching last night in the moonlight, and figured you needed a little push toward your *true* love. Sometimes people don't go after what is theirs unless someone else is going after it. Don't worry about me, Rusty. I'm always moving on—and I think you're the only one who saw it, and that's why you liked me. But I think it's time we all start going after what's possible in our lives. For me, it's career. For you, it's Ethan."

At this moment I realize that I've never really known who Brandon is. We've dated for a year, and I don't really know him. I'm not sure any of my friends do either. It dawns on me that there is a reason for his lissome friendliness, his primary overtures, his interest and questions of people, his ebullience and pluck. His sweet nature, I think, is calculated. It keeps him protected. People never question him because he's so busy being the questioner. But at this moment I realize there is a measurable amount of disconnect in his behavior. We haven't had a single fight in the entire year we've dated. That can't be normal. And I think it's because we've never really connected. My gut reaction would be to think that it's been my fault—that I was still secretly pining away for Ethan, so I wasn't capable of bonding with Brandon. But maybe it was Brandon who was incapable of bonding with me.

Brandon smiles, pulls my arms out wide, then steps in and gives me a kiss. "Get going," he says. He pulls away, picks up his bag, and turns to board the flight. "Oh, gosh!" he says suddenly. "I almost forgot!" He takes a piece of paper from his back pocket. "This is a note that explains things a little more. But promise me something—promise you won't read it until the plane takes off."

I nod.
"Promise?"
"Promise," I tell him, taking the note from his hand.
"Bye, Rusty!" he sings, trotting toward the loading bridge.

I ask Ethan if he wouldn't mind taking me down the service road, on the edge of the pineapple field, to the chain-link fence that borders the airport. We race the DC-10. As it taxis out to one end of the runway, we speed along to the other end, kicking up a trail of dust as we go. We make it to the runway's far border and Ethan shuts the truck off just in time to hear the engines of the jumbo jet spool up, two miles away at the other end. I get out of the truck's cab, and step into the bed of the truck, and stand there as the huge jet points toward me, seemingly stuck in place. But then I see smoke from behind the engines, and through the heat waves rising off the runway, I see that the jet is finally moving. As it approaches, the noise of the engines begins to catch up, and a low hum grows nearer and nearer until it turns into a moan, and then a rumble as the nose of the jet lifts and it releases itself from the force of gravity. Moments later it passes over our heads, the wheels retracting into its belly, the noise from the engines blasting our ears, and I turn to watch my friends fly away, toward the mainland, toward their main lives.

I reach into my pocket and take out Brandon's note. It reads:

> *Your wallet is hidden in the drainpipe on the left-hand side of the house. Have a great summer.*
>
> *Love,*
Brandon.

It is late afternoon. We drive along the coast on Highway 30, past the forehead area of Kaanapali, down through the eyes of the island, Lahaina, the old whaling town where the smokestacks at the sugar mill billow the dun-colored smoke of burning cane. We keep the windows of Ethan's truck fully open, and the pungent smell of the burnt cane fills the car and singes our noses. We bypass the throat and head north, across the neck, until the green spikes of the pineapple fields surrounds us. Off to our left, in the distance, sits the airport, but this time we head west and begin our gradual climb to the heart, Haleakala.

We pass through the cattle and ranch upcountry of Kula, climbing until the eucalyptus trees end and the big mountainous volcano starts looking like a desert, with nothing much growing on either side of the two-lane highway. As we go higher and higher, I keep looking back at the rest of the island and try to grasp how beautiful it is.

When we finally make it to the top, Ethan is like a bird that has been let out of a cage. He flies out of the truck and by instinct picks the trail that leads to the summit. Up he goes, his feet barely on the ground. I yell for him to go ahead, and promise to meet him up there in less than a moment.

I head into the bathroom and pee, and when I'm done I walk over to the mirror and look at myself. I won't tell you what I see, because Mrs. Chris, my English teacher back in high school, said that when you're writing something you should never have a character look into a mirror and describe himself because that person can never be honest about what he sees. But I will tell you that looking at myself makes me start to cry, and it has nothing to do with failure. And if I can't tell you what I see, then I should be able to tell you how I feel. I feel like the guys and me, when we got back to Los Angeles that summer six years ago, were forced to start living our lives in straitjackets again. School started in less than a month, and going into our junior year we felt the need to start acting like juniors, whatever that meant. Karl and I were good at sports, and Robby was passable enough that we didn't plan to get hassled. Besides, we were all liked by the people we gave a shit about. But there was that whole girl thing, that stupid phony world between guys and girls our age, and the three of us just didn't fit into that whole system. And then word got out about our summer. Ethan painted us pink to his posse of wrestling buddies, and they spread it from their school to our school. And we got squeezed on both ends, like we always did, and it was torture. Finally there wasn't any question that we were exactly what everybody thought we were. We were boys like us. It was painful and disheartening—and necessary.

So I think I'm crying because for the first time in our lives, six scab-covered years back, here on Maui in our little rented beach house, we took off our straitjackets and tried on our gay ones. And for years after, suffering the pain of Ethan, I thought it was a big mistake. But now I realize it was the smartest thing we ever did. There was nothing wrong with any of it. Our giggles, our music, our cooking, or our taste in men—it was all just fine. And Ethan was just fine too. He did what our culture—and his parents—had driven him to do. They'd backed him against a wall and he came out fighting—against what everyone told him he couldn't be, and against those that showed him what he *could* be. Karl, Robby, and I were lucky enough to know ourselves a little better. We had the acceptance of one another and we knew it. In the end, it doesn't matter. We've all come out of our straitjackets.

When I catch up with the Ethan, my eyes must still be red because he gets this real sweet look on his face, and he puts his arms around me on the summit of the heart. We stand above the patches of clouds that hang hundreds of feet below, and we look out onto the curvature of the blue world while neither of us says a word for what seems like forever. And then, out of nowhere, Ethan sighs and quietly tells me, " 'Someday, after we have mastered the winds, the waves, the tides and gravity, we shall harness for God the energies of love. Then for the second time in the history of the world, man will have discovered fire.' "

I start crying again, and Ethan does too. I can't believe such words from him. They are so romantic, so noble. I can't imagine them rising out of the mouth of the cruel boy I met six summers ago. When I ask him where he learned the words, he says he stole them from a French philosopher, and he tries to act like it is nothing. But I know if he's taken the time to memorize it, then it is something. I wish I could tell Karl and Robby how much they mean to me.

We hike over to a rock and sit down together, pointing ourselves toward the west. "Where do you live?" I ask Ethan.

"In my truck," he says, watching the sun inch away. I look over at him to see if he's serious. He is. "I came with hardly any money, and it's almost all gone." He looks back at me. "Why do you think I buzzed my hair? I don't have to take showers so often with it short. When I do, I go over to the YMCA. I know things have to get going. I've been coming out of shock. I'll get on my feet soon."

"I've got some money in my savings account," I tell him. "It'll last us for a while."

He takes my hand, slips his fingers in between each of mine. "I was looking in the paper the other day. There's construction work in Kahului."

I laugh. "You're too butch to be queer."

"Was I butch last night with my legs in the air?" he asks, squeezing my hand.

"Hell yes," I tell him. "We've all got to switch our thinking on that one. It doesn't get any butcher, as far as I'm concerned."

"Don't get too comfortable in your thinking," he tells me, smiling. "Or in last night's position."

"Variety is the spice of life," I assure him.

"Damn straight," he says.

We both laugh at that one.

"I've heard of these guys over on the Big Island," I tell him. "Outside of Pahoa, where the fresh lava and the sea make new land. They have this sort of all-male commune thing. There are macadamia nut trees and coffee trees on the mature part of their plantation. If we work, we can stay for free."

We hold on to each other, as the orange sun appears to touch the blue water. Ethan makes a hissing sound as it does, and we wait while it slips into the ocean, little by little, then surprisingly fast. But we hold tight to each other's hand, and neither of us looks away. Though we missed the beginning of the day, we're determined to see it end together.

Satisfaction

Ben Tyler

For Kevin Howell

Chapter One

"This is your brain on drugs," Dusty shouted to no one as he drove through the Southern California desert en route to Palm Springs. It was August. Late Saturday morning. The top was down on his black Mercedes 300 CE, and the sun was intense. Sizzling. But it felt great, even erotic. It penetrated his gym-pumped bare skin, which was bronzed from this weekly driving ritual. Alone in the car, Dusty pounded the hot steering wheel, beating out the rhythm to Air Supply's *I'm All Out of Love* blaring on the oldies radio station. As he sang along he was wondering how he'd manage to get through another combative weekend with his lover, Chad, and where he'd gone wrong in finding Mr. Right in the first place.

Although he usually drove out to Palm Springs on Fridays, a crisis at the office had kept Dusty working late the night before. By the time he left the film studio where he served as speechwriter for the corporate communications department, he was too tired to drive anywhere but home and to bed. He called Chad from his car cell phone and promised he'd be in the Springs by one o'clock the following day.

Dusty expected a big complaint. "No hurry," Chad said. "I'm hitting the hay myself so don't bother to call again when you get home."

That was refreshing, Dusty thought as he hung up the phone.

Morning came, and, not wanting to endure the toaster-oven temperatures of midday, Dusty forced himself to get up a little earlier than usual and drive out of town before the blazing sun and the lung-choking smog in San Bernardino had the chance to give him the double whammy of a stroke and emphysema.

As much as Dusty resented the long drive each weekend, he gave in to his lover's arrangement of living at his Palm Springs condo for the summer.

When the subject first came up three years ago, Dusty had complained, "For Christ's sake! It's a furnace down there! And the scorpions! I'm supposed to see you only on weekends?"

"Just for the season," Chad reasoned, as if it were a *fait accompli*. "Your heart'll grow fonder."

"And your dick'll grow fonder—of all those hunky guys who flock to the Springs! I know you. You'll be at every circuit party!"

But Dusty eventually surrendered, giving in because Chad insisted it was unfair that he should have to stay in town doing nothing all day, while Dusty was at work.

"You could get a job," Dusty challenged. "Maybe as a pole dancer at a geriatric bath house." That last remark was hurtful because Chad had once been a model. He'd had his moment, even his own month on a swimsuit calendar. But that was during his Paleolithic youth. Now, at age 45, those days—and Chad's youth—were long behind him.

"Whatever Lola wants, Lola gets," Dusty mocked Chad, who bragged that he didn't have to work because he had more money than the combined yearly salaries of the cast of *Friends*.

Driving along Highway 111, through the San Gorgonio Pass, with the San Jacinto Mountains looming on the right, Dusty drove past miles of what was affectionately called the Mercedes-Benz graveyard: Hundreds of windmills with three blades that resembled his own car's distinct emblem. Each was rotating and generating enough power over the course of a year to feed electricity to twenty-two thousand homes.

Eventually on the main drag of Palm Canyon Drive, he finally arrived at 11422 South Caliente Road. He parked alongside Chad's BMW. Dusty emerged from the car with his gym bag, which held only the few essentials he needed for the weekend: a change of shorts, underwear, socks, and SPF 30 sunblock.

He entered the condo. The cool air inside made the place feel like an igloo. "Sanctuary!" Dusty called out in his best Charles Laughton/ Quasimodo impersonation. He was happy to be out of the heat.

The living room was decorated in a southwestern motif with a lot of faux Native-American trinkets. Obligatory Georgia O'Keeffe color prints dominated the plaster walls. Except for the sound of the environmentally irresponsible air-conditioning unit dumping chlorofluoro-carbons into the precariously flimsy ozone layer, the place was quiet. It was deserted and a tad unsettling.

"Chad?" Dusty called out as he dropped his bag on the tile floor of the foyer next to the door. "Hey, sweetie. Don't tell me you're still humping the pillows at this hour!" His voice echoed throughout the house.

The condo was eerily quiet. The atmosphere set off Dusty's internal bells and whistles of suspicion. Chad had to be around. His Beemer was parked in its usual space. The front door of the condo was un-locked. Antarctica was flowing through the air vents.

"Chad?" he called again, now in a tone of apprehension. He peeked around corners. The huge condo was designed for entertaining, and boasted vaulted beamed ceilings, custom-tiled floors, French doors leading to a courtyard and atrium, a media room, stone fireplace, spa-cious kitchen and three bedrooms and bathrooms.

Suddenly he stopped and pulled himself up short. A guttural sound issued from his lips. He spotted the stuff: a pair of khaki shorts, a tank top shirt, dirty-white tennis shoes, all discarded in a heap by the bar in the living room. The clothes weren't Ralph Lauren so they didn't be-long to Chad.

Not again! Dusty said to himself. *I'm such a damn fool.*

He stealthily made his way down the hallway corridor to the master bedroom suite, expecting the worst. Empty. The king-size bed was an unmade tangle of sheets, pillows, and blankets. No surprise, consider-ing Chad's lack of domestic responsibility. "We have people to do the menial stuff," he often said, dismissing Dusty's complaints that "neat-ness counts." He often liked to call Dusty, "Harriet Craig," after Joan Crawford's role as a perfectionist wife.

As Dusty turned to leave the bedroom he noticed a glass on the nightstand. A cigarette butt had been dropped into two fingers of an amber liquid. Scotch. Chad neither smoked nor drank. Next to the glass was a nearly squeezed-empty tube of Probe-Lube. Two wet condoms, shriveled like burst party balloons, were on the floor.

"Bastard," he muttered and left the room.

Dusty ducked into the guestroom. It was as neat as it had been the weekend before, obviously unused. He poked his head into the master bathroom off the main corridor. A couple of towels were piled on the floor. A contact lens case sat on the sink vanity. Not Chad's. He'd had Lasik surgery last year.

As he continued prospecting from room to room, Dusty's breathing became heavy. His adrenaline pumped him into warp overdrive. His blood pressure was climbing, if not to Everest, at least to Mt. McKinley. Finally, after two dozen paces he found himself in the bright, white-tiled kitchen, standing at the sliding glass door that led to Chad's secluded, fenced backyard with the pool and Jacuzzi.

At last, there was Chad, standing in the shallow end of the pool—with someone else—who he embraced, sharing deep kisses. The sound of water lapping against their tanned and naked busy bodies and the hum of the motor sending refrigerated air into the condo and the screeching of noisy insects were too much of a din for them to have heard Dusty call out Chad's name.

Dusty stood at the glass door for a long moment. To his surprise, he wasn't shocked, merely disappointed. Inured, really. This scenario had played itself out too many times.

He took a good look at Chad's sexy trick. The boy was too typical of the guys Chad was turned on by: Late teens—practically jail bait. Long, bleached-blond hair. Not beefy, but certainly a well-defined physique. *Probably some wannabe guitarist in a rock band,* Dusty abstracted from the guy's appearance. The kid's alabaster ass was contrasted with his tanned torso that tapered at the waist. He was young enough to eat meals of three-cheese pizzas and double burgers and Cokes, and never gain an ounce. He could be a mannequin window display for swim suits at The Gap.

The boy's endowments were in contrast to Chad's mid-life build—which was above average for his age, but not without its hints of the handles, the sags and wattles that came with time and gravity. Still, whatever Chad's physical condition, he had no problem picking up guys younger by more than half his age. Dusty had once been one of them.

As Dusty stood watching Chad make love, he was resisting an urge to retreat to the living room and pick up the guy's clothes, find his wallet and money and car keys and grind them in the trash compactor. He imagined sliding the door open and asking, "Three for brunch?" *Isn't that what perfect Martha Stewart would do if she came home from a quilting bee and found her lover in flagrante delicto?* he asked himself.

Dusty stood by the door a while longer. When neither of the men noticed him, he finally turned away.

He decided to leave. Not just leave the condo, but leave Chad—this time for good.

Dusty had tried breaking up a dozen times before. But Chad was a charmer, when he wanted to be. His smile. His sparkling green eyes. The way he held and kissed Dusty, telling him how Dusty was the only man who had ever loved *him* so much. "They all leave me eventually," Chad sobbed after one of the times Dusty threatened to pull up stakes and dissolve the relationship.

But Dusty was both an optimist and a romantic, and he had perpetual hope that Chad might eventually recognize his devotion and make some serious concessions toward monogamy. However, as Dusty's mother often said, "A leopard can't change his spots, dear." The same axiom applied to Chad's wandering dick—it never changed the spots it enjoyed entering. The bad times with Chad out-weighed the good.

Dusty walked back past the discarded clothes and reached for his gym bag. He opened the front door—then stopped.

No. He couldn't just depart the scene as if nothing of major consequence had happened. He had to leave behind some sign that he'd been there. He needed to send a message to Chad that he'd seen it all.

His first thought was for something memorable, like spray painting, I KNOW WHAT YOU DID THIS SUMMER, in floor-to-ceiling-size red graffiti dripping down the wall. But he'd have to go out to buy the paint.

Rather than vandalize the condo, Dusty opted for subtlety. He wished his quickly devised scheme could be directed squarely at Chad, not so much at the kid who probably didn't know Chad was in a relationship. But it couldn't be helped.

He walked into the master bathroom, picked up the contact lens case, and unscrewed the caps to make sure the contacts were inside. "Blue," he said aloud, looking at the colored tinting. "Figures." Then he held the two small wells of the case over the black porcelain toilet bowl and turned them upside down. For added measure he let the caps and case drop into the commode as well. Perhaps they would clog the pipe when flushed. He'd leave that up to providence, and hope for the worst—or in this case, the best.

Dusty returned with purpose to the kitchen. He checked to make sure Chad was still preoccupied, then retrieved a pair of sharp scissors from a catch-all utility drawer. He went to the living room, and, play-acting that he was Anthony Perkins in *Psycho* mutilating Janet Leigh, cut the guy's tank top. Finally, he went back into the bedroom, picked up the glass of Scotch and soggy cigarette butts, carried it into the living room, and poured the contents on the khaki shorts. Spent of energy, he let the glass drop to the floor.

Once again at the front door he took one last look around the condo he'd been sharing with Chad for untold weekends. He opened the door for the final time, said, "Bye-bye, cocksucker," then walked out into the killer heat of a smeltery.

The temperature was excruciating. Dusty got into his car and, still shirtless, burned his skin on the blistering leather seatback. He hadn't bothered to put the top up on the vehicle before going into the condo. He blasted on the air conditioner—as if it would serve any purpose with the interior so exposed to the sun—and quickly reversed the car out of the driveway and backed onto the street. He was fighting time, in case Chad had already torn himself away from his boy toy and witnessed Dusty's aggression.

Dusty just wanted to race back home, pack what he could and get the hell out of their house. He'd crash on a friend's couch for a few nights if he had to. Anything but stay another moment near Chad.

By now, the desert was literally the *Backdraft* attraction at the Universal Studios Tour. No way did Dusty want to drive all the way back to Los Angeles, especially in his current state of anger, sadness, regret, and self-pity. From spending so many weekends over the years in Palm Springs, he'd made a few friends. Although Chad would argue that they were mostly *his* friends, the guys genuinely liked Dusty. He had insinuated himself into their circle, which consisted entirely of couples who were in long-time committed relationships. Although on weekends they often ventured to Arenas Road, the gay strip in P.S., to hang out at Hunters, *the* hot dance bar, they never went without their partners. They were just out to have fun, cavorting under sparkling mirrored globes suspended from the rafters, innocently ogling the shirtless, nipple-pierced, gym-devoted studs who gyrated and sweated to the heavy rhythms blaring from enormous house speakers.

As Dusty drove his car on to Palm Drive toward Desert Hot Springs, not really knowing where he was going, he dialed his cell phone to call Peter and Rod, two of the guys from their group whom he liked best. They were always teasing Dusty that they'd like to fix him up with this wealthy doctor, or that rich interior designer. Dusty knew they weren't serious. Or at least not serious enough to actually try to bust up his relationship with Chad.

"In humor there is truth," Peter had once philosophized, when Dusty commented on his suspicion that while he recognized their constant badgering was good-natured, it sometimes slipped into double entendre, indicating at least a hint of seriousness.

"You guys probably know more about where the bodies are buried than I do," he said, acknowledging Chad's conspicuous philandering. "But I'd like to keep the cadavers under the stairs, at least for now."

This conversation had occurred one evening when Peter had addressed the issue at a poolside party. He was playing a favorite game of "With whom would Chad sleep if his partner would never find out?"

"Let's turn it around," Peter suggested. "When you have a chance," he coaxed, "nonchalantly take a look at the six-footer by the tiki torch. The one in the white silk Donna Karan."

Dusty raised his glass of Merlot to his lips and swiveled his hips to the right. Casually he lowered his head just enough to see the main attraction.

"Ah, yes. Mr. Gillette razor commercial. One could certainly work up a lather with him."

"'It's alive!' Peter imitated Gene Wilder in *Young Frankenstein*. Then in his own voice he declared, "Your libido isn't *Abby Normal* after all!"

"Just on hiatus, I hope," Dusty deadpanned.

"I thought you should know that he asked about you," Peter offered.

"Me?"

"Why not?"

"'Cause I'm nowhere in his league."

"Just 'cause he's Stuart Richards?"

"Exactly. *Famed* Stuart Richards. Best-selling author, Stuart Richards. One of the most attractive men in Palm Springs, Stuart Richards."

"Give yourself a little more credit, Dusty," Peter said. "There are plenty of guys who find you incredibly attractive."

"Must be the hair," he said, sardonically flipping non-existent locks, imitating an obnoxious TV commercial for a national chain of cheap hair styling salons.

"I'm serious. Rod and I agree. Don't play innocent ingenue with us, boy," Peter said. "Your virgin days are long over."

"Actually, my virgin days have *returned*." Dusty tried to laugh. "I think I've grown a hymen!" Then as an aside, Dusty asked, "So what did you tell Stuart about me?"

"That you were one of Dr. Laura's authentic biological errors. A mistake of nature."

Dusty rolled his eyes. "Seriously. For once. I may be married, for the moment, but I can still be intrigued."

"I told him you're the man that got away—from everyone but Chad. I pointed out your Prince Charming. Chad was . . ." Peter's sentence trailed off.

"Chad was, what? Like a dog, sniffing some other dog's ass? You can say it. I have eyes. I've tuned into the same scene—many times. Even reruns of 'Vitavetavegimen' gets boring after too many viewings. It's just the way he is. He needs all the attention of an insecure actor."

"Mind if I tell you something the good man of letters said?"

Dusty shrugged. "As if I could stop you?"

"He took a long look when I pointed to Chad. Then he turned toward you. His exact words were: 'Such a waste. That cute guy'—you—

'living in a fool's paradise. Everybody I know has had that Chad character.'"

At that moment Stuart wandered over to join Peter and Dusty. Peter introduced the two men.

Stuart sniffed. "I sense Peter's been gabbing about me? Or am I just paranoid?"

"You two get acquainted," Peter said, making his getaway, saying he had to refill his wineglass.

"In your haste, don't spill the full one you have in your hand," Stuart joked.

Dusty smiled at Stuart. Standing close to the edge of the pool, they were far from alone, as dozens of other men and a sprinkling of women—"The golfers," as Peter had euphemistically referred to them—mingled about. But to Dusty the two men seemed in a sort of open cocoon. There was a moment of awkwardness, but it lasted only seconds because Dusty was adept at breaking the ice. "I'm an ardent admirer," he finally said.

"You haven't heard of me, unless it was from Peter," Stuart said, smiling.

"Seriously," Dusty continued. "You've probably heard this a gazillion times, but, in my case it's absolutely true. I thoroughly devoured A *Four-Sided Triangle*. A beautiful novel. I probably reread it at least once a year."

"It's only been out for two. Sorry. You're very kind. After all these years I'm just beginning to be able to accept a compliment. And you're too cute for me not to wish I could make a pass."

"And you're so hot that I wish I was in a position to accept a proposition."

"I know you're with someone."

"Yes. Someone." Dusty sighed.

"Excuse me for being forward," Stuart began again. "I hate to be the bearer of bad news, really, I do. But I feel . . ." He stopped midsentence. "It's none of my business. Not my place. Please, I apologize. It was nice meeting you."

He started to wander away. Dusty immediately pursued. "No. Wait. You're a friend of Peter's and Rod's. Consider me a friend, too, if only by association. If you have something to tell me, please, I'm all ears." He secretly hoped it was a confession of undying adoration. He needed someone—other than Peter—to affirm that he was still desirable.

Stuart sighed now. "Please don't misunderstand. I swear I'm not out to gain anything here. Although I sometimes wish I were that type. But it's not my nature. It's about your boyfriend."

"Lover," Dusty corrected.

"Your *lover*. He's left the party."

Dusty looked over to the far side of the pool where he had last seen Chad talking with a facsimile of a *Days of our Lives* stud.

Stuart followed Dusty's eyes as they searched the yard. "He's probably in the house getting a 7-Up, or something," Dusty said.

"As a matter of fact, he is getting *something*. To put it bluntly, he's having sex with another guest in a car out in the driveway. Notice how the crowd's thinned? The lemmings are out there viewing the free entertainment. I RSVP'd in the negative."

"Not into *theatre of the absurd*?" With forced casualness, Dusty swallowed what remained of his Merlot. "Mind if I have a splash of yours," he asked, holding out his glass.

Stuart obliged, pouring half of his drink into Dusty's glass. "I'm sorry," he said.

"Don't be," Dusty dismissed. "I'm the Glad Girl, Pollyanna, and that perpetually cheerful governess Maria Von *Tramp*, all rolled into one." Dusty tried his best to sound optimistic. "Anyway, maybe tonight he can pretend I'm someone else and deign to be interested in me. We can role-play handsome Baron and horny nun."

Stuart considered the insinuation that Dusty and Chad were no longer having sex, but simply said, "If you ever have a fantasy about being kidnapped, Peter can give you my number."

"Afraid I'm all out of fantasies," Dusty said. "But if I ever need to be abducted by a handsome kidnapper, you're at the top of my list. I promise. You've got that sexy, Ryan Philippe thing going for you. And your talent alone gets a ten plus on my *OUT* survey of what turns me on most about a man."

"We could leave, too, you know," Stuart suggested. "Tit for tat."

"And give the asshole something else to lord over me? Nah. As much as I'd like to feel your bare skin against mine . . ."

"Don't stop!"

"And suck on that hard cock that's bulging through your slacks, until my lips are ready for Chapstick, and my tonsils are bruised, I'll have to save that pleasure for a rainy day."

Stuart grinned. "It doesn't rain much down here. But I sense a storm is brewing. I hope for my selfish sake there's a monsoon on the way."

"I'll send up a flare if I'm foundering without a life vest," Dusty said. "I think I'm heading into the perfect storm."

Now, recalling that evening—and so many others of similar nature—Dusty pushed the last digit of Peter and Rod's number. He heard the phone ring twice before the answer machine picked up. "Hey! Thanks for the call. You know the drill. Here's your roadrunner. Beep, Beep."

For a moment Dusty's throat was constricted. He suspected that if he tried to speak he'd start crying. Finally, he began to talk. And as he feared, he sobbed too.

"Hold on! Hold on!" It was Peter's voice. "We're here. Is that you, Dusty?"

Silence.

"Dusty? Are you okay?"

"No."

"Where are you?"

"Don't know. Indian Wells, I think. Chad."

"Something's happened to Chad?"

"Some *one*."

A pause. "Dusty, can you get yourself over to our place, or do you need me to come for you?"

"Can I see you now?"

"Get your ass over here, ASAP!"

Dusty hung a right on Tachevah Drive and headed back along the highway into Palm Springs proper. The main drag, Palm Canyon Road, was jammed with cars, many of them convertibles and Jeeps occupied by sexy, shirtless guys, getting hotter by the moment from the ferocious sun. Finally, he passed one of the ubiquitous Denny's restaurants, and turned right onto a secluded street. Mammoth bushes of oleander and bougainvillea hid estates from view. Taking a circuitous route, Dusty drove on to Via Veneta to Peter and Rod's home. *The Hacienda,* as the bronze plaque on the entry gate announced, was sequestered like so many other homes, behind palm trees and walls of green vegetation against chain-link fencing.

Braking at the gate, Dusty pushed the call button on the intercom box. "C'mon in," Peter said without asking who it was. The gate slowly opened into a car park, then just as slowly closed behind Dusty's car.

Peter and Rod, both wearing only shorts and sandals, revealing their fortysomething but still well-toned bodies, emerged together from the house. Dusty continued to sit in the car, until Rod tapped him on his bare shoulder and stirred him from his stupor. Dusty put on a smile as he looked up at the men. "I'm sorry, guys. I've made a mistake. I've bothered you for no reason. Really. I don't know what happened to me. I'm really fine."

"Your ass," Rod said. "Your eyes tell a way different story."

"Yeah," Peter agreed. "Either you've been smoking some awesome weed, or you've been bawling your baby blues out."

At which moment, Dusty burst into tears.

Chapter Two

Chad reluctantly took his mouth away from the full lips of the young heartthrob he'd coerced into spending the previous night with him. He looked at the wall of the stuccoed cabaña to a large, round, thermometer/clock. The temperature needle was broken and had melted years ago at the 120 degrees mark. The time however, was correct. Almost noon. Chad knew that Dusty should be on his way into Palm Springs by now. In fact, he could be here any minute.

Chad embraced the young man once again, running his fingers through the boy's long, wet, golden hair. Then he placed his open hands on the stud's chest, caressing his smooth, wet skin. He bent down to taste the boy's nipples for the umpteenth time then submerged his head underwater and found the kid's feisty sausage of a dick, which slid into his mouth.

Chad held his breath as he sucked, and the guy quickly discharged his load. To Chad, the velvet pudding-textured semen tasted of Clorox. *Pool water*, Chad realized.

God, kids can cum so quickly, he said to himself, as he finally came up for air. He gargled with a mouthful of water and spat out what little of the guy's load he hadn't swallowed. "Afraid I've got to call it quits," he gasped, catching his breath. "I have a business meeting in just a little while."

"How 'bout if I just stay here by the pool and wait 'til you get back?"

"My mother's due over for cocktails, then dinner."

"Right. Okay. So what about after she leaves?"

Chad hesitated. "She's spending the weekend."

"Right. Okay. Guess this is it."

The boy hoisted himself up on the side of the pool, his biceps, triceps, and deltoids flexing. Chad watched, transfixed, as the boy walked casually over the skillet-hot concrete to a patch of outdoor carpeting on which rested two chaise longues and a wrought-iron-and-glass patio table and chairs set. He picked up a yellow striped beach towel from a chaise and, still hard, turned to face Chad as if to drive home the message of what the older man would be missing. He began drying his hair. Beads of water on his body were quickly evaporating into the warm air, but he made a display of blotting his flaxen pubic hair and crotch. Chad, with a full erection, watched, aching as the boy showed off his physique one last time before tossing the towel aside and going into the house.

"Christ," was all Chad could say, as he too, emerged from the pool. Unlike his young friend, however, he had to hop over the concrete as if dancing on white-hot coals, until he reached the safety of the carpet. He used the guy's towel to dry himself, taking a moment to inhale the scent of chlorine and sweat. He then followed the boy into the house.

Just inside the sliding glass kitchen door, Chad donned a pair of shorts from off the granite kitchen counter and slid his feet into a pair of Top Siders. "Can I have a drink or something before I go?" the still-naked boy called as he stood at the wet bar in the living room ready to help himself to another round of Scotch.

"I'm kinda rushed," Chad said, joining him and observing their reflection in the gold-veined mirror behind the bar.

"At least let me pee and then help me find my contacts. Can't see worth a damn without 'em."

"Where'd you leave 'em?" Chad asked.

"If I knew that I wouldn't have to ask for your help," the boy mocked. "I thought they were in the bathroom, but I just checked."

"Check again," Chad said.

He accompanied the guy into the master bathroom, then watched as the boy yanked on his succulent cock and began to pee into the toilet. The kid involuntarily groaned from the pleasure of emptying an obviously full bladder. The sound echoing in the toilet bowel was not unlike that which a horse makes during the same procedure. *Youth*, Chad thought with amazement and envy, as he leaned against the vanity, enjoying the view.

"My contacts," the kid said again. "I *know* I left 'em in here."

"Why'd you take them out in the first place?"

"I didn't want to chance swimming with 'em in. If I opened my eyes underwater they'd be history." He shook the last drops of urine from his cock and reached for the handle to flush the toilet.

Chad cried out, "Don't!"

Too late. The kid's reaction wasn't quick enough and he pushed the handle.

"They're in the toilet, you dumb ass!" Chad cried. "The contacts! Get 'em out before they go down!"

Nearsighted though the guy was, as the lenses and case swirled in the commode and the water in the bowl began to rise, he could see that what Chad had said was true. "Fuck!" the boy shouted. "They're going down the toilet!"

"The case is caught! It's backing up the water, you fuckhead!" Chad wailed as the water rising to the rim of the commode began gurgling over the side, and flooding the marble-tile bathroom floor. "Grab some towels! Clean this up!"

"I can't see anything, you prick! How'd my lenses get in the fucking toilet? Christ, I can't drive without 'em!"

"Just go get your clothes on and get out of here," Chad commanded.

The kid angrily threw a soaked towel at Chad, then stormed out. A severe fear of germs made a urine-soaked towel as nauseating to Chad as being doused with plutonium.

Cautiously swabbing the floor with a towel of his own, under his shoes, Chad suddenly heard a tirade from the living room. "Hey, man, my shirt!" the kid shouted. "It's all ripped! What the fuck did you do that for? And my shorts! Jesus Christ, they're soaking wet!"

Chad stopped sopping up the yellow toilet water and raced into the living room.

Still naked, the boy stood in the middle of the room, fuming. "First my contacts, now my clothes! What the hell kind of kinky asshole are you?"

A cold hand clutched at Chad's insides. He looked at the ravaged shirt. Then he looked around the room. "It's not my fault. I didn't do this!"

Then, "Dusty?" he called out. "Dusty? Where are you?"

Returning to the condo after driving his nearly blind trick a half-hour away to his house in Palm Desert, a nervous Chad picked up the kitchen phone and dialed Dusty's cell number. Voice mail answered. "The cellular customer you are calling is not available. If you wish to leave a message, please do so at the tone."

"Hey, guy, where are you?" Chad said, feigning naiveté. "You should have been here at least an hour ago. Hope everything's okay. Call and let me know. Love ya." He hung up and dialed their number at home. This time his own voice on a machine answered back. "Not in. Leave a message." He hung up.

For the rest of the day, Chad puttered around the condo. He tried to watch television—VH1 and MTV. As a last resort he attempted reading a celebrity autobiography, but he fell asleep in the media room before the star's grandparents had emigrated from Poland to some hellacious tenement in New York. He awoke to the sound of the telephone ringing. It was nearly four in the afternoon.

He picked up the cordless phone beside the sofa. "Dusty?" he said.

It was Peter. "Is that a question or an answer?"

"Dusty was supposed to have come down this morning," said Chad. "He never showed up. I'm worried."

"You're a lying asshole," Peter said. "You're only worried about yourself."

"I'm worried that something might have happened to Dusty. He's punctual to a fault."

"Something happened all right, and you damn well know what it was."

There was a long moment of silence. Finally Chad said, "Christ. What did he see?"

"Nothing out of the ordinary. Just your average, gutter variety, asshole Chad-like display of splashing around in the pool with your dick up some slut's asshole."

"Shit." Chad paused. "But it's really *his* fault, you know."

"Dusty's?"

"Well, yeah."

"How the hell do you come to that moronic conclusion?"

"If he'd been here last night, as he was supposed to be . . ." Chad paused again. "He'll get over this. He always does."

"You're right. He'll get over it. He'll get over you, too. We *all* will."

"What?"

"How can you be so stupid, Chad? You have all week when you're here alone to make out with whatever piece of garbage a fly like you can attract. You're no spring chicken, man. Dusty, however, is. You had the golden goose but you had to have more. If you keep wanting everyone, you'll end up with no one."

"Confucius say?" Chad said in a sarcastic tone.

"Someone with brains and compassion."

"Dusty'll come back. We've been through this before. He loves me."

"Jesus Christ," Peter snorted. "He does, or did, love you. But he'll get over it."

"What have I done that's so fucking abominable it's making the earth rotate off its axis, for Christ sake?"

"If you don't know, you're even more scummy than I thought you were."

"I haven't done anything that a billion other guys haven't done before me, and after me. You're not so pure yourself. I've seen you leer at Dusty."

Peter ignored the remark. "Don't bother calling Tony and Steve, or Martin and Leonard, or Barry and Gene, or any of the others. We've held our own little 'tribal counsel.' You've been voted out, man. You may as well leave Palm Springs, because you'll be an outcast, like some home-wrecking slut infiltrating Pasadena society. And if you're insinuating that the way I look at Dusty has anything to do with this, you're more fucked up than we thought."

Chad heard a sharp click as the line disconnected. He blinked at the phone. "So what am I going to do?" he whimpered.

A suffocating silence enveloped him. He was completely alone. He felt like Scarlett O'Hara, to whom a reasonable facsimile of Rhett Butler had, though not in so many words, just declared, "Frankly, my dear, I don't give a damn."

Only the sound of the air-conditioning motor clicking off could be heard—along with a soft hiccup of sadness to accompany the tears that welled in Chad's eyes.

Chapter Three

It didn't take Dusty a week to find another place to live because he didn't care where it was. He made an offer on the first condo his realtor showed him in Toluca Lake. The agent kept insisting it was a prime location. "It's so close to the studios, and Bob Hope lives just a few blocks away over there." She pointed in one direction. "And Jo Anne Worley is a few blocks over there." She again pointed to some nebulous corner of the earth. "I just moved Denzel Washington's old property, which is around over there!" The woman sounded relieved as though a major laxative was responsible for the purge of real estate.

Bob Hope. Denzel Washington. Big deal.

The day that Dusty moved out of the house on King's Road in West Hollywood, Chad was there to keep an eagle eye on what the movers were taking. He needn't have been concerned. Dusty had packed only the items he'd brought with him when they decided to cohabitate and the things he had personally purchased during their three years together. The only argument came when a separate moving van arrived to take the baby grand piano.

"That stays," Chad commanded. "It's part of the furniture. I need it for parties."

"Wanna pay me the ten thousand dollars it cost me?" Dusty said with equal defiance. "Take it away," he instructed the piano mover with a flourish of his hand.

"It stays, or else I call my attorney and sue you for stealing property from my home. I can make you very sorry you ever got involved with me."

Dusty laughed in Chad's face. "As if I haven't already had regrets?"

He walked outside to his car, retrieved his briefcase and brought it back to the house. He snapped open the locks, lifted the leather lid, and withdrew a piece of paper that he waved directly in front of Chad's face, which made him flinch. "Receipt," Dusty declared. "I've got a lot of these, even for some of the things I'm leaving behind. So don't fuck with me!"

Then, in an act that was both generous and sensible, since the new condo was really too small for a baby grand piano, Dusty took his checkbook from the briefcase, wrote one out to Melody Movers and handed it to the dumbfounded man who had already draped a heavy blanket over the shiny top of the piano. "Leave it here," he said to the man, handing him the check. "Sorry for making you come all this way."

As the piano movers departed, Dusty looked at Chad and said, "It's yours. A gift."

Then he picked up a screwdriver belonging to one of the movers and climbed on top of the piano. "What the fuck?!" Chad screamed, as Dusty, kneeling on the lid, began carving a huge heart on the shiny black surface. He gouged a deep arrow with the head pointing to hell.

Chad stared in horrified disbelief, as Dusty chiseled their initials in its center. "May it always be a haunting reminder that you had the opportunity to live your life with someone who loved you and who only wanted a little respect and consideration in return."

"You've ruined my piano!" Chad gasped in utter shock.

"It'll still play. Try 'Rhapsody in Blue.' The title will suit you the moment I leave and close the door."

With that said, Dusty left Chad caressing the disfigured instrument, and followed the last mover outside to the truck. He gave the man directions to the new place.

"I'll try to avoid seeing you around, Chad." Dusty waved from his car and drove down King's Road to Sunset Boulevard.

*   *   *

Dusty's weekend ritual of driving to Palm Springs continued. Now that Peter and Rod had "adopted" him, he found he actually looked forward to getting away to the desert. He realized that for the past three years, it had been *Chad* he hadn't wanted to see on weekends. That was the real source of his resentment about making the weekly commute.

Peter and Rod had become his best pals, and they kept their guest-room ready for his arrival each Friday night or Saturday morning, whichever was more convenient for Dusty. The guys hosted intimate dinner parties, inviting old friends as well as new ones. They often peppered their soirées with a celebrity or two from their client roster, and they always seated Dusty beside whichever eligible bachelor they had stalked through the aisles of the Stater Bros. supermarket during the week and then charmed into attending an alfresco supper.

Dusty usually hit it off with whomever Peter and Rod had foisted on him, but he made it clear to all that he wasn't ready or interested in reentering the dating world. This didn't stop his pals from keeping their eyes and ears open for potential matrimonial mates, however.

Given their computers, faxes, cell phones, and video conferencing capability, Peter and Rod's public relations firm in Beverly Hills didn't require that they ever leave Palm Springs. They worked out of The Hacienda. Even though their clients were a Who's Who of film, television, and recording stars, there was seldom a need to venture into what they considered the Calcutta of the West: Hollywood! Dusty, too, began to resent having to return to the city on Sundays. He would much rather stay in Palm Springs. But his work schedule was such that he had to be in town daily for meetings, writing speeches and press re-leases, and holding the Religious Right at bay. His life in the city also made it difficult to maintain more than telephone or e-mail contact with the guys with whom Peter and Rod attempted to match him.

Then one balmy Saturday night in the Springs, Dusty bumped into Stuart Richards at the home of magazine publisher billionaire Hershel Moses. Moses was throwing a party at his estate in Rancho Mirage, in honor of his friend Barry Manilow.

The scene between Dusty and Stuart played similarly to their first meeting. Dusty was talking to Peter beside the pool. Suddenly, Stuart appeared by his side. Dusty was surprised because, as he admitted presently, he had just that morning asked Peter, "Whatever happened to Stuart?"

"A new book and a long promotional tour," Stuart answered.

"Just for your reference," Peter said to Stuart, "Dusty's no longer with Chad. And he's down here most weekends. Why don't we all get together?"

"I've been pretty occupied," Stuart said, almost as if he hadn't heard a word Peter had spoken. "I want you to meet Jeremy."

From a few paces behind Stuart a young man in his early twenties approached. He was totally West Hollywood: tight jeans that hugged his perfect ass; a dark T-shirt a size too small, which made obvious his well-pumped muscles. A portion of a tattoo peeked out from the short sleeve of the left arm of his shirt. His attire was completely inappropriate for the current affair, but most of the guests seemed quite appreciative of Stuart's eye candy.

"Nice to meet you, Jeremy," Dusty said with a wide smile, being the first to give his blessing to the couple.

"Likewise," Jeremy said without a trace of a smile, as he swallowed the last of his flute of champagne. "Think I'll grab another," he said to Stuart, making an excuse to immediately leave the clique. As Jeremy wended his way around the pool, the eyes of everyone he passed followed him toward a catering server at the far end of the property.

"Was that a Beavis moment, or what?" Peter joked.

"Yeah. The bar's right behind us," Dusty said. "What gives?"

Stuart shrugged. "He does as he pleases."

Dusty offered to Stuart, "I'm really excited to see you again. I never forgot our last conversation. I've thought of you a lot, truth be known."

"Me, too," Stuart said.

"What about the new book? Sorry I haven't kept up with the latest releases. What's the title?"

"*Too Late to Forget You,*" Stuart said.

"Apropos," Dusty said, giving Stuart a look he hoped expressed both lust and affection.

"It's just out. I'll send you a copy."

"Oh, no," Dusty countered. "I have to support your sales. But I will ask you to inscribe it for me."

"I'd be honored."

Peter jumped in. "We're having a little repast next Saturday at The Hacienda to celebrate the publication of Isabel Sanford's new autobiography, *Movin' On—Down*. She just retained us. Horrible book, but it's filled with juicy gossip about Sherman Hemsley, Marla Gibbs, and Norman Lear. Stuart, we'd love it if you—and Jeremy, too, of course—could drop by. The local literati'll be there. Probably a lot of people you know. What do you say?"

"Sounds great," Stuart said with more enthusiasm than he'd displayed since arriving. Then a light in his eyes went out. "I'll have to check with Jeremy's schedule. He's fussy about our weekends. It was pulling teeth to get him here. The carrot was the possibility that David Hasselhoff would be attending. Jeremy thinks he'd be right for a role on *Baywatch*."

"Is that series still on?" Dusty asked, amazed.

"Reruns. He doesn't know the diff," Stuart said.

"So, Jeremy's an actor?" Rod piped in.

"Wannabe," Stuart explained.

"Any roles we may have seen him perform?" Peter asked, thinking he looked familiar. Most likely from an Encounter Productions porn video or two.

"Possibly," Stuart said. "*The Butler Did It*," he said facetiously. "As a matter of fact, he's currently onstage and getting raves. See?" he said, cocking his head in the direction where Jeremy had faded into the crowd.

All three men looked past groups of the rich and famous—mostly rich—who were grazing on canapés to where Jeremy was flirting with a guy no older than himself. They observed what appeared to be a deep conversation, Jeremy and the newcomer knocking back flutes of champagne as though their host might imminently run out of Cristal. Dusty was uncomfortable for Stuart.

"He's certainly handsome enough to be on a soap," Dusty acknowledged. "Does he have talent?"

"When you look like that, talent's not part of the equation," Peter interjected.

"He is awfully good-looking, isn't he?" Stuart admitted. "And he does have, as they say, 'A talent to amuse.' If you get my drift."

"So, you guys are 'lovers'?" Dusty finally asked.

Stuart snorted. "Isn't it obvious?"

"I'm just a tad obtuse about some things. How long?"

"Six weeks, maybe five centuries. Who knows? Seems more like centuries though. I'm no longer sure about anything." Stuart's voice was now distant, as if he were under interrogation, trying to remember the specific facts of a crime scene to which he was the sole witness.

"He seems great," Dusty said not very convincingly, with Peter immediately chiming in with, "Oh, absolutely. Great. And we're really happy for you, Stuart!"

Dusty sighed. "Now that my dance card is empty, yours is filled. But if you ever need to be kidnapped, Peter and Rod have my number."

Stuart simply nodded in appreciation, obviously recognizing what had been *his* pick-up line.

As word spread that Barry Manilow had agreed to sing a few songs, the crowd assembled inside the great hall of the estate. Dusty, Peter, and Rod were unable to find a seat by the time the impromptu program began, so they stood together. Dusty was a huge admirer of Barry Manilow. To his thinking there were only two pop recording stars of the '70s: Dusty Springfield and Barry. Mentioning this didn't often score him any points, if he made the mistake of announcing it while in casual conversation. Not ordinarily starstruck, he could hardly believe he was in someone's private home, in Palm Springs, with Barry only a few feet away from him, playing "I Write the Songs."

Although he could hardly take his eyes off Barry, who still looked great—Dusty also scanned the room for Stuart, whom he eventually discovered leaning against a marble Ionic column. Stuart looked uncomfortable and lost. There was no sign of Jeremy.

The program concluded with a long medley and, after thunderously appreciative applause, the evening quickly ended. A receiving line had been casually arranged for guests to thank their host and their entertainer before departing for the night. A swell of tuxedoed men and their partners waited outside the house for the valet to find their cars and deliver them to the porte-cochère.

As Dusty and his pals were waiting for their vehicle, they noticed Stuart up ahead, giving the valet a tip and driving away—alone.

"What do you make of that?" Dusty said *sotto voce*.

"Jeremy must have found something—or someone—else to do," Peter said.

"It's this damn desert air," Rod said. "It makes guys horny as hell." He rubbed a hand up and down the back of Peter's tux jacket to make his point. Peter smiled.

Dusty frowned. "He doesn't deserve the sort of treatment Jeremy gave him tonight."

"Oh, I think he does," Rod said. "He's rich, he's famous, he's talented, but he doesn't value himself. He really doesn't know how great he is."

"I had the feeling he was insecure," Dusty said. "In a way, it's kind of refreshing. But it makes him an easy target for guys like Jeremy. Hell, I don't even know Jeremy, but he seems like some aberrant species from a documentary on *Animal Planet*. Although maybe I shouldn't cast aspersions."

"Go ahead and cast," Rod chuckled.

"Let me know when Stuart's free again," Dusty said.

"It may be right now," Rod said.

Just then, Peter's Rolls Royce arrived. The three men said their good-byes to the few people they knew who were still waiting for their cars.

For a time, as Peter's elegant vehicle slowly moved down the long driveway, the men were quiet. Finally, out on Frank Sinatra Drive, Peter called to the backseat, "Darling? I think it's time to start dating again."

Rod agreed. "If Stuart had been alone, you would have gone home with him. Am I right, or am I right? I could see it in your eyes—and his."

For a long moment there was silence, until Dusty finally admitted, "Probably. It's definitely time to take myself out of the cedar chest, iron out the wrinkles, and cough up those mothballs. Anyone have a mint? I can smell mildew on my breath."

"Oh, God," Rod said. "She sounds like Barbra in *Hello, Dolly!* begging Ephraim for permission to marry Walter Matthau!"

"Dead, you know," Peter added about one half of the Odd Couple.

"Pul-ease!" Dusty laughed. "Tell you what, find out about Stuart's relationship. And the next time you find someone who you think I might like, or vice versa, I promise to make an effort to get something going. Any thoughts for next week's Isabel Sanford soirée?"

Peter and Rod chuckled. "We'll think of something," they said in unison.

Chapter Four

Once Dusty made the decision to start dating again, it suddenly seemed that eager and sexy men were more abundant than badly made Hollywood movies released in January. He suddenly became aware of great-looking guys at the studio, guys at the supermarket, guys at the gym, and guys making eye contact with him at stoplights. It was like a revelation to Dusty, who had never been particularly aware of other men cruising him. It was as if some late-blooming pheromones had finally kicked in. He was like a profusion of pollen exploding from a field of goldenrod, saturating the air in springtime. And he was very much enjoying his newfound popularity. The decision to say "yes" instead of making excuses about being too busy for a social life changed his entire perspective about sex.

Dusty had long had a secret desire to sleep with a different man every night for a month, just to enjoy the full range of possibilities. He wanted to know what it would be like to go wild in a candy store of diverse sexual activities and then make a decision, based on experience, about what he really wanted from another man. When guys asked him, "What are you into, man?" Dusty didn't know. His few-and-far-between dalliances usually consisted of him and a partner jacking each other off. Once when he was in college, he went crazy and 69'd with a guy in his dorm room.

Then along came Chad.

Chad was twice Dusty's age, but his physical good looks, charm, sophistication, and, Dusty admitted, his money, were alluring. After only a few perfunctory dates, Chad invited Dusty to move in with him. At the time, Dusty was too naïve to realize that *he*, Dusty, was the catch, not the other way around. Living in L.A. there were plenty of men with Chad's credentials who could have offered Dusty the kind of relationship he claimed to want. But he had accepted the first offer—from Chad.

And so Dusty, now newly adventurous, decided to take a sort of *National Geographic* expedition of the "Undiscovered World of Homosexual Sex." He was more than willing to accept offers from a range of guys: younger, older, straight but curious, and anything in between. He wanted to experience it all, and he quickly filled up his calendar for the month—with the exception of his weekends in Palm Springs, which were reserved for any make or model Peter and Rod had selected for him to test drive.

After the first two weeks of meeting guys for dinner and ending the evening at his condo or their house or apartment, Dusty thought he'd seen it all. There was Michael—lean and hairy and well hung, but passionless. Roger, the carpenter, was deeply tanned from outdoor labor, and had sexy tattoos on his strong arms and chest, but he pounded Dusty's ass as though he were driving spikes into cement. Ray was a tad overweight, but he had a tongue that tasted like peppermint. But he was also boring, and he talked incessantly about innovative ways of obtaining frequent flyer miles. Jerry was black and endowed with a cock whose head seemed to reach halfway up his sternum when he pulled it up and over the waist of his blue jeans. Dusty enjoyed the novelty of trying to play sword swallower, but there was no way he'd let Jerry attempt to sheath that weapon with his ass. Clark was balding, and he got off only by rimming Dusty. Sandy lay in bed as if he was in a coma, making Dusty do all the work. All were pretty much disappointments. A second date with any of them was never a question. Dusty began to wonder how on earth the right guys ever connected with each other!

Then, at last, the mountain came to Muhammad.

* * *

Dusty was at LAX preparing to fly north for a one-day meeting in San Francisco. While waiting to board the plane, which was delayed because of fog, the unwashed masses of humanity crowding the terminal like Main Street at Disneyland suddenly, for Dusty, faded to black—with the exception of one man.

As umpteen passengers griped and swore at airline personnel, a pink pinspot of light seemed to illuminate one lone guy. Dusty's eyes were drawn back to him time and time again, the way one's vision is magnetized to Fourth of July fireworks exploding in the night sky.

The man looked to be around thirty-fiveish and about five feet nine inches tall. His brown hair was close-cropped, like a dachshund's and looked as though it had been petted a lot. He wore faded blue jeans, a light green T-shirt that, although it showcased his gym-pumped arms and chest, didn't appear to be worn to advertise his endowments. The man carried a red backpack, and he sat on the terminal floor against a large pillar, with his knees drawn to his chest, looking the epitome of Buddhist tranquility.

His countenance alone made him an object of attraction. He was a color slide in the View-Master of life at which Dusty could stare for hours as if seeing postcard-perfect sights of El Capitan at Yosemite, or a crystal lagoon on Bora Bora. The guy stood out from every other traveler at the airport. He wasn't movie-star handsome, just punishingly sexy—which of course was a purely subjective response from Dusty. The man appeared to be utterly at peace with himself and the time and place in which he existed.

After the marine fog layer finally burned off around the airport, Dusty and his fellow passengers were herded like cattle onto the plane and buckled into their seats. The jet began to taxi down the runway. Then it stopped.

Dusty, a frequent flyer, knew it wasn't uncommon for aircrafts to be lined up on the runway, like a queue of fashion models waiting to strut the latest Paris haute couture. After a few minutes, a voice identified itself as the captain's and made an announcement. "Due to mechanical problems with our number two engine, we'll be returning to the terminal until the situation is resolved. Thank you for your patience and understanding."

During the ensuing five-hour delay, Dusty kept his eye on the man with the red backpack. If he stood up to stretch, or take a walk around the gate area, Dusty's eyes accompanied him. When the announcement finally came to re-board the airplane, Dusty was delighted to hear that rather than waste time seating people by rows the commuter flight would be open seating. Dusty made the snap decision to maneuver his way into sitting next to the man of his—current—dreams.

Dusty succeeded.

Once again buckled in his seat for the flight to San Francisco International, Dusty opened a book and pretended to read as the plane taxied down the runway. From the corner of his eye he saw that the man in the seat beside him was reading Joe Keenan's novel *Blue Heaven*. When the plane was racing down the runway and ready to lift into the air, Dusty leaned closer, pretending to be looking *over* his seatmate and out the window. A musky body scent emanated from the man. Dusty was close enough to feel his warmth radiating like microwaves. He was practically cooking Dusty from the inside out, or at least defrosting his cock.

Once the plane leveled off at cruising altitude, Dusty collected his courage. "Excuse me," he said and leaned over to the man, who turned and smiled, seeming to welcome the diversion. "I never do this, but I've got to say that I've been observing you all morning."

The man's grin widened.

Dusty went on. "What I mean is, I've watched how calm you've been throughout this whole ordeal and I wanted to commend you. You must be anxious as everybody to get to your destination. I've got a meeting myself, that I'm probably going to miss."

"If there's nothing you can do about a situation, there's no need to be moved," the man said. "I just go with the flow, as retarded as that sounds to some."

"No. Not retarded. Enlightened. I take it you saw how most everyone else responded to the delay."

The man gazed into Dusty's eyes. "Aren't you glad we're not like everyone else?" he said in a voice that expressed confidentiality. He smiled a radiant smile that revealed a dimple on his left cheek as well as full lips and straight, gleaming teeth. Dusty's navel ached. At that moment he wanted desperately to know what this man's lips felt like pressed to his own.

"I'm Jon," the man volunteered and held out his hand.

"Dusty."

He reached over and accepted Jon's hand in his own, feeling his firm grip and noticing that Jon's green eyes were looking into his the way men do when they're in deep concentration. Their hands remained clasped a moment longer than necessary.

"I see we're both reading Joe Keenan," Jon said, holding up his copy of *Blue Heaven* and acknowledging Dusty's edition of *Putting On the Ritz*.

"I noticed that too."

"The guy's amazing. Hilarious."

"The episodes he wrote for *Frasier* were the best of the series," Dusty said. "Don't you think?"

For a time they talked and laughed about particular episodes from the show they thought brilliant. Within the first few minutes of their conversation they were like old friends. They discovered mutual interests—reading and swimming, hiking; certain films from Ireland and Britain. They were so engrossed in conversation—picking apart Jennifer Love Hewitt's small talent compared to the greater gifts of Blythe Danner and Kate Nelligan—that the beverage service cart passed by them unnoticed. In what seemed like mere minutes the captain was instructing the flight crew to prepare for landing.

Out of the blue, Jon said, "What are you doing for dinner tonight?"

Dusty's heart leaped. He stammered, "I . . . I'm booked on the six o'clock flight back to LAX."

"We need to get to know each other." It wasn't a question, but a declaration.

Dusty's faced turned bright red. "Somebody once said, 'Don't say why, say why not?!'"

"Sally Bowles?"

"Probably."

As the two slowly deplaned through the jetway, Dusty announced that there was a car and driver waiting for him. "Can I give you a lift anywhere?"

"You already have," Jon said with a grin. "Thanks. I should have a ride waiting too, if they haven't given up on me. Are you seriously interested in dinner? We could meet at Stars. Or . . ." Jon hesitated a moment. "I'm a better chef than at anyplace you'll find in the Bay area. The choice is yours."

Dusty joked, "*Chez Jon?* I hear it's a tough place to get into unless you know somebody."

"I have clout."

"*Chez Jon*, it is, then," Dusty said. "I seem to remember reading about it in *Bon Appetit*. Or was it the InsightOut web site? Sounds great. Let me bring some wine."

"I have a little cellar, but if you'd like to, you're welcome." Jon nodded in appreciation. "I trust you'll find the right ambrosia to go with whatever I'll whip up. Here's my phone and address." He removed a card from his wallet. "Shall we say six-thirty? Or whenever you're available?"

"There's not much I can do to spruce up. I expected this day to end back in Los Angeles."

"Just loosen that tie a little, and you'll be fine."

Dusty reached into the breast pocket of his suit jacket and withdrew a business card holder. "My cell number's on here in case . . ."

"In case I need a strong man to share a heavy load?" Jon smiled. "The only thing I'll change is the shirt I've been wearing all day." Then as if he'd read Dusty's mind, he added, "The *specialité de la maison* is the aperitif—and a fully loaded dessert tray."

They were still discussing the details and imagining their evening together when they finally left the jetway into the terminal.

Just then they noticed an African-American man dressed in a black suit and tie, appropriate for funerals and chauffeurs. He was holding a sign that read *Dusty Hunt*, hand-written in black ink.

Dusty signaled to the man just as he heard squeals from a woman calling, "Jon! Jon!" from a crowd of smiling people welcoming family or friends off the flight.

With a wide smile, Jon waved to acknowledge an attractive woman who appeared to be in her early thirties. He shook Dusty's hand and whispered, "Come over as soon as possible."

"Sure I won't be interrupting your reunion?"

"My sister. We're best friends. She's just kind enough to pick me up. See you in a while."

The driver escorted Dusty through the terminal. Once inside the hired black town car, the driver announced that Dusty's secretary had tracked him down and left a message to call his office. He could use the car phone rather than his cell if he liked, the driver told him, but Dusty automatically flipped open the cell and dialed his assistant's phone number.

"Mr. Greggson's upset because you missed the meeting," his assistant, Ginny, announced.

"He knows it was unavoidable," Dusty explained. "I called ahead to let those f'ing Lions and Lambs for Christ know I might not make it."

"You know Mr. Greggson. He doesn't want excuses. He wants results," she echoed the company line. "Want me to patch you through to him? He's called a dozen times, but your cell was off."

"Go ahead. Spoil an otherwise perfectly wonderful day and let me talk to him."

Once the two men were connected Dusty simply listened to the tirade coming from the other end of the line. At last he responded, "I've explained it was unavoidable, Mr. Greggson," he said in a calm voice. "Another flight on another airline? I suppose I could have tried to arrange that, but there was no way of knowing how long we'd be . . ."

He listened as his boss shouted about Dusty's important job as the liaison to the press and how imperative it had been today for him to smooth ruffled feathers of the heads of this minor league Lions and Lambs religious coalition that was threatening to boycott the studio's films.

"They said they understood the circumstances, sir," Dusty continued. "It's not as though we're ducking them. In fact, I've rescheduled for next week. It also buys us more time to . . . Look, I'll get a note from the airline if it makes you feel any better. No, sir, I'm not being sarcastic. But with all due respect I think you're overreacting. When have I ever missed a meeting before? Yes, I'll see you when I get in. Good-bye, sir."

"Busting your chops, is he?" the driver said. "Sorry, I couldn't help but overhear."

Dusty sighed. "I was a no-show at an important powwow because the flight was delayed. A room full of Donald Wildmon clones just aching for some free publicity by harassing our film product. Won't he be surprised—and lost—when I resign and accept another offer. Could we go straight to the hotel?"

"The Renaissance, right?"

"Is that where my assistant booked me?"

"She called me earlier with those very instructions, anticipating that since you were arriving late and would probably miss the meeting, she didn't want you to be stuck waiting for another flight back if you were too tired. She's top-notch."

"Yeah. A regular Gunny Bricker. Couldn't do my job without her." Dusty thought of something. "By the way, is the hotel anywhere near."— he pulled out the card Jon had given him and looked at the address— "Sea Cliff?"

"Fancy!" the driver exclaimed. "That's way up in the hills. Great views of Alcatraz and, on a clear day, Angel Island. Primo property. My mother worked up there for the Gettys, until Danielle Steel absconded with her."

"How long will it take to get there from the hotel?"

"Depending on traffic, an hour."

Dusty looked at his watch. It was already half-past four. "Could you call your dispatcher and see if you could arrange to wait for me at the hotel while I change and then you, personally, drive me there? You won't have to stay. I just need to be there as quickly as possible."

"Not a problem, sir. What time are you expected?"

"I'd like to arrive no later than six-thirty."

"Shouldn't be a problem. Just check in and do what you have to do as quickly as possible. We can make it, no sweat."

At that moment, Dusty's cell phone rang. It was Ginny again. "Sorry to bother you, Dusty, but Mr. Greggson's being an asshole, excuse my language. He wants to know what flight you're coming back on tonight because he wants to see you, regardless of the time."

Dusty took a deep breath. "I've decided not to come back tonight. Tell him it's been an exhausting day and I just want to check into my hotel and get some rest. Thanks, by the way, for the reservation. I'll see him in the morning."

"He's not going to like this, Dusty. He's been mean as spit all day."

Dusty sighed. "Put me through again."

Dusty wailed. Then, "Mr. Greggson," he said, "is there something we can discuss now, or after I've checked into the hotel? I'm sure you can understand that this has been a very nerve-wracking day for me. I'm drained. Sir, I don't think there are any more flights out tonight. Yes, sir. Yes. I'll see what I can do. I'll get back to you. Ginny, are you still on the line?"

"Yes, Dusty."

"Do me a favor. Call Alaska and United." Then he added in a whisper, "Call me back with news that there are no more seats available tonight on any carrier, but book me on something noonish tomorrow, okay? I'll get in touch with the boss myself and let him know I'm stuck here."

"You really want me to lie, Dusty?"

"Of course not. Sorry. If there really is an available seat I'll take it. But please, God, don't let there be anything until tomorrow."

"I think someone's got special plans," Ginny sang.

"You have no idea," he said with the lilt of someone soaking in a warm bubble bath of romance. "Call me as soon as you can, okay?"

When he hung up, the driver said, "Here's an idea. If your assistant gets you a seat, you can just use the excuse that you're too far from the airport now. Which is true. With traffic and such, it'll take you another hour and a half to get back there. All this damn construction and stuff. It's time that will be wasted, when you could be doing other company business. Also, you'll probably have to forfeit at least some part of the hotel tariff for late cancellation."

Dusty thanked the driver for his concern. Within five minutes the cell phone rang again. "Hi, Ginny. Oh, fuck! And why's it so important that I get back tonight? What's with this guy? Would you call him on the other line while I hold and tell him I'm nearly at the hotel and there's no way for me to return to the airport in time for that flight. Also, tell him the company will have to pay for my hotel room whether I use it or not. I'll hold."

When Ginny came back on the line, she said, "Dusty, I have Mr. Greggson for you."

"Yes, sir?" Dusty rolled his eyes. "I know this isn't a pleasure trip, sir. Trust me, being delayed for five hours is no picnic. With all due respect again, sir, I'm so far into the city now that I'll probably miss that flight too. No, sir, I'm not being difficult. I'm simply explaining that the time and logistics are prohibitive. My driver tells me there's no way to make that last flight. Yes, sir. I'll see what I can do. See you later, sir."

"Tough luck!" the driver exclaimed. "Now you can't make that date with the backpack guy."

Dusty laughed. "You're pretty observant! I'm sorry, I haven't even asked your name."

"Reggie," he said.

Dusty unbuckled his seat belt and leaned forward, extending his hand into the front seat. Reggie took his right hand off the steering wheel and shook Dusty's hand.

Dusty said, "Thanks for being so understanding. Now, where can we get a couple of bottles of really good red wine?"

"I know just the place."

"I smell a big tip for you, Reggie," Dusty said.

"All in a day's work, sir. Ah, here we are, sir, The Renaissance."

"Call me Dusty."

"Dusty. Okay, check in. Jump in the shower, lose the tie, unbutton the collar, and be back here within half an hour if you can. I'll get you to Sea Cliff as fast as possible."

Dusty smiled at Reggie, as a hotel porter dressed in a burgundy uniform with gold epaulets opened the door to the car. "I'll be back down in a flash," he said.

"We've got time," Reggie called out before the door closed.

Chapter Five

Dusty's room in the club section of the hotel was as lavishly decorated as a colonial home in Connecticut, complete with hunting prints on the walls.

He quickly undressed. The pristine bathroom had floor-to-ceiling mirrors. Dusty studied himself for a moment. He acknowledged that the private physical fitness trainer he'd hired after his break-up had helped give him the shape he'd always wanted but somehow could never achieve even with devoutly strenuous workouts on his own.

"Fuck you, Chad," he said, a statement that came from out of nowhere. He hadn't thought of Chad in weeks, and his own voice startled him. Why was he thinking of Chad just before a date with a man who'd aroused him merely by smiling—and divining his lascivious thoughts?

Then, just as suddenly, he announced, "I hope someday you find out what you're missing," as if Chad were within earshot and could see how much Dusty's previously boyish body had been transformed into something most other gay men would find more than acceptable.

He turned on the shower and adjusted the hot and cold until it had reached its ideal temperature. Stepping into the tub, the refreshing water came lashing down from the chrome showerhead. He stood under the flow until his skin was bright pink. Then he tore the paper off a small bar of soap and lathered himself from toes to forehead. He then reached for a washcloth and added shampoo from a little plastic bottle and washed his ass.

After rinsing off, he stepped out of the shower into a completely foggy room. He reached for a towel and then opened the bathroom door to let cool air surge in to quickly dissipate the steam clouding the mirror. He dried himself then removed the complimentary toiletry kit from a wicker basket which contained a small toothbrush and a tube of Colgate that was not much larger than the head of the brush itself. He hoped there was also a complimentary bottle of cologne or at least anti-perspirant, but neither was included in the kit. At least there was a one-swish-only size bottle of Scope.

He redressed and, as Reggie had suggested, he left the first three buttons of his now-wrinkled white dress shirt undone, which revealed a sparse crop of chest hair. He had practically made record time for his ablutions—twenty minutes from check-in to redressing. Dusty was definitely in a hurry, but he made certain he had his hotel key, his wallet, money, and the card with Jon's address, which he kissed like a gambler smooching dice for Lady Luck. Dusty left the room, hurried down the carpeted hall and stairs rather than wait for the elevator, and headed out of the hotel. Reggie, anticipating his arrival, was standing by the opened back door of the town car.

"Off we go," Reggie said, buckling his seat belt and turning on the radio to a classical music station. "But first, a wine that will impress your host. If he's a connoisseur of the better things, and considering his tony address I'd bet he is, he'll know Silver Oak Cabernet, or a nice Heitz Martha's Vineyard." Thinking aloud, Reggie said, "That's not from Massachusetts, despite the name. I think Heitz's wife was named Martha." He was quiet for a moment, then added, "You wouldn't want to bring anything Gallo is trying to foist off on an unsuspecting public!"

"No *Turning Leaf*!" Dusty laughed "I want the best for tonight. Let's find the Silver Oak, or Martha Plimpton, or whatever."

As the car slowly ascended, winding its way up Pacific Crest Drive, high above the city, Dusty decided to call Peter and Rod with his news.

"Reggie," Dusty said, "will it bother you if I make a personal call that might sound a little, shall we say a little like a conversation between . . ."

"Chatty Cathies?"

Dusty laughed in agreement.

"We're on the same team, Dusty. But I won't hear a word. I'll be concentrating on finding this address, and Vivaldi on the radio."

"I feel a little self-conscious."

"I think we know each other well enough by now, Dusty." Reggie chuckled.

Dusty flipped open his cell phone and dialed the familiar number in Palm Springs. The answering machine clicked on with its same old message. He said, "Guys! Guys! If you're there, pick up. It's Dusty."

Click.

"Dusty!" It was Peter's voice. "Sorry. We get so many solicitations at night we have to monitor our calls. What's up?"

"I've met someone!"

"As in 'him Tarzan, you Jane?'"

"As in 'him Perfect, me in Shock.'"

"Lord almighty! Let me get Rod on the other line!"

Dusty could hear Peter yelling into another room for his lover to pick up an extension. He finally heard a click. Peter said, "Mother, it's your incorrigible son calling."

Rod chirped, "Dusty, darling! What's going on, pal?"

"I'm in San Francisco! It was supposed to be business, but it's metamorphosed to Cinderella at the Palace!"

"Not to be confused with Judy at the Palace," Peter joked.

"That too! Everything wrapped into one big life-altering event!"

"Are you saying we're ga-ga over someone?" Peter added.

"Since real words can't describe what I'm going through, ga-ga sums up everything."

"Details, details," Peter said.

"Think of the lyrics to the song, *One*, from *A Chorus Line*. I'm in a car right now, on my way to Singular Sensation's house for dinner!"

"You don't even know him!" Rod piped in. "You haven't even tried on the glass slipper. It might not fit! Plus, you unfledged thing, all first dates should be in a well-lighted restaurant. You know the rules!"

Dusty countered, "We were going to a restaurant, but he twisted my arm with the promise of something 'whipped up' at home."

"Your shoulder's in a sling from the dislocation, I presume?" Rod offered.

"No doubt the main course is animal, rather than plant or mineral," Peter chirped. "What's his name? What's he do? Which kingdom are his people from? Does he have a tiara or a crown? How long is his scepter?"

"Peter, you sound like a yenta!" Rod said. Then, back to Dusty, "So, what's his name? What's he do? *Does* he have magic wand?"

"Jon. His name's Jon. I hardly know any more about him than what I've just told you. But we're like just the right combination of vowels and consonants that bring big prizes on *Wheel of Fortune*! You know me. I don't *do* this. Which means . . ."

"You're either in lust or in love," Peter finished the sentence.

"We were both reading Joe Keenan, for crying out loud!"

"*Blue Heaven* or *Ritz*?" Peter asked. "This is the only thing your damaged gaydar has tracked since Chad?"

"There was Stuart, but we were never simultaneously available."

"Then I can see why you'd confuse Keenan with a burning bush as a sign that you two were destined for the Promised Land of love."

Dusty insisted, "You're kidding, but that's exactly what I'm trying to say. I think it is love at first sight. Not that I've ever believed in love at first sight."

"Maybe you're just especially horny tonight," Peter offered.

"Or the moon's in your seventh house," Rod suggested. "Whatever that means. We're just really happy for you, Dusty. You'll have to bring him over on Saturday."

"He lives here in San Francisco," said Dusty. "Depending on how the date goes, perhaps I can coax him down to the Springs."

"San Francisco!" Rod bellowed. "I hope you're not thinking of abandoning us for the Castro!"

"Of course not! I just wanted to share my good news with you. Oh, and in case he's more Ivan the Terrible than Richard the Lionhearted, and I'm cut up into bite-size tasty morsels and ground into a can of meat by-products for Alpo, here's his address and phone number. If you don't hear from me again, I'm either dead or in heaven."

"Or both," Peter and Rod said simultaneously.

Dusty read them the information from Jon's card, just as the car pulled up to a high wooden fence covered in creeping fig, with an arched entry door cut into the center.

"Holy smokes, guys, I'm at the palace. Looks like he's rich, too! He's at the very top of Sea Cliff! Can't tell from out here, but I'll bet the view is to die for. Listen, I'll be back in the office tomorrow. I'll call you then."

The three said good-bye, with Peter and Rod wishing Dusty good luck.

"Here we are, Dusty," Reggie announced. "It's been a pleasure."

"You've been incredibly swell, Reggie. Let me give you my card. If you're ever in Southern California, let me know. We can have dinner or something. You're a pal."

Collecting his bottles of wine, Dusty reached into the breast pocket of his suit coat and withdrew his wallet. His hands were shaking from nervousness. "Here's a little something extra for your efforts."

"A hundred dollars? I was just doing my job."

"And a good job should be rewarded! Now wish me luck."

"You have my positive vibrations for a life filled with health, wealth, happiness, and love."

"Thanks, Reggie."

Dusty stepped out of the car and closed the door behind him. Once again he looked at the number on the gate. It matched the card. He looked at his wristwatch. Six forty-five. The sun was setting.

The gate didn't have a doorbell, or a brass knocker or an intercom system. Instead, there was an old-fashioned bell with a pull chain dangling from a rusting decorative iron arm. Dusty pulled on the metal links, which made the bell toll an F-sharp.

Within moments, the gate opened. Jon was standing on the opposite side of the fence wearing the warm smile Dusty had hoped for. "Perfect timing. Any trouble finding the place?"

"No problems. I had a great driver."

Jon beckoned, and Dusty stepped through the opened portal onto a carpet of grass in a landscaped yard. The house was huge, a perfectly maintained '60s contemporary glass box. The lights on the inside were dimmed to enhance a plethora of candles that could be seen throughout a spacious common room. "Come on in," Jon said.

"A little something," Dusty said, presenting Jon with the wine bottles.

After a quick examination of the labels Jon said, "You certainly know your wines, Mr. Sexy. It's impossible! I couldn't have told you that Heitz was my absolute favorite. I'll open it and let it breathe for a few minutes. In the meantime, why don't you go out on the deck and look at the sunset? The moon's rising. It's full tonight."

Dusty followed Jon as far as the kitchen area, then went on his own through the house to the opposite wall of twenty feet of tall glass panes. "Must be hard to keep this glass clean with all the rain and salt air," Dusty called, making small talk.

"Kind of. I've got it down to a science." Jon was removing the foil cap and cork from the bottle as expertly as a sommelier.

"He does windows too," Dusty deadpanned. "I figured you'd need to have a crew come to do the work."

"Nah. I'm very domestic. I actually enjoy the challenge."

"Wa-hoo!" Dusty exclaimed when he got to the door leading to the deck and looked out. By now, Jon had sidled up to Dusty and opened the sliding glass door. He took Dusty by the hand and led him onto a wide redwood deck. At first Dusty was a bit nervous to go near the wood railing. "How high up are we?" he asked.

"Practically the highest spot overlooking the Bay." Jon motioned, as if giving a docent's tour of the panorama. "You're in luck tonight. It's clear. The lights below will be spectacular." He pointed. "There's the Golden Gate Bridge of course, and Alcatraz, Angel Island in the distance; and over there is Marin County, Sausalito, and Tiburon. Many times, all I can see are the two 700-foot-high towers of the Bridge sticking up when the fog is low. When it's like that, you feel like you're in an airplane looking down. You can hear the deep mellow tones of the foghorns located around the Bay."

Dusty was mesmerized by the sound of Jon's own deep mellow tones. His voice was sexy and masculine.

"Better hold my hand," Jon cautioned. "I don't want you jumping over to get a better view, or ending up like Norman Neal Williams investigating poor ol' Mrs. Madrigal! If only he hadn't been wearing that damn clip-on tie, Laura Linney could have saved his blackmailing ass instead of him falling over the cliff!"

Dusty and Jon laughed simultaneously, acknowledging the scene from *Tales of the City*.

"You're the only view I see," Dusty said. "The way I feel, I'd scale this vertiginous hillside or the Chateau D'If to reach you."

"He's literary, too," Jon cried into the air, as if to an audience hundreds of feet below. "Vertiginous, eh?" he repeated to Dusty. "Sounds sexy. I know what it means, but I've never had a date who used it in a declarative sentence! And no date has ever mentioned Dumas!"

The two men faced each other, staring into the other's eyes. "I'm so glad you invited me," Dusty said in a whisper.

"I'm glad you hustled to take the seat beside me. I had to shoo away two other passengers while waiting for you."

"You were expecting . . . ?"

"Hoping."

Dusty laughed. "God, I'm such an open book!"

Jon leaned in and placed his lips onto Dusty's. The men let go of each other's hands and enfolded each other in their arms. There was heat from their lips, and their ravenous tongues fought one another in a kind of wrestling match.

Still inhaling each other's exhalation, Dusty broke the embrace. He moved his hands to hold the treasure of Jon's face. Dusty could hear the waves of the Pacific Ocean crashing far below them.

"God, Dusty!" Jon said, panting, "You're a dream that I pray I don't wake from! You taste *so* good!"

"I've always been looking for you, Jon," Dusty returned. "I just didn't know it until I saw you. You're all I've thought about this entire day. I've had a non-stop hard-on since before take-off."

Jon grinned as he pulled Dusty's hand down to the crotch of his jeans. "I've been hard since you leaned over my seat *pretending* to watch the earth disappear below the plane!"

"The earth *did* disappear, the moment I saw you. But," he asked coyly, "was I that obvious?"

Jon chuckled. "I'm afraid so. Even inside the terminal. But you were so armored in your Brooks Brothers uniform that I was afraid I'd have to make the first move."

"Would you have?"

"If you'd passed by my seat, I was prepared to reach out and tug at your sleeve and say, 'This one's available,' hoping you'd take the bait. My line was going to be really stupid. 'Oh, I see we have the same taste in books.'"

"Mine was going to be equally inane. 'Excuse me, have you read his other stuff?'"

Both men laughed again. They then took a long hard look at each other. "It's that old devil moon," Jon said, pointing to the sky. His smile morphed into a dimpled grin. "The wine should be ready," he said. "Shall we?"

"I've been ready all my life," Dusty said solemnly.

"For the wine?" Jon teased.

"For you," Dusty said. "For this feeling of inebriation."

"Come inside. It's getting chilly. I'll light a fire. Sit back and relax. Do you have a favorite style of music you'd like me to play?"

"Surprise me."

"My choices aren't very hip. I was born before my time. Ella. Lady Day. Doris Day. All the Days, except perhaps Dennis," he joked. "A singer or a piece of music has to speak to my soul, otherwise it's just noise. Silence can be just as fulfilling. I'll put on what I like and you tell me if you want something else. You're my guest. I can accommodate almost anything but hip-hop and that queer bashing Eminem, or the noise of LL Cool J or whatever his name is. I know they're famous and I should be more up on pop culture, but I'm sorta stuck in a time warp. I know what I like."

Jon seemed able to do a dozen things simultaneously. While serving the wine he placed three CDs on the stereo's carousel, lit a match to strike a fire in the gas fireplace, then turned on the oven. He sat beside Dusty on the living room sofa just as Karen Carpenter's voice issued from the speakers.

"No way!" Dusty exclaimed. " 'I Can Dream, Can't I?' The *Horizon* album! Perfect!"

Jon looked at Dusty in amazement. "Neither of us are supposed to be old enough to know the Carpenters, let alone this album! What are you, a veteran *Name that Tune* champion? No one else I know would have recognized this song."

"I'm not just anyone," Dusty said in a tone of voice that made it clear he wanted Jon to realize he was special. "I'm a voice that speaks to your soul. And yours to mine, too."

Jon took another sip of wine, set his glass on the coffee table in front of the sofa, and took Dusty's glass and placed it beside his.

Then he leaned over and embraced Dusty. Their lips locked and Dusty held Jon's face with both hands.

By the time the next song began, Eydie Gormé's *Don't Go to Strangers*, Jon had maneuvered his body into another position, pulling Dusty on top of him. He began unbuttoning Dusty's shirt.

Dusty simultaneously reached for the bottom of Jon's T-shirt, which he pulled up over his arms and head. Dusty was stunned at the sight of Jon's smooth muscular chest. He was everything Dusty had ever fantasized about in another man—only better. His skin was velvety and Marine Corps-solid all at once.

Jon quickly helped Dusty remove his own shirt, and the two of them rolled onto the floor, which was cushioned by a plush, palace-sized oriental rug. They lay one on top of the other, their bare flesh pressing into the other's like artists kneading and molding clay. The sensation was unlike anything Dusty had ever experienced. He couldn't control himself from exploring every centimeter of Jon's body.

They took turns licking each other's chests, underarms, necks, navels, and stomachs. Surely, Dusty thought, this must be the feast for which *Chez Jon* was most famous. The cuisine couldn't have been more sumptuous.

When the CD carousel switched to A *Brand New Me* by Dusty's namesake, Springfield, Jon whispered, "Let's go to bed."

He stood up. The outline of his cock was prominent in his jeans, as was Dusty's in his slacks. Jon reached for Dusty's hand and pulled him up off the floor. They picked up their wineglasses.

As they passed through the kitchen, Jon surreptitiously turned knobs on the oven and stove to prevent food from burning. He grabbed the half-empty bottle of wine and led Dusty to a room with many lighted candles. Dusty hardly noticed the spectacular display of lights from the cities, and from boats dotting the bay far below the house. However, he did notice the massive handcarved four-poster bed.

"Copied from one at the Hearst Castle," Jon whispered. "Something big—to play in."

Both men quickly shed their remaining clothes and climbed onto their playground. They embraced and began making love—slowly building to a crescendo of uncontrollable ecstasy.

To Dusty it was as if some long-held inhibitions were freed from more than three decades of shackles.

The next eight hours were spent in dimensions of the mind and body where nothing and no one other than themselves existed. They wrestled, soaking themselves in each other's perspiration, exploring every sinewy fiber of muscle and every inch of skin that the other had to offer. Each time they climaxed, it was more powerful and fulfilling than the time before. They had the mutual desire and stamina to continue until just before dawn.

"This is what's called 'making love,'" Dusty heard a loud voice in his head repeating over and over.

"Is it you?" Jon wanted to say aloud, Jane Seymour's line when she meets Christopher Reeve while strolling along the lake in *Somewhere in Time*. Instead, he expressed his staggering attraction to Dusty in non-verbal cries and voracious sexual needs.

Chapter Six

Dusty's taxi ride from Sea Cliff to the San Francisco International airport was melancholy. After a marathon night of sex, a breakfast that consisted of the meal originally prepared for the night before, and the prospect of returning to "the real world," Dusty was morose. He absolutely hated to leave Jon. Figuratively, the clock had struck midnight. A long, passionate kiss good-bye affirmed their continued mutual adoration for each other. The spell that occurred between the two of them last night was not to be shattered. They had more than just a one-night lover's waltz between them. They were both assured of that. It was the beginning of a new life, for each of them.

Back in Los Angeles, Dusty picked up his car at the airport's short-term parking lot. Stopping by his condo, he quickly shaved, showered, and dressed in another business suit. He was in his office by three o'clock, and was finished being bawled out by Mr. Greggson by 3:20.

Dusty sat patiently throughout Greggson's tirade, tuning out the geezer's vitriol by replaying his night of passion with Jon and knowing that if this stupid diatribe was what he had to pay for his awesome encounter with Jon, it was worth the price. He also thought about the job offer from the Palm Springs Chamber of Commerce and how pleasant it would be to turn the tables and upset Greggson with an acceptance of the new position.

Fortunately, it was also Thursday. Tomorrow he'd head back to Palm

Springs for the weekend and, more important, Jon had agreed to fly down and join him.

Presently, ensconced in his office, Dusty closed the door so he could call Peter and Rod. "Mind if I bring a guest this weekend?" Dusty asked, when Peter answered the phone.

"Who?" Peter asked coyly.

"You know who. And I know you're gasping to meet the man who's changed my life. He's coming into Palm Springs airport tomorrow night. We'll be at your place by eight at the latest. If that's okay."

"Guess we'll have to turn away our latest acquisition for you," Peter said in mock dejection. "And Ph.D.s in ornithology are so hard to come by in Palm Springs these days."

"I'm officially off the endangered species list." Dusty smiled. "Tell him to fly over to The Crow's Nest. He's bound to find something *foul* over there."

"Fortunately for you, the guest wing of The Hacienda is far enough from our quarters," Peter said. "Otherwise, Rod and I might be peek-ing though keyholes. You'd better check the intercom in the room before you start screwing each other's brains out. Some less-than-benevolent host might take advantage of the situation and glue the intercom speaker button to a permanent 'hold' position in order to hear every disgusting, 'God, oh, God! Don't stop! Harder! You're the man! You're the king! I'm ready. I can't hold it! I'm coming!'"

"Are you through with the juvenile histrionics?" Dusty joked. "I know you're going to love him as much as I do."

"If you guys can tear yourselves out of bed by late afternoon, we're invited to Eddie and Dexter's for a sit-down. They're hoping you'll be there. I'll call and tell 'em to set another plate, and make sure the place cards are arranged so that you and the White Knight are side by side."

"Informal?"

"Come as y'ar, Blanche. You know the drill here in the Springs."

Dusty fled the office at precisely five o'clock Friday evening, praying he wouldn't get a last-minute call from his nefarious boss. He ditched into the men's room, à la Superman in a phone booth, and changed into what he hoped was sexy casual attire in which to meet Jon.

The drive to Palm Springs airport was the usual weekend getaway bumper to bumper, from the 134 in Burbank, out the 10 freeway past Raging Waters and bedroom communities in the San Bernardino area that he couldn't imagine finding himself living in. He'd almost rather die than be stuck in a trailer park in Duarte!

By seven, Dusty was standing in the Alaska Airlines terminal at Palm Springs International, waiting impatiently for Jon to exit the aircraft which had just arrived. With each passenger who came into view through the jetway, Dusty's smile widened. He knew that Jon had to be next.

Next came and went. As did Next. And Next.

The yellow rose wrapped in cellophane with a couple of sprigs of baby's breath that Dusty had in his hand as a token offering to Jon seemed to be wilting as he waited . . . and waited. Dusty stood on tip-toes trying to peer into the tunnel of emerging passengers but there was no sign of Jon. Finally, an airline attendant closed the door.

"Wait a minute," Dusty said, hurrying up to the uniformed Alaska Airlines employee. "Is everybody off the plane?"

"Everyone except the maintenance workers scrubbing the toilets," the woman said, sounding like a very bored Marsha Warfield. "Wanna wait for one of them?"

What could have happened? Dusty nearly cried to himself. He walked over to the monitors that listed arrivals and departures. He checked the flight number that Jon had left as a message with Ginny. Sure enough, beside #128, ETA 7:00, San Francisco/San Jose/Palm Springs, the word ARRIVAL was flashing.

Dusty's heart sank. He sat down in a chair as the custodial crew began vacuuming the carpet.

Should I call him? Dusty thought. *He must have a good reason. I know I wasn't missing any signals. This was a date. Maybe he . . ."*

"I thought you'd given up on me!"

Dusty turned around. "Jon!" he cried, loud enough for anyone remaining in the terminal to hear.

"I thought you prided yourself on punctuality," Jon teased.

"What?" Dusty said, confused and excited. "Yes. I got here just as your plane came in. But you didn't walk off!"

"I was on Flight 281 at six o'clock. I left the message with your secretary."

Dusty rolled his eyes. "I'll kill 'er! Ginny's one flaw is that she's dyslexic. She must have transposed the flight numbers!"

"I should have called your cell. It's my fault."

The two men embraced and kissed passionately, not caring that they were in a public place. "You had me so worried! I thought you'd changed your mind!" Dusty almost sobbed.

Jon smiled. "I felt the same thing when I got off the plane and you weren't waiting for me. Finally I called your office and got the machine. Then I went to the bar, thinking I'd go on standby for the next flight back to SF."

"What made you come back to the gate?"

"A little voice inside my head said to pass this way en route to the ticket counter. I always listen to that voice. It's never steered me wrong." Jon paused. "Gorgeous rose. For me?"

"I'm just so glad you're here," Dusty said, handing him the rose and enfolding his arms around Jon's T-shirt-clad body once again. "Okay, let's get on our way! Any other bags?"

"Nope. Just this carry-on, and something for our hosts."

On the drive into Palm Springs proper, Dusty and Jon held hands and talked non-stop about everything from how gloomy both had felt when Dusty left San Francisco, to the plans for the weekend. Dusty provided bios on his friends Peter and Rod, as well as the other guests expected at tomorrow's dinner party.

"You don't mind my accepting the invitation for us," Dusty said.

"I want to get to know all your friends. Aren't they going to be my friends, too?" Jon replied.

Along the final stretch of road toward The Hacienda the outside temperature was still so warm and the stars above so sharply defined like diamonds on a swatch of black velvet, that Dusty pushed a button to release the convertible top, which folded neatly into a well behind the backseat.

"This is really awesome, Dusty," Jon remarked as he looked up at the stars. "I haven't been down in a decade. I've missed it."

"So you know what you're getting yourself into."

"I do know what I'm getting myself into. Same thing I got myself into the night before last. And I've been counting the minutes."

Dusty grinned, an expression of self-satisfaction. "I'm here practically every weekend. I've come to really love Palm Springs. I'm only in the city for business and I'm seriously considering accepting another job down here."

"It used to be that way for me too," Jon said.

"Did you come down a lot?"

"I lived here. I had a lover who *adored* Palm Springs. Claimed the air was good for his health! So, I bought us a condo in Rancho Mirage. During the week, before I sold my company, I'd stay in his house in West Hollywood. I'd come down Friday night, if I wasn't too swamped, and then drive back late Sunday. Turned out it wasn't just the desert he liked so much. It was what the desert attracted. And I don't mean the tarantulas and scorpions. He turned out to be a snake!"

Jon paused. "There I was, busting my butt to make my business work, supporting this guy, who I admit was a real calendar model—then I find he's spending his days at C.C.B.C., Vista Grande, The 550, Cobalt or Inndulge, those 'clothing optional' places! He was using their gyms and pools and picking up other guys!"

"Sounds like *my* life story," Dusty confessed. "But fortunately, I made great friends with my ex's chums. They got me as part of the package in the divorce settlement."

"Lucky them. When I got away from my *bête noire*, I closed the door on practically everyone we knew together. I ran away and relocated to San Francisco. I'm glad I'm coming back here—with you."

Dusty squeezed Jon's hand in empathy.

Jon sighed. "He sued me for palimony. I settled a big chunk of change out of court and let him keep the Palm Springs place. It was a small price to pay to never have to see him again. But that was so long ago. And if it hadn't happened I would probably never have met you. I always land in clover!"

By eight they were at The Hacienda. "Peter's the one with the mustache, and Rod's the one who everybody says is a dead ringer for Campbell Scott, although I don't see it, myself," Dusty explained.

"Gotcha."

Dusty pressed the intercom button and a crackly voice asked, "Dusty?"

"Vickie Lester will appear!" Dusty announced. "And she's got Norman Maine in tow!" He laughed as the gate slowly opened, like the pages of a story book in a Disney animated fairy tale.

By the time Dusty and Jon parked in front of the house, popped the trunk to retrieve their overnight bags, and walked from the driveway into the garden through a curtain of fine mist that was watering the tropical plants, Peter and Rod were both at the open front door.

"Welcome," they announced in unison.

"Come on in before half the winged creatures of the night join us," Peter said.

Introductions were made, and Dusty noticed immediately that Peter and Rod were telegraphing their mutual approval of Jon, or at least their satisfaction that Dusty hadn't been overreacting to his daz-zling physical appearance.

"I brought you both this," Jon said to the two men. "It's just a wee token. Something to express my appreciation for the invitation to spend the weekend with Dusty at your beautiful home."

"What is this?" Peter asked, as Rod accepted the string-handled bag lined with tissue paper and containing a wrapped present.

"You don't have to open it now," said Jon. "As I said, it's just a token."

"Are you kidding?" Peter pretended condescension. "We *adore* pre-sents! We *live* for them, don't we, baby!" Then, in a stage whisper to Dusty, Peter said, "We love this boy already!"

"Let's take it into the living room and open it along with a bottle of wine," Rod suggested. "Red or white, Jon?"

"Anything. Red if it's available, please."

Presently the men were settled into comfortable plush chairs in the living room/entertainment center of the house, which was furnished like a Connecticut farmhouse, instead of the too-typical (for Palm Springs) desert motif of potted cacti and sun-bleached skulls of cattle that had long ago died of thirst and starvation. No O'Keeffes hanging in this home.

Rod had melted a wedge of Brie in the microwave and topped it with a sauce of sundried tomatoes. He'd placed small, creamy dollops on tiny pieces of toasted pumpernickel and served each of his guests an individual diminutive plate and cocktail napkin. Peter served the wine.

Once they were all seated around a low, antique oak coffee table, Peter demanded in a playful tone, "Open it! Open it!"

"First," Jon said, "may I propose a toast?"

Everyone raised their glasses. "To our wonderful hosts, and to the beautiful man who has allowed me the opportunity to meet his Peter and Rod."

"So you've met his Peter," Rod quipped.

"And his Rod," Peter deadpanned.

"Oh, God, that didn't come out right!" Jon blushed.

"What didn't come out right? Dusty's Peter?" Rod continued.

Peter and Rod and Dusty smiled playfully, and leaned in close together. When the elegant ribbon, wrapping and bow were off a white box with "Valkenbuerg" written in gold script across the top, Peter said in awe, "I know this shop!" He held the box reverentially, making a ceremony out of the procedure, weighing the box, holding it in a way to prove that whatever the contents, it was heavy. "I can't imagine," he said.

"That's your big problem," Rod teased. "You have no imagination. Just open it!"

Peter lifted the lid off the box, he pulled aside more tissue paper, and all three men stared inside.

"My God," Rod breathed.

"It's Lalique!" Peter cried.

Jon nodded. "They had to overnight it from France. It's the only nude sculpture they design with two *men*. I didn't think you'd appreciate the embracing man/woman thing that Macy's has on display."

Dusty smiled and looked at Jon to show he'd selected the most appropriate and extravagant gift imaginable.

As he withdrew the crystal glass sculpture from its box and held it worshipfully, Peter's eyes were as wide as if he'd just seen the most exquisite cock and balls in all of Palm Springs. "I'm speechless," he said. Rod removed the heavy bronze Remington steed from the center of the table and Peter replaced it with this masterpiece of glasswork.

"As I said, it's just a token but I was certain it would be different."

After the surprise expressions of appreciation subsided, and the conversation became more comfortable, Jon started answering Peter and Rod's nosy questions about himself—questions Dusty had never asked.

"I grew up in Switzerland. Had very understanding parents who didn't flip out when I opened the closet door, even though they were with the diplomatic service. Got my master's in biochemistry from Cornell. Did research with the CDC for a few years. Fell in love, or so I thought, and settled down—here in Palm Springs, as a matter of fact, for all of about a minute. Long, boring story there. Left the relationship. Went up to Stanford to study Eastern philosophy. Then patented a little something I cooked up in my home lab, and now it gets prescribed by about a zillion oncologists every day to HIV+ patients. That's me."

"Let me get this straight," Peter said, feigning sardonism. "You're handsome—that's obvious. Well educated. Brilliant. Close to your family . . ."

"My parents are dead. But I have the best sister in the world," Jon amended.

". . . and you're stinking rich! All I can say is, welcome to the family, son!"

All four men simultaneously exploded with laughter, including Jon who was embarrassed by the list of his accomplishments, which he never thought much about.

"I'm just a normal guy," Jon uttered, as if gleefully dismissing the notion that he was in any way special, which further endeared him to the other men, especially Dusty.

At that point, Dusty stood up and stretched, feigning fatigue. He looked at his wristwatch. "Jeez. Midnight already!"

"Guess this means sack time," Peter said with a hint of mischief in his voice. "You two boys run along and have some fun. We geezers will just hit the hay and dream of what it must be like to be young and cute again. There's no agenda around here, except for dinner tomorrow night. So if we don't see you all day, it'll be our loss. But we understand."

*   *   *

Dusty's and John's guest bedroom suite was as luxurious as the best room at the Ritz-Carlton. The king-size bed was covered in a cloud of a plush paisley comforter and down-filled pillows. A television and VCR were hidden in an antique armoire, and the opulent bathroom was as large as the sitting room.

Dusty and Jon fell into a quick wrestle on the bed. Then, not wanting to deplete all their energy, Jon said, "You use the facilities first. That way, you'll be in bed waiting for me when I come out."

Dusty quickly completed his ablutions, and returned to the room minus his shirt and socks. "I'll hurry," Jon said and closed the bathroom door behind him. Within moments he returned. He crawled into the bed beside Dusty and they eagerly embraced one another. "I've been impatient for this since the day before yesterday," Jon moaned.

The two were as ravenous for each other as they had been the first time they made love. They had already fallen into an understanding of what specific acts of sex pleased the other, in a way that takes many couples months if not years to understand.

Although they were equally versatile, Jon knew that Dusty was especially turned on by him slowly and gently but with purpose, pressing his hard, throbbing, fervid cock into Dusty's tight anal lips which opened gradually and cautiously to accept Jon's eight inches of pleasure. Reversing their roles, Dusty was at first inhibited, because of his lack of experience being a dominant lover. But Jon expressed his satisfaction. Dusty's technique was more developed than he gave himself credit for. They were perfect lovers, satisfying each other in every conceivable way.

When they were finally physically and emotionally spent, Dusty and Jon fell asleep, curled in each other's arms.

Chapter Seven

Peter and Rod didn't see much of Dusty and Jon the following day, until five o'clock when they all gathered poolside for a glass of champagne. The hosts were dressed only in swimming trunks but the guests were more discreet, wearing shorts and colored T-shirts. Peter and Rod would never admit as much, but they were dying to see Jon without his shirt on. Without Dusty's knowledge, they had conspired to coax him into the pool at least once before he left the next day.

Rod hovered, pouring flutes of champagne and passing homemade munchies tasty enough to please Julia Child. "And not a calorie or gram of fat in any of these delicious goodies," Rod announced in a tone that implied they were loaded with the highest caloric ingredients imaginable. "Some of us don't have to watch our waists, do we, Jon?" he said hoping Superman would lift his shirt to reveal the truth, that he could be the model for some new stomach cruncher on an infomercial.

Instead, Jon merely raved that the treats were the most delicious he'd ever enjoyed, bar none, and that included what the finest bistros in France had to offer.

"Should be an interesting evening," Peter said, sipping his champagne. "Just to fill you in, Jon, we're going to our friends Eddie and Dexter's. They give a little soirée practically every Saturday. Eddie's a retired—at 45—former CEO from some Silicon Valley computer company. Dex teaches English lit at a high school somewhere in Rancho Mirage. Although why he works, when they've got more money than God, I'll never understand."

"He likes to feel independent," Rod offered.

"But they should be traveling and enjoying all those lovely dead presidents," Peter countered. "Anyway, they're *fabulous* and they *love* Dusty."

"Any competition for me?" Jon smiled.

"If they weren't committed to each other—what's it been, twenty-five years?"—Peter looked to Rod for corroboration—"you'd get a run for your money. But no. I think they just like that he's Dusty."

"I know the feeling," Jon said. He took Dusty's hand in his.

"Any idea who else will be there?" Dusty asked.

"Eddie said something about the new ambassador to Thailand."

"Finland," Rod corrected.

"A Republican?" Peter said, incredulous.

"Log Cabin, too!" Rod added. Then, not knowing Jon's political party affiliations, said, "Hope we're not offending you."

"Far from it. I gave a ton of cash to Al's and to Hillary's campaigns. Mr. Puppet from Texas can 'kiss my grits,' as Flo used to say. I think he'd just as soon shoot all the queers with pink bullets than acknowledge that fags even exist. God only knows the cuts he'll make to funding for AIDS research. We'll get Hillary into the White House and then we'll see change!"

"I'll drink to that," Rod said, as they all raised their flutes and sipped the bubbling ambrosial vintage.

"Time for you and me to put on our party frocks," Peter said to Rod. "We'll catch you guys in about an hour. Should give you enough time to do whatever you have to do." He grinned.

"I think we can manage," Dusty said. "We're big boys."

"Don't get me started on that line!" Rod said, fanning his face with his hand.

The opulence of Eddie and Dexter's private estate exceeded that of Rod and Peter's. Both hosts were happy to see Dusty again, and thrilled to have what Dexter playfully called "fresh meat" around the house. Meaning Jon.

After an hour of enjoying the Shangri-La-like setting of the ostentatious but stunning formal gardens that Eddie and Dexter had created in the desert, and meeting old friends and a few new faces, Dusty was suddenly taken aback when Dexter escorted another guest into the garden: Stuart Richards.

"Oh, my gosh! Stuart!" Dusty enthused as the two embraced and exchanged kisses to their cheeks. "How've you been? Dare I ask where Jeremy is?"

Stuart faked a wince. "Ouch! Your memory is too sharp!" Stuart smiled. "That's not a topic for a fun evening. I'll accept all the blame and simply say it was entirely my fault, that I was just too busy with my work to keep him occupied—and satisfied. But you, my sexy friend, are looking fantastic! Oh, oh." He drew back. "You've got a playful puppy grin and that distinctive glow of a queer in love. Hope I'm wrong, because I've been looking forward to playing Gene Kelly to your Niña! I've been practicing my swashbuckling all afternoon, hoping I'd finally have the opportunity to be your Macoco!"

Dusty looked chagrined. "I am. In love I mean. Come meet him."

"Don't do this to me, Dusty," Stuart complained, throwing a feigned tantrum. "Not when I'm finally available!"

Holding his glass of champagne in one hand, Dusty placed his other hand in Stuart's and guided him over to where Jon was holding a conversation with Dexter about the possibility of building a new home somewhere in the Palm Springs area.

"Excuse me," Dusty interrupted. "Jon, I'd like you to meet my friend, the very famous author Stuart Richards."

"Oh, don't," Stuart blushed. "Famous maybe, but not 'very.' "

"Stuart Richards? Wow! I'm an ardent admirer." Jon rose, smiling, to shake Stuart's hand. *"The Four-Sided Triangle, Judge Lest Ye Be Judged, Holiday Lodge.* I've read all your books. They're fantastic!"

Stuart blushed and looked down at his feet is if to say, "Aw shucks." Then he added, "I hope you didn't see the movie version of *Triangle.*"

"Catherine Deneuve was a triumph. Don't let anyone take that away from you," Jon admonished.

"That's a very gracious way of saying the novel was great but the movie sucked," Dexter piped in.

"I heard that the screenplay was barfed up by the producer's slutty girlfriend. Then Neve Campbell was her usual one-dimensional caricature of a Barbie Doll," Stuart added.

"She really should be working at the cosmetics counter at Bloomies. Or at a Ninety-Nine Cents Only store," Eddie bitched.

"And that director! Barry Sonnenfeld? As always, he was scared shitless because he was in over his head." Dexter frowned. "The studio's marketing division got his wrath at the flick's failure. I have a friend who works there. I can't figure out how they're supposed to get asses into movie seats if the film's a bloody mess. And this one was, from that inane opening montage to the end credit crawl? Give me a break!"

"Isn't Dex a dear friend," Eddie interrupted, joining the group. "Always knows how to make a guest feel like leaving! Sorry, Stuart. Dex, please, darling, watch yourself. Perhaps you've had your limit of cock-tales?"

"It's what I deserve for being a whore," Stuart laughed. "When Warner's offered an armored truckload of cash for *Triangle*, plus a healthy back-end deal, I couldn't refuse. I don't have an ounce of integrity when someone wants to option my books. I tell my agent, 'Screw the so-called talent.' I don't even want to hear that Parker Posey is starring as the lead, even though I wrote the book with Judi Dench in mind. I only ask how many zeroes are on the check. I'm happy to cry all the way to the castle I bought on Malta!"

Dexter patted Stuart on the back. "But Mr. Brilliant Author here is exonerated because at least the novel was a finalist for a Lambda Book Award."

"I feel guilty that I never did send *Triangle* to you for an inscription as I promised," Dusty said. "I'll do it during the week, I promise."

"And I said I'd send you one, which I didn't do, but I will, this week. *I* promise." Stuart looked at Dusty with longing.

"I'm starving!" Eddie segued. "When's Mathilda going to serve?"

Dexter answered, "I told her to give it another fifteen." Then to Dusty and Jon and Peter and Rod he said, "When we heard we'd have the pleasure of Jon's company at our table we invited one more to make it an even twelve. As soon as he gets . . . Oh, here he is now! Oh, Chad? Chad? Over here. Be right back, guys. Don't go 'way," he said as he literally skipped off to the other side of the garden—and Dusty dropped his flute of champagne.

Jon didn't flinch or make a move to help pick up the shards. He was lost. Peter turned to Rod, who was looking at two stone figures: Dusty and Jon. "Fuck! It's Chad!" Peter said in a sickened whisper.

"I have to go," Dusty said.

"I have to go," Jon said at the very same moment.

"You guys *have* to stick around," Peter admonished. "Dusty, don't give him the satisfaction of making you run away. Impress him with how well you've succeeded without him and moved on with your love life."

It was too late anyway. Dexter was returning to the group with Chad by his side. "Guys, this is—"

Chad interrupted his host. "Dusty, what a surprise," he said in a condescending tone. "Although if I'm to play the noble ex-lover I'll have to admit you've never looked better. I see you've been working out. And probably screwing your way across the state, eh?"

Ex-lover? The news wasn't lost on Jon, as Dexter introduced Chad to Jon. "It's certainly my pleasure," Chad said with a warm smile. Taking Jon's hand in his, he pumped with a tight, suggestive grip while staring into Jon's eyes and giving him an obvious and lascivious once-over, sensing that perhaps they had met before.

Jon simply nodded to acknowledge the introduction. "Dusty," he said, "may I talk to you for a moment?"

Dusty, who was equally eager to escape the group, was about to agree. But just then, the maid, Mathilda, called out, "Dinner is served!"

As Dusty and Jon turned to find a quiet spot to speak, they were swept up in a human wave—Dexter on one side and Eddie on the other, escorting them inside, along with Chad, Peter, and Rod. Dusty and Jon were prisoners unable to speak or break away.

Inside the luxurious, oval-shaped dining room, which featured a cut-crystal teardrop chandelier over the center of the table, Dusty and Jon found that they were not to be seated beside each other as Rod had promised. Instead, Stuart was at Dusty's left and Peter was on the right. For Jon, it was Dexter to his left and Chad to his right. Although Dusty and Jon made eye contact and returned smiles during the first course—gazpacho—they were eventually and unavoidably lost in conversations with their dinner partners.

Dexter and Eddie, gracious hosts that they were, made a great show of being overly attentive to the "new boy," Jon. They included him in all their conversations and used him as the mediator when any disagreement arose, such as the sorry state of new musicals on Broadway, or puppet President Bush's latest international relations faux pas. Jon was gracious in all his remarks, doing his best to remain neutral. "I'm more impressed with Laura than I expected to be," he stated, trying to sound positive about at least one aspect of the White House charade.

"With the world blowing up around us, he's got an unthinkable challenge," stated another guest.

"Laura'll never get over the anxiety and fear of what her idiot husband might do, not only to the country, but to the planet," another man suggested.

Chad was being overly solicitous of Jon, asking if he'd like another glass of wine, even as he was pouring from the bottle. His interest in Jon manifested as someone obviously putting on airs, pretending to want to know everything about him. "How do you know Dexter and Eddie?" Chad asked Jon. "Where do you live?"

"San Francisco."

"What brought you all the way down to Palm Springs this weekend? A business trip?"

Clearly, Chad had set his sights on this man and wanted to attract the prize. Later, he'd do his damnedest to seduce this most handsome man among all the others in the room.

"What brings me down to Palm Springs, this weekend?" Jon reiterated the question. He looked Chad square in the eyes and, nodding to the opposite side of the table, said, "My lover, Dusty Hunt, invited me."

Chad's eyes grew wide and his mouth agape like a character in a television commercial who was shocked that his best friend didn't use the popular brand of medicated hemorrhoid itch-soothing cream.

"What a coincidence. Dusty was *my* lover until about a year ago," Chad said. "Surprised the hell out of him when I showed up, didn't it? Surprised me too, the bastard."

"Excuse me," Jon said. "I'd appreciate your not referring to the man I love as a 'bastard.'"

"I have the experience to calls 'em as I sees 'em," Chad said. "He's trouble, with a capital T. Just my opinion, as Dennis Miller would say." Chad quickly turned to his other dining partner.

Noticing that Jon was suddenly abandoned and was no longer in conversation with Chad, others invited him into their diverse discussions. He became engaged in so many simultaneous conversations with the other guests that he didn't have the opportunity to keep his eyes on Dusty during most of the remaining time at the dining room table. Because he wanted to both make a good impression on everyone and avoid Chad remembering their past, he allowed himself to be caught up in every critique and bitchiness that the other men proposed, from Cher's television version of *Mame*, to Bette's failed series to where in hell was Meryl Streep these days? Still he didn't fail to notice how Stuart was looking at Dusty. And how Dusty was often looking across the table at Chad. Jon couldn't tell if it was contempt or an expression of annoyance for each.

If Jon had been able to pay more attention, he would have seen that as the dinner progressed, Stuart Richards, with the aid of several glasses of wine, had become more animated. He touched Dusty often. At first it would be simply a lively tap on the arm when Dusty referred to Stuart's track record with men, and managed to sum up the short relationship with Jeremy in a word: "delinquent." But as they continued their conversation about life and love, Stuart's aggressive behavior became more overt, until he rested a hand on Dusty's thigh under the table.

"I'm involved now, Stuart," Dusty whispered. Stuart didn't seem to get the message, or at least it didn't deter him. "You met my lover, Jon."

"He's not officially your *lover*," Stuart snorted. "You guys only just connected. You and I have known each other much longer. You have to confess, we've both been attracted to each other."

"It's just rotten timing again," Dusty whispered to Stuart. "If you hadn't brought that 'delinquent' to the Manilow party, things might have turned out differently. I was all ready to go home with you that night. But you had someone else."

"I went home alone. And things haven't 'turned out' for you. Not yet," Stuart said.

"I promised if I ever needed kidnapping, you'd be the first man I'd call," Dusty offered. He politely removed Stuart's hand from his leg. "That's still a promise. But for now, I don't need to be rescued."

"Well," Stuart conceded, "I can't blame you for how you feel about your new boyfriend. He appears to be passing this audition with flying colors. For looks, ten. For personality, ten. He's a charmer, and this is a tough audience to please. Even your ex-jerk, Chad, seems to be enamored of him. Smitten even, I'd say. I wish you guys luck. But I'm holding you to your promise. Because, frankly, Dusty, I've always been attracted to you. Perhaps even in love with you."

Dusty blushed. He hoped the din of silverware against china and the gulp-gulp sound of wine being poured and swallowed, had prevented the disclosure from being picked up by Jon's ears. There had been a time when Dusty felt the same about Stuart. The man's creativity and sensitivity—not to mention his being endowed with extremely good looks—was a big turn-on for Dusty. And Stuart was right. Although Dusty seemed in paradise now, there was no guarantee about the future with Jon.

But he couldn't bring himself to think past the next time when he and Jon would be flesh on flesh—two virile men with vital bodies, enjoying what God had given them: the appreciation of being able to recognize that love is not subjective. It's an absolute. And they were in love—absolutely.

When Mathilda finished removing the dinner plates from each guest's place, Dexter tapped his water glass with a spoon and asked, "Who wants coffee, decaf, tea and/or a nip of Grand Marnier?"

"I'd like to know how Jon enjoys being back in the Springs after all these years," came a voice from the opposite side and end of the table. The query was from a once-famous sit-com star whose biggest success was in a series about a widower whose television kids played practical jokes on his dates in each episode. The actor's face was now marked with many white spots where moles—the result of his sun-worshiping days—had been removed. "I didn't recognize you until just a little while ago, Jon, I'm sorry. It's Franklin. Remember from when you and Chad used to live down here? It's nice to see some things never change and that you're still together."

"Franklin!" Jon said enthusiastically. "I'm so sorry. I've been away for so long, I didn't recognize you! But you still look great! As for Chad and me . . ."

Chad blanched. "What?" he cried out in bewilderment, turning his head to Jon and taking a long look at him, as though the man by his side was someone believed to be long dead.

Chad suddenly thundered, "Jon? Jon Willows? Jon the biggest ass-hole on the face of the planet?"

"Obviously, I didn't leave that great an impact on you, Chad. We've been seated together all evening and you didn't recognize me."

"Because I'd put you entirely out of my mind. What's it been, about a decade?"

"And I'm still counting my blessings," Jon said.

Franklin said, "Did I miss something? You guys aren't . . ? I just assumed because you were seated beside each other . . ."

By now the table was alive with every guest trying to figure out what the gist of the situation was. What was all the fuss about? A couple of ex-lovers were unexpectedly reunited?

"Just don't start throwing the Fitz & Floyd, darlings," Dexter chided. "Personally, I'm thrilled. These unplanned episodes are what make for dinners the guests talk about for ages afterward. Eddie and I are in your debt!"

"Talk, yes," Jon said. "In fact, will you all excuse us for a few moments. Dusty and I need to have a small chat outside."

Both men simultaneously pushed back their chairs, placed their napkins on the table, and walked out of the formal dining room into the garden.

＊   ＊   ＊

"My God, Dusty," Jon began. "Chad was your lover too? This is too far-fetched to believe."

"I was absolutely shocked when he showed up," Dusty said. "I never in a million years expected to see him again. It was a horribly bad break-up."

"As was mine with him. Remember? I mentioned it last night."

"It's funny, but when you started telling me about your previous life in Palm Springs, it sounded so similar to what I'd endured that for a split second I thought I was in the *Twilight Zone* or that it was *déjà vu*. But I figured the idea was too absurd. No way were we ever involved with the same guy."

"I recognized him the moment he walked in," Jon said. "I'd never forget the man who caused me the most pain I'd ever endured. But he's so self-absorbed and egotistical, if it hadn't been for Franklin, he never would have remembered me."

"I don't buy that he'd have forgotten you," Dusty countered. "How does one forget a lover—even after ten years?"

"There were so many men in his bed while we were together, and so many since then, including you, they all blend into one giant surrealistic kaleidoscope of busy bodies, I suppose."

"You heard that he'd been my lover. Would you have told me about you and him eventually?"

"I tried to tell you right away," Jon said. "Remember? I tried to get you away? But then Dexter and Eddie hauled us into the house. I was going to tell you and ask if we could leave."

"We couldn't have left. It would have made me look as though I was running away from my past," Dusty said. "Pretty much everybody at this party, except Franklin, I guess, knows that Chad and I used to be together."

"So what do you want to do?" Jon asked.

"Do we both agree that Chad's not an issue in our lives?"

"You're the only man in the universe, as far as I'm concerned," Jon said.

"That's all I need to know."

"What about your friend Stuart? He was pretty much all over you during dinner."

"Stuart's a lovely sweetheart, but he's very messed up. He's so wrapped up in his work I doubt he'll ever find anyone who'll put up with him for too long. I used to find him sexy. And I thought it would be romantic to play the supportive lover of a talented man, idolized by the world. But although I love his writing, I don't love him. I love you."

Dusty and Jon embraced. They kissed as fervently as they had their first night together on Jon's terrace. They were in the garden, but not hidden from the floor-to-ceiling glass dining room windows where all the guests had assembled as if to view a pair of giant panda. With the exception of Chad, all were sighing a collective, "Awwww!" as they watched the two men absorb themselves in each other's passionate kisses.

"Think our hosts would mind if we disappeared?" Jon asked, breathless.

Dusty shook his head. "We've got to go back inside and face the group. We can't be rude to these people. They're Peter and Rod's friends, and ours, too."

"We'll go back hand-in-hand, proving to one and all who's with whom."

"But what can we do about Chad?" Dusty said.

"Revenge isn't a pretty sight," Jon mused. "In the end, it's bad for the soul, and really quite unfulfilling. But if we're going to live together, here in the Springs, I'd rather not have him within a hundred miles of our lives."

"Last I heard, he was practically broke," Dusty said.

"After all the palimony money I settled on him?"

"A spendthrift."

"Then it shouldn't be too difficult to send him on his way."

"Peter and Rod will know the full extent of his up-to-the-minute life story and finances."

As Dusty and Jon slowly walked back to the house they caught a glimpse of the other guests scattering away from the window back to their respective seats. "Appears we've been the evening's entertainment," Dusty said.

"For an encore, let's make a big show and make us the most envied of men. We're young—"

"Relatively," Dusty japed.

"And completely in love. We'll make everyone see that it was Chad, not either of us, who could possibly have been responsible for our leaving him."

"What's your plan?"

"When we return, we'll both make a point of holding Chad up to virtue. Anyone who knows him—especially Peter and Rod and Dex and Eddie—will see his juvenile behavior as something no rational man could live with. And in the meantime, they'll all be impressed with our graciousness."

When the two men returned to the dining room, they made appropriate excuses and requests for forgiveness for interrupting an otherwise perfect evening. "You must let us play hosts to all of you the moment Carlos can build our new home," Jon said to the gathering.

"Of course, we'll have to impose on each of you for guidance about exactly where to build," Dusty said.

"The decorating. All the elements that go into the establishment of a new residence. As the newest couple in the group, I hope you'll accept me and Dusty as gracefully as you've accepted me alone this evening," Jon added.

The entire room was charmed by Jon's statement—plus, Dusty knew, it would give the men a project to embrace, what with all the time on their hands. They were mostly a group of middle-aged retirees who desperately needed to fill their days with rewarding activities.

"And Chad," Jon continued, "perhaps you can introduce us to the members of the country club."

"I don't belong," Chad muttered.

"Then maybe you can help us select someone as marvelous as Mathilda to accept a position with us. We'll need help in the house, since Dusty and I are so busy."

Mathilda was serving coffee and beamed at hearing that she was the standard by which these men were judging the type of efficient help they wanted in their own home.

"I don't have a domestic, either. You'll have to find your own."

"Perhaps your lover would have some suggestions."

"I don't *have* a lover," he huffed.

"I'm so sorry," said Jon. "Everyone here has a partner; I just assumed you wouldn't have wasted any time after you drove Dusty away. It's nice to have someone with whom you can share your life."

"Don't worry about me. I've got plenty of men to choose from."

Peter piped in. "Chad, what exactly have you been up to since the last time we saw each other? It's been about a year, and frankly, since you spend so much time down here, I'm amazed we haven't run into you again before now."

"I don't get down much anymore. I'm far too busy."

"Telemarketing, isn't it?" Dexter said, quietly sniggering, which prompted others to follow.

Chad was silent for a moment and poured himself a glass of wine.

"Since when did you start drinking?" Dusty asked. "You were always the teetotaler. You used to get so angry when I'd have something with my meals. Hope you haven't taken up smoking too!"

Chad turned scarlet. "If you'll all excuse me, I have a long drive back to the city," he announced.

"Not staying at the place in Rancho Mirage?" Jon asked.

"Oh, Chad doesn't have that place anymore," Dexter baited him. "Wasn't it a foreclosure, Chad?"

Chad abruptly stood up, threw his napkin on the table, drank what remained of his Merlot in one quick gulp and started, a bit unsteadily, to leave the room. "It was a voluntary foreclosure!" he snapped. "And it was Jon's fault." He angrily pointed a finger, which the group followed to their new friend. "If he hadn't bought us such a big condo, and had paid me more in the palimony suit—"

Palimony! The entire room offered a collective gasp. The long-time committed couples at the table didn't have to worry about palimony, but a number of their friends had been the victims of nefarious gold-diggers. Chad had just revealed himself to be among that breed of op-portunists.

Jon said mildly, "If you recall, Chad, I gave you everything you and your attorneys insisted you wanted."

"It still wasn't enough to last forever!"

Dusty eyed the faces of the men in the room. Most were snobs, no doubt about it. Some of them were from old money—or as in the case of Jon and Peter and Rod and Dexter, they'd worked up to twenty hours a day for years to make their respective businesses successful. The idea that someone could insinuate themselves into their class and beguile them and then take them to court for half of their assets was abhorrent. Palm Springs was filled with hard bodied, handsome men who were very tempting to touch. But the risks were too great.

Chad finally stormed out of the dining room and left the house.

"N.O.C.D.," Mathilda called dryly as she passed through to the kitchen. All the men chuckled in agreement.

Dusty got up from his chair to sit next to Jon. All eyes were on them as they embraced.

Without anyone saying a word, the room was filled with vibrations of envy. Although most of the men were happily married, the reminder of what it was like to be truly in love for the first time brought pangs of jealousy.

Franklin had tears sliding down his cheek. He stood up with his glass of wine. "I know what love is," he said. "I had the most wonderful man who gave me the most meaningful moments of my entire life. I'm also very perceptive, and I see in Jon and Dusty two men who I believe are soul mates. May I propose a toast. First of all, welcome to our family here in beautiful Palm Springs. Second, may you both enjoy all the years of your new life together as much as I did with my Marc, and as much as most of the rest of my friends at this table share with their loved ones."

Words of sincere approval could be heard as Jon and Dusty embraced again.

Stuart Richards cleared his throat. "Dusty," he said, "congratulations. The proper kidnapper has abducted your heart."

Chapter Eight

"Your friends are great," Jon said later that night after he and Dusty had made love. "I especially enjoyed meeting Stuart Richards. I hope I didn't sound too much like a sycophant."

"They all loved you," Dusty said, snuggling closer to Jon and feeling his hard muscled chest as they lay in post-climax satisfaction. "You were a sport to go along with the whole evening. I just hope you didn't feel as though you were being scrutinized too heavily."

"I knew what I was getting myself into. These people love you, and they wanted to make certain you were with someone acceptable. I think I passed the initiation. I just thought, screw it, I am who I am and I'm not playing games. I just didn't want to disappoint you."

Dusty placed his lips over Jon's and gave him a deep, passionate kiss. "You only make me love you more, as if that's possible, when I see how you are with everyone else."

Jon smiled gratefully. "Sorry for making plans to move us both down here without consulting you first."

"I'm going to make you pay for that," Dusty whispered. He ran his hands over Jon's chest and down to his cock, which was reemerging from fifteen minutes of hibernation.

"You'll be sorry," he teased. "I'm interviewing contractors right away."

Dusty sat up and straddled Jon. Imitating an overly zealous realtor,

Dusty began a guided tour of a marvelous property. "A grand and sophisticated desert residence for year-round living and entertaining, this is a home that friends and family will enjoy for many years."

Jon smiled as he listened to the sales pitch.

"This rare, two-story Spanish-style house features six bedrooms, six bathrooms, double-height cathedral living room opening onto a stunning Olympic-sized pool and a Jacuzzi."

"Will you let us keep the place in SF?" Jon smiled.

"Perhaps," Dusty said vaguely. He continued his guided tour of the dream house. "Fountains and statues that are stone representations of Ricky Martin and Jon Willows, accent the lush Edenesque landscaping. Of course, there's a panoramic view of the mountains and valley floor."

He started stroking Jon's erect cock. "The 'great' room," he continued, "boasts not one, but two, count 'em, two, stone fireplaces. There's a formal dining room that looks onto the tennis court. A media room, with floor-to-ceiling bookshelves and every electronic toy imaginable accents the exclusive property of Messrs. Jon and Dusty."

"You joke," Jon whispered, looking up at Dusty and wincing with the pleasure of his eight tumescent inches being lovingly stroked, "but I'll top that by building us an indoor pool, as well. Plus an eat-in state-of-the-art kitchen. A steam room is de rigueur, as well as a gazebo and a dramatic waterfall!" At that instant, he groaned loudly and the volcanic action of his penis erupted into another orgasm.

After a moment of catching his breath, Jon said, "Dusty. It's you. I know it's you who I want—no, I need—to spend my life with."

"I won't play games and pretend to be hard to get," Dusty responded. "I know what I want. And what I want is to spend my life with *you*. Here in the Springs, or Timbuktu. I have in my arms the only man I can imagine being with intimately, now and forever."

Dusty's cock was throbbing. He lubed it with the puddle of semen congealing on Jon's chest and slowly and methodically massaged his own member. In little time, he was moaning and then all at once crying out and ejaculating onto Jon's beautiful chest.

"And that's why Stuart Richards—author, lecturer and somewhat attractive fairy—will never bury his thick quill in your ass!" Jon said. "Because I'm all the man you'll ever need. And vice-versa!"

Dusty wrapped his legs around Jon's waist, and soon they were unconscious, depleted of energy and sleeping with the secure feeling that they were safe in another man's strong-yet-tender arms. Their hearts continued to pound, and guttural sounds emanated from their larynxes throughout the night. At dawn, they awoke and made love until the afternoon.

"God, we can hear them all the way on this side of the house!" Peter said to Rod, as they were reading the Sunday *Times* by the pool during breakfast. He leaned over from his place at the table and kissed his own lover. He saw that under Rod's bathrobe he had a hard-on.

"Surprise, surprise!" he added. "And it's not even our ritual Tuesday or Saturday morning! You must be fantasizing about Jon!"

"After all these years, it's certainly not *you*!" Rod cracked.

"Okay, wise guy. Let's go inside," Peter demanded.

"I'll play Dusty. You play Jon."

"I want to be Dusty!" Peter pouted.

"You can be Dusty the next time!"